D042692

River of Secrets

TRADE
Books & CD's
BOOK NOOK.

River of Secrets

SASKIA HOPE
& GEORGIA ANGELIS

BLACK
lace

Black Lace novels are sexual fantasies.
In real life, make sure you practise safe sex.

First published in 1994 by
Black Lace
332 Ladbroke Grove
London
W10 5AH

Reprinted 1995

Copyright © Saskia Hope & Georgia Angelis 1994

Typeset by CentraCet Limited, Cambridge
Printed and bound in Great Britain by
Cox & Wyman Ltd, Reading, Berks

ISBN 0 352 32925 4

*All characters in this publication are fictitious and any
resemblance to real persons, living or dead, is purely
coincidental.*

This book is sold subject to the condition that it shall not,
by way of trade or otherwise, be lent, resold, hired out or
otherwise circulated without the publisher's prior
written consent in any form of binding or cover other
than that in which it is published and without a similar
condition including this condition being imposed on the
subsequent purchaser.

Chapter One

I came into the office like the English summer, late and lousy. Charlie called over saying when should he arrange my resignation party? And when I snarled back at him, he told me Big Mac wanted to see me.

Big Mac is the editor. Fat, fast and expensive.

I got myself a coffee at the machine and went into his office.

'You're late,' he said grouchily by way of welcoming me in.

I get paid because it don't bother me to rile people. 'I'm late, boss,' I drawled, 'because I went to this party last night with my sights set on a real gorilla. Then this girlfriend of mine blocks me in a corner and tells me why her husband doesn't understand her. The gorilla gets snapped by someone else and I'm mad, so I drink too much, so I sleep in, that's why I'm late.' I injected some coffee into the vein.

'You're disgusting, Sydney,' said Big Mac in more genial tones. He likes me sassy.

I like my name. It's unusual for a woman. My

1

parents had no hang-ups about not having a boy. They just wanted to give me an edge in the world.

I smiled toothily. There's no point paying the earth to have them fixed and not flaunting them.

Mac flinched. 'I've got this assignment for you,' he said.

Charlie's words came back to me. 'Whoa, boy,' I said. 'No way.'

'You haven't heard it yet.' He was trying to be patient.

'I've got this journalist's nose,' I said. 'I know when I'm being dumped on.'

'There's plenty on the staff would give their eye-teeth for this,' grumbled Mac. He has this really original way of speaking which is why we hacks and the subs write the paper. Mac reserves right of veto. He knows he can't write.

'So let them.' I drawled.

'I'm assigning you, Sydney, and there's no choice in the matter.'

'I'm frightened,' I said in a squeaky voice.

'Carl's in Charing Cross.'

'Train spotting?'

'Hospital.'

I leaned back in my seat. 'Oh yeah? What with? Rabies? He should stop biting strange dogs.'

'Shut up, Sydney,' said Mac, trying not to laugh. 'It's serious. He fell off one of those bungey jump things.'

'You're kidding.'

'I'm not. The guy fell a long way. He's broken quite a lot of bones.'

'At least it's a story,' I said consolingly.

'The hell it is. A kiddy falls, it's a story. A hack falls and no one cares. They figure it's a fix.'

Mac was right. Hacks write about things that happen to other people, not themselves.

2

'I don't see,' I said carefully, 'what Carl being in hospital has to do with me.' Carl is travel and adventure. He goes all round the world. To me, travel and adventure is going to Norwich.

'We had him booked, Sydney, and it's very expensive and we can't trade the ticket.'

'Nuts,' I said in sheer disbelief.

'It'll be weeks before he's ready and it's topical now. Someone has to go.'

'Not me, boss. I'm features. Remember?'

Mac leaned towards me. 'Every paper's doing this story so we have to do it different.'

I stared at him wide-eyed. 'Should I take notes?' I said breathlessly. He was speaking to me like it was my first day on the job.

'Carl would have done it differently,' said Mac. He didn't have much patience left and I was getting a very bad feeling. 'Carl is a talented, original writer with a great deal of personal bravery.'

'He has to be, the size of his expenses.' Carl's expenses were legendary in the office and they made him unpopular. Every time he got back from a trip, accounts exploded and we all had to trim our sheets. Carl made it tough on all of us. The management put up with him because he was, as Mac had just said, a very talented and original writer. He was a screwball, too, and nasty, in my opinion – speaking as one who knows.

'We could send environment,' said Mac. 'But that would give us the same thing as everyone else. So we had a meeting and decided who we could spare who would be guaranteed to come up with a different viewpoint.'

'Mac, I love you,' I said. 'But I earn my money writing articles like how a woman in her forties doesn't get illnesses diagnosed because the doc

3

can't see past menopause and hormone replacement therapy.'

'Is that true?' asked Mac, diverted. I think he's having wife trouble at the moment.

'Try reading the paper you edit,' I said sourly.

He pulled himself together. 'Sydney,' he said. 'You do this job. You understand? You have no option. Surely the thought of travel is exciting to you?'

By now I had a really sick feeling in my stomach. 'It's Africa, isn't it?' I said. 'One of those places where they have non-stop civil war and starving children. I can't do it, Mac. I can't. I'll resign.'

'It isn't Africa.'

'It's an ex Soviet republic full of people who think women should wear the veil and not drive. I will resign. I mean it.'

'Don't be stupid. It's one of the most beautiful places on earth and very lightly populated.'

'The Antarctic,' I moaned. 'Penguins, snow and scientists. I bet the penguins have more conversation.'

'Shut up, Sydney.'

'Thank heavens a woman's already climbed Everest. And been in space,' I added, my mind leaping upwards and outwards in horror.

'You're hysterical,' said Mac coldly.

'Therefore, totally unsuitable for the assignment,' I said with low cunning. I snickered.

'You fly to Miami tomorrow,' he said.

I gaped. 'Miami? Lightly populated? I know the murder rate is very high but I didn't know it had got that bad.'

'You needn't leave the airport. In fact, you mustn't. You only have two hours to get your connection.'

'Connection?' My voice was faint.

'To Belém.'

4

'Bethlehem? Send the religious correspondent.'

'Belém, Brazil. You get the first plane out of Belém to Manaus. There you pick up the boat.'

'The boat?'

'Up the Amazon.' Mac was genial again. He leaned back and smiled at me. 'Go and look at the rain forest, Sydney. Decide what you think about it first hand. Don't worry about the statistics. We've got all that on file. We want your impressions. We want what an ordinary person might think, the sort of person who thinks the slogan "Save whales" means cleaning up a beach in Rhyl. If we send someone from environment they'll be too sentimental. We need a tough mind here.'

I ignored the insult about being ordinary. 'Mac,' I said hoarsely. 'They have insects.'

'We have insects.'

'No.' I was positive. Bonhomous bastard. 'I mean insects. People-eating insects, things like World War One airplanes. They bite and suck and poison. They carry all these fancy diseases that interest scientists because there's no cure for them yet.'

'You can get shots.'

'I don't like trees,' I whispered like it was a big secret.

'That's why you're going. You'll have an original viewpoint. Frankly, we would have preferred Carl, but we don't mind cutting our losses with you and taking it from a new angle.'

'I'm on the side of the loggers,' I said desperately. 'I like my trees with the fluffy bits cut off stacked sideways with door holes and windows in them, a neon sign flashing Pizza Hut up top.'

'Fine,' said Mac, smiling.

'And I like gold,' I said. 'I hear the gold miners are really bad people.'

'Write what you like,' said Mac expansively. 'We'll print it.'

'No,' I moaned. 'No, no, no.'

'They're laying bets on you in the office, whether you'll leave the paper or go and do as you're told.'

'Who's running the book?' I looked Mac in the eye.

'Claire. The odds she's offering, she figures you'll resign.'

Clara the cow, I call her. She wants my job.

'Sydney,' he said, knowing I was going down. 'Write it sharp. Write it spunky. We'll do you proud. Maybe several articles, big fat ones. Like your bonus.'

'Pics,' I gasped. 'I'm no photog.'

'That's arranged. Carl fixed it. There's a guy already in Brazil who's going on the trip, which is a private one, by the way. Obviously he's not a staffer, but Carl says he's good. He knows him from way back, I think, and I gather he's the one knows the rich bitch who's paying for the show. You might get a book out of it,' Mac added casually. 'We wouldn't mind. We could serialise it.'

'You liar.' This was outrageous.

'Can you take the risk?' He smiled sweetly. 'Go and tidy your desk, Sydney. Jenny will give you all the stuff. Then take the rest of the day off to buy clothes and have holes put in your arm. You'll have to backdate your anti-malaria pills as it is.'

I found time to visit Carl. I don't like him but I'm not so cruel I can't feel sorry for someone who looks like an escapee from a Tutankhamun movie. Every bit was bandaged and he was in traction.

'They're sending me in your place,' I said gloomily, wondering if he could hear through the bandages. 'You want me to go?'

His jaw was wired. I contemplated what I could see

6

of his face. 'Blink once for yes, twice for no,' I suggested.

He blinked twice.

I set aside an hour to say bye-bye to my neighbour, Tyrone, who lives in the basement flat beneath mine. He was a friend. A *very good* friend. I love Jamaican, and I don't mean the food.

We had a simple relationship, based purely on sex (not that sex could ever be termed 'pure', some would say), seeking each other out when the itch struck us and there was no one else readily available to scratch it.

See, it's like this: some nights I'd watch a video, the way you do, alone, bingeing on crisps, chocolate and a bottle, or even two, of wine. And there before you would be Johnny Depp, Denis Quaid, Nicholas Cage or Richard Gere, making *it*, hot and sultry with some screen siren. I'd imagine it was me, get that hungry feeling, you know what I mean, your tail getting restless, your pussy making its presence known. Then I'd bump down on the floor three times with my slipper and Tyrone, if he felt obliging and was at home, would be up those dingy stairs in a trice.

Sometimes he came up without being asked, to quench a need of his own and I'd return the favour, quickly excited into acquiescence by the rigid cock he'd unzip from his denim jeans.

Sometimes he wasted no time, stripping off my tights and panties, stabbing it into me up against the door to my flat, lifting me and sinking deep into me between my spread white thighs. Tyrone was a body beautiful, worked out every other day in a gym two streets away. He was usually the one to choose the position. I liked it that way (with him), saw each fuck

7

as a novel gift from a genuine friend. Just like every other muscle in his stocky black body, his cock was well disciplined, a thick, long tool that never let him down. Tyrone rarely lacked female company. He was much appreciated.

Before leaving for South America I knocked on his door, bags packed, my lascivious smile an unmistakable signal of intent. He wore nothing but navy and white polka-dot boxer shorts. His musculature was perfect, his Medusa-like dreadlocks a dancing chaos around his head and shoulders.

An eyebrow raised at the luggage. 'Hey now, Syd, I don't mind servicing you like a good neighbour but, I'm sorry, y'aint moving in. No way. Ty gotta hang loose, gotta spread it around, be fair, honey. You can understand that.'

'I'm gutted,' I sniffed on an imaginary tear. 'Guess there's nothing for it then, I'll put myself on the first plane out of Heathrow and throw myself into exploring the Amazon in the hope of forgetting you. But how about a little fun first, for old times' sake?'

'Y'know I'll break off from press-ups any time for some strenuous heavy breathing with you.' He hauled my luggage inside his front door and kicked it shut behind me.

My skirt was tight and short. I wriggled it up, undid four buttons down the front of my crush-resistant travelling blouse.

He was back on his bench press, feet braced either side, flat on his back. He lifted a weighted bar up and down above his head with ease. His shorts were lying on the floor discarded now, his black joy-bringer was pointed at the ceiling, wagging in friendly fashion.

I wriggled a bit more in my skirt, hitched it higher, and removed my panties, swinging a leg over him, running my tongue over his pecs, taking his length and putting it to my hot and aching spot. I lowered myself onto it, giving an 'Umm' of appreciation as it slipped up and in, going gratuitously deep. I tightened about it, rising, falling, gyrating.

Tyrone was grinning broadly, neck corded, sinews taut, the weights jerked up with arrogant assurance. 'Keep in time, gal,' he complained. Like a good girl, I tried, up down, up down, taking all, then gliding up to the tip, a hand groping, cupping his balls, toying, encircling.

He pumped iron, pumped me, a supreme athlete, the sort who would have made Mr A. Hitler snort with fury back in the thirties. Black and beautiful.

My breasts danced in his face and Ty laughed, enjoying the teasing way they remained just out of reach. He couldn't pump iron and suck on my breasts at the same time and he was too well disciplined to abandon the jerks. In fact, I think he achieved an even greater pleasure by being denied.

'Fifty,' he puffed with satisfaction and set the weighted bar back in its cradle. Fastening his chalky hands on my thighs instead and jerking me up then down, deliciously hard, grinding as our bodies bumped softly together, raising his head then to suck at my breasts noisily.

I started to come and, right along with me, so did he, jerking, making cat-like noises of delight. 'Ow! Wow! Meow!'

I tightened about his meatiness, throbbing, squeezing, my flesh in turmoil. It was several moments before I could bring myself to slide off his lovely softening length and pad off to the bathroom to get cleaned up. He joined me, climbed beneath the shower while I applied a red-for-danger lipstick.

'So where you going?'

'I told you – up the Amazon.'

'Oh yeah,' he chuckled, not believing me, I could tell, thinking it more likely that I'd booked a fortnight in Majorca to enjoy the more stud-like and least inebriated of the lager louts. I blew him a kiss as I hefted up my luggage and headed for the door.

'Do me a favour will you. Cancel my papers.'

I hate flying, but I flew. I wanted to move around, please myself, eat decent food, have conversation, entertainment and a shower. Instead I flew in an aeroplane. Then I flew to Belém.

Belém is very modern, very lively, very Brazilian and a thousand times better than being in an aeroplane though my own London suburb has the rest of the world beat, as far as I am concerned.

I bought some more stuff on the firm. I was determined to beat Carl's expenses.

I flew to Manaus, inland. I preferred this plane because it didn't pretend to be comfortable. At Belém the Amazon is so wide it's hopeless. I mean, how can you get emotional over something that might be the sea, if you added salt. The water disappeared from view. At Manaus, I could see over to the other side.

It was here at Manaus that I had to wait to meet my contact, the photographer Carl said was coming along, name of Tom Matheson. The paper had made a deal to buy his snaps. The lady-boss whose idea of a holiday this was was evidently perfectly happy to have a professional writer and a photographer along subsidising her expenses. He wasn't at my hotel when I checked in so I imbibed some night-life and decided this *tropicalismo* business had something going for it. The men were very sharp, very forward. They acted the way the lady liked it, like it was a joint adventure into fun. This is an approach I can handle.

10

However, it wasn't the time nor the place and so I slapped them back amiably and waited for *the* man.

It was one hell of a place, nearly one million people, many living high-rise, all out in the middle of the jungle. The river rises and falls forty feet each year, so the docks float. I went to the Opera House. Unbelievable. Jenny Lind sang there in 1910 and the Ballet Russe danced there in its hey-day during the rubber boom. Now it has works of art and stuff. Helluva place.

I wouldn't be writing about it, though. I wasn't doing a holiday piece, I'm no travel writer. Nor am I reduced to writing guide books. I went back to my hotel, itchy with the heat and humidity. My room was air-conditioned. I put on a white bathing suit, a silk wrapper, and went down to the pool.

It was dark all of a sudden. I was very close to the equator. The pool was almost empty. It was lit from below and the edges seemed dark because the pool-side lighting was set in the tiled surround so you could only see it from above. From below you could look up from the sapphire glowing water and see the night sky.

I surfaced, enjoying myself, and slicked my streaming hair back. Then I began to climb out of the water.

A man was watching me. He was sitting at one of the poolside tables, smoking, alone, watching me.

I looked for my towel and wrapper. They weren't where I had left them. Finally, I looked over to the man.

My towel lay on a chair beside him. My wrapper was over the back of the chair.

I don't like being bullied.

I went over to him and picked up my towel, wiping my face with it. The fragrant night air was like warm oil on my cool skin.

11

'You want one?' he said, offering his pack.

'I'm already smoking,' I said. I rubbed my hair.

He raised his eyebrows. The light wasn't so good but he looked in his thirties, craggy, wearing a creased tropical suit. He wore no tie and the open-necked white shirt and pale suit made him look very dark.

'When I feel pushed around,' I amplified, 'it makes me angry.' I smiled, showing my teeth.

'Sydney Johnson,' he said.

'Hey, that's my name, too. What a coincidence.'

'I asked the waiter to identify you. I thought Sydney was a man's name.'

'I had the operation. Same as John Wayne. He started out as Marion.' I was speaking to an American, I knew by now. Or a Canadian. My ear isn't that quick.

He ran his eyes down my bikini-clad figure. 'Some doctor,' he said and gave a soundless whistle.

I put on my wrapper. 'You want lady's clothes, go and buy them, mister,' I said softly. 'The next time you take mine, I tell the police.'

'Why isn't Carl here?' he said abruptly.

My heart sank. He was my contact.

'He had an accident. The paper sent me instead.' I added in a baby-voice, 'I'm a reporter, too.'

'The deal was with Carl, who is primarily a writer.'

'Your deal is with my paper. Carl isn't the paymaster, buddy.'

He was annoyed. 'I don't want to take you up the Amazon.'

'You're not *taking* me anywhere. I'm going along.'

'Why didn't Carl tell me himself?'

'His jaw is wired. He's in traction.'

'He get beat-up?'

'My,' I said mildly. 'You must come from a very

12

rough part of the world. Where I live a road accident would spring to mind. As it happens, it was neither. He fell off a high platform. I mean he jumped. The rubber rope broke, that's all.'

He thumped the table. 'I don't believe it,' he said.

'I do tell lies but it's early in our acquaintance for you to know when,' I snapped. Did he hate all women or was it just my raspy manner? Personally I love my raspy manner.

He looked at me sourly. 'You shouldn't be here. It ought to be Carl. If not Carl, a man. One who can write.'

'Huff puff,' I said cheerfully. 'You're getting me all upset.' I batted my eyelids.

He laughed suddenly. Hey, he wasn't so bad, I thought, lightening up.

The night was like honey. I could hear some crazy music inside. I was hungry and the menu, when I had sussed it earlier, looked terrific. The water in my bikini bottom gathered in the crotch and dripped slightly.

I felt horny.

'You don't look like someone who readily accepts discomfort,' he said.

'Tell you what,' I said all soft again. 'Forget the character assassination and take the pics, yeah. The rest isn't your affair.' I walked away.

I dressed nicely and had a drink in the bar before eating. Here I allowed myself to be picked up by this really smooth type, a businessman, he said. He looked and dressed really well. I felt it was time I sampled the country. We shared our food and a few more drinks. Then I took him up to my room.

I can hold back. I'm not a sexaholic. I like it, though. I really like it. And all the time the photog watched me, watched me eating, drinking, dancing and then going off with my man.

Voyeurs, these photographers. They watch. The rest of us *do*.

My Brazilian was superb. He undid my silk shirt and kissed my breasts, holding me close and swaying to the music all the time. Brazil is a wonderful country for music and it seems to flow in the veins.

I felt him big through his trousers. I love this, the feel of an excited man when I am too, and he's OK and we're going to make it together. This guy was clean, really clean and he smelled good.

He stripped me, dancing all the time, and then he stood back and clapped at what he saw. 'Beautiful,' he breathed, 'so beautiful.'

Well, I'm not, but it does me no harm to be told it.

He slid his jacket off but then he went overwhelmed again and knelt, kissing my belly, kissing my crisp curls, kissing my thighs till my breathing quickened, and I thought travel wasn't such a bad thing.

His shirt was very stiff and white against the colour of his skin. I undid the buttons and kissed his smooth, hairless chest. I heard his breath catch as I undid the buckle at his waistband. It's nice to feel appreciated.

He wasn't much taller than me but he was muscled and firm. I stood facing him, rubbing my naked breasts against his naked chest. My hands undid his clothing and released it. I pressed my stomach forward. I get like this, proactive you might say, but he didn't mind one bit. His sex was hard between us, caught between us, and we were kissing and breathing a little crazy as we got more and more excited. He stepped out of his clothes. My hands closed over his buttocks. He was wonderful, firm and tight. He

14

kissed my throat and I could feel my own hair hanging down my back as I bent my head back and exposed my throat.

We were getting down on the carpet now, too greedy to make it to the bed. He was hung sweet and big, how I like them. The hell with this 'it's not what you got, it's what you do with it' stuff. If the key's too small for the lock, it ain't gonna open any doors. That's how I see it.

My door was opening. The man was kissing it sweetly and I writhed with pleasure. He pussy-kissed me till I was wet and he checked my humidity by putting his tongue inside. I tried to kiss his gorgeous pole, I love the taste of a man when he's hard and starting to drool, but he needed to get it inside.

Ah, it was sweet. It slid like a velvet-gloved iron bar, slick as an oil spill and sweet as a rose inside me. I clenched all my muscles and moaned softly with happiness. He moved it, sliding easily, pressing me open and filling me squeeze-tight, then pulling back till I cried with the loss. Then in he came again.

He didn't so much fuck with it as dance with it in me. He slid it about, now fast, now slow, now funny, now clever and then hard and tender in one shot. He began to push, getting greedier. I was coming back at him, trying to make it good for us both. My pussy-muscles sucked his lolly and sucked some more till he came. The man kept at it as he softened till I was there too.

I lay dreamy and pleased. He kissed the valley between my breasts and then he turned around and played with my toes, sucking and nibbling at them. I'd never reckoned them as an erogenous zone but this Brazilian, he could have made a carbuncle feel in the mood.

Idly I lifted his equipment. It was sticky up front

naturally enough, but behind the main event lay his velvet, swollen, soft fun-bags. I began to dip and toy with them.

I watched his gorgeous tool swell and slowly grow again, the soft wrinkled skin filling and becoming shiny. I began to kiss it, I love the feel of a man's sex in my mouth, and he reacted by getting up onto his hands and knees over me, facing the opposite way.

My legs came open. The dear man had everything hanging below the way nature intended and I could fill my mouth as much or as little as I wanted. Meanwhile, he dipped down between my legs and I felt his hair brush warm on the sensitive inner skin of my thighs.

He began to suck me properly. This wasn't a lazy wind-up to penetration. The man was taking me all the way. I felt pleased and surprised. Then I felt excited. He was licking me from my anus all the way round till he found my clitoris. He would stop here and nibble and chew on it a little till my hips bucked a bit because I was climbing the slope too quickly under this expert treatment. On the way back he lingered, biting gently at my labia and pulling my sex-lips, then kissing my pussy-mouth and sucking a little, before going on round to where I found it wriggly.

How many men know how to do this right? I put my hands over his buttocks and pulled his dangling cock down into my mouth. I began to suck very seriously, my fingers penetrating his tight cleavage and scratching gently at his anus.

He was putting his tongue in and sort of suck-pulling it out. At the same time he jigga-jigged with his chin on my clitoris. Just when I felt like bursting, he moved totally onto my bud and working it he made me come so I was wet and weak, my belly soft and yielding, all my senses ravished with his cleverness.

Sometimes I think they should start a school for men, teach them how to do it properly. This man could be Principal.

I was a player, too. I went on with him till his hips started to tremble. I even slid a fingertip into his tight rear orifice. Then he was jerking, thrusting uncontrollably and I was tasting his man-salt and taking it down.

We showered together after this. I was happy he didn't want to stay, I don't like men in the morning. I don't like anyone in the morning, even me. We agreed we had work to do and then we went to the door, him dressed again and me wearing my silk wrapper.

At my open door he kissed my lips and murmured something in Portuguese that sounded nice.

I watched him go down the corridor to the lift. As I did so, leaning on my door-frame like a trollop, with my hair all mussed and an idiot expression of repletion on my face, the photog came along the corridor.

It seemed he had the next room to mine. He looked at me as he went by. 'Good, was it?' he asked.

I had to hand it to him. The guy had nerve.

'It was so good even you look appetising,' I said. I said it to annoy, but there was an element of truth in it. He was tall, stood up, and he walked sort of easy, like his body was a friend.

He looked coolly at me, leaning there all fat with good sex.

'This is a mistake,' he said.

I gave him a lizard stare.

'Not that,' he said coldly, nodding over his shoulder at my departing lover. 'I mean you being here instead of Carl.'

17

'Don't mix up the side-show with the main action,' I said. 'I didn't want to come and I still don't.'

'I'll see you half-eight in the dining room. We have things to talk about.'

'Half-eight is for work,' I said, cold in my turn. 'If it's abuse, you can wait till past nine.'

His eyes narrowed but he couldn't think of a retort. I was grinning to myself as I shut my door. With sexy men it's simple. If you can't bed 'em, bait 'em.

My, I thought, falling asleep. So I think he's sexy.

I dreamed endlessly, the pics-man insinuating himself into my subconscious meanderings and causing me to awaken with muttered irritation. Once awake it was impossible to relax again and drop off.

Every insect for a thousand miles seemed to be buzzing or rubbing its legs together beyond my balcony. God knows what it would be like when we entered the jungle proper. Perhaps I should go shopping tomorrow for ear-plugs and a ten-gallon drum of insect repellent instead of the economy size I'd bought at Boots.

I sat up, switched on the light, cursing the fact that this wasn't the kind of hotel that had mini-bars in its rooms. In my silk pyjamas I padded barefoot to the louvred window and opened it, stepping out onto a wrought-iron balcony. Denied a stiff drink I'd decided upon some fresh Manaus night air. Almost at once my thoughts found a diversion: a drink, unwanted intrusions by a rude pics-man into my dream-world and the fact that Manaus night-life was of the air-borne, biting variety, were forgotten as I spied the goings-on in the room next to mine.

I'm no snooper. No Peeping Tom. What caught my eye was there, right before me, hard to miss. I didn't think I was a voyeur either, but for the life of me I

18

couldn't help but stand and watch, spellbound, intrigued to know what would happen next.

The wrought-iron balcony of our two rooms was a single structure, separated midway by an iron railing. Standing at the railing I could see right into the bedroom next door. The lamps were lit, casting a soft coral light over everything, the louvres opened to let in the night air. In the room were two waiters and a maid. This much I knew, for I'd encountered each of them earlier, going about their tasks.

The waiters were Julio and Ricardo. The chambermaid Constanza. They wore no uniforms with name badges now though, they were stark naked.

I was riveted. Bug-eyed. Was glad no one could see me. I felt like one of the dirty raincoat brigade but just couldn't stop myself. I had to see, watch, stay until the lights went out or the action ended.

Music played, it had a samba beat, and they danced, each man taking the girl into his arms in turn, holding her, twirling her, rubbing his erection against her, the other male pulling her from caressing hands into his own.

Constanza was beautiful. Dark, petite, her hair like sable, her eyes like Irish velvet. The men adored her, couldn't take their eyes off her, nor their hands.

Ricardo lifted her, hands about her tiny waist, speared her upon his slim blade of turgid flesh, swayed with her legs wrapping around him, her arms around his neck, his head ducking to suck on her breasts. Ooh my, I was getting hot all of a sudden. As hot as hell. I clenched my sex muscles repeatedly, ran a palm over my squirming mound. Lucky Constanza. I was doing some heavy breathing.

Julio was scrumptious. Indeed, I'd eyed him covetously when he'd carried my bags to my room. So was Ricardo. They might have been brothers. Dark skinned, black haired and eyed, tall, lean, as graceful as bullfighters, they were like Rudolph Valentino in stereo. Just a smouldering look from either of them made a woman wet, left her quivering. When I'd watched Julio pouring wine at a table adjacent to mine in the hotel's restaurant, I'd seriously contemplated inventing some debilitating ailment so that I could stay behind instead of taking part in this insane expedition up the Amazon, lie abed and make ample use of room service.

What Julio, Ricardo and Constanza indulged in was obviously no one-off bout of sexual gratification. I got the distinct impression that such get-togethers were a regular delight.

Ricardo lowered her to the rush matting beneath the air-conditioning fan that twirled endlessly from its ceiling mountings, making a rippling pattern circle over their bodies, his flesh filling her, thrusting at her, me watching his thick length bury itself deep in her compact juiciness. His shaft was hers, his balls bouncing tautly against her rectum. She jerked her body energetically, greedy, impatient. Such a perfect male specimen didn't awe her, obviously, the way he did me. Perhaps it was that his Latin beauty being novel to me added something to the basic act he performed. While to Constanza, Ricardo and Julio must have seemed handsome yet commonplace. Confronted by a blue-eyed, blond-haired Nordic type, doubtless she'd have been as ecstatic as I now felt.

I groaned inwardly. Must have groaned aloud too. The three people in the room paused, looked out through the opened French Provincial windows, looked straight at me. I began to mumble an apology for disturbing them.

Ricardo paused where he was, buried deep within Constanza, taking his weight on golden brown arms.

Julio came out onto the balcony, smiled at me and nodded his head deferentially. 'Does madam require anything?'

'I'll have what she's having,' I requested, leering, remembering that line from *When Harry Met Sally*, thinking myself real clever.

'She is having all,' said Julio, putting his arms around me and swinging me over the railings that separated us.

'All?'

'All. Yes. It is so, madam.'

'I can see that.'

'No, not yet. Ricardo *and* Julio are all. You watch. Perhaps you like, yes?'

'Umm. Maybe.' I was intent on the coupling taking place before my eyes, the sight of Ricardo sheathing himself up to his balls in the greedy little Constanza.

Julio advanced upon them, lying beside the copulating pair, smoothing the satin of an already erect penis, drawing it down to expose the sensitive, bulbous head, offering it to Constanza's mouth.

While Ricardo slid in and out of her, Constanza took Julio into her mouth, her pouting lips making a tight little circle about his cock, her mouth rising and falling to match the thrusts and jerks from his rigid member.

I hovered nearby. Spare, embarrassed to stay, yet too excited to leave, undoing the buttons of my silk pyjamas with fingers that seemed to work of their own volition, touching my own breasts, my sex which felt as if on fire. Compared to their deep, coffee-browness I was milk white, insipid, I felt.

The maid gave little squeals of delight around the midnight snack in her mouth, her pelvis rising, meeting Ricardo's relentless, piston-like performance. She came in spasms of pleasure, her groans loud at first

21

and typically Latin, dying away to a contented series of tremulous sighs.

Still hard, Ricardo beckoned with a crooked finger and a grin, showing off a silken rod of yummy proportions, coaxing me to the white-sheeted bed beneath the wispy white veil of mosquito netting. I didn't need any coaxing, was aquiver with good old uncomplicated lust. I dropped my silk pants and moved pronto.

Ricardo pulled me alongside him, a hand running from my cheek, down my neck, shoulder, hip and thigh, then back up on the inside. He wasted no time. He traced a finger feather-light through my bush and kept on going, up over my navel, my flat midriff (jee was I glad I'd kept up with the aerobics), to my lolling breasts. The Latin blade smiled, leaned forward and fastened his teeth and lips delightedly around a stiffened, perky nipple. His tongue ran over my generous white flesh, already red-spotted here and there from insect bites. Ricardo's mouth was definitely the most welcomed object to land in that vicinity since I'd got off the plane in South America.

While he made ravenous sorties at my breasts, his knee nudged my uppermost leg wide so that his rigid member could insinuate itself between my pussy-lips and caress me gently there, moving lightly, its progress moist and easy, his hand around the throbbing girth, guiding. He found my place easily, slipping into me with ease, I was so wet with hunger. I made an appreciative noise in the back of my throat and Ricardo laughed, kissing me fleetingly, his tongue jostling with mine.

His whole body was a gliding pleasure-giver, as pliant as a serpent. His body touched mine from head to toe, filled me too. I ran my fingers over him, loving the silken, damp lustre of his dark skin, licking his ear, his shoulder, clutching at his slim hips as he stroked into me. He slipped out of me. I groaned, mortified, squeezing my muscles against emptiness, clutched at the man possessively.

He laughed teasingly, gave me a mock frown, black eyes glinting. 'Madam is impatient. You must wait. The pleasure is all the sweeter for the delay.' His body moved over me, hardly touching, just a taut nipple glancing off my jutting shoulder. I tried to lie on my back, taking up the *numero uno* position for the action, but Ricardo held me still, on my side. As smooth as silk down my back now, his engorged penis slipping between my buttocks, sliding in the moisture, plunging back into me.

I grinned broadly, happy again, shivered as he licked around my ear, kissed my nape lingeringly.

Then Julio was on the bed as well, his penis now flaccid, Constanza looking replete and happy as she drank a glass of cool wine.

Julio finger-stroked my pink folds, touched where Ricardo moved in and out, setting off an electric shock of pleasure within my head. He opened the sex-lips fully, flickered with his tongue. I gasped, contracting around Ricardo and making him groan with pleasure. He was mvoing harder now, jerking with a violence I adored. Julio's tongue cut down across my bud, his fingers holding back the folds, exposing every secret sensor of delight, making me cry out as I came with amazement at the intensity of my pleasure, then cry out again as he continued and Ricardo thrust and thrust; in me to the hilt, yet trying to give more, go further, his hands holding my hips so that I took the full force of his love-strokes. He yelled, jerked, jerked like a dog mounted on the rear of a bitch, his movements reflexive, beyond his control. And I came again, gurgling with delight, catching at Julio's hair and tugging at it wildly as his tongue stroked me to exhausted rapture.

I hit the next day wearing this gorgeous number in twill which apparently the beasties can't burrow through. That is, it slows them down enough for you to swat them away. Or scram, yourself.

I considered wearing my snazzy rubber boots to breakfast to show the pics-man I was all equipped. These are *de rigueur*, I'd been told, for strolling in the rain forest while you watch the monkeys and the parrots.

In the event, I didn't. The man was so easy to tease, I didn't need props.

It was about eight forty-five when I sat down with my bath-tub of hot, sweet, milky coffee. At home it would have made me feel sick. Here it was gorgeous.

Ol' Sourpuss was right there opposite me. I took a good long look at him.

'What's the matter?' he growled.

'Neat shave. Good tan. Hair *au naturel*. You got some good points after all.' I considered. 'Those your own teeth, are they?'

He was silent for a moment. 'You are some pain in the ass,' he said eventually.

See? Easy to tease.

I drank my coffee and felt a sense of life and well-being invade my cells. I seem to remember that in Brazil they grow the stuff. Sinatra did the number.

The waiter brought a menu. 'You wanted to talk,' I said after ordering.

He had bacon, eggs and potato waffles with a stack of toast to follow.

'You talk to Carl about this business?'

'I told you, he had his jaws wired. The man could hardly blink. I went to see him but it was hopeless.'

'So what do you know?'

I shrugged. My croissants arrived, warm and flaky. 'Nothing,' I said. 'That's what I'm being paid for. I'm not replacing Carl, because I can't. What I can do is offer a fresh, unsentimental approach to the rain forest. No eco-tears, and the Chico Mendes T-shirt stays in the drawer.'

Chico Mendes was this rubber-tapper, a good guy. The snots shot him.

He looked at me. 'Are you for real?' he asked.

I grinned craftily. After a minute he gave up.

'You'll have to meet our patron. Our patroness.'

'Who's she?' Big Mac had mentioned her but he had been shifty over details. It was time I knew why.

'Martha Andersen Turner. She's a very rich lady and she's the piper paying the tune.'

'What's in it for her?'

He looked at me carefully. 'She likes to travel but she does it in comfort. She wants to see what all the shouting is about. She is not unintelligent nor is she unreasonable, but she's spending a lot of money and she intends to get value for it. She heads the Turner Trust. Occasionally when the New York Metropolitan can't afford a picture, the Turner Trust will buy it for them and donate it. She's not Carnegie and she's not Rockefeller, but she's not Little League, either.'

'She knows I'm a hack?'

'She knows and she doesn't mind. She didn't mind Carl, that is. But she vets the copy. That won't be your problem. Your editor will deal with her.'

For a mere photographer this man was bossy. And verbose.

'You mean if I say it's hot and the insects are biting, she tells my editor back home if that's OK?'

His eyes flickered. 'She won't care about stuff like

that. You leave me to deal with her. I've worked with her before.'

'Why's she tied up with a London paper?' I was bemused. 'Is there something I'm not understanding here?'

'She's not tied up. It was Carl she wanted, on my recommendation, as a writer and a useful man when civilisation is a long way away. Carl has the tie-up with your paper, not Martha.' He pushed away the remains of his breakfast and lit up without asking. 'Don't worry about it. Carl plays his own game, you know. Maybe he planned to syndicate stuff.'

'He didn't want me to come,' I said slowly. 'Am I queering his pitch?'

'The point is, she has the say-so whether you come along. I'll take you to meet her today. See, Carl knew what he was at. He could work his passage. You, you're just excess baggage.'

It seemed to me this was no more than the truth so I wasn't offended. It was Big Mac who was screwing up here. I looked at this peculiar pics-man. 'Who else is going?'

'Her step-daughter. Her secretary. A sort of male assistant stroke hired muscle to keep her safe. He's the organiser of the expedition. Then there are a couple of guys to tell her about the flora and fauna. A motor-man stroke cook. You and me, babe. The writer and the picture man.'

'Nine of us.'

'Hey, you can count.'

'Three women, six men.'

'Four women, five men. The secretary's a female.'

I considered. Finally I looked under my eyelashes at big-boy opposite. It was bugging me he got tastier the more I saw him. 'So what are the guys like?' I asked demurely. 'Any chance of some action for me?'

He smiled the way I imagine a crocodile does it and actually answered. I'd only been winding him up. 'Madame, as paymaster, expects first crack of the whip. The step-daughter seems mousey but she has that hungry look, if you know what I mean. The secretary's quiet, but me, I kind of like females that way. She's pretty, too.'

'Whew,' I said cheerfully. 'A double whammy.'

'I don't expect they'll bother with the cook. You might have a chance there.'

I grinned. 'When do I meet the boss-lady?'

'This afternoon. There's a meeting between all of us. That's when we'll find out when we're leaving.'

I finished my coffee. 'Where is the meeting?'

'At madame's hotel, the Rio Palace, near the airport. At three.'

'I'll be there.'

I wouldn't say that at this stage I knew something was going on. Certainly various things seemed odd to me, but then I knew Carl had the habit of playing a lone hand and I guessed I had fallen into a situation he had set up but one where I didn't know the rules.

Tough. Mac needn't have sent me blind like this. He had mentioned this Martha Andersen Turner to me but had given me to understand I was along on the paper's behalf, primarily. She was the free ride and none of my business. Now it was obvious Carl had a ploy going even if I didn't know what it was, but my best bet was to be sweet to the lady, write what I pleased and take it from there. Teasing the photog was just a little by-play to spice up an unwanted assignment. I could behave when I wanted to. It had seemed to me that the man was making assumptions when we met, that's why I had slapped him down so hard.

It was necessary but it was a pity. He was OK shape- and looks-wise. I just can't stand men who assume I'll come running when they crook the finger, and his ploy with my towel had had that smell.

So now I had this meeting to look forward to, when I'd meet the gang.

I shuddered. The sooner this whole trip was started and finished the better it would be. Then I could go home. I know it looks contrary, I didn't want to go and yet here I was preparing to make the effort to be accepted. But that's one of the things about me. It was OK for me to refuse to go in the first place, but having said I would go, I was damned if someone else was going to prevent me. I have this urge to control my own life, see.

It was an urge that was about to be unsatisfied for a very long time.

It was night-time. I'd had the meeting with Martha and the others. I felt I had an astonishing amount to think about. I am a hack, as I keep saying, and I could smell the sub-text. I just couldn't figure it out.

The heavy warm heat everywhere had made me dopey and I fell asleep in my cool room in that nasty way, sinking down through layers like I was suffocating. I was roused from this stupor by someone in my room.

Ho. Not me. I'm not your average vulnerable pigeon for the plucking. Metaphorically-speaking, if you get my meaning, I file my teeth and wear knuckle-dusters just to say hello.

I slid the flick-knife out from under my pillow. I'm not dumb enough to travel equipped through customs but I had fixed myself up in Belém. This pussy had claws.

'Sydney,' said a soft voice. A male voice. 'Miss Johnson.'

I eased the knife down by my hip and kept one hand on it. 'Who is it?' I asked unemotionally.

'Don't be frightened. It's Rory. Rory Duncan.'

'Mr Duncan, we're compatriots. I know you know to knock before you enter a lady's bedroom.'

'Put on a light. I don't want to trip over and make any noise. You have that American next door to you, don't you? I don't want him to know I'm here.'

I put on my bedside light and sat up. The air-conditioned room was a nice temperature, unlike the rest of this town.

I had found a specialist silk shop in Manaus and bought lavishly, charging it all to the paper. I'd bought my wrapper, some shirts, a couple of skirts and dresses and two pairs of gorgeous silk pyjamas. I was wearing one pair now, the cream material shining softly in the yellow glow of my bedside lamp.

A girl likes to look nice in bed, especially when someone like Rory Duncan is in the room.

I'd thought Matheson, the photographer, a reasonable looking man. Rory had him beat. Rory had most men beat, and beside him Matheson looked like a gargoyle. His looks weren't pansy at all, he was all male. He reminded me of the young Sean Connery.

As I said before, he was British, as was the other flora/fauna expert coming along on the trip. Martha sure knew how to pick 'em.

'I needed to speak to you privately without the others knowing I'd done so.'

He stood in the middle of the floor. He wore black trousers, a black T-shirt and sneakers. Sneakers for sneaking into bedrooms. I don't like being taken for granted but a man who looks and moves like Duncan might find he can overcome my prejudice.

'Can I sit down?' he asked. He spoke sort of soft public school, a flower of England's finest. Me, I'm a weed out of Brixton, hoarse and coarse.

'This couldn't wait till morning?'

He sat on the end of my bed. I restrained myself from feeling how messy my hair was. The flick-knife was hard by my right thigh.

'I'm sorry. Look, you can trust me.'

Oh? Certainly, Doctor Crippen. But I didn't say it out loud.

'It was such a shock when Tom brought you along this afternoon. I don't understand why your paper sent you instead of Carl. I mean, he was coming along as himself, not as a reporter.'

'You explain that to my editor,' I said. 'Carl's editor. Maybe he presented himself as more of a free spirit than he was in reality. We're all hired help, Mr Duncan, one way or another.'

'Call me Rory.' He inched up the bed. His weight was nice. 'Martha took to you,' he confided, 'else you would have been out on your ear.'

I looked at him steadily. 'I liked her. A gutsy lady. Not softened by riches one bit.'

'You understand her. She's a good judge of character. Still, I was surprised. This trip could get uncomfortable. Have you been remote before?'

I considered. 'I've made it to Croydon once or twice,' I offered.

He laughed. 'Martha's not the only gutsy lady,' he said softly.

There was a moment's silence. My itch to know is strong. Sometimes it's stronger than my other itch.

'So, call-me-Rory,' I said. 'Just why are you here?'

He stopped the romancing immediately. I gave a mental sigh and unplugged my ears.

'Er, just how well do you know Carl?' he asked. 'I mean, I know you are colleagues.'

'I'm features,' I said flatly. 'Carl's travel. I see him across the office maybe once, twice a year.'

Rory was bright-eyed, like a blackbird. 'You'll have discussed this trip, though. I mean, he chose you to come in his stead.'

Sometimes you have to trade information to get it. 'Not exactly,' I said, lying through my teeth. You don't have to trade correct information. 'He was badly hurt, Rory. He couldn't say much. He just gave me a rough idea.'

'A rough idea of what?'

Oh ho, I thought. My little nostrils were quivering like a hungry shrew's.

'You know Carl,' I said, shrugging my silk-clad shoulders. 'The man isn't straightforward.'

Rory leaned forward putting one hand on my blanket-covered thigh. With his sort you do it with the light on. You don't want to miss the visual input. Black hair, broad brow, humorous eyes. I couldn't even remember Tom Matheson's name.

'I don't know Carl,' he said softly again. 'That's the trouble. I have thoughts about Carl, thoughts that make me uneasy. I don't trust this American pho- tographer he was so friendly with, either. I tried to advise Martha against them both but she knows best, she says, and I daren't say any more.'

'You feel like sharing these thoughts?' I invited. This is the nearest I get to fishing.

'How do I know whether to trust you?'

'You don't. But Tom Matheson doesn't like me and tried to send me back where I came from. Does that help things?'

He grinned. 'I think Carl has something going. This is supposed to be a trip up the Amazon, maybe taking in a tributary or two, trying to spot as many animals and birds as possible. Carl acted as if it was something quite different, or so it seemed to me. Martha is a tough lady but in one sense she's vulnerable.'

'And that is?' I prompted.

'She's rich. She's a commodity.'

I had it in a flash. What if clever old Carl had fixed for Martha to be kidnapped. He could save her, claim a reward and write something thrilling for the paper, for the world.

It fitted with my estimation of Carl's sneaky character. Carl and I were a little hotsy-footsy once, though I don't bring the subject up if I can help it. The man was nasty between the sheets.

Information shared is information weakened. I opened my eyes wide. 'You think Mrs Turner might be in danger in some way?' I gasped coyly.

'It's possible.' The man was gorgeous when he was solemn. He was gorgeous full stop. He also knew a good deal more than he was telling me.

There would be time to find out.

'Might the rest of us be in danger?' I cooed, trying not to overdo it.

Rory oozed up the bed a little. 'You have a friend now,' he said. 'You have to believe this.'

Knee-jerk script, huh? 'I'm a fair judge of character myself,' I said and fiddled with my jim-jams.

He stroked some hair back from my face. A moment later his lips brushed my cheek, by my ear. I shivered suddenly. This was a beautiful member of the species.

He was whispering. 'You have a pretty adult mind,' he said.

Hoo, boy. Was it masturbation with birch rods or just that he liked to wear women's clothing?

'Can you understand what it means to me, to come

on this trip?' All the time he spoke his lips caressed my cheek-bone.

'What do you mean?'

'It's very hard to get funding. I'm not independently wealthy. Like you, I'm hired help.'

'So?' I said, relaxing back and closing my eyes. Every nerve-end the guy touched sat up and wanted more.

'Martha doesn't only have a vigorous mind. She has a vigorous body.'

I held still. He nuzzled my hair and delicately licked my ear. 'I can't please myself,' he whispered. 'When Martha buys help, she buys it all ways.'

I kept silent. There's not a lot to say when the man you lust for tells you he's a prostitute.

'I didn't mind till you came along. I mean, I like her. It wasn't a penalty. Far from it. It was a pleasure. But it leaves me in a bad position now.'

I liked his position, frankly, pressed against me, kissing my face, his hand gently touching the silk of my pyjamas.

He kissed my eyelids, the corner of my mouth. 'I want to make love to you,' he said, his hand gently scrunching the material at my breast. 'But if Martha finds out, she'll sack me.'

'She didn't strike me as possessive,' I said. Frankly, I was out of my depth.

He kissed my jaw-line, my throat. 'All rich people are possessive,' he said. 'It's a law of nature. Darling, I'm going to have to go.'

I was angry suddenly. Clit tease, that's what he was. Then I looked at him and my heart melted. He looked beautiful, rueful and knowing. 'I won't always be on the company's pay-roll,' he said. 'Really, she's a nice lady in lots of ways. I have to go along because

I'm sure she is in danger. Can I take it you're on my side?'

I looked at him steadily, willing my pussy to calm down. 'I'm on my side,' I said.

He grinned. 'That'll do, Sydney Johnson. What's good enough for you is good enough for me any day of the week.'

After he was gone I had such rich food for thought I nearly had indigestion. I got up and paced my room, leaving all but my bedside light off. The trouble with pretty people is that they can't help manipulating. The thing was, did one hold it against a dog for barking. If I'd been a beauty, I'd have done it too. It wouldn't have made me any less honest or decent than I might otherwise happen to be, but as an extra weapon in the armoury, I'd have used it.

What I'm trying to say is that although Rory the Fair was specious and manipulative, he wasn't necessarily wrong or bad. It was just his way, like eating and drinking.

Anyway, why make such a story up? There was no benefit that I could think of. Certainly I had felt from my brief dealings with Tom Matheson that something was going on.

Should I tell this to Rory? If Tom and Carl were partners, then Carl being absent would surely have put paid to any plan they might have hatched for the greater glory of themselves. I certainly didn't believe Carl was an out and out villain. It was just simply that I knew he was a man who liked things tricky, he enjoyed living on the edge, he was a damn fine writer and he quite enjoyed other people's pain. That he had a scam going was eminently believable.

What if Matheson went ahead without his erstwhile partner? He wasn't like any photographer I'd ever

34

known. As a rule, they are a dumb breed watching the world through a Nikon lens and misanthropic to his fellow man. Sad, sour and silent they tend to be, with their whole world contracted to two dimensions with artificial perspective.

Matheson wasn't that way at all. He was lippy and lively. Suspicious as hell.

I'd just reached this point in my thoughts when I heard a noise. As Rory Duncan had known, sound travelled through the walls of this hotel. Now I heard movement next door. Then I heard the unmistakable sound of a key turning in a lock. In a split second I was at my own door. I heard the door next to mine close in its frame. The key turned, more quietly this time, and footsteps receded down the corridor.

I eased my unlocked door open and peeped. Matheson was just vanishing into the fire escape.

I slid my feet into sneakers, pulled a linen jacket over my pyjamas, grabbed my room key and some money, then I was out and running.

I ran down the concrete stairs as fast as I could, slowing down cautiously at the bottom. I slid into the lobby and looked.

It was three in the morning. It was hardly surprising the place was dim-lit and quiet. I ran lightly across the lobby and out onto the street.

I could see him, moving fast, already some distance from the hotel entrance.

I was on the Praça Adalberto Valle, in the central district of the city. Matheson, as best I could tell, was heading for the docks.

I had to run to keep him in sight but he never looked back. We quickly left the high-rise modern area and entered the older, low stucco-built town. Matheson went a little slower here and I closed up,

35

moving silently on rubber-soled shoes, always ready to dart into one of the plentiful door or alleyways.

There was a smell of rotting vegetation and bats swooped between the buildings and the trees. We passed what was in the daytime a busy market-place. We went into a yet older part of the town, all residential, with ghostly lines of washing hung above between the tenements.

I had to keep close now but he never looked back.

Suddenly, he turned through an archway. I followed and found myself in a courtyard with an old dry fountain as a weedy centre-piece. Somewhere music played even at this late hour and when I looked up, one or two of the balconies showed a gleam of light through shuttered windows.

The smell was of cats and urine, the night warm and heavy as a mouldy damp blanket.

Matheson was gone. I searched round the dark doorways quickly. They were passages through the buildings with doors in their walls leading into common stairwells. By one of these was a square of light and I heard voices.

I peeped over a high sill. I was looking into a dirty room, the most notable feature of which was a huge flypaper hanging from the ceiling embedded with thousands of black corpses.

I cast round me and found a wooden slatted box in some rubbish. I put this under the window and stood on it, praying no one would come. I was perched in the main entrance to this section of the building, after all, even if it was very late at night. Or early in the morning. There are two ways of looking at everything, as all news-people know. And neither of them might be the right one.

Matheson was there, all right, with a dwarf. I kid you not. The little guy wore a royal blue, glazed cotton shirt with white dots all over it and dark trousers. His shirt was open at the neck and he wore jewellery there, at least three gold chains, one with a medallion on it.

The little guy was dirty and he had terrible teeth. I'm not anti the vertically challenged in life, I'm just reporting facts. Since both he and Matheson spoke Portuguese, I didn't understand a word.

The little guy had something in a package. Matheson wanted to see it. There was an argument and Matheson became so threatening the little guy pulled a knife.

I had my flick-baby in my jacket pocket since I'm a lady who likes the freedom of the streets without a bodyguard. I considered whether Matheson needed help and if so, whether it was my place to supply it. If I could have understood, maybe I would have rooted for the dwarf.

Matheson had his hands up, evidently placating the irascible little fellow. It must have worked because the knife disappeared and grudgingly, or so it seemed to me, the dwarf handed over the package.

Matheson unwrapped the filthy paper. He held the object up to his face. He scrutinised it. The dwarf hopped up and down with anxiety. Finally Matheson reached into his pocket and pulled out a fat wad of paper money.

Then the pain exploded in my head and I fell slowly off my box into the void. I'll get blood on my pyjamas, I thought, before losing consciousness.

I woke up and was sick. Someone held me over as I inelegantly emptied my stomach. The pain in my skull was crucifying. My face was wiped with a paper towel and then I was laid down again. Something freezing and wet was laid on the back of my head. I began feebly to yelp and whine.

'Shut up,' said a familiar voice. 'I knew you'd be trouble,' it added.

'You skunk,' I said, all muffled straight into the pillow.

'You're feeling better.' There was satisfaction in his voice. He allowed me to sit up.

My eyes felt like someone had stamped in them. My teeth felt loose. The back of my head was on fire. Even my eyelashes hurt. I peered blearily at Matheson who was sitting over me where I lay propped on my bed. 'So what happened?' I croaked.

'You don't remember?'

'Remember what?'

'Someone broke into your room, presumably to steal since no man in his right mind would tangle with you in bed. You must have woken up and been sapped.'

'Where's the doctor? Where's the police?'

'Don't whine, girly, it's just a bump. You can call the medicos and the police if you want, but I won't. Mrs Turner doesn't want attention being drawn to this trip yet. She'll make good anything you lost.'

'My health.'

'You'll feel better in the morning.'

'Which is when?'

'A couple of hours.'

The back of my head was wet where he had put an ice-pack on it. I lay back gently. They call it referred pain, I think. My whole body was very referred while my head had hot fireworks going all the time.

'Give me some aspirin,' I whimpered.

'No. Just sleep will fix you up. Take aspirin tomorrow if you are sure you're getting better.'

'I hate you.'

'I'm not crazy about you.'

I lay with my eyes shut. He did things, clearing away the mess I'd made. Presently I began to snore but even that didn't wake me up. I slept.

I felt better in the morning, though not by much. Matheson wasn't there but I had the feeling he had only just left. There was a smell of cigarette smoke in the air and the ashes in the ashtray still seemed warm.

I eased off on the air-conditioning. You aren't supposed to feel cold in Brazil but I was shivering.

I dialled room service and ordered coffee. My gummy eyes swept the room indifferently. I couldn't see signs of any sneak-thief.

I drank the sweet milky coffee greedily when it came. Then I ran myself a bath. I was in this when Matheson came back.

'You in there, Johnson?' he roared through the door.

'Go away,' I said feebly.

He came in anyway. I was lying soaking under a mountain of bubbles and I glared at him.

He started to snigger. 'You look terrible,' he said. 'Like an angry albino slug.' He sat on the edge of the bath.

'I feel terrible. I got hit, remember?'

'Sure do. You make a lousy next-door neighbour. I've hardly slept for mopping up your ghastly body fluids.'

'You want me to say thank you?' I gasped incredulously.

'Hey, toots, I saw off the bad man and saved your personal effects. At least I reckon I did. They didn't look mussed up to me. Then I brought you back to the land of the living and performed disgusting and

39

menial services for you. Yes, goddammit, I want you to say thank you.'

'Thank you,' I said, subsiding.

He trailed a hand in my bubbles. 'You remember him yet?' he asked casually.

'Nope. What was he like?'

'Twenties, thin, broken nose, tight jeans, shirt with parrots on it, Nike trainers.' He regarded me for a moment. 'Let's look at the bump, then.'

I sat forward obediently and rested my forehead on my knees. Gentle fingers explored the back of my skull. I winced when they got too intimate.

'You're already fossilised,' he said eventually. 'A blow like that would have killed a lesser man. You, it hardly broke the skin.'

'How long was I out cold for?' I asked, blowing bubbles.

He tugged my shoulders and made me lean back in the bath. My bare, wet breasts dripped foam.

'Ten minutes. Not more. Or I would have called out a doc.'

I made no move to duck my breasts under. After a while he touched the one nearest him, running his thumb over the nipple when I didn't say anything. 'It's not a bad body, considering,' he said.

'Considering what?'

'You're a werewolf. One who doesn't change back, either.' He bent and kissed my breast.

My face must have been red as a turkey-cock in all that heat and steam. The bath was as hot as I could bear it. I looked at the top of his brown head of hair as he kissed my secondary sexual characteristics.

Did he think I believed him? I could see the yellow square of light right now in my imagination, clear as I had seen it for real last night. He must have carried me back to the hotel. It was a town you could do that sort of thing in and not be interfered with.

I must have been out a while. At least he had sat with me till I came round, making sure I wasn't dead. Making sure I didn't remember.

The thing was, I didn't. I mean I remember thinking the transaction was complete and I'd better get off my box and hide as he might be coming out at any moment. Then I was slugged. But I couldn't remember if there had been an interval between the two events.

In other words, who slugged me? It couldn't have been Matheson if my memory had no gaps because I was watching him when it happened. But I couldn't be sure. I was certainly thinking about hiding and maybe I had done so and Matheson had spotted me at the window, slunk out and biffed me one.

To kill me? Surely not. He could have carried me down to the docks and thrown me over, end of story. Instead, he'd brought me back and brought me round. Then he'd checked up on what I remembered.

What would he have done if I'd admitted remembering? Slugged me again? Had he a story ready? He'd had plenty of time to concoct one.

It was strange to think thoughts like these when the man concerned in them was kissing my breasts. His hair tickled my nose. He looked up and we were almost nose to nose.

'If I kept my eyes shut all the time I think I could get to like you a little,' he said softly.

'I'm always grateful when a man says he likes me.' I was going cross-eyed.

'I'd have to shut my ears, too.'

He bent right forward and kissed me on the lips. Gently. I kissed right back. The kiss grew hot and sexy, firming up in a meaningful way.

41

I put my wet arm round his neck. I pulled.

He fell into the bath and it was very messy, water everywhere. He cursed and struggled while I laughed and groaned as my head hurt. When he had extricated himself he stared down at me, dripping.

A whole lot of water had gone, including most of the foam. My naked body was revealed.

'Gee, your suit's a mess,' I said.

He started to speak and stopped. He tried to start again and again he bit it off short. 'Oh shit,' he said and pulled off his clothes.

He turned me over and took me from behind. If you figure it, there aren't many comfortable ways to make it in a bath-tub. His cock was wet and foamy as it slid into my soft, aroused pussy and he took me quickly, working his anger and his lust off together.

It's hard to say why I let him. Partly it was revenge. I had been aroused by Rory-the-Fair the previous night and the memory of his gentle tender kisses was very sweet. He had made me feel womanly and desired in a way not many men can do, especially when they're telling me they ain't gonna do it.

It's cruel to a man to use him to satisfy the lust aroused by another but we're all cruel some of the time and they do it to us, of course. If Matheson made me mad in the near future, I might tell him what I'd done. Meanwhile, it felt nice having my sex filled with a throbbing heavy cock, knowing the man didn't like me and couldn't help himself. Queen pussy ruled over king cock. I felt horny, he had the equipment.

He sat down afterwards and had me sit facing him while the water refilled around us. He kissed me a little, the poor sap had it hard. 'We could declare a truce,' he said. 'We're leaving tomorrow and really we have to get along.'

'I'd like that,' I said demurely. I touched his shaft. 'You're quite handy with that.' A little ploy was starting to develop in my mind. If I inflated his ego he might not spot it.

'You're a terrible woman.'

'I'm weak with concussion. I'll spend today in bed, I think.'

'Good idea. It might keep you out of trouble.'

Whoops. 'But I was in bed when trouble struck,' I said innocently.

'It won't strike again. Can I bring you something to eat?'

'Mmm. A nice head on a plate.'

'I knew you reminded me of someone,' he groaned. 'I bet Salomé said thank you without being asked when she was rescued.'

Rescued, huh.

His cock floated up with the water. Have you noticed how the Plimsoll line on men varies with the state of their erections?

I stood up and he bent forward and bit gently at my wet and streaming mound. Then he nuzzled it slightly and licked so that my knees felt suddenly weak.

'Hey,' I said feebly. 'I'm going to dry myself and lie in the sun on my balcony. Croissants and coffee would be wonderful.'

I stepped out and took a towel. I rubbed myself carefully. The truth was, I didn't feel good.

He brought me breakfast and then he left me. He said he wanted to go round the town snapping it before we all set sail tomorrow.

That was good. Very good. I wanted him well away from the hotel. I had long since formed the intention of breaking into his room and finding the package he had bought last night from the dwarf. I wanted a closer look. The whole thing was a bit like a dream sequence now. I wanted to straighten myself up mentally before going on. I'm nosey, too.

What would a man who was about to go up the Amazon bird-spotting with his camera want with such a thing? What was so special about it? Very much he was the sort of man who might smuggle a little, find the angle in a given situation. But how could the thing I had seen him buy be worth clicking me over the head? Did he really think I was so upright and law-abiding that I couldn't shut up at the sight of a little illicit wheeler-dealing?

Where had it come from? Why had the dwarf had it? How had Matheson known about it? Was this the scam I half-believed must exist for this whole thing to be worth Carl's while?

Did Martha Andersen Turner know about it?

What was it? Well, as best I could tell in the poor light with my head about to be half-broken, it was a mask.

A mask.

Now where could be the harm in a thing like that?

Chapter Two

I broke Matheson's door lock with cunning subtlety. I trotted downstairs and took a nice flat-sided rock out of the hotel flower-bed. I used this as a hammer on the handle of a screwdriver, a thing I have by me always, chiselling the woodwork away from the bit that held the door shut.

No one came along the corridor during the crucial few minutes. I surveyed my work with satisfaction, blowing little curls of paint and chips of wood off my fingers. I put the makeshift breaking and entering tools inside Matheson's door. Humming to myself, I began to search his room.

Men aren't subtle at all. They rely too much on brains and brawn. Me, I rely on being sneaky.

I pulled the room about. He was neat and his stuff was orderly, until I passed through it. It didn't take me long to find the mask hidden in his clean boxer shorts but by the time I did the room looked as though a small tornado had passed that way.

I examined the thing. It was made of a wood so hard and dark and close-grained it felt like warm metal. There was an intaglio design carved into it, a little like tribal markings. It was a long face, not expressionless exactly, but one that left me without the words to describe it. The cheek-bones were high and emphasised by the carving. The long almond-shaped eyes sloped upwards at their outer edges. The Roman hooter wouldn't have shamed a horse.

It was terrifically alien, superficially simple and it felt as old as hell.

I didn't exactly like it but I was reluctant to put it down. I waltzed through the mess I had made and stood myself in front of a mirror.

I put the mask on. It had no evident means of fixing, no thong or thong-holes for that matter, though the wood curved round in imitation of the human face. I had only meant to hold it to my face but I found my face fitted into the curve of the thing quite comfortably and then it seemed lightly to clasp me, so that I could let go.

My eyes shone from the eye slits, giving it life. The warm breath from my nostrils clouded the dark, glossy upper lip. The wetness on my inner mouth was a half-hidden gleam.

The incised cheek-bones glittered slightly.

I saw the waters stained dark with tannins and toxins from the endless abundance of trees. Leaf-litter floated in sluggish whirls on the sullen surface. On either side the trees curved and bent towards us, their tops closing in an embrace full of subtle menace. Half-submerged logs lay forward of us, blocking our way. Behind us the water bubbled slowly, settling after our rough passage.

The men were in the water chest-deep, pulling the fallen trees aside, hacking with machetes at the greedy fingers of vegetation threatening to overwhelm the silent, narrow, jungle-deep waterway.

'Anhinga,' someone said. The bird rose with a noisy self-

important flurry from the surface of the water, its long thin neck and head extended, its tail fanned. It was a dark oily green, messy with white splashes.

We entered the lagoon. The men climbed hurriedly back into the boats. There would be piranha here.

We fished and rested for some time. Then we could not find the right exit to the lagoon, not for a long time. The current was weak and sly . . .

'What the hell!' roared Matheson.

I turned to him and the mask smiled. He went white, the skin so bleached at his cheek-bones that they shone as if fleshless. I removed the mask.

I had made my cream silk pyjamas messy the night I trailed Matheson. That had only been the previous night. My time sense was screwy. Now I was in my peach pair.

I felt the material slide cool against my skin. I saw Matheson slowly regain his colour. His face was lean and the skin gleamed. His jaw-line was strong. His ears were set neat to his skull, the brown hair pushed carelessly back.

He carried his hat in one hand. I saw the long, sinewy fingers. The shirt was open-throated and I could see river-dark shadows at the base of the neck.

I wetted my lips.

'My room,' he said hoarsely. His eyes had a queer glint to them. They were fixed on my face.

'Tom,' I said softly. Wonderingly.

He took a step back and put a hand up as if to ward me off.

I smiled. I unbuttoned my jacket. My breasts hung, not heavy but light and swingy, pointing forwards, slightly apart, as if to embrace.

Matheson croaked slightly and moved towards me. A humming started in my mind. I stepped out of my pyjama bottoms. Matheson closed with me, putting his arms round me and holding me pressed against his body so that I felt the hardness of him.

His mouth found mine. I moved my body against his. He made a small noise deep in his throat. Then he looked down into my eyes and his hands slid up under my open jacket so that they were warm against the satin of my skin.

I pressed into his groin and felt him there, wonderful. Ready. He shivered slightly and kissed my throat. I backed off my hips a little and ran my fingernails lightly over the front of his trousers. He expelled air sharply and I undid his belt.

We fell slowly to the floor in a tangle of his strewn possessions. He licked my belly and then drew his body up so that he could enter me, between my long legs. Long he was, long and wide and satisfying. I felt him slide into me so all my body wallowed in the teasing pleasures of desire. He fucked like champagne, slightly fizzing, and I lifted to each stroke and absorbed it deep into me.

His weight was delicious, heavy but not pressing, a sort of sprung strength.

Afterwards, after his own urgent thrusting and my soft bubbling melting, we lay, warm.

Matheson came round first. His cock had half slid out of me and lay damp and slightly sticky against my thigh.

'What the hell, Johnson?', he mumbled, bemused.

My mind tingled. Prickled. What the hell, indeed. A storm had passed over me leaving me naked and wondering why the hell I was on the floor with him. Sweet charity, was I crazy?

I struggled to sit up.

His ugly, slightly rugged face looked up at me, letting me have the first word. Letting me set the tone. 'I can't think why I did that,' I said flatly. It was true.

He drew breath. 'You're the only woman I know turns into a frog when you kiss her.'

'Kiss? Is that what you call what we did?' I was mad at myself.

'Fuck.' He sat up. 'Succubus.' He pulled his clothes together, not looking at me.

It was like we were teenagers, embarrassed at the consequences of fledgling passion.

'I woke up,' I said cleverly, getting in first, 'hearing this muffled noise from your room. Of course, it could have been you masturbating, or whatever your sort of primate does by himself, so I didn't rush to investigate. Then I opened my door and I saw your door was open. This guy was wrecking the room. When he saw me he did a dive over the balcony. On the way he dropped your little ethnic curio.'

'You saw him? What was he like?'

'Skinny,' I said. 'Young. Squinty nose. His shirt was all over parrots. I didn't get the make on his trainers.'

There was a moment's absolute silence between us. I mean, the guy couldn't say he knew I lied because it was his lie to me I was giving right back.

He swallowed painfully. 'The same guy,' he muttered.

'You told me he wouldn't be back,' I said, wide-eyed with innocence.

'I didn't think he would be,' he growled. In an objective way I wondered if it was the sex impairing his thought processes or that he simply wasn't quick enough in the mental sphere. Whichever, I felt comfortably superior.

'You'd better report this to the management,' I said sagely. The room sure was a mess.

'No,' he said grimly. 'I'll have to see if anything's

missing. But like I told you, I don't want to draw attention to us.'

'He didn't look as if he had anything when he took a dive off your balcony, unless it was small, like papers or money. He dropped the mask.'

'The mask,' said Matheson, oddly.

I yawned. 'I didn't take you for a sucker,' I said.

'You've changed your mind?'

'Market trash. Made for tourists. Act your age, camera-man. It was probably made in Hong Kong.'

'Out of my room, frog. You bring me bad luck.'

'Ribbet,' I said amiably and left him to it.

We all met for drinkies in Ms Turner's palatial hotel out by the airport that afternoon. This was our last dose of air-conditioned decadence. We were due to leave at dawn the next day.

Martha drew me to one side. Rory watched us. I winked. Sydney, I told myself, you're dazzled. And I was.

'I hear you were hit over the head,' she said. She had snappy black eyes and a fine-lined skin that looked great from a distance. It wasn't so bad close-up, either. I guess Rory didn't have to shut his eyes or anything.

'A thief in my room. I'm better now.'

'You can still back out.'

'You can forbid me to come with you,' I said courteously, 'but if it's up to me, I'll swing along.'

She looked a little restless. 'What if something goes wrong?' she suggested. 'We might have to live rough for a while, hunting, eating only a little, you know what I mean?'

She had fifteen years on me. Mind you, she looked tough as a tortoise.

I shrugged. 'I might not like it but I promise to keep

the whining under control. It'll be my fault I'm there, or my editor's. I'll have no one local to blame.'

'There are biting ants. Wasps. Hornets.'

I smiled. 'Blotches suit me. Ask Matheson. He thinks I'm a frog already.'

'Are you OK with snakes? We can't have hysterical women along.'

'There's no snake in the world,' I said firmly, 'can say a bad word about me. I can show respect. I even hold doors open for them and give up my seat on the bus.' Why was I saying all this? They terrify me.

Martha grinned unwillingly. 'It's against my better judgement,' she said. 'I want a writer along very badly. Carl would have been perfect. We had this little thing going, too.' She put her head on one side and eyed me, waiting.

I looked her in the eye. 'I can write,' I said flatly. 'There are enough men along, surely, to provide the full requirement for muscle.' I hesitated just a fraction before saying this final word.

She read my lips. I had accepted the pecking order. She was first and intended staying there.

I kept pretty quiet for the rest of this apparently festive occasion. I found myself watching the step-daughter, though.

Her name was Carla Mignari. I was to find out that she was actually the daughter by a previous marriage to Joaquim Turner's wife, before Martha. That is, rightly Carla was Joaquim's step-daughter. Her mother, former wife to Joaquim Turner, had died and he'd remained as guardian to the young girl. Later he'd married Martha who had herself become fond of the girl. When Joaquim died, Martha sort of inherited her, but it seemed a willing inheritance, for Carla, though young, was of age and had independent means. They remained together by choice.

She was quite unlike her surrogate mother in every possible way. Physically she was dark haired to Martha's harsh blondeness, with a pale creamy skin and big, dark, dreamy eyes. She was quiet and soft spoken, shy even. Her smile was gentle and rare. Martha's aide-de-camp and male assitant cum muscleman, Big Jacko, was protective towards her.

I knew the look in her eyes, though. Every so often they dwelt expressively on Rory. Me, when I go for a man and allow myself to let it show, I narrow my eyes greedily and think dirty thoughts. Carla wasn't like that. Her eyes became vast and haunted. We had the same basic feelings, though, even if they came out different. We had the hots for the man. And it wasn't conversation we were after. It was the physical connection that was our goal, fitting those rude bits together the way they went so snug.

We split up and went to bed early. We would be meeting at the docks with our gear in the pre-dawn to go aboard our boats. There were two because they were both small, small enough to go up narrow riverways.

I could not get shot of the feeling that strange things were going on, things under the surface of an innocent expedition. Heaven knows, it was complicated enough on the bureaucratic level. Martha had had to arrange authority for our departure from Ibama, the State environment agency, from Funai, the Indian Institute, from the Superintendency for Amazonian Development and from the newly formed Extraordinary Ministry for the Articulation of Actions in Legal Amazonia.

All to look at parrots. Phew!

I was sweetly sleeping when Matheson beat on my door. 'Wake up, viper-pants,' he called. 'Time to go mess about on the river.'

I moaned and turned over. My bed felt fantastic. Matheson reached in and put my main light on.

'Pox on you,' I snarled.

He grinned. 'I already got it,' he said cheerfully and vanished.

I showered and dressed rapidly. I knew deep in my gut this was a very bad idea and I had suckered myself into going along. My gear was packed and ready when Matheson reappeared like the bad fairy bearing coffee and doughnuts.

'I eat croissants for breakfast, not children's cakes,' I said ungraciously.

He ate a doughnut whole. 'You could do with sweetening,' he observed. I bared my teeth and snarled at him. 'She can smile,' he said happily.

My pussy lay quiet, a warm slug under my belly. I was embarrassed about screwing this man. What had come over me? It made me want to hurt him. I didn't want him running off with the idea I liked him.

We shared a taxi to the docks. We were the only two in our hotel. The rest of them had stayed with Martha in her five-star doss, with the exception of the cook and motor-man, who lived local.

The boats were small, horribly small. Maybe only thirty foot long, or so it seemed to me. In the front one went Martha, Carla her step-daughter, Big Jacko her personal bodyguard, Rory and Colin Brown, the other bugs-and-flowers man. In our boat, the second one, came Pablo the cook-boatman, a Venezuelan. There was me and there was the pics-man, Tom Matheson. And there was Marguerite Halloran, Martha's secretary.

We left before dawn, just. The sky was suddenly gold and purple. A couple of bits of lint up there pretended to be clouds. The river surface was wide and smooth save for the ripples of the front boat.

'Tonina,' said Pablo suddenly.

'Dolphins,' said Marguerite.

I stared. The river dolphins tumbled about us. There was some noise and laughter from the front boat. After a while the dolphins left us.

It grew hot. The banks of the river were all tall trees hung with lianas. Flowers spilled into the light area of the river bank, the jungle itself looking dark and unwelcoming. Little birds with white wings flittered to and fro over the water. There were great big things on long stalky legs, species of heron and egret, I guess. Suddenly two blue and yellow birds flew across the river.

'Parrots,' I yelled.

'Macaws,' said Pablo and winked at me. He had broken, blackened stumps where you and I keep teeth.

I realised I was going to have to work harder at not being impressed.

Matheson took pictures. Marguerite checked the stores in our boat. I lay on my back and slept. Pablo steered the boat. After a while Matheson relieved him.

We ate packed lunches supplied by the hotel. We went on. The river went on. There were more birds. There were lots and lots of trees. We had big engines on the boats and we went fast.

Funny way to take a holiday, I thought, half asleep. You'd almost think we were heading somewhere.

The water was a very peculiar colour, part murky brown, part black. Pablo explained. 'Is Rio Negro an' Rio Amazon,' he said. 'Wedding of the waters. They not mix like man an' wife, ha?' He grinned, having evidently made a joke. I grinned back. It occurred to me we had something of a naturalist on board, even with our second-class boat.

At last we turned off this giant waterway and entered a smaller river. The green walls came closer on either side with trees and branches growing in the water itself, and navigation was more difficult because there were many straggly vegetation-covered islands in the stream. Some were just rocks with toupees. Others could have hidden entire tribes of blowpipe-carrying Indians, or so it seemed to me. Maybe I just have an overactive imagination.

We stopped and a camp was made. It seemed the ladies slept on board while the men were consigned to the bank, which in this case was some granite boulders sticking up. Martha brazenly took Rory off with her in an inflatable to explore, she said. They were paddling so as not to startle the wildlife away before they could see it.

Paddling. Yeah, a good name for it. I had to admire Martha. I hoped for Rory's sake she'd got a mosquito net in the rubber boat. I didn't want Rory's bum bitten while he was performing his duties.

We all had hammocks to sleep in. You slept across these rather than along them but wrapped in a blanket they weren't so bad.

Too hot by day. Cold by night, in the pre-dawn. I slept badly, sinking into vivid and unpleasant dreams, jerking awake.

The river chucked and gurgled. The men kept a fire lit on the bank. Pablo said it was against jaguars.

Dawn came with clouds smoking up into a sky which settled to be hard blue and hot.

For two days nothing happened. I saw more fresh-water dolphins, a turtle, some crocodiles, huge irides-cent blue butterflies, macaws, parrots, herons, king-fishers, bats and once, looking like badly stuffed toys, toucans. Pablo cooked rice and meat messes by night and flour cakes hot for breakfast which we also ate cold at lunch. It was OK. Matheson shot some pictures. Marguerite counted stores and made notes. Martha got noticeably excited. She continued to take Rory off every day to perform his duty. No one passed any comment on this.

Flying hypodermics periodically stabbed us in the back and off-loaded a superabundance of venom into our inoffensive bodies.

On the fourth day, under a green tunnel of foliage up a small river I didn't know the name of, Martha said: 'It's time to tell Sydney what we're up to.'

We had camped early. Pablo fished, pulling large things over a foot long out of the water with ease. They had big, deep bodies, sort of dinner plates on their sides, and small heads with red-ringed eyes. Until whacked with a machete they horribly hiss-screamed at us, beating their tails. Verbals from a fish is an experience to miss. Matheson took their photos after they were dead, Pablo holding the mouths open for him.

'What's the big deal?' I asked casually. The teeth were surprisingly large and flat, triangular with very sharp points. As Pablo let the mouth shut, keeping the lips back, I saw how the upper and lower teeth fitted perfectly, leaving no gap.

'Some dentist,' I said admiringly. 'You'd never have known as a tadpole he wore a brace.'

'Is piranha,' said Pablo, grinning.

I felt sick. 'No,' I said huskily. 'They're little. I saw the movie. Little fish. Not these sharks.'

Matheson smirked. I looked at him. 'You fall in, cowboy, you don't look for help,' I said in deadly earnest.

'You needn't be frightened,' he said. 'From you

they'll swim away. It's blood attracts them, lady, and you have poison-juice in your veins.'

'Pablo,' I said.

'Yes, Seednee.'

'You cook anything?'

'It move, I cook it.'

'Tried gringo?'

He chortled with laughter. 'I thin' this gringo, he would taste bad to you, Seednee.'

'You're right,' I agreed.

The piranha made very good eating and I felt a kind of primaeval satisfaction. I could at last understand those cannibal tribes who ate their enemies. It was nothing mystical about ingesting the spirits of their enemies, like all that anthropological claptrap would have us believe. It was revenge, pure and simple. The more frightening the enemy, the greater the gratification. We had here the ultimate winner and loser situation, the winner eating, the loser being eaten. You can't lose more thoroughly than ending up as barbequed munchkins for your erstwhile enemy. Those piranha were lip-smackin' good, all the better because the damn things would have eaten me given half a chance. For now, I had the drop on them.

I looked up and caught Matheson's eye. It seemed to me he understood and was amused by my thought processes. But it was then that Martha made her announcement. It was time to let Sydney into the secret.

'So, what are we up to?' I asked in a lazy voice. My eyes flicked round, checking up on the others. No surprise anywhere. They all knew, even Pablo. Just dumb ol' Sydney was in the dark here.

'You see, Carl knew,' said Martha. She wore a classy, tailored safari suit, the trousers tucked tightly into thick socks with lightweight rugged boots. You had to work to keep the insects out, here. Her hair was tied back with a silk scarf, a brilliant flash of colour. Her tough tanned face and white teeth gave her overall an impressive, handsome appearance. Me, I was limp and damp and eaten by insects, despite liberal applications of jungle repellent.

We were gathered to eat on the bank under a rigged tarpaulin in case snakes fell on us out of the trees. It was these sort of details which made camping such fun here. Rory and Colin were already in their hammocks, swinging gently and smoking small cigars. Pablo was filling his pipe. Matheson sat by Marguerite, whom he seemed to fancy, poor woman. Carla rested just outside the firelight, watching Rory.

I kept silent.

'This isn't just a holiday,' said Martha. Rory offered her a cigar and she took it. He bent forward from his hammock and lit it for her. I saw his head turn fractionally and he looked at Carla's shadowed face.

So he knew, huh. That made sense. It must be the standard reaction from females he met.

It's my opinion it rots a man's soul, knowing a woman hungers for him. Don't let on, that's the secret.

'Rory and Colly here,' Martha went on, 'aren't primarily naturalists at all.'

She let the silence grow. 'They here to sell encyclopaedias or what?' I asked.

'We're archaeologists,' said Rory.

'New World, pre-conquest,' said Colin.

I thought of the mask. 'You want Indian artefacts, you buy them in the market,' I said flatly.

'That isn't what we're after,' said Martha. 'We want to find a place.'

Something coughed over the river, a sort of boomy cough that echoed slightly. It coughed three times.

'Jaguar,' said Pablo. He put more sticks on the fire and rested his hand by the handle of his machete.

It was hot and humid with a compost-heap smell of rotting vegetation.

'A particular place?' I asked.

'Vilcabamba,' said Carla suddenly and there was a moment's awed silence, as though she'd said something holy.

They're crazy, I thought, my spine trickling with cold. *I'm in the jungle with a bunch of obsessives.*

'The last Inca city,' said Rory. His face was lit from underneath by Pablo's fire. His eyes were black sockets, his mouth an empty hole. Again I thought of the mask, a dead thing. Perhaps.

'Archaeologists can't find it,' said Martha, her voice dry and level. 'After their defeat by the Spanish conquistadores the Inca regrouped briefly east of the Andes, down in the jungle, under their last Emperor, Tupac Amaru. They still had a great deal of gold, of golden treasure. The Spanish had melted down most of what they took, of course.'

'You think you can find it,' I said. I kept my voice colourless. I didn't want them to hear I thought them crazy.

'Carl heard about this map.'

My patience snapped. 'Grow up,' I shouted. 'Ancient cities in the jungle. Hidden treasure. Maps. Who gets the money out of this? Who's pulling the con?'

Martha laughed. 'That's a very healthy attitude, Sydney. To answer your questions, no one is pulling a con. The Turner Trust will ensure that all finds go to the legal authority to which they rightfully belong, whichever country we end up in. We would hope to set up a travelling exhibition, however, in the fullness of time. I'm interested in museums, in history, in art,

59

my dear. I have all the money I could ever want or need.'

Bully for her. 'And this pair?' I said nastily. 'Your pet archaeologists. What do they get?'

'It would make their careers. This is like opening Tutankhamen's tomb. It will be news around the world.'

'News,' I said.

'Yes, Sydney. News. That was Carl's job. He was to be an independent witness and our first controlled leak of news. You are our independent witness now. You can tell this story, if it becomes one, the way it happened.'

For a split second I had sympathy for Carl. If he believed in this twaddle, then my going in his place must be giving him apoplexy.

'This map,' I said. 'How could there be a map? Martha, you aren't dumb. Anyone having the map would use it themselves. If you've bought such a thing, you've been conned.'

'The map is unusable. I bought it for a few dollars. It was worth its price as an artefact, even if we can't read it.'

'This is the map,' said Matheson. He held out the mask.

My eyes flicked from Matheson to Martha and back again. 'That pair authenticate this?' I asked, referring to Colin and Rory.

Colin said: 'It looks right. We can't date it objectively, of course. It wasn't bought as an antique though it is startling. It was bought as a map to which we might have the clue.'

I took the mask and felt its warm hard wood again. The firelight flickered behind it, showing through the nose, eye and mouth holes. It was the reverse effect to what I had just witnessed in Rory's face. *It's just theatre*, I thought. *Special effects*. The thing had seemed to change expression.

'I saw this in your room, the day I found the intruder,' I said to Matheson. If you tell a lie, stick to it.

'I've been looking after it for Martha. Carl found out about it and he told me. I knew Martha slightly. I worked for her once in the past. I got Carl to meet Martha. This expedition has grown from that meeting.'

My first thought that it was an obvious con faltered. The angle for Carl was that all this was for real. Then he could tell the story and enter the history books. If he had found the mask and was playing games with Martha, then there was no story. It would do him no good in the long run to be associated with a fake.

'That intruder,' said Martha. 'That's worrying. We've preserved total secrecy here. We wouldn't have got permits if we'd told the authorities what we were really up to, and we would have found ourselves in a race.'

'A caucus race,' I murmured.

'What's that?' said Martha.

Matheson intervened. 'This intruder, he was just serendipity, Martha. I'm sure.' Of course, Matheson knew I was lying because there had been no intruder before and I'd used his own mendacious description. The interesting thing was that although he must realise I'd wrecked his room after breaking into it, he still didn't think it worth his while to confront me. To prove he knew I was lying, he might be forced to admit to my having seen him buy the mask from the dwarf.

Did Martha know where the mask had come from? I decided to ask. 'Where has the mask come from?' I said subtly.

'Carl traced it,' answered Matheson.

'Have you had it long?' I asked Martha.

'Not long.'

'If you think it is a map, how can we set off without being able to understand it?'

Martha leaned forward. I caught the smell of her excitement, pungent as her cigar. Her eyes glittered. 'If it was easy, who'd want to do it?' she rasped. 'We figure we have to have the right jumping off point, the place the mask was found. That's a mountain, a particular mountain, out here east of the Andes. It's in the middle of the jungle. It's barely been seen by anyone except the Indians who live round there. We take the mask there. Then we have to interpret what it tells us.'

What it tells us. Sweet Jesus. I felt cool reason flow back. These people were mad.

I let it go at that. It was time to turn in. If I was to sleep easy, though, I had something to do before beddy-byes.

'Matheson,' I said quietly, while the others were making their moves for their hammocks.

'Yes, viper-pants?'

'A walk in the jungle. Pronto.'

We strolled out of the firelight and blundered a short way into the mess of trees, saplings, vines and hanging fruits. The space down here under the canopy gets very little sunlight and surprisingly, it can be quite easy to penetrate.

We found a snake-free tree trunk and switched off our torches. 'Some straight talking, lover-boy,' I said.

'I thought you wanted to get inside my pants again.'

I wasn't going to beat about the bush. 'Are you a fruit-cake like the others on this trip?' I asked. 'The others except Pablo,' I corrected myself, 'who is doing this, most sensibly, for money.'

'I don't think I am a fruit-cake, no.'

'This is you and Carl, conning the old lady.' My voice was rough. I had to keep it low, we weren't very far away from the others.

'She's not old. Ask Duncan.'

I punched him lightly in the chest. 'I couldn't speak one damn word with Carl before I came. His jaw was wired. He was bandaged like a mummy. I came in all innocence. So where did the mask come from?' There was a prolonged silence. 'I don't believe it's a treasure map,' I said.

'How do you explain Duncan and Brown?'

'Martha's paying. They can look around an area hard to get into. Possibly El Dorado exists. What does it matter to them if it doesn't? They're no worse off.'

'You're very cynical,' he said. His breath stirred my hair. Something far off began to call. Um um um ooh ah, it went. Again and again and again.

'I'm a newspaperman.'

'So's Carl.'

'No. He's a writer. An adventurer. A myth-maker. Me, I'm just a hack.'

'Some hack,' he said. He wasn't giving an inch.

I stood close because the jungle was scary and it made me less frightened, being up against him. 'You buy the mask?' I asked. 'Or did Carl?'

'Carl heard about it. I think it's very old. Truly, frog-princess. I truly believe it is a genuine Inca artefact, dating from the last days of the empire. I think there is a possibility it is what it claims to be. It contains a clue to where they hid their treasure, a clue only they could read. A clue for their people, their descendants. I don't think we'll unravel it, if

63

you want to know. But this isn't a con, not the way you mean.'

'Something's coming,' I said, my voice rising to a squeak of fear.

His arms closed round me. He heard it too. I turned round to face whatever it was, Matheson's arm protectively across my chest.

The tree we stood against was vaulted. Huge extra root supports buttressed the main trunk. Stuff here is shallow-rooted and trees often grow these extra supports. We withdrew behind one, into the embrace of the tree.

I saw the flicker of torchlight. I started to relax, I drew breath to call out but Matheson squeezed me. 'Shh,' he breathed in my ear. So I kept quiet.

Two people appeared. The torchlight made them hard to identify at first. One carried a lantern burning kerosene. They shone it around after switching off the torch and then one of them laid something on the ground.

They put the lantern down low and hunkered down on the tarpaulin they had laid. I made a small movement of protest but Matheson hung onto me tightly, forcing me to keep still.

I kept quiet. Clothes rustled. Voices murmured. I saw long pale limbs move in the glow of the lamp. It was too late to intervene. Matheson had prevented me at the point where it still would have been decent.

I saw lips trail slow over belly and thigh. Legs parted in welcome and the man's head lay between them. I saw the lift of a hip, the outswell of buttock, touched and kissed and tongued in a lingering ravishment. A breast was fruit crushed between the bodies. Sighs and swelling shapes were liquid in the night.

The lamp cast strange shadows. Leaves bifurcated, denticulate, storm-beaten and torn, cast shadows and travelled cloud-fashion over the moving geography of writhing bodies. Little murmurs of passion bubbled like night-jars. Breath came in quick grunts. There were small explosions soft as sin, sobbing cries, and then the smooth satisfactions of post-coital pleasure.

All the time Matheson held me tight against his taut body. I felt the swell of his sex against me. Sweat ran warm between my breasts. His breath was on my skin. I felt my heart and his heart thud.

Before us the naked pair knelt facing each other, the man's body curved as he bent to kiss the upturned face of his lover. He kissed gently, trailing his lips lightly along her cheeks, her jaw, across her lips.

They muttered together for a moment. Then they dressed. The man collected the tarpaulin and shook it carefully. He folded it and taking the girl's hand in his, they set off back to the campsite.

I was trembling. Matheson turned my stiff body round and pressed me against him. One hand was under my collar against the nape of my neck. I kept my hair knotted up and under my hat most of the time.

His fingers stroked my sensitive neck. His lips were against my cheek.

'What do you think of that, Sydney?' Each speech movement rustled his lips drily against my skin.

'You voyeuristic bastard.' My voice shook. 'You pervert. You, you Peeping Tom. Peeping Tom Matheson.'

He shook with silent laughter making no move to release me. His other hand slid over my buttocks. 'Didn't it turn you on, Sydney? Come now, be honest for once. Aren't you just a little bit horny?'

I made a feeble effort to withdraw. Our noses bumped. 'You're a bag of pus, camera-man. Too bad you didn't have the Nikon along to do a shoot. You into blackmail?'

He turned me round. His hands bit into my upper arms. He was angry now. 'Look,' he hissed.

I looked. Black on black. Horrible sinking vertiginous blackness, swelling to swallow me, to suck me into its depths.

I gulped.

'Now look.' He flashed on his torch. A thousand pinpricks stared, ruby dots. Then they winked out.

Matheson switched off his torch. 'Everything watches,' he said into my hair. 'It's the name of the game. Duncan fucked you yet?'

I made a movement of protest. A kind of paralysis held me. I couldn't break free of this damned man. The jungle scared me, too. Really scared me, deep down atavistic stuff.

'The man is making it with our lady patroness. Now we know he's stuffing the daughter on the side. That's information, hack, and you know it.'

'Carla isn't Martha's daughter,' I managed. 'There's no blood relationship.'

'If you think that's relevant, you've got it worse than I imagined.'

I came to my senses. The queer paralysis of will left me. I wrenched myself free of Matheson's grip and turned in the dark to face him. My voice was quiet and controlled when I spoke. 'You're sick, cameraman. Rory goes with Martha because she says so and he wouldn't be along otherwise. She's probably a very good lay, too. If he goes with Carla for fun, that's up to him and none of my business. As far as I am concerned, men as sexual partners don't have to be celibates till they meet me. I like a man hung big, with the body and brains to use his equipment right. The rest I don't give a shit about. Am I getting across to you? I use men for sex. When I want friends, I go to people. Friends and sex don't have to coincide, just like men aren't always people, which you ought to know, nonperson. *Zé Ninguem*.' I spat this last.

Matheson was surprisingly mild under this onslaught. 'Joe Nobody. Very good. You're not as ignorant as I thought. So when Rory Duncan crooks his finger, you'll add yourself to his tally.'

'You can't get it, can you? You're so damned self-important. Sex is just an appetite for me and I prefer my food pretty. Rory looks and moves sweet. The rest means nothing. Nothing.'

He laughed softly. 'Come on, frog,' he said, 'I'll walk you back to the camp.'

I turned, intending to stride out ahead of him, Miss Independent, Miss Keep-Your-Bloody-Distance, fell headlong over an exposed tree root. The air rushed out of me with a whoosh and I lay still a moment, winded *and* wounded in the pride department, swearing horribly in an under-the-breath mumble.

Matheson, of course, was laughing, a low, humiliating chuckle. 'Do you like your sex objects to have a streak of gallantry', he asked sarcastically, extending a hand.

I was on my knees by then, spitting vegetation litter out of my mouth. I slapped the hand away. He tried to grab me up by the scruff of my neck, or rather my twill collar. I attempted a judo throw but it went spectacularly wrong, Matheson landing heavily on top of me, knocking me windless again, my elbow smacking him in the eye.

'Ouch!'

'Yowch,' he exploded, the outcry sending the roosting birds up out of the treetops to flap and squawk noisily.

'You clumsy sod!'

'Me! What about your elbow, viper-pants? I'm gonna have a psychedelic eye come tomorrow.'

His knee was between my legs, his mouth too close to mine. I was already hot and bothered after being held captively close to him and forced to watch Rory and Carla. I tried to heave him off.

He laughed, pinned me down.

'Pig!'

He thought about it. 'No. Don't quite see myself in that zoological guise. How about stallion?'

I sneered. 'Your conceit is truly unrivalled. I'm awfully impressed.'

Obviously he didn't have a suitable reply to that, so he held my head still with hands that clamped like a vice, and kissed me savagely instead. It was such an assault to the senses that I didn't even attempt to bite his tongue or knee him in the groin, though usually that would have been my speedy response to such a liberty taken with my person.

So what was happening? Why didn't I? I didn't have a clue. His kiss was like the zap of a Martian's ray gun; it completely stunned me. Worse still, I could feel my hips straining up against him, was grappling with his trousers, with mine. He wriggled, we fumbled and then he was in me, sliding in long and deep, his hands never moving from the sides of my head, the kiss going on and on, deep, bruising, robbing me of any belated attempt at gaining the mental upper hand. I hated him, loathed the mastery, but I had no will to stop it.

Mouths moved, bodies moved. If suddenly we'd found ourselves in a sci-fi 'beaming' that transported us to the Royal Albert Hall and an audience of several thousand, we wouldn't have been aware, wouldn't have cared.

No man had ever kissed me like that before.

We moaned, we gasped, very quickly we both came. My hands at the back of his head, raked his dark hair, holding him to me, mirroring his own embrace. For several seconds we both lay without moving, then, as embarrassment set in, we sort of wriggled apart, doing up clothing and prolonging an awkward silence. We didn't look at each other.

We walked back to camp with no mention of what had just occurred, nothing said apart from one query by Matheson. 'So tell me, with your culinary approach to sex, frog, where does *that* figure: A quick treat? A stir-fry maybe?'

I'd regained my senses, was relieved by his return to acid banter, had a suitable reply. 'Tee-hee. Oh no, nothing so substantial, oh clumsy one. You were the aperitif. Rory's the main course.'

The next day Big Jacko found the radio wouldn't work. He had been at pains to keep it dry in the steamy atmosphere but something inside it was broken, broken beyond his ability to repair. He became mulish and insisted the damage could not have happened accidentally.

'Come on,' said Martha reasonably. 'I'm not blaming you, Jacko. Any of us could have been careless and knocked against it.'

'It was between the sacks of rice,' he persisted obstinately.

'You're trying to blame Pablo? This isn't healthy.'

'Pablo hasn't used stores from our boat, ma'am. The rice sacks have been moved. I say it's deliberate.'

Martha looked round us all gathered for breakfast. We were all listening.

'Does anyone have anything to say?' she asked quietly. When the silence continued, she turned back to Jacko. 'Why did you examine it today?'

'I check it every three days to make sure it is dry and safe.' The man was sullen.

'It was OK last time?'

'It was fine.'

Martha came to a decision. 'It doesn't matter. We probably won't need it. I don't understand what has happened here but I cannot bring myself to believe that malice has been involved. Someone has been unknowingly careless. It's a shame, but that's all there is to it.'

Carla spoke. 'Jacko is very careful, Martha. He should know he's the last person we'd suspect of clumsiness.'

Jacko cheered up at this naïve statement. I wondered if he knew what Rory was up to in the woods by night. I presumed Martha didn't know.

That day our progress was interrupted by rapids.

Martha was perplexed. 'They shouldn't be here,' she said, staring with hands on hips at the foaming white water confronting us. We had pulled into the pebble-beached bank disturbing clouds of brown and red butterflies. Occasionally we would see something larger and iridescent blue or green flashing like jewelled fire in the sunlight.

No radio, I thought dully. *Wrong river. We're lost.* The heat was oppressive. My clothes stuck to me. Little sweat bees kept trying to drink from my eyes and mouth.

I took a couple of steps into the jungle. The river vanished from view, the sound of the rapids muffled even by this short distance.

It was hushed. The blood thudded in my ears. Each day I tuned into Radio Dawn Chorus as the frogs and insects slugged it out against the birds. As the sun beefed up, this tonal variety reduced and concentrated itself into a constant ear-drilling shrill. That was on the river, though. Here the shrieks and churrucks of the bird life had stopped. None of us had seen a monkey yet nor heard one call.

It was hushed, I thought eerily, rather than being quiet. This was no summer afternoon's drowsing quiet like you might get in the temperate regions of the world. This was a bated breath, a held artificial silence of unseen watchers. Watching me. Silently. Waiting.

Carefully, I went back to the others, to the river and the biting insects.

Marguerite was sitting silently on a rock, composed and peaceful. 'What's happening?' I asked.

'The men might cut logs and roll the boats along the bank.'

I looked at the river bank. Part of it was bare rock. Most of it was covered in ultra-lush light-greedy vegetation bursting with red flowers and nectar-crazed butterflies. A sudden clout under my guts told me that emotionally the place was getting to me. Too hot, too humid, too full of ants, snakes, scorpions, man-eating fish and reptiles, altogether too much. It was also breathtakingly, savagely beautiful. It had a raw brilliance about it, a shallow-rooted fecundity run riot.

Matheson came back to join us and squatted by the secretary lady.

'We're going to warp the boats up,' he said.

'Warp them?'

'Unload them first, Margie, to lighten them and to prevent loss if they overturn. We're going to wrap ropes round trees on either bank, one end of each attached to the boat. Pablo will steer using the engine. The rest of us will pull on the ropes round the trees on each bank. Human winches, you see.'

'Will it work?'

Her trust in him was cute, I thought sourly. She probably still believed in Santy Claus.

He smiled down at her. 'Maybe.'

Martha came back and confirmed what Matheson had said. We began to unload the boats.

It took the whole of the rest of the day, back-breaking work. We removed everything from the boats and stacked it all under tarpaulins on the bank above the flood zone. A sudden storm upriver could raise the water level by several feet in less than an hour. Leaving one boat moored, ropes were attached to the prow of the other. Rory and Colin forded the river where it was quiet and walked up the other side, slashing the over-hanging vines and branches out of the way, spilling grey clouds of small bats from their roosts as they went.

The men found roughly matching trees about half-way up the broken racing water. There was only about a hundred yards of it altogether. There were two ropes to each bank. The first was wrapped around these half-way trees. The second two lines would be put round trees further up when the boat had got so far.

'You crossing, girls?' called Martha. I looked at Margie and then patted my pockets. There was nothing worth a damn that hadn't already been emptied out. We shrugged and grinned nervously at each other. Then we plunged into the water.

The current under the placid surface was strong, tugging at our feet. Rory and Colin watched from the bank. The water was thickly warm. I shut my mind to the possibility of piranha and crocs.

My chest felt tight. I didn't like this. The water was so dark, anything could lurk there. A whole lot of snakes could swim, too.

Margie said nothing as she struggled, though I

could hear her panting breath over the noise of the angry water upstream of us. Some big insects with armour-piercing equipment up front whizzed by. My concentration lapsed, my feet started to skid and I yelped and went under.

I whirled in dark green bubbles. I kept my mouth shut and my chest heaved, wanting oxygen. Suddenly my limbs were tangled in something limb-thick and mobile.

Anaconda.

They squeeze when you breathe out, I thought hysterically, and my breath sobbed out between my clamped lips.

No one would know if I cried. This was my death. I was entitled to let the side down and show fear.

My head broke the surface and I saw rainbows in the water-filled light. Sleek as a seal, Rory's head surfaced beside me. He held me upright and my scrabbling feet found purchase. We had tumbled twenty yards downstream in as many seconds.

He held me, his wet face by mine. I puffed and panted like a grampus. 'I thought, I thought you were . . .'

'I know. It's all right.'

'Anaconda. I was so frightened.'

'Darling, it's OK. I know. We'd all have been frightened. Poor girl, poor girl.'

'Rory,' I said and laid my head on his shoulder. For a moment I forgot I was a tough wise-ass.

He held me there in the middle of the river. Then he was leading me across, holding my hand.

Margie had arrived safely and without drama. We stood steaming by the rope, waiting to pull.

Pablo cast off and manoeuvred the boat left of centre stream, where he thought he could see the beginnings of a path through the foam-sprayed rocks.

73

We all took up the slack on our ropes, four to each rope, two men and two women. We dug our boots into what purchase we could find. Pablo shouted and opened the throttle wide. The boat leaped forward, the nose instantly covered in broken water.

I thought my arms would come out of their sockets. The worst bit came when they tied off the rope and we went forward to the second upstream warp. The boat danced mid-rapid in a welter of foam. As soon as the slack was taken up, the knot on the first rope had to be jerked loose so the boat could go on. This rope had to be retained, though, and not allowed to fall in the water where it might tangle with the prop.

We did it. Having succeeded and reached calm water above, we had to do it again.

We rested and ate, discussing whether it was worth losing a rope puller on the second boat by using the first to partly tow the second. It meant two people at the helms, and everyone agreed that Pablo had to guide the second boat through the rocks, he'd been so superb with the first. Bailed out, it was dry and as watertight as it had ever been.

It was agreed. Martha took the helm of the boat upstream. The second boat was therefore partly driven, partly warped and partly towed through the rapids.

Wearily, with arms that felt they had been stretched on a rack, we trudged up with all the stores and gear.

I wasn't close enough to see what happened. Suddenly there was a screaming row between Rory Duncan and Matheson, the latent hostility between the two men spilling raw and ugly in the sunshine. Hostility on Matheson's side, that is. I'd no evidence for thinking Rory thought twice about the man.

A precious rifle had been dropped in the water.

Matheson blamed the Englishman. The Englishman blamed Matheson. They almost came to blows.

Martha intervened, shorter by a head than them both but compelling in her authority. I couldn't catch what she said to them but her tone was quiet and bitingly angry.

Margie was white. Carla closed up to Rory afterwards. Matheson looked sulky. Big Jacko stood, the picture of amiability, by his boss. It was clear that if either of the men had not obeyed her, he would have stepped in.

I was near Colin when it happened. We spent the day in different boats and he was not conversable like his colleague. Yet he seemed a pleasant man.

He looked shaken. 'We can do without this,' I said.

'We can do with the rifle. If anything holds us up we'll need to hunt.'

'What about the Indians?'

His head swivelled and he looked at me. 'We can't shoot the Indians,' he said, shocked.

'What about all this stuff about blowpipes and curare?'

'You're out of date,' he said shortly. He looked back at Rory and Matheson. Both had picked up their gear and returned to porterage work between the equipment dump and the boats.

The next day was barely better. We entered a wide slow area with shallow water full of submerged broken vegetation. Pablo said we mustn't use the engines and Big Jacko agreed. The men punted the boats, having cut themselves poles from saplings growing in the forest.

It was suffocatingly hot and clouds of little black flies settled on us, biting frenziedly. I tied mosquito netting over my hat and face like an Edwardian motor veil. The heat inside was intense but fly-free.

When we were able to return to deeper water, the river was narrow, so narrow I felt confirmed in my belief that we were lost. The overarching vegetation met above us. Trees torn up by their roots had fallen across the stream. The vine-strangled bushes contained wasp nests, conical suspensions in yellow clay.

Big Jacko and Matheson waded ahead with machetes, clearing a path. There was an absence of birds and although Pablo pointed out evidence of otters, we saw none of the giant beasts.

I could have believed in dinosaurs here. It was unearthly, not of our time, not of any place on earth I understood. Sound echoed slightly as though we were in a green, watery vault. Pale veined butterflies bumbled between clusters of rotting fruit.

I saw the waters stained dark with tannins and toxins from the endless abundance of trees. Leaf-litter floated in sluggish whirls on the sullen surface. On either side the trees curved and bent towards us, their tops closing in an embrace full of subtle menace. Half-submerged logs lay forward of us, blocking our way. Behind us the water bubbled slowly, settling after our rough passage.

The men were in the water chest-deep, pulling the fallen trees aside, hacking with machetes at the greedy fingers of vegetation threatening to overwhelm the silent, narrow, jungle-deep waterway.

'What's the matter?' Margie asked, looking at me strangely.

We had left the blood-greedy flies behind. I wore no veil so my face could be seen.

I felt faint and semi-conscious. 'I don't know,' I whispered. 'Was I sleeping?'

'You look ill. Is it fever? You've been taking your malaria stuff, haven't you?'

Pablo said: 'Anhinga.' He pointed.

The bird rose with a noisy self-important flurry from the

surface of the water, its long thin neck, and head extended, its tail fanned. It was a dark, oil green, messy with white splashes.

'Yes,' I said. 'Yes.' I drank some chlorinated water. I felt terrible. Visions flickered double-imaged in front of my eyes.

'Lie down here,' said Margie. 'There's some shade.' I wanted to pull off my sticky, heavy, sweat-dampened clothing and roll in cool silky water. I felt like snivelling.

I think I did sleep. When I came round we were in an open piece of water with clear sky above. Something large hung in it, a bird of prey, I suppose.

I felt too sluggish to find out whether it was a kite, an eagle or a vulture. On the whole I reckoned it would be a vulture.

I felt enormously far from home.

We pulled in to camp, though it was early. Rory came to see me, looking worried.

'What's wrong?' he murmured. He had untied the hankerchief he wore round his neck and soaked it in water. He wiped my face.

'The heat, I guess. Is it safe to swim?'

'Yes. Pablo and Colin have been fishing for an hour. No piranha. Will you be cross if I stay by you?'

We entered the lagoon. The men climbed hurriedly back into the boats. There would be piranha here.

We fished and rested for some time.

'I won't be cross,' I said weakly. 'I thought there would be piranha here.'

'So did we at first. But it's fine.'

We all swam. Margie did my washing for me. Pablo gave us corned beef and rice. I was hungry, feeling better now.

Martha went off to explore the lagoon, or so she said, in the rubber dinghy with Rory. I was drowsy, meaning all the time to go to my boat and arrange my hammock and mosquito net. I put it off, a lethargy holding me where I was, with the others. The truth was, I didn't want to be alone.

Pablo made a whistle and played it. Its plangent notes were not unpleasant. Margie and Carla began to sing.

I caught Matheson's eyes on me, dispassionate, like I was meat. I thought of Rory's kindness to me and how he had saved me in the river below the rapids.

For all my brave talk I was falling for the guy. It was my most important personal rule. Never get emotionally involved. Never sucker yourself. Stay invulnerable. The bastards are always out there ready for the moment of weakness. That's when they go for the kill.

Matheson fetched out a mouth-organ and found the key. He began to play along with Pablo and the girls.

I felt lonely and far from home. I felt peculiar in my head. I didn't trust my companions to make rational decisions in the face of their obsession with treasure.

That was all it was, I reassured myself. I was frightened and ill at ease. My weak subconscious wanted to latch me on to a protector. Rory was just any old gorgeous, beautiful, intelligent, sexy mover, one who made love like a dream as I well knew, having watched him screw the girly Carla. That he thought quickly and was personally brave was neither here nor there. It was just a temporary weakness on my part.

He and Martha returned. He came over to speak to me, to ask how I was.

'Dopey,' I said. 'Tell me, is there a beauty salon round these parts? I could do with a once over.'

He grinned down at me. 'You look fine to me,' he said.

I felt a moment's irritation that his own personal beauty was unmarred by insect bites and if anything, slightly enhanced by the stubble on his cheeks. It pleased me he didn't shave before screwing her. Mind you, I wouldn't have put it past her to like it with texture.

He smoked for a minute. I felt Carla's eyes on him. 'We couldn't find the main exit to the lagoon,' he said. 'Entrance, I should say, since I mean upstream. There are several possibilites and it's hard to find the right one. They're all much the same.'

Then we could not find the right exit to the lagoon, not for a long time. The current was weak and sly . . .

My mouth was dry. 'The current,' I whispered.

'Not strong enough. You OK? I shouldn't be worrying you.'

'I'm fine. I think I'll go to bed now.'

'Shall I put your hammock up for you?'

'That would be very kind.'

Matheson was smiling sarcastically as we went by to the boat. I felt too tired to bother with him. I felt too tired to bother with anything.

I dreamed. Psychedelic nightmares featuring an aunt I hadn't seen since I was ten. She was baking fancy cakes with cherries on the top. When they came out of the oven they looked just like fleshy breasts with aroused nipples.

I awoke, tossed and turned uncomfortably in the hammock, dropped off again. Now I dreamed of Carl with whom I had once had the briefest of flings. On reflection I don't know why. Anyway, in the dream Carl and I, Martha and Colin were hacking our way through the humid jungle with machetes. I felt an air of anticipation, was sure that at last the mystery of Vilcabamba was about to be laid open before us.

Carl sweated, his twill safari jacket patched darkly at the armpits and down the middle of his back. He'd always had a problem with his body odour, was the sort of man who brushed his teeth thrice a day yet only freshened up his dick once a week in the bath. He dominated the jungle smells.

Up ahead we broke into a clearing where Colin (and this my overactive mind subconsciously tried to make sense of and failed) stood bound by fat green lengths of vine to the huge trunk of a mahogany tree. He was naked and looked somewhat distressed by the overtly sexual advances of Margie, who danced about him singing 'Tie a Yellow Ribbon'. Yuk, how I hated that song. Even in my dream, as I trudged behind the pongy Carl – who now, for no good reason, sported assorted bandages around his head and torso – I grimaced noisily at the nauseating singing coming from Martha's secretary.

'Take a letter,' said Martha, but Margie only sang the louder, making me put my hands over my ears, running her hands over Colin's unimpressive chest. He was the same size all the way down and his stick-like arms and legs made me feel a litle sorry for him. Puny was the word, exceptionally so. In my dream he grew, ballooning before my appreciative eyes until handsomely proportioned.

Unfortunately, a change of shape didn't change his mind about Margie.

'Don't. Stop it,' he pleaded, his face contorting with disgust as Margie broke off from singing and did the Hula before him, reaching out a hand to play with his penis, try to make it grow. It seemed to wilt more if anything. 'Get off me! Help! Go away. You're a *woman*!'

Margie sobbed with hurt and frustration, collapsed to the floor and beat her hands on the ground.

'That was rather brutal, Colin,' chided Martha, looking sternly at him. 'Couldn't you have told the truth in a more gentle fashion? Really, I'm surprised at you.'

'Sorry,' said Colin, pouting.

The vines dropped away from him and Colin was on his hands and knees before the masterful blonde and Rory was at his rear. Where had he come from? My heart pitter-pattered as he unbuckled his belt, whipped down his zip, then his trousers. His shaft was huge, given several extra inches in my dream and as fat as a cucumber. He caught hold of the cheeks of Colin's arse and worked the bulbous head of his member past the tight musculature, a look of joy seeping over Colin's refined features. Rory pushed home, his pubic curls caressing Colin's bottom. He caught the man about his slim hips and started a slow, deep screw.

'I'm glad we're all getting along so well,' said Martha with relief, watching vaguely. 'It's nice that we're such a happy, comradely band.'

I wasn't happy, not happy at all. The sight of Rory buried to the hilt in Colin's rear made me horny as hell and madly jealous.

I ran up to them, tried to pull Rory off. He laughed, pumped on, the huge penis withdrawing and then sinking forcefully into Colin as I watched. They were too determined to be thwarted. Colin offered his rear as a woman would her sex, presenting it, raising it, and Rory kept deep within it, withdrawing perhaps eight of the twelve awesome inches I gauged to be springing from between his legs, then burying himself deep again. They seemed as if superglued at the thighs.

81

I put my hand down the front of my twill trousers and stroked myself with a knuckle and finger, desperate.

'I need a man,' I cried, not too proud to beg.

Carl came running, unzipping his trousers as he did so.

I shook my head, no, he wouldn't do. From the vegetation behind Martha came Matheson, smiling devilishly. He looked good – downright ugly – but oh-so good. I felt myself weakening, my body straining, but I wouldn't let myself give in. Especially not to him. He had even less respect for me than I did for him. He started to unzip his bulging trousers. 'No,' I said, determined, and he disappeared, along with the surplus Carl – shazam – just like that.

'Here, dear,' said Martha, cool and practical, handing me something from her crocodile handbag. A handbag that was alive, was an opening and closing tooth-filled mouth into which had been placed all those little things a woman might need on safari. She'd given me her dildo to borrow, an antique piece carved of ivory, smooth, off-white, sensuous to the touch.

I wriggled it into place and pushed it home, sighing at the generous fill, watching the humping males as I worked the bone within myself, pleasured my clitoris with my spare hand. I was on my hands and knees, swaying back and forth, lost in my delight. My crisis was quick in coming, and I jerked, breathed quickly, heavily, gasped as the waves of bliss crashed over me.

I awoke.

It was strange to find myself on the boat, took me a second or two to remember what I was doing there, my breath still ragged, my heart beating fast. I looked furtively around, praying that my erotic dream had woken no one, began to sigh with relief, then stopped. No one stirred except Matheson. He stood ashore smoking, the burning tip of the cigarette glowing red as he took a deep drag. He was smiling knowingly. 'Pleasant dream, huh?'

I glared, wouldn't snarl back an answer in case I woke someone, poked my tongue out instead.

'Put that fork away.'

I rolled my eyes furiously, struggled until I felt comfortable in a new position and slammed my eyes closed. If I pretended to be asleep long enough he'd go away, I hoped.

'"No" to what or whom, I wonder?' he chuckled, and as I thought about it, going back over the limited dialogue in the dream, I realised I must have spoken aloud, just hoped I hadn't given the loathsome Matheson more ammunition to goad me with.

The next day I was back to normal, my excessive weariness gone in the night.

It had rained heavily, a thunderous wall of solid water dropping out of the sky for an hour. The boat had rocked and swayed but I saw Pablo up with the lantern loosening the painters.

After breakfast we investigated how to get on out of the lagoon. There were five possible exits, all with what seemed to be identical amounts of current.

'It's that one,' I said quietly to Pablo. The one I pointed out was rather smaller than the others.

'You think so?' he said and smiled.

'Why d'you pick that one?' asked Margie. She was fanning herself with her hat.

I shrugged.

Those in the front boat in consultation with Pablo picked one of the others. I said nothing.

It took us half a day. Half a day to get back to the

lagoon. The men were angry and frightened because they had been in the water clearing ahead with machetes when a croc had spilled off the bank and come for them.

Carla screamed, standing up in the front boat at the rail. Big Jacko gave the helm to Martha and went forward with the boat hook. Matheson came over the side in a scrambling rush, dropping his machete in the water. Colin helped him get his flailing legs over the rail. I didn't see it myself, being back in the second boat, but Carla described it later.

Unable to reach the boat fast enough, Rory had turned on the croc and hit out with his machete. The beast had stopped in surprise. Rory struck again and then the boat was nudging up at his shoulders, Big Jacko dropping the boat hook and picking Rory clean out of the water and hauling him over the rail.

Soon after this we nosed into clear water. It was Pablo who broke through the cries of relief. 'Is the lagoon again,' he said.

It was, too. We'd gone round in a circle.

We rested and ate. Then we recommenced discussion about which way to leave the lagoon.

'That one,' I said again.

Pablo looked at me. 'Why you say so, Seednee?'

I shrugged. I had goose bumps down my spine as it was. Nothing would have allowed me to elaborate.

We tried another exit. By nightfall we had entered a swamp.

Pablo nosed our boat round the muddy edges looking for firm ground. He couldn't find any. The water was between the tree trunks, so that vegetation sprouted from it and all apparent edges were queasy ground, soft and treacherous.

He consulted with Martha. 'I thin' this wrong way,'

he said. 'I thin' this marsh very wide. This not main river.'

We had to camp in the boats. Pablo cooked using precious kerosene instead of lighting his usual fire. The boats were crowded with all of us in them. Martha sent Colin back to sleep in ours and was plainly out of temper. This was unusual. I ascribed it to her missing her usual evening paddle with Rory.

It was a vile night, the um um um ooh ah bird calling with mind-numbing persistence for all the hours of darkness.

We saw spider monkeys in the morning. They watched us from the canopy and then swung away chittering on immensely long arms and legs.

Pablo grinned. 'Good to eat,' he said, rubbing his stomach.

We went back to the lagoon.

Matheson cleared his throat: 'I think we should choose the way Sydney suggests.'

Martha looked at me from the other boat. We rocked gently side by side. 'Why?' she asked.

'I dreamed it,' I said nervously.

There was a moment's stunned silence. Then Matheson gave a great shout of laughter and slapped his thigh. 'She's flipped,' he said. 'The girl reporter's flipped.'

Martha looked at me carefully. I showed the whites of my eyes.

Pablo said: 'Why not?' and looked resigned.

'We might as well,' said Carla tiredly. 'It's no sillier than anything else we've been doing.'

'It's the smallest exit,' said Colin, aggrieved.

Rory said nothing, watching me intently.

An hour into the waterway, it broadened. The

current was slow but sure. We began to motor faster and no one, no one at all said anything to me.

Pablo winked, though.

We found a beautiful campsite. The air seemed fresher that night, the forest thinner and friendlier. We all felt we'd passed some terrible obstacle.

Before turning in, Matheson came up to me and took my arm. 'Walkies,' he said brightly.

'No, schmuck.'

'Come now, don't be an old sourpuss.'

'Go play with the crocodiles.'

Matheson was startled. 'That's not funny,' he said primly.

Rory ambled over. 'Come on, Sydney,' he said. 'It's not a bad idea. Stretch the legs, huh?'

'Sure,' I said, getting up at once and grinning at Matheson. 'You take some snaps, camera-man. Earn your keep for once.' I strolled off with Rory.

We walked silently but at ease, Rory marking our passage with swipes of his machete so we could find our way back. Macho stuff for a honky, huh? Cut the insects, put him inside a Calvin Klein loincloth and Bo Derek, and things would be hot.

With suchlike thoughts I allowed myself a mild pleasurable expectation. I didn't seriously think this was a sex gambit but it was nice to be in his company. If Matheson was a hair shirt, Rory was velvet, deep pile.

In between the scattered forest giants were straggly saplings and vine-hung, fan shaped palms. One strange plant Rory suddenly told me was the chambira palm, prized because the leaf can be split like raffia and then rolled on the knee until it becomes string-like. The Indians weave hammocks and carrying baskets from it.

I listened indulgently to this nonsense. Was the man shy of me?

Finally, he stopped the fact-dribble and gazed at some glossy leaves. 'Tell me, Sydney,' he asked casually, 'you often dream things?'

'Never.'

'Till now.'

'Till now.'

'When was this dream?'

'Back in Manaus.'

He looked at me. 'You saw the events of yesterday and today?'

'Some of them. I saw the lagoon and the bit before we came into it. I dreamed Pablo calling anhinga, though I didn't know who said it in the dream.'

'That's the cormorant sort of bird, isn't it?'

'Yes.' I agreed readily. 'And common where the river is reasonably wide though we were at a narrow bit then. That was because we were about to come into the lagoon, of course.'

'You knew the way out.'

'I knew it,' I said steadily. He was easy to talk to. Perhaps I needed to get this off my chest. I was spooked, me, the founder of sceptics and cynics incorporated.

He sighed and slashed a little vaguely. 'You believe in second sight?'

'Nope,' I answered. 'Nor honest policeman, colonic irrigation, tooth fairies and kind men with open car doors and sweeties.'

'Is this anything to do with when you went poorly yesterday?'

'That's when it started coming back to me. I felt ill for a bit.'

Rory looked at me sadly. I saw the sensuous line of his lip, the slight dragging on his eyelids.

A passionate man. A man of appetite. I could seriously lust this man. He was wasted out of bed.

'Tell me the truth, Sydney,' he said quietly.

The words bubbled. 'I wore the mask,' I said and looked down at my feet.

The silence stretched. When I looked up his face was closed and shuttered. He reached out and touched my arm. 'You're one hell of a woman,' he said.

I said nothing. There was nothing to say. Why didn't he take my clothes off?

'Are you making it with the American?'

I was startled. 'None of your damned business,' I said smartly.

'I don't trust him, Sydney. Do you?'

'There is no issue of trust between us.' I was stiff. Trouble was, it was he who needed to be that way, not me.

'Have you told him about this? About the mask, I mean.'

'No. No, I haven't. I've told no one, as it happens. I don't believe it myself.'

'Why don't you keep it to yourself for now?'

I looked at him. I stopped thinking about sex. 'Why should I do that?' I asked carefully.

'Need to know basis? There are big stakes on this trip, for all of us except Pablo. Perhaps even for him.'

'Martha runs things. It's her mask.'

'Martha can find things out for herself.'

I began to walk back the way we had come. I was already wishing I had said nothing. Rory followed me.

'Tell me about Vilcabamba,' I said.

'Yes, it's time we talked about it,' he said, but then he shut up and I didn't feel like asking again.

That night Martha talked about the mountain, the mountain in the jungle we had come to find.

'It's big,' she said. 'Big and flat-topped and straight-sided, though I believe it is climbable. I hope so. We have to get up it. It has to be climbed.'

'Is this where the mask came from?' I asked.

'Yes. So Carl was told. I'm sorry he isn't here with us. He should be. He deserves to be. This will be his triumph as much as anyone's.'

'The directions,' said Rory, 'if directions there truly be, start from the mountain. It's called Cloud-maker in the local Indian tongue. *Kaliké.*'

'If it's a big mountain, how do you know where to start?' I asked.

'The mask came from a cave,' said Martha. Her eyes glistened with excitement. 'There were gold prospectors out there. They got frightened by something and began climbing the mountain. Then they found the cave. There were drawings of llamas and stuff on the walls, rock paintings. They found this mask but it was only wood, so they didn't value it. But they brought it back with them the next time they returned to civilisation. Comparative civilisation, that is. Carl came across it in Mexico, he said. He liked it and the story attached to it and bought it. He took it to an expert who said it was Inca in style. Carl knew enough to be surprised that Inca relics should turn up so far to the east as Kaliké was supposed to be, though its precise location, like everything else in this damned puzzle, is unknown.'

'Carl consulted a few historians of the Sun king-doms of the Americas.' Rory smoothly continued the story. 'He heard about the lost city of Vilcabamba soon enough. That's common knowledge. The Inca have a legend that it lies between the condor and the jaguar.'

'Between the earth and the stars,' translated Martha. She was glowing.

Rory went on. 'Then he heard about the story of the map, the secret map made by the last lost people from Vilcabamba who escaped the Spanish. There had been a neo-Inca state for some years co-existing with the Spanish. An important envoy was killed and war declared. The Incas abandoned Vilcabamba, sacking it themselves ahead of the Spanish who found it burned and treasureless. The Incas fled east to be swallowed by the jungle. Tupac Amaru was the Lord-Inca but he was slowed by his wife who was heavily pregnant and frightened to go in a canoe. The Spanish finally caught up with them under the captaincy of one García de Loyola. The rest of the Incas fled and were eventually murdered, no doubt, by Amazonian Indians. It was said subsequently they sheltered on the flanks of the Cloud-maker, starving, lost, landless, threatened on all sides. But they knew where the treasure of Vilcabamba had been hidden and they made their cryptic map so that future generations of their own people, after the Spanish were defeated, would come east to find it and understand. Some were murdered there on Cloud-maker. Some went back and passed on the word of the map's existence. And that was that.'

Not one word about dwarves in Manaus. Ho, boy, was there dirty work afoot.

'So why hasn't this Cloud-maker been searched before?' I asked in my naïve way.

'No one could find it.' Colin took up the tale. 'The Spanish at the time sent a few half-hearted expeditions but the Amazonian Indians, the Manari, got them. The same tribe that had betrayed the fleeing Incas to the Spanish, incidentally. It dampened people's ardour considerably. Then the story was substantially forgotten. It turned up again in the nineteenth century when interest in the pre-conquest Americas began to get going. But this area, the Amazon basin, was still closed and dangerous. It's only in the last thirty years that missionaries have come out to the Indians, that governments have tackled them, that gold prospectors, oil-men, loggers and botanists have penetrated this region. Now rumours of *Kaliké* turn up, but there hasn't been a proper expedition yet.'

'You here are the only ones to add the pieces of this puzzle together?' I asked, still sweetly innocent. 'And Carl, that is.'

'No,' said Martha tensely. 'That's the point of all our secrecy. We had to come under cover of a holiday. We'll say after the event we got lost, it won't be a problem. But we would never have got authorisation, we don't even know what country the Cloud-maker is in. It could be Brazil, Colombia or Peru. These governments are so changeable and corrupt that we didn't trust them to do the proper job, either. We had to guard against looters. This is an architectural treasure, Sydney, just waiting to be found. Think of it. Just waiting there, somewhere. We have to be first. Then we can protect it.'

I looked from one to the other in the leaping firelight. A jaguar coughed and none of us noticed except me. 'It's one hell of a story,' I drawled. 'Hard to believe.' I meant the bit about Martha being interested in old buildings rather than golden artefacts.

Matheson said: 'Think of the film rights. Disney would love it.'

Margie laughed and the spell was broken. We turned in.

Next morning I was in the forest dealing privately

with the calls of nature. Plumbing and dentistry are two of the marvels of our century, I think. I hoped I wasn't going to get toothache.

I heard noises and stayed where I was, meaning to walk back to the river as soon as the other had passed, no doubt on the same errand as myself.

Then I saw. I saw and was not seen.

A man was there. A terrible man. He stood and I could not look past him. He called to me but when I would have gone forward, I saw there was another there.

Carla.

The man wore, I think, the costume of us all except Pablo, a safari shirt and trousers tucked into boots. I could not see his face. I could only see the mask.

He stood calling silently and I found my limbs trembling with the desire for me to go forward, but then Carla was there in my place, standing before the man, gazing at the mask.

There in the ant-strewn, scorpion-infested leaf-litter under the cathedral vault of the eternal rain forest canopy, in the hushed stillness of watching beasts, Carla took off her clothes and danced naked for the mask.

I heard the music like I heard the calling of the mask, with my mind, not with my ears. Carla loosed her dark hair so that it tumbled over her pale shoulders and she danced with her arms raised and her head thrown back, making strange small cries in her throat.

She hopped as she danced, a repeating arrhythmic hop that struck a dull drum-note in her dance. Her arms crossed at the wrists high above her head. Hop, turn, twist, bend at the waist left, bend at the waist right, hop, clap hands softly, twist the head round now slow, now fast with hair flying, hop, arch the back, hop, caress the breasts . . . It went on and on, her young breasts swinging, her dark fleece a smudge on the paleness of softly rounded belly and thigh.

The mask watched.

She danced closer, hop, bending more, hop, touching the legs of the man imploringly, hop, now on her knees, stroking his body, caressing it, weaving patterns with her hands in the air before it, bending back, throwing her head gradually round so that her hair fell slowly and her breasts stretched up to the man before her. To the mask.

She undid his trousers. Her hands fluttered over him. She drew out his sex.

It was big, jutting clear of him as he stood.

She stroked it. She touched it with her hair. She tried to reach her breasts up to it. She put her lips to it.

I saw her tongue pink as a baby croc's mouth. The tip flicked over the swollen head of the penis before her. Her hands came up and took the heavy swinging balls. She began to milk them gently, pulling first one, then the other.

Her tongue flickered. She pressed it tip to tip with the penis and pushed the great member up and caught it as gravity pulled it down.

She kissed the bubbling end of the organ. I saw the foreskin retract. I saw the red head bulge. I saw the pink mouth open. I saw the tongue snake-quick before the mouth closed over the heavy head and I saw her cheeks suck in.

The mask stood unmoving.

Carla twisted on the ground and stood up, bending over to put her hands on the ground. She backed onto the penis and speared herself with it. She began to shake herself so that she pleasured the thing in her, pleasuring herself, doubled over.

She stopped suddenly. She eased slowly forward so that the fat thing slid from between her tight buttocks. She came round again, falling once more to her knees.

It was very big now. She pushed her breasts forward, letting her head hang back so her hair streamed down her back. On her knees she advanced. The penis slid into her mouth, her lips closing on it. She brought her face up and absorbed all that she could. Her cheeks sucked in. Her mouth opened and I saw the rapid movement of her tongue. Then she sucked again. Her fingers were in his testicles. One hand now held the stem of the penis. Sucking hard, she masturbated the thing. I saw the white of her teeth.

Then her mouth was open. The man's hips jerked. She sucked and swallowed. Still his hips jerked. She opened her mouth again, her head falling back. I saw the pearlised stream for a moment given to her open mouth. Then she closed it again and swallowed, her throat gulping. She sucked, sucked again and shuddered into stillness.

The mask drew his slackening member from her mouth. He passed back into the forest.

Carla knelt naked. For a moment she seemed stunned. I saw her wake up and look around. She looked down at herself and gasped audibly. She got to her feet and feverishly pulled on her clothes. Then she ran back to the river.

I stood shaking at what I had seen. Then I too walked back to the river. I had no desire to be alone in the forest with the mask.

I looked round the campsite. Pablo was smoking his post-breakfast pipe. Martha was talking with Big Jacko, their heads close together. Margie was writing something in a notebook, I think she was keeping a diary.

Carla wasn't there. Nor was Colin, Tom Matheson nor Rory.

It rained for five hours and we motored upriver through the brown swirling water, seeing nothing but greyness. Margie and I took turns at the helm to give Pablo a rest in this safer stretch of water.

I was cold but it was a day blessedly free from insects.

About five in the afternoon the rain stopped. The sky boiled briefly and the clouds rolled excitedly, pink galleons, before tumbling away and releasing the blessed hot sunshine. The river was wide and complacent and we rounded a bend.

A terrific shout from the boat ahead of us sent a cloud of angry birds chittering up into the sky. We looked up, startled.

At first I thought it was another cloud, smoke-black and louring before us. Slowly the tops turned sugar-pink even as I watched.

'*Kaliké*,' said Pablo with satisfaction.

'Cloud-maker,' said Margie, staring.

Golly gee. The mountain. This easy. Right on schedule. Who was playing god on this expedition? Who was pulling the strings?

Mentally I shrugged. Maybe it's just my disease, my inborn urge not to accept things the way they look.

Objectively speaking they looked fabulous. We motored on, always making to the west and south though we twisted east and north some of the time, the river was so bendy. The Amazon basin is huge with very little drop from the eastern flanks of the Andes all the way to the Atlantic ocean. Several thousand miles. In the rainy season there's even one river that reverses its flow.

Now, as we snaked our way onwards, we saw Cloud-maker again and again, always at a great distance it seemed to me, dreaming in the dawn of tomorrow.

Uncannily, as if reading my thoughts, Matheson said: 'The Incas called it the evening mountain.'

'It lay to their west,' I said uncertainly.

'That's right.'

I looked at him. He looked bronzed and ruggedly fit from these days in the jungle. His ugly, humorous face was peaceful.

Peaceful because a young girl had cock-sucked him among the trees that morning? Carla wasn't quite twenty yet.

Peaceful because he knew the angles and had it under control?

Peaceful because his con was working and he'd got me off his back?

Or was he peaceful because he was crazy like the rest of them, a fanatic thinking his dream was about to come true?

'What's in this for you, Matheson?' I asked suddenly.

'In this for me? The excitement, I guess.'

'You're above financial considerations, are you? How noble.'

'I'm never above money, sweetheart. That's what it's all about.'

'This excitement. It's the thought of the treasure, is it, or does the archaeology turn you on?'

'Treasure?' he said casually. 'I'll believe it when I see it.'

'But you believe in the map.'

His eyes were golden brown and secret with knowledge. 'You think it's just a hunk of wood, do you?' he asked.

My nostrils quivered with distaste. So he was the man in the woods, the green man, the masked man. The mask.

Tom and Margie disappeared. Martha was looking at me and winking after watching their backs recede. 'A romance, d'you reckon?'

'With Matheson?' I balked, wearing my aghast expression. 'A woman would have t'be crazy or desperate.'

Martha cocked an eyebrow. 'I thought you two . . .' She shrugged her shoulders. 'Never mind. Forget it.'

She was a decent, sensitive lady, Martha, knew when it was best to drop a subject.

'I'm gonna take a nap,' she decided, going off to stretch out on the deck of her boat. Big Jacko hovered near, as usual, and Pablo was already snoring, propped against a tree, his woven straw hat pulled down over his face to shield his eyes from the sun.

I looked around, not quite sure what to do with myself. Colin was studying a particular orchid he had found at dawn. Carla and Rory had their heads together. This Carla female was turning out to be one helluva gal for the men.

She rubbed against him, her inside leg caressing his, one breast hard against his arm. This wasn't a friendly closeness, but a sexual come-on. And Rory, with his healthy appetite for woman-flesh, wasn't the sort to ignore such an offer, not when the pussy was as cute and inexperienced as Carla's. Almost, I envied her naïvety. But not quite. There was something to be said for the losing of innocence and the gaining of experience. Thinking about it, though, I wouldn't have swapped, wordly-wise and jaded though I was. I'd have hated to be a teenager again and in love.

Boys behaved so badly and there were other things to contend with besides broken hearts – spots, body hair. No, your thirties weren't so bad, I decided. At least it wasn't quite so easy now for men to make a mug of me. I was wise to them, even a smidgeon immune.

Colin watched them, his orchid entered and drawn in his notebook, measurements taken and colours arrowed to different parts of the waxy, strange flower. When Rory and Carla wandered off, Colin followed slowly, at a distance. I watched, intrigued, and curiosity eventually got the better of me. I had nothing better to do. I wanted to see what they were up to. Had a feeling. I was right.

In a clearing not far from camp Carla had put on the mask now and was already acting with characteristic oddness, well under the influence.

I hung back in the trees, hoping the greenery hid me and that, also, the strange power of the mask wouldn't affect me at such a distance.

Her clothes came off. So did Rory's. And, I saw at the edge of the clearing, Colin was dropping his trousers as if in a trance, his slim penis already standing up like a tent pole.

I began to feel too warm, strange, my clothing uncomfortable. Without being aware of it, I too stripped naked, began to move towards the strangely entwined group. They circled, arms clutching other arms, like a coven, under a deep spell, the mask, seeming to me, to change its expression, to grin at me. I held hands with Rory, my big breasts squashing against his firm chest.

Carla spoke. 'Pleasure me. Take her.'

Rory obeyed instantly, throwing me on my back and positioning himself over me so that his tongue could work up and down Carla's sex-lips as she stood at my head, legs wide, awesome in the Inca mask.

'Do it,' she commanded.

Something in my head told me I didn't altogether like the way things were going, that I had lost control, but I couldn't seem to show any wilfulness, just let the beautiful, naked Rory do what he wanted.

He took my legs, pulled them up so that my knees were against my chest, put his engorged member to my totally exposed sex, which quivered and contracted in anticipation, all glistening and pink. He was big, hard with desire, a pearl of juice seeping from amidst the angry red head. He placed it at my opening, caressing me fleetingly, sliding a finger into me, then, when he started in earnest to suck and lick at the overshadowing sex of the succubus, Carla, he pushed it forcefully into me.

In such a position it filled me almost to the point of discomfort, pressing at my very core, filling me. Too much. I felt like a trussed up chicken, tried to move my legs at least, but no, Rory held them firm, a willing, powerful servant of whatever demons had possession of us.

Over Rory's shoulder, between Carla's legs, where all the action seemed to be taking place, I saw the slim and pale form of Colin advance, kneeling behind Rory, caressing his rear, his balls, stroking the penis that thrust in and out of me. He licked Rory's anus, working a finger in, and stroked up some of the wetness from me to lubricate the tight, puckered opening, then he bided his time, sticking a finger up my exposed bottom as well, watching Rory's penis intently, adoringly. The added stimulation made me come almost immediately, exploding into a thousand little pieces. Overwhelmed by sensation I contracted, throbbed, relaxed in a happy stupor. Only then did

Rory release me, go onto his hands and knees, allowing me to squirm languidly free of the body tangle.

He licked still at the fearful person in the mask who had possession of Carla, bringing forth one pleasure crisis after another, then cried out in shock as Colin forced the fat head of his penis past Rory's puckered muscles and sank to the hilt, withdrawing hardly at all, making little, precise jerks at his mount.

Carla laughed at the astonished look on Rory's face. It was obvious that no one had ever tried such a thing on him before. He didn't like it, but was as much a subject of the deviant mask as the rest of us. He stayed obediently still as Colin steadily sodomised him.

I'd never seen two men at it before, was all eyes, watching the flesh withdraw and then push in again, Rory's cheeks held apart, caressed by the ecstatic Colin.

Poor Rory. Such an indignity. He'd lost control just as I had. I felt some sympathy for him, but not a great deal. He knelt there, rear in the air, testicles hanging and penis in a state of semi-arousal again. In thrall of the masked Carla, he licked her endlessly and plunged his pointed tongue into her wetness, making her cry out for the umpteenth time, her spread legs trembling, her crotch pushed hard against his face. At the same time Colin came, with a cry and much frenzied jerking. It seemed to last for ever.

I was already retrieving my clothes, beginning to feel more normal again. I snuck off, dressing hurriedly, had already decided that it was probably best to act as if nothing had happened.

Chapter Three

I was languid in my hammock where we had pulled up early for the night, under my mosquito net. I was hot but not as hot as I had been earlier in the day. I had swum, done my washing and hung it to dry, put on clean dry clothes and was almost comfortable.

My thoughts were of home. Wisecracking with the staffers. Buying lunch from the deli near my flat. Interviewing targeted people and teasing the information I wanted out of them. Drinking red wine with a man who was going to make love to me later in the evening.

My hand slunk under my trouser belt and slid inside my panties. I was hungry for sex again, truth be told. The forest was frightening but it was sexy as hell.

All those penile trees stretching up greedily to the light with long straight stems, then bursting into a green exuberance that fought for the light, gave me very Freudian thoughts. Clusters of plum-shaped fruits all purple and red hung like testicles one hundred feet up in the air. The creepers were creepy, long woody vines growing parasitically up the forest giants to wind through the canopy, twisting and strangling their hosts in their own domestic urge to reach the sun. There were flowers up there, orchids, violets and others that never bothered with rooting in the ground. They lived in the debris caught in branch forks and made their own play for the light we were denied down here below. It was like a forest upside down. All the nutrients were up top. Down below was starved and humming-quiet.

The silent ferocity of all this was daunting. Some hundred different species of parasitic plant-life can cling to a host tree and wind through its crown. Some of these looked alive and purposeful, cable-thick as they looped and coiled and snaked about above my head.

It scared me. But it gave me hot thoughts. It was a fight to succeed like sperm swimming frantically in semen. The leaf litter was full of frogs, toads, lizards, scaly things, bugs and beetles, food for the snakes that hung about pretending to be vegetation. Up top were pretty birds and butterflies chomping the fruits in the canopy, and monkeys and sloths and ant-eaters and all kinds of diverse creatures living without us, without humankind.

I smelled something.

Pablo told me about horrible things, like the huge green ticks that live on the tapir's belly and if you shoot a tapir, they swop over and climb up a man's legs till they can get cosy in his groin, sinking their jaws into his penis. Pablo was Venezuelan but he told me he could travel, he had papers, and he was the best motor-man in the Amazonian basin. Back home the Orinoco, the Siapa, the Casiquiare were all really bad for flies and biting insects, for *hormiga*, *jejenes*, *zancudos*, *tempraneros*, and down here in Brazil he could make more money and be bitten less.

The thing I smelled, I should do something about.

I lifted the corner of my mosquito net and sniffed. It was stronger. It wasn't horrible. It wasn't decay or rot or anything like that. But it said danger.

I put my head over the side of the hammock and took a real lungful up through my nostrils.

Matheson was wandering towards our boat smoking a small cigar. I lifted my head and stared at him.

'Put the cigar out,' I called.

'You just declare a no-smoking zone, vulture-lady?'

'Tom, put it out, behind you.'

He looked at me and did it. Gingerly I climbed out of my hammock and tiptoed across the boat. I climbed over the rail and jumped for the bank. Matheson stood there and watched me. 'I smell kerosene,' I said.

I didn't have to say any more. The boats had no cabins but were capable of carrying an enormous amount of stores and equipment for their size. This began with the huge drums of kerosene, fuel for the engines, used as ballast and as each was emptied it was refilled with river water to trim the boats. Everything else was arranged on top of these drums in a more or less orderly fashion. Big Jacko and Pablo supervised the packing of the boats and Margie kept records as we used stuff up. We humans sort of perched on top, out on deck. We slept, we girls, in hammocks strung from the masts used as little loading derricks, and an awning was rigged when we stopped to provide shade and protection from the heavy rain showers.

In other words, the boats were bombs.

Tom leaned over and sniffed delicately. He turned and called to Big Jacko. Pablo ambled over, too.

Some kerosene was leaking in our boat somewhere.

The cooking fire was doused and the smoking members of the party put out their cigars, pipes and cigarettes. Then we set about unpacking the boat.

Every day some kerosene from one of the big drums was emptied into smaller cans which were used to fill the fuel tanks during the day. The culprit was one of these cans which had a hole in it.

We contemplated the hole. It looked punched with a sharp implement, the gaudy paint flaked off and bare bright silver-coloured metal showing.

It was the sort of hole my screwdriver would make, the one I left in Matheson's room back in Manaus.

Rory said: 'I'll get rid of it. We'd better check none of the food stores are contaminated.' Without waiting for an answer he grabbed his machete and strode off into the forest.

'Shouldn't we use the kerosene?' I asked stupidly. I knew it was a diminishing resource that was vital to us.

'I have already filled the boats' tanks,' said Pablo, who indeed always left the boats ready to use though with the engines lifted out of the water. 'It might have dirt in it. No good for carburettor, huh?' He grinned.

Margie looked ill. 'We might have been killed,' she said huskily.

Matheson put his arm lightly on her shoulder. 'Hey, there,' he said, 'more people die crossing the road than by being blown up in boats.' But the picture in our minds was vivid, the boat going up in a series of violent explosions leaving us passengers as kebab-meat.

The jungle exploded. About three million startled bats, birds and insects hit the sky making it momentarily dark. It was the first time I truly realised that the Amazon basin is a device for arming each cubic metre of air with venomous and toxic teeth, darts and spears, mobile and on the wing. The place exists for these darting armoured crunchy chitinous predators, it is their environment. We humans pass through this hell-hole like the buffalo on the plains when the white man came. We are meat on the hoof, bovine, stupid and available. We make the insects happy.

'I wonder if he took himself along for the ride,' said Matheson happily.

'Don't be jealous, sweetie,' I cooed. 'I'm sure you have some very fine characteristics of your own. Somewhere.'

'How old are you, Johnson?'

'Not your business, camera-man.'

'I guess you'll reincarnate as a flu virus.'

'*That's* what you were last time around,' I said wonderingly. 'At last I understand. The way you are now is your punishment.'

He started to laugh. For a moment I felt tempted to ask him about the mask. He had experienced something peculiar, same as me, in his hotel room. I wanted to know if he had tried it on.

But he had. That time, in the forest with Carla, I was sure it was him.

I swallowed the impulse. I was sorry I'd told Rory as it was. I sounded loopy because the mask was nothing, just a creepy old artefact from a past culture which the Spanish defecated on. (I'm not anti-Spanish. All top-dog nations have done it where they could and still do it today.) I'd seen Matheson and felt a sexual urge, and being a normal man and me not a gargoyle, he'd responded. The guy was intact and fully working, something I would have guessed from the outside anyway.

It was this country, this place, I thought irritably.

Maybe I was a little feverish all the time. I hardly knew myself, this far out of my natural environment. I wanted decent, honest screwing with naughty frills from a nice sophisticated urban type. These macho jungle-men wielding their machetes, they had the sexual vibes of a used tissue. I told myself this very firmly. They weren't for real, even Rory, work of art though the man was.

I like my men tainted, with a touch of the devil in them. Honesty and muscle can go in the romances but in real life give me sneaky, funny men who suck good.

Matheson was very close to me. 'You're missing it, aren't you?'

'I'm missing everything. Good food, fine wine, real work, fun men.'

'Sorry you came along?'

'I'm sorry you came along.'

'Is the itch bad today, honey?' He was sniggering.

'May your dong be infested with ticks,' I returned pleasantly.

'Here's lover-boy back.'

I saw Rory ambling to join us after his arson experience.

'I think Margie's a very nice girl, Matheson. Pity she's no judge of character.'

'She just uses me for sex. Like Martha uses Rory. You won't catch Martha muddling desire with reality.'

I looked at him soberly remembering what I knew of the provenance of the mask. 'Martha can make mistakes,' I said.

He looked puzzled then, as though we'd gone beyond the fun exchange of insults and moved into a new ball-park. Which, of course, we had.

* * *

Kaliké continued to hover at the edge of our vision for days. We crept snail-paced along a good-tempered, lazy river who knew it'd got itself down out of the mountains of its birth and had a couple of thousand miles to go before it need fuss its way into the sea. Sometimes we would see the mountain smudging the distant sky. Sometimes we would only see the dark confusion of clouds it drew about its flattened head. Sometimes, often, we would be turned the wrong way and snaking pointlessly about still miles from its feet.

I heard a helicopter in the night.

I woke feeling cheered and it took me some time to work out why. The night was velvet pitch and I was snug within my mosquito net. My ears snagged in memory, a comforting, familiar memory.

My dream-feeling left me and I felt hollow and homesick. It occurred to me I really had heard something, it wasn't just a dream noise.

What out here could sound like that? There are two million square miles of these overgrown matchsticks and helicopters don't fly that far without fuel, especially at night. Even a plane over-flying has to take care. Loggers' camps and gold-mining areas are dots in this immensity. They built a road through it, all the way from the sea to the mountains, as far as Cruzeiro do Sul in the far west of Brazil where you bump your nose on the rocky wall of the Andes. But this TransAmazon highway got renamed by those who made it and those who tried to live beside it. They called it the Transamargura – the highway of bitterness.

I had heard a helicopter and been comforted by all that it suggested in the way of technological achievement and creature comforts. That's what was wrong with this place. We couldn't win. The trees beat us.

The insects saw us as lunch. So did the snakes, the jaguar, the piranha, the giant catfish, the electric eel and even, I'd been told, a sting-ray. I wasn't used to being considered edible by my environment. It spoiled my backchat.

'Margie,' I called softly, sticking my head out from under the netting. 'Margie.'

She didn't answer. I wanted to know if she'd heard it too or whether I was just hallucinating. Out here, a girl needed an objective check on her sanity once in a while.

I tumbled out of my hammock. No silk pyjamas out here. I wore a dry set of clothing at night leaving my boots off and the knobbly bits loose. Now I put my boots on and gingerly picked my way over the decking.

The night creaked, croaked, gobbled, hissed, barked, coughed, screamed and churrucked. Bastards. Give me urban quiet with a little traffic and the odd passing drunk. No one has any consideration for others out here, I thought crossly. What the hell were their mothers doing when they were little.

I began a piece in my mind about how to deal with juvenile offenders, the sort that stole cars and terrorised housing estates. Send them out here, I thought gleefully. No, better, send them to the north of the Amazon basin where Pablo told me the flies and ants and hornets and mosquitoes bit worse than any gummy old Brazilian insect.

Margie wasn't in her hammock.

Call of nature? Sure. What aspect of nature, though. I stepped quietly off the boat and onto the shore.

This was a lovely campsite, a broad sandy playa or beach in the river that had been all over butterflies when we moored, yellow and black, blue, green, red, brown – beautiful things. They didn't eat people either which made them a rarity in these parts.

I kept away from the embers of the fire where the men slept and moved quietly down the sand spit. The moon was up and riding high. Despite the fearful noise all around as the nocturnal things got a word in edgeways, I felt a kind of peace. Coming to the Amazon was going to be one of those experiences like reading meaningful fiction – not enjoyable at the time but you were glad you'd done it afterwards.

I heard a noise, a different noise I mean, and my heart turned over with a spasm of pain. *Crocodiles. Did they eat at night?* I drew breath to yell even as I remembered that all the men were up in hammocks. I was the only meat attached to the ground here. I scrubbed the scream scenario and turned to bolt.

And stopped. And stood. In the moonlight ahead of me sat two people with their backs to me. Their heads were together and they were whispering.

I took a delicate scrunch-free step forward, easing my weight onto the foot and bringing the other one up and past it. My ears doubled in size and flapped. Secret night-time conversations, huh. Sydney wanted to know.

Matheson turned his head and kissed Margie on the lips. Her head was back, her eyes closed and her mouth fastened on his. His hand was down the front of her shirt.

She gave a little moan of pleasure.

As well she might. The guy could fuck, as I certainly knew. I stepped delicately backwards, connected with something moving, tripped and fell on my back.

A light sprang up. Momentarily I was blinded. It swung away from me to the thing I had tripped over.

I am not a screamer. If I do scream, and it's very

109

rare, it's to warn others or to get immediate help for myself. I do not scream in fear. Never. Except, that is, when I fall over a crocodile. It might have been a cayman. That's the Amazon all over. You can't even be sure what it is that's eating you.

It opened its mouth and I had a really interesting view of its dentition. It would have benefited from Listerine, though. From the smell, it had pyorrhoea.

I screamed. I was going to be the noisiest dinner ever. I even screamed with an echo.

You wouldn't think things could get worse. They could, though. The light went off. I scrabbled backwards in the sand and *felt my boot connect*. You cannot feel worse than lying on your back in the dark and knowing you have just kicked a croc on the snout. I mean, it would be angry now.

My vision returned adjusting to the moonlight proving my beta-carotene quotient was up to par. The croc would get the benefit, of course. It opened its mouth again and waddled forward.

Paul Hogan stuck his machete between its jaws. It closed its mouth and ate knife. It opened its mouth again and made this really terrible noise. The machete was withdrawn and I saw it slash down across the beast's nose. My echo was still screaming. The croc swung its head round and made for its attacker.

Matheson stopped being Paul Hogan and back-pedalled smartly. The croc put on speed. There was a bright flash and a loud noise. The croc stopped. Accompanied by some tail-lashing, it died.

Margie stopped screaming. If the croc had a pal along, the food was on the plate. I could not move.

Pablo came towards us with a gun. He had shot the thing, waking from sleep, grabbing the rifle and shooting in one smooth and successful action. What a guy.

Matheson came over to me. 'You OK?' he said, his voice queer and wobbly.

'Help me up,' I whimpered.

He hauled me to my feet. 'It didn't bite you?' he asked.

'You stopped it in time.'

He hit me hard round the face. I heard, through the buzzing in my ears, Margie give a shout of shocked surprise. Otherwise, only Pablo saw. The others were still rolling themselves out of their hammocks and finding torches to see what the hell was going on.

Pablo's head switched sharply from me to Matheson and back again. I put my hand to my face and held it there stupidly. I had never been hit in my adult life, not once, not ever, and certainly not by a man.

Suddenly everyone was there. I turned trembling and pushed through them till I got to my boat. It took me two goes to get on board. I stumbled over to my hammock and fell into it, wrapping my mosquito netting round me.

I pictured myself upstairs in The Bottle in Wine Office Mews off Fleet Street. I pictured the whole crowd in there, all of us drinking champagne or something equally stupid because we'd pulled off some coup. Jessica, our astrologist was bitching in the corner. Maria who did fashions was undulating against a sub. Damien the human Rottweiler, our news editor, was sniffing up the skirts of the newest rookie hackette. Marvin the barman was making champagne cocktails and Celia, my immediate boss, was on her mobile ordering strawberries to make the champagne taste nice. Nicer.

My thumb slid into my mouth. I huddled on my side, curled as foetally as my hammock would allow.

Deep in my fantasy I let sleep wash healingly over me.

The next day Margie said: 'I'm furious with Tom for what he did to you. It was disgraceful.'

My cheek was tender and reddened. I put an extra layer of jungle repellent on it and hoped no one would notice.

I didn't want to talk to Margie. I didn't want to talk to anyone.

'He said you were spying on us. I said that was no excuse.'

'I wasn't spying on you,' I lied. 'I heard a helicopter in the night. That's what it sounded like, anyway. I wanted to ask you but you weren't there. Then I got up and took a walk. I'd just seen you and was trying to back off when, when it all happened.' One way of telling when I lie is by how much I talk. It's very sussy if I gabble. I was gabbling now.

'He shouldn't have hit you.'

'It doesn't matter,' I said wearily. 'We don't get along. You must know that.'

She looked at me oddly. I took my smoked piranha, hot flour cakes and coffee down the playa. Arranging myself so that I could see any crocs a fair way off, I began moodily to munch my breakfast.

Pablo had skinned the croc and was proposing to Martha we eat it.

'What's it taste like?' I heard her ask.

'Rubber,' he answered. 'Weeth a hint of feesh.'

Matheson joined me. 'I'm sorry I hit you,' he said. Hubby was obeying orders, was he? I hadn't reckoned him as the conjugal type.

I shrugged. 'You saved my life first.'

'Margie told me you heard the helicopter, too.'

'You heard it?'

'Yes.'

'And Margie heard it?'

'Yes.'

'All three of us heard it.'

'Yes.' He was sounding impatient now.

'I guess it was real, then,' I said, nodding sagely.

And so we reached the mountain. The river ran round its rocky base. The trailing vegetation was sparse here, the water having washed away all the soil. To climb it we would have to abandon our boats leaving Pablo in charge to protect them, and make our way through the rain forest till we could climb the western flanks of Cloud-maker, hopefully to find the cave of the mask.

I wasn't so sure about this walking lark. It involved back-packing, for a start. I hadn't realised how fond I had become of the piranha infested river and my life of ease in my hammock. All the humid damp had made my feet a little rotten, despite anti-fungal powder, and I don't like walking further than the nearest form of transportation at the best of times.

We would have to cook for ourselves, too. Pablo was motor-man and cook. Now he would have a little holiday.

I got myself beside Rory that first day. 'The mountain wasn't so hard to find,' I opened conversationally.

'No one's looked very hard before,' he said. 'It hasn't mattered precisely where it was until now, except for overflying planes.'

'You hear that helicopter the other night?'

He turned his bright eyes on me. 'The night you nearly got eaten?'

'That night. I remember it clearly. It was the helicopter woke me up.'

'I heard it. I guess he was lost. Pity the radio doesn't work. Of course, it could have been a government aircraft, but I wouldn't expect such a thing to fly at night. It's surprise mountains like this one that make flying dangerous here.'

'Nowhere to land, either.'

There was a short silence. 'I couldn't figure out,' Rory said carefully, 'why you were out with Matheson that night. I mean,' he added hastily, 'it's absolutely your own affair, but somehow I had the idea you two didn't get along.'

'We don't,' I said flatly. 'He was padding palms with Margie.'

'I'd have thought she had more sense.'

I shrugged. 'Needs must. There isn't much choice here, is there? She's a red-blooded girl.' Actually I thought she was a girl in search of a husband. She had the eyes of an ash-tray emptier and cushion-plumper.

We had dropped slightly behind the others. Colin and Matheson himself were up front with their machetes clearing the path and incidentally showing us all the way back to the safety of the boats. Now Rory suddenly stopped.

'Jesus,' he said with quiet violence.

'What's the matter?'

'The pay-roll. It's not compensation for this.'

'I'm not with you,' I said, but my heart started thumping irregularly.

He shrugged off his pack and put his hands on my shoulders, pushing the straps off mine too.

I let him.

He took my face between his hands. He drew it towards his own. I was passive, shaky. His mouth came onto mine. My eyelids fluttered closed. His mouth touched mine, teased at it and opened it. I felt myself sag slightly into his body. He took a step in and let go with his hands. His arms went round me. I tasted his tongue and he increased the pressure and kissed me hard. Hungrily.

He shivered suddenly and held me tighter. *You sweet bastard*, I thought. *You really want me.*

We kissed like we were starving. I guess we were. He opened my shirt and kissed my breasts. 'You're so beautiful,' he breathed. 'So beautiful.'

My hands wrenched at his shirt and I got them in against his body. I hadn't realised the depths of my own hunger for this man. Touching his bare skin was bliss.

He loosened his belt hurriedly. 'Touch me, Sydney. I need you.'

I put my hand down inside his trousers. His penis was up and hard. Its hot, silky length fitted the groove of my curving hand. I squeezed gently and bit his shoulder. 'I want you in me,' I said fiercely.

He dropped my trousers. He pushed his own down and lifted me onto a tree root. My hands were on his shoulders, my face down in his hair. He slid his penis up between my legs and I felt it enter me. My vulva spasmed and my pussy seemed to suck him greedily in. He began to take me in long, thirst-quenching strokes, his face in my neck, his lips kissing my throat.

Maybe it wasn't anything great in the technical sense. We were pushed for time, it was a bad place and we were too hungry to be refined about it. But it was beautiful, just beautiful. That hungry man feeding hard from my body and satisfying me at the same time was the summit of my desire at that moment. When he came, his long cock thrust hard to fill my place with honeyed sweetness, I pulled his hair till his head went back and then I kissed him fiercely, his

115

eyes, his mouth, his ears, tasting him and smelling him the way I had been wanting to for so long.

He pulled up his trousers and fell on his knees kissing my belly. 'Sydney,' he said. 'I've got to have more of you. This isn't enough. I can't stop now. You can't make me stop now.'

'No,' I said, between laughing and crying with happiness. 'We can't stop now.'

He pulled up my clothes and hugged me close for a moment. 'I'm going to make love to you properly,' he whispered in my ear. 'I'm going to pleasure you like a woman needs, like a woman such as you deserves.'

'Huff puff,' I said, laughing.

'What's that?'

'What I say when men boast to me.'

He kissed the tip of my nose. 'I'm not boasting. You'll see. I'll make you see. We were made to do this together, Sydney. You can't deny it.'

I looked into his face, my arms lightly clasping him round the neck. 'You are such a lovely man,' I said soberly. 'It kind of frightens me.'

'Why does it frighten you?' He was teasing me now.

'How can I keep guard over myself with you around?'

'That's what I want,' he said, fierce in his turn. 'I want you defenceless. At my mercy. I want to screw you till I go blind with it.'

We were kissing again. It was crazy. At any moment the others might be back. We were surrounded by things wanting to eat us. But I wanted to have this man again inside me and I wanted him properly, in bed, with time and cool wine and long lazy hours to explore each other's bodies, to tease and

116

arouse all smoky with passion, limbs tangled, my pussy sweet and swollen with desire and excess.

I wanted excess.

He stopped and stood back. He looked a little shaken. 'We'll find a way,' he said hoarsely. 'By Christ we will.'

'Yes,' I said, nodding my head slowly, happily. At that moment it seemed fine that we must slide and deceive to have our way. It would keep my lust secret, close in to my breast.

Rory picked up my pack. 'Put this on, beautiful woman,' he said. 'Stop looking so happy. The others will know just what we've been up to. You're indecent.'

I laughed. 'You're some character,' I said. 'You'll need razor wire to stop me pouncing.'

He was sober suddenly. 'Not long, Sydney, I promise. I'll play out my part in this farce but quite soon nothing, nothing on this earth is going to stop me claiming you. You'd better watch out.'

I trotted off up the path the men had cleared. Rory hung back so we shouldn't reappear together. I trotted past hairy trees, trees with fat string round them, trees with flowers sticking straight out of their trunks, trees like giant pineapples, trees with huge flanges round them propping them up, trees with extra roots out away from the main trunk supporting them from a distance.

Hell of a place.

My euphoria started to subside. I heard the others up ahead bashing through this eternal cosmic-sized conservatory.

My body calmed down and my brain switched back on.

After all, where was the problem? What could Martha do if he stopped playing toyboy? Sack him?

Send me away? Things were too far gone for that kind of nonsense.

Then there was sweet Carla. Who had twisted Rory's arm to get him inside her panties?

Just what farce had he been talking about? The sexual farce? Or this farce of treasure maps and lost cities full of gold?

I wished I wasn't so hungry for the man. It was sapping my judgement. Should I go the way my leathery old heart was telling me? I had no practice of the tenderer emotions, I had kept them successfully out of my life.

I had kept myself safe.

It seemed to me I needed something proprietary here, some emotional equivalent to the all-purpose jungle repellent we smeared ourselves with. I needed a man-repellent. Well, that is, ol' Sydney wasn't giving up on the game, but game it had to stay or I was in danger. Men were for playing with, for using. It was one very big mistake to get involved with them.

It was hard to keep this sane and defensive attitude in operation with something as luscious as Rory wanting to raid my locker. I was lusting for him in a really big way. His cock was magic in me, a wand of pleasure.

I could tell myself feebly that all this was just deprivation, Rory had no competitors out here in the land of a billion insects. It was a lie, though. He'd fit snug as a bug into my London life. The guy moved, he had brains, he was sneaky.

Yes, he was sneaky. I could sense it. But I liked my men clever, playing the angles.

If Rory had appetite, serious appetite, he could gobble Martha's tough ol' pussy, kiss Carla's tender little pouting flesh, and keep some fuel in his tanks for fierce love-making with me.

Did I really care? I was not and never will be jealous. That way lies madness and worse still, old age. What gave me a squeamish feeling was being played for a sucker, if all his protestations of lust were so much hot air.

I could swear that man meant it. He was as trapped by this inconvenient and unlooked for passion as I was. Play-time was always welcome. But things were looking serious.

We camped that night at the foot of Kaliké. What had looked sheer from a distance was broken and ridged this close. Even I thought I could manage a toughish upward scramble, given enough time.

We cleared a patch of forest and made saplings into poles to support the tarpaulin cover. Big Jacko lit the fire and he and Margie settled to cook the evening meal. Matheson and I strung the hammocks.

We dined lavishly on tinned meat, biscuits and dried fruit. As a special treat Martha dished out muesli bars for us to chew on from the stores. We drank coffee, for once not tasting the chlorine-treated water because Martha gave permission for one of the bottles of brandy to be opened and we all laced our drinks.

Lying there in my hammock in our company of eight, this seemed to me to be the finest meal in the world. Looking back, this strikes me as an objective measure of how far down the fruit-cake path I had strayed myself. Matheson started to play his mouth organ in a bittersweet bluesy fashion. The um um um ooh ah bird started up its monotonous call, settling in for a few solid hours of repetition in case anyone missed it first time around. Even that didn't trouble me.

'Will you be very disappointed if you don't find Vilcabamba?' I asked Martha. I had to admit she intrigued me, being such a mixture of good cynical horse sense and romantic wishful-thinking.

'Disappointed? Yeah. Sure thing, Sydney. Heartbroken? No. We're making a play here. Not all plays come off.'

'How'd you pick the team?'

'I travel a lot, Sydney, partly on Trust business and partly 'cos I like it. Carla likes to come with me and Jacko and Margie usually accompany me, too. They didn't have to come this time but I'm glad they chose to. It seems to me this kind of trip is beyond the normal pay-roll.' She grinned, baring her designer-white teeth. She was a tough cookie. 'Tom introduced me to Carl in the first place, of course, which was what started all this business. It was Carl who found our two available experts.'

'You're enjoying this, aren't you?' I asked.

'Sure am. Ain't you?'

'Except when I'm being bitten by insects and scared half to death by hungry crocs, I guess so. It's quite an experience.'

'That's my bag, Sydney,' said Martha quietly. 'Experience. You know, I don't say this much, but I don't believe in fuck all, you know that?'

'Can I quote you?' I was laughing.

'I grew up in the Bible belt and it seemed to me that every little innocent thing I wanted to do, some guy with his collar back to front said no.'

'How innocent were your innocent things?'

'Garden of Eden stuff. I wanted to lie under the cottontails and find out what the boys five years older 'n me kept under their fig leaf. My ma wanted me to

120

get married 'n have babies. Pa used his belt on me. The sheriff tol' me off and put his hand in my panties. It's a miracle I didn't set up shop and sell the commodity they all made so much fuss about.'

'But you didn't.'

'Nope. Despite all that religion telling me sex was shit, I knew they were wrong. So wrong, baby. I knew it was a happy thing, a good thing, and a proper thing for men and women to do together. I don't know how I knew because sure as hell, no one felt like that around me. Then I met Charlie. Charlie was thirty years ahead of me in the game and he ran a bookshop in the next town to ours. I moved in with Charlie who was gentle and kind and liked what we did together. No fireworks, honey, but sweet-sippin' whisky day after day. That man taught me a lot. I'm not talking technical here, Sydney. I'm talking lifestyle.'

'What happened?'

'Charlie had a heart attack but he left me the store. I sold it and used the dough to move north. I bought some education, art education specifically because Charlie had taught me that older things could be nice, and I married my teacher. By the time that bust up I had met Joaquim.'

'You ever go back home?'

'Papa calls me a whore and ma weeps over me. I don't bother no more. My money's good enough for them, though. Joaquim's money, I should say. Ain't no trouble with that.'

The following morning we struck camp and moved up Cloud-maker. Every thousand feet up takes four degrees off the temperature. The forest changed its character as we moved upwards. The silent strangled forest giants gave way to smaller, more slender trees with silvery bark. The palms I was used to, and all that stuff that looked like house plants with real big ideas, disappeared. There was moss. There was moss everywhere, covering the trees, the ground, covering rotting broken branches, and there were ferns. It was cooler and wraiths of mist curled vapourishly between the gnarled and twisted trunks.

We climbed between huge rocks carpeted in soft thick moss. Flowers nodded in the quiet dampness. At a distance things shrieked, but not near us. The canopy was close above. It was like a very ancient English wood, intertwined and furry-soft.

I shivered. A druid wouldn't be out of place here. Or a troll. It didn't help that we went in single file, without talking.

It grew steeper and the vegetation gave way to barish rock and open vistas. It was shaped and layered and grooved as though someone had carved it. It was lighter than the stuff we had camped on beside the river and Colin explained. This was sandstone. The river ran through outcrops of ancient shield granite.

A pebble is a pebble is a pebble to me. 'Are the Andes granite?' I asked.

'They're Andesite,' Colin replied.

Ask a stupid question.

It became nastily like real climbing, steep enough to use hands as well as feet, and I took care not to look back or down. At the periphery of my vision I could see the rolling canopy of the rain forest stretching forever like endless green cloud seen from above on a long flight.

We were climbing a broad sloping slab of rock, fissured and ridged to make foot-holds easy, like climbing stairs. It was alarmingly steep. The slab gradually narrowed, becoming a spur. Then it became a tooth. I drew to a weary halt beside my companions.

'We'll have to go back,' said Matheson.

'Is there no way to get across?' asked Martha.

They were arguing about this chasm that had appeared between our flake of rock and the main mountainside, now some six feet away from us. This doesn't sound much, but that six feet continued down for some forty feet or more, narrowing to a mere crack. Anyone not making it over the gap would wind up a collection of small bones in a loose bag of skin down there. It was a horrible drop.

Colin looked this way and that. The little summit we were on was blade sharp at the top and sheer on the inside where it had split from the mountain. 'If we could get a rope across,' he said.

'It's down and back,' said Matheson. He took a couple of shots with his Nikon, panning the spectacular vista with a fancy lens. It made me feel ill.

Rory paced up and down. Then he took one of the coils of rope and laid it on the ground. I watched him tie it to a little notched pillar of rock. He tied the other end to his waist.

The others argued. Carla lay with her eyes shut, pale and interesting. Margie watched Matheson like he was lunch. Martha listened to what everyone said, making up her mind while we rested.

Rory moved back a little from the edge.

'Hey,' I said suddenly.

He grinned and blew me a kiss, dancing lightly on his feet. Then he ran and jumped.

There was a concerted gasp of horror. Rory landed four-footed, grabbing for hand-holds. His boots skidded sickeningly. A moment later he was in balance. He stood up and turned to grin at us in triumph.

I felt sick. I loathe macho tricks. Martha was on her

123

feet clapping and laughing. Matheson had gone very quiet.

'Stupid berk,' called Colin. He was grinning, too. It had been amazing to see.

The rope was tied off and a second one sent across. The packs were sent over, including Rory's. Then it was our turn.

'Ladies first,' called Rory, cheerily.

'I'll go first,' said Matheson, 'and test it.'

'I'll test it,' said Big Jacko. 'If it bears my weight, we all get across.'

He tied a loop of rope round his waist and round one of the ropes. He edged out over the chasm head-first, hanging from his waist loop with his feet hooked at the ankles over the bridging rope. He held the other rope and hauled himself across. I felt ghastly just watching. But it was no distance, of course. His head was touching the far side even as his feet left our side.

Martha followed, then Carla, then Margie and then me. Hands pushed me off and hands collected me. It wasn't so bad. Matheson moved forward.

'Colin next,' called Rory. He was anchoring the rope his side and making sure it didn't fray under our weight. 'It's only fair. Matheson wanted to go back.'

Colin stood up. He had had the ropes tied round him as well as the rocky pillar, anchoring this side of the chasm. Matheson took his place and Colin crossed.

Now we were all over except for the camera-man. 'Are we leaving the ropes in place for coming back?' he called.

'I'll jump it again.' Rory was laughing.

'Don't be silly.' But Martha was pleased at his vainglory, I could see.

'Seriously,' said Rory. 'We may well need the ropes

again and we only have one more apart from these here. I'll jump it, don't worry. We might even find a better way down.'

Matheson untied the ropes and advanced to the edge. He tied both ropes round himself, tucking his precious cameras inside his shirt. Then he crouched down, bent at the knees. There was a moment's silence. He launched himself.

I couldn't see what happened. With Rory and a rock buttress taking the strain, he should have swung easily across the gap. Instead, he was slipping, going down into the chasm, his boots sending showers of friable rock debris off as he turned upside down on the rope.

Rory, anchoring the rope, had slid forward. One hand held the buttress. The other held one of the ropes.

Big Jacko moved forward and took some of the strain. Then Colin was holding Rory. From the chasm we all heard Matheson swearing horribly.

Jacko braced himself and dug his boots in. He hauled and Rory got to his feet and hauled behind him. I lay over the edge and put a hand down, hooking it under Matheson's arm as he slowly worked his way up. Margie sat on my feet.

When he was up top, he sat down. He untied the ropes. He took his cameras out of his shirt and checked they hadn't got bashed. Then he looked at Rory. His face was grey and greasy with shock. 'You son of a bitch,' he said.

'Hey,' said Martha sharply. 'It was an accident, Tom. Rory did what he could.'

'It was Jacko saved him, Martha,' said Rory. 'I was slipping. See, I had the rope tied off here. The rock broke and that rope went. I couldn't hold it. The sudden strain on the second rope pulled me over.'

Matheson stood up. 'Let's keep going,' he said roughly.

Martha said: 'You might say thank you to Jacko. And I think you should apologise to Rory.'

'Jacko knows how grateful I am. He saved my life,' said Matheson. There was a long silence.

'It doesn't matter,' said Rory lightly. 'You can't blame him. I dropped him, after all.'

We all stood up and shouldered our packs. We continued on and up. Cloud-maker began to live up to its name. We entered a dense, wet, thick, grey drizzle.

We went steadily upwards. We came out the other side of the cloud, above it.

I gasped.

Before us the mountain rose in a series of broad, stepped ridges. Seen like this, rearing skywards, the sides were fluted and rippling as though the rock was soft, creased material. Below and behind us lay the cloud we had walked and scrambled through. Its thick fluffy tops were pink-stained for miles around from the setting sun. Across this candy-floss vista a dark shadow lay sombre and grey. The mountain itself cast its shadow over the cloud tops, for we were on the eastern flanks and the mountain reared between us and the sun.

'We had better camp,' said Jacko. 'It'll be dark soon.'

It was cold. We would sleep on the ground here wrapping our hammocks around us for warmth. We found a wide lichenous ledge under an overhang that could give some shelter if it was stormy in the night.

'We'll collect sticks for fuel,' said Rory, and taking my arm he walked us both off brazenly together.

He climbed swift as a cat ignoring the dried and wind blasted bushes we passed on the way. Without my pack I felt able to keep up with him, at least for a short way. We were nearing the saddle and there were larger stretches of comparatively flat rock up here, loose and scree-like. The mountain had looked flat-topped from a distance, but the centre of the plateau summit sagged in the middle. The geography was considerably more complicated close up.

Rory jumped down into a small dip and wriggled under a ledge. 'Room for two,' he called.

'What are you doing?' I said, amused and exasperated. I wanted the warmth of a fire and my supper.

'Come here, Sydney.' The inflection in his voice made my heart hammer.

I dropped into the declivity and went on hands and knees to join him. He reached out an arm. As I came within it, he pulled me close.

I stretched my length against his body. 'I want you long and slow with all the trimmings,' he said.

His lips were against my skin. 'The others are waiting for us,' I said, stupidly.

'Sod the others.' He kissed my mouth. He opened my shirt and kissed my breasts, holding me above him so he could take my nipples into his mouth, turn and turn about, and suck them lingeringly.

How much of the day had he spent thinking about me, planning this?

'Are you cold,' he murmured.

'No. Not any more. That's not why I'm shivering.'

'You darling. You sweet darling.'

He stripped his shirt and made me lie on it. His body was warm and firm and I found my own lips grazing his skin, tasting him, so that I could enjoy at last the unhurried feel and smell of the man.

He was not particularly broad nor tall, but his muscles were firm and well developed. It was a lovely body, a warm marvel of strength and agility.

It was very good. He moved down my body opening my clothes, kissing me as he went. I felt his lips in the soft places on my waist, on my belly, I felt his tongue in my navel and I felt his chin graze my sexual mound.

He moved up me rubbing his naked chest against mine. His hand closed over my fleece. He looked into my face, his own dark and quiet, while his fingers curled and curved into the groove under my pubic bone. 'I'd like to shave you here,' he whispered. 'You would be like fruit. The plump outward thrust *here*, the soft succulent split of the flesh *here*.'

His fingers pressed into me. He opened me and let one finger lie in the length of my vulva. His face was very close to mine. 'I will fuck you and suck you till you cry,' he said.

'I never cry.'

'You will cry for me.'

His fingertip vanished into the hot little mouth of my vagina. His tongue was out between his teeth and his breathing had become less regular.

How strange this was, on a mountain in South America.

'How do you want me to do it?' he whispered. 'With my fingers, like this?' He teased my clitoris and passion jolted like electricity through me.

'Or with my tongue?' He put out his tongue further and entered my mouth with it. I kissed him.

'Or with my cock in here?' He slid a finger into my pussy and pressed.

'Or with it in here?' He moved the sex-wet finger round. I felt his teeth on my neck. The finger penetrated my anus. My body jerked in reflex, pressed tight against him.

He laughed.

I pushed him far enough away to wriggle out of my

boots and trousers. I came round on top of him then, astride his waist. His eyes glittered in the gloom below me. His dark face was alive and devilish.

I swayed forward so that my breasts drooped and brushed across his face. He caught the nipples, kissing and sucking them, waiting for me to make the next move.

I lifted my hips. His penis was hard. I rocked back squatting on my toes. Holding myself above him, I lifted his cock and put the tip to my vagina. I pressed down slightly so that he was almost but not quite within me.

'Kissy-kissy,' I said. I bobbed slightly. The two sticky places pressed together and parted, pressed together and parted. I neither let him penetrate me nor did I release him. His cock kissed my pussy and my pussy kissed him right back.

'Beautiful lady,' he said, his voice low and warm and wicked. He jerked his hips so suddenly I couldn't withdraw in time. The head of his penis, his glans, entered my body and stopped there.

The feel of it was bliss, fat in my restricted place.

We looked at each other. 'Who will give way first?' he said and licked his lips.

I squeezed my pussy muscles.

'Ah,' he said softly, with pleasure.

I squeezed again.

'I think you're cheating.'

I began to sway very rapidly, just a tiny amount, so that I masturbated the end of his cock with my labia, neither letting him drive right in nor allowing him altogether out of my clasp.

He began to pant. 'Witch.'

I continued. He licked the ends of his thumbs and put his hands up to my breasts. His thumbs slid over my nipples. I frigged the end of his cock and then suddenly stopped and sank down so that his shaft penetrated up, up and up into the deep heart of me.

His face was wiped of emotion. His penis in me was so good I felt frightened. We began to screw properly.

For a moment he was satisfied to thrust deeply into me, as though our sex-play had starved us and for a moment we must gulp our pleasure. Then he took my hips and lifted me.

I let him. He lifted me slowly, his arm muscles bulging. He looked down between us as he did so, the pale shining rod of his penis coming gradually into view, bridging our two bodies.

I felt every nanometre of him as he came out of my body.

He pulled me forward and lowered me over his face. I had gone onto my knees. I could feel the warm silk of his hair on my inner thigh.

He still held me above his face. His tongue came up and walked in my swollen vulva.

I felt its hot tip teasing me. He ran it round the entrance to my pussy. He moved it between my labia. He touched my clitoris, several times, with a stabbing movement. He slid his tongue back and penetrated my anus.

He lowered me slightly. He kissed my clitoris. He kissed my vagina. He bit gently at my sex-lips and pulled them softly. He pushed his tongue further into my pussy and lapped my juices. He kissed my anus, puckering his lips small to match its own little, pink, puckered state.

He put his lips to my sex and sucked. Then he bit my clitoris.

'Rory,' I whispered, my voice unsteady. He'd done this before.

His head came up sharply and he sucked really

hard. Unable to control myself I started to come, my body throbbing and pulsating as my juices flowed. He sucked hard, drinking my nectar, nibbling my bud, and then he moved me sharply down his body and dropped my open spasm-wracked sex over his hard thick penis.

He thrust up very hard and I jerked upright hitting my head on the ledge over us. I hardly noticed it. I was squeezing as hard as I could. I felt him come. He grunted slightly as he did so. After several strong thrusts he began to soften and relax.

I pulled off him and moved down. I opened my mouth and took his soft, wet sticky member right in. I licked and sucked him. I took his balls in my mouth and sucked them gently.

He drew me up alongside him and we lay facing each other in the confined space. It was dark now. He put his hand down between my legs and felt into my wet pussy. Then he moved his hand on and under me. Using the lubrication of my sex he penetrated my rear. He brought his head down and began to suck one of my nipples. He fucked my rear with his finger while rhythmically sucking my nipple.

I began to re-arouse. I felt his cock first soft against my belly, and then hardening. When it was hard, he left my rear and worked me under his body.

I lay with him on top. I opened my legs wide. He took each leg and pushed it up over his shoulders so that I was doubled under him, my sex lifted in offering. He held my wrists so that I was pinned to the ground. He raised himself up on his toes so that his whole body was off the ground, his weight taken by his hands and his feet.

I lay open beneath him.

He gave a small grunt and drove his penis hard into my sodden, aroused pussy. Using the strength of his hips without help from knees or elbows so that his body was taut and sprung, he took me like a train with hard deep thrusts that were almost savage.

It was wonderful. I was fully lubricated, fully open. It felt as though his penis went into me forever. Each violent blow made my teeth rattle and brought me closer to my second orgasm. I began to see stars as he speeded up. It was an orchestration of sexual violence that contained no pain. My body was powerful enough not only to absorb each blow but to give back at him.

I came with my breath whistling out of my lungs, my head twisted back and everything I had given up to the moment of blazing glory. He felt me and let himself go so I felt his heat and power and the abundance of his lust.

He let my legs down and lay on me, easing his weight onto his elbows. He kissed my face.

'I want you to cry because I'm so good for you,' he said.

'You vainglorious bastard,' I said, half-laughing, half-sobbing.

'I knew you'd be good,' he said with glee in his voice. 'I could see it the way you moved, how you held yourself. I could see it in the look in your eye. In the way you spoke. You're a dirty lady, aren't you, Sydney? You like it dirty.'

'I guess so.' I grinned.

He rubbed noses with me. 'I have all sorts of dirty tricks up my sleeve. I don't want you to fuck with Matheson.'

I was astonished. 'You get jealous?'

'Not usually. Screw anyone else. Jacko. Pablo. You won't get Colin, of course, wrong persuasion. Play with the girls if you like, as long as I can watch.' He kissed me again. 'But not that damn American. That

132

weasel, cowardly, whining, trouble-making American. He has his eye on you. You know that, of course.'

'It's Margie he's after.'

'He doesn't give two farts for Margie. He's using her to make you jealous.'

'What?'

'Believe me, Sydney. And it isn't just that your beautiful, clever tricksy, naughty body would be totally wasted on that nothing of a man. It isn't just that. He'd seek to poison you against me. That's what he's after. He's the jealous one, baby. He sees we go for each other and he wants to split that. And there's worse.'

'What do you mean?'

'He's a trouble-maker. He's a wrecker. He'll spoil this little expedition if he can.'

'But he and Carl set it up.'

'What he and Carl set up, Sydney, what they *tried* to set up, was a deal to cheat Martha. The idea was that we use her money to find Vilcabamba but having found it, we ditch her and come back later ourselves and divide the excess loot before announcing to the world how clever we were.'

I could see several problems with this. 'Martha isn't stupid. If you find Vilcabamba, she'll know it.'

'You wait, pussycat. When we get close Colin and I will strike off. There'll be quarterings of the ground. If Carl and Matheson and we two were all in cahoots, one of us would have found it first. Jacko always guards Martha. You girls won't venture out alone. Pablo will stay with the boats.'

'Why are you telling me this?'

'I told Martha. We wouldn't play. Matheson pretended it was a joke then, he hadn't meant it seriously. He denied it to Martha and she needed to

133

have Carl along because he had the mask at that stage. She reckoned she could outplay Matheson and in a way she's right. She's a wily old bird.'

'What do you believe about this mask?'

'I believe its genuine. I believe it will help us.' I felt his lips curve into a smile against my skin. 'I am consumed with my own cleverness, you must realise that. At this stage I believe seriously I can unravel the mystery of the mask. Do you find me too arrogant?' He rubbed himself against me, cat-like and smug.

'I find you too everything.'

He chuckled. 'No, you don't, toots. You are smart as paint and every bit as clever as me. I couldn't fool you if I tried. That's what is so gorgeous about you. I probably will try, of course.'

'Why? Why should you want to fool me, Rory?'

'For fun.'

I caught his mouth in the dark above mine and kissed him, opening it and tasting his tongue. 'We'd better go back to the others,' I said.

'In the dark. Aren't we naughty?' His voice was complacent. 'We'll think up a story on the way back. Shall we have been attacked by a leopard?'

'Jaguar, you mean.'

'It carried you off and I attacked it with my bare fingernails.'

'It carried *you* off,' I said smartly, 'and I rescued you by filing its teeth with an emery board and blocking its nostrils with tissues.'

We got dressed and climbed out into the gloom. Rory flicked on his torch and arced it over the sky and mountain. It was clear and when he left his torch off, the stars came out brilliant and shouting at us.

Rory flicked his torch some more, waving it about. It was very cold and I shivered. He took my hand and we began to clatter back the way we had come.

I knew it was the way we had come when we arrived close enough to hear the others and see the firelight. How Rory found his way, I do not know. He was sure-footed as a cat and his eyes seemed able to pick up the least detail in our black and broken environment.

When we saw the light he stopped and put his arms round me, holding me close.

'Don't make me unhappy, Sydney,' he said.

'What do you mean?' It was luxurious to stand almost sagging against his wiry abundant strength. The man didn't seem to feel the cold and all his body was warm against me.

His lips were in my hair. 'I'd given up thinking there were women like you around. Spunky. Sexy. Brave. Funny. Sharp.'

'Bullshit,' I said, kissing him.

'Darling, I wish it was.' He broke the clinch and we went forward to join the others.

Chapter Four

M artha said: 'Where have you been?' Her voice was level. She was angry.

'We got stuck. My fault,' said Rory lightly. 'I was showing off. We didn't have packs on. I led Sydney up this really tight spot. Then we couldn't get back down. We got lost trying. It got dark. End of story.'

'This isn't a picnic,' said Martha. She looked up into Rory's handsome, sardonic face.

Involuntarily I glanced over at Matheson. Matheson the cheapskate, the man who had planned to cheat Martha. He was leaning on his elbows with his face well away from the fire. Margie sat near him, her hands and arms clasped lightly round her knees. I felt sorry for her, if what Rory said was true. It all went to prove the general proposition: men were snakes. You could admire the fancy scales but don't believe the forked tongue.

Rory dropped on his knees by the fire and picked up a mess-tin full of food there. He began to eat. 'We might have found the cave,' he said. 'You would have been pleased then.'

'But you didn't.'

I squatted in my turn and took my lukewarm food. I was ravenous. I felt terrific, all my fur stroked the right way. I was trying hard not to let it show.

'If I didn't like taking chances I wouldn't be here, Martha,' said Rory through a mouthful of rice. 'You can't run a crazy trip like this and not expect some of us to dance on the fringes.'

'You want to take care you don't fall off.'

He grinned, looking at her. 'I never fall off,' he said mock-solemn. 'Haven't you noticed?'

My eyes fell on Colin as I ate. He too was watching Rory. I remembered what Rory had told me about him. It occurred to me Rory would be pleased to have both boys and girls wanting to play with him. His arrogance, his vainglory, fed on admiration.

Hell of a man, though. It was like sex with an angel, one who had a secret thing going about Lucifer, wanting to play where it was hot.

I finished my food and stretched. 'I'm bushed,' I said. 'I'm turning in.'

We spent the next day hunting for the cave. The gold-miners' description was vague. The cave lay on the eastern flanks, near the summit plateau, where Cloud-maker bulged and then crimped herself like a gummy mouth.

We worked separately and I understood how when we searched for Vilcabamba itself, if we ever got that far, Martha could be deceived.

Martha was being deceived already. Even Rory, clever Rory, was being deceived. Matheson had bought the mask in Manaus. Carl hadn't bought it in Mexico. What astonished me is how they could have strung Martha along so far without her seeing the thing.

It was so astonishing it was unbelievable. At this

point I realised a possible answer to the conundrum. The conundrum was, how could a wise and cynical lady like Martha, head of a large and valuable Trust, let herself organise and equip an expensive expedition without having seen the mask that was the *raison d'être* of the whole shooting match first?

The answer came back pat. No way. She would see and examine the artefact first. She would have independent experts examine it. Once believing in it, she would gloat over it.

Yet Matheson had delivered it to her barely a day before we left to paddle up the Amazon.

There was a solution to this puzzle that suggested itself to me.

That afternoon, finding myself temporarily out of sight of the others, I made a rapid beeline for the camp. Once there and sure I was unobserved, I began to go through Matheson's pack.

I knew Martha was carrying the mask. When I found it in Matheson's pack, I had the answer.

There were two masks.

It looked like the one I had handled before. Every detail, as far as I could remember, was the same. The dark smooth wood felt the same. It smelt the same. The incised pattern looked the same. I put it on.

It held itself lightly on my face and I looked through the eye holes at the bare grey and brown mountain, the scrubby yellowish-white thorn bushes, the vast heaving sea of green below that spread for endless uncountable miles.

A shadow fell across me. I looked up and saw Matheson.

I took the mask off. He held out his hand and I gave it to him. I was hunkered down but he stood, towering over me.

I didn't feel threatened. Size doesn't impress me.

Well, shit, it does, but only where it counts, out front at belly-base.

'Duncan tell you to pilfer my stuff?' he asked.

'Which one came from the dwarf?' I asked.

Having asked it I found my hand slipped to the knife at my belt. We were alone. This man was possibly very dangerous.

Matheson saw my gesture. He crouched down in front of me, holding my eyes with his. His hand came out and eased the knife from its sheath on my belt. He reversed it and gave me the handle. He opened his shirt, clearing a way between his camera straps. 'Do it, Sydney, if you want to. That's what was in your mind, wasn't it?'

I held the blade forward. The tip lightly touched his brown skin. I saw the skin indent. Matheson leaned in over the knife and kissed my lips.

I didn't respond. I was frozen with surprise. As he moved back I saw his action had punctured his skin. A bright bead of blood showed, crimson, rich.

He was looking at me, his head on one side. 'Got what you want, now?'

'How would you know what I want?'

'We all know. You got it last night. Good, is he?'

'He's a marvel. It's beautiful with him.' My voice was suddenly warm with memory. I smiled at Matheson and ran my tongue lightly over my lips.

Matheson's face went tight. He did up his shirt and stood up. I stood up, too. I took a step back away from him, the knife loose in my hand.

'I think I should tell Martha,' I said, looking at the mask.

'You do that.'

'Was it you hit me over the head that night?'

'If I'd have done it, you wouldn't have survived.'

The man looked very ugly. My grip on the knife tightened. He turned and walked away.

We didn't find the cave. We saw strange birds that hopped and croaked at us. Overhead kites wheeled and a harpy eagle looked hungrily at us from a crazed far-seeing eye. Exploring cracks in the mountainside was horrible because bats wheeled out thick as smoke, bringing a reek of ammonia with them.

It was cold. We would run out of food soon. That night an enormous storm built up and we huddled together pressed back under our ledge, watching the clouds below us boil and fret in the moonlight, huge flashes of lightning brilliantly lit the heaving ominous mass at frequent intervals. The storm cracked and roared and the wind whirled manically round the mountain, tearing and plucking at its stony indifference.

Watching from above I felt like God.

In the morning Martha sent Big Jacko, Margie and Colin for food. It was one day down the mountain and one day back to camp. Then two days back again. The actual walk through the jungle would be much easier than on our outward trip because the path had been cleared.

They would be taking a different track down the mountain, though, to avoid Rory's jump. If they had trouble finding our camp at the base after this, those four days might stretch to five.

The five of us left up top tightened our belts and searched harder, casting above and below the patch we had already searched.

At night Matheson played his mouth organ quietly to himself. We were tired and we ate hungrily what little we were allowed, before turning in.

I wondered why Martha kept Matheson up there

with us. Maybe she didn't trust him back at the boats without her watchful eye. I couldn't know.

On the second night we saw the helicopter again. Maybe it was a different one. If lifted above the dense, apparently unbroken canopy some miles to the north of us. It hung there, not moving, or so it seemed. There was no perspective to judge by. After ten or fifteen minutes it sank and disappeared.

Martha said: 'Let's clear a cave of bats and move in. We should get the fire inside. I have the feeling we're being watched.'

'How much does it matter?' I said. 'I mean, how many government regulations are we breaking by being here?'

'None as far as I know. We're still in Brazil, I think, so we haven't crossed a border illegally.'

'Why do they worry you, then?'

It was Rory who answered. 'You haven't got it, Sydney. You aren't understanding.'

'Understanding what?'

'The potential prize we are after.'

'Oh. That.'

Carla laughed. 'Does any of this interest you at all?'

I was surprised. 'What do you mean?'

'The Amazon. The jungle, how incredible it is. The marvellous birds, the parrots, the monkeys . . .'

'The tarantulas big enough to eat the marvellous birds, the exotic illnesses comma incurable,' I said.

'Have you no romance in your soul?'

'Didn't you know? I'm a news-person.' I bared my teeth. 'We have no souls.'

'But this is the story of the year, of the decade,' Carla persisted. 'Finding Vilcabamba will be like finding Tutankhamen's tomb and El Dorado all in one go. This is wonderful stuff, Sydney. You can't be that cynical.'

141

I grinned. 'Try me.'

'Sydney,' said Rory. 'Other people might be on the trail.'

Martha sucked smoke from her cigar and blew it out into the night. 'That's it,' she said. 'That's why I didn't tell you the truth about this trip till we were so far along you couldn't get back and tell anyone else. That's why we had the holiday cover in the first place. That's why we got going with the minimum of fuss. I could have put us on this mountain on day one using a helicopter, but the whole damned river would have known about it. We've approached this catty-cornerwise, Sydney, so no nosey Joe has the least idea what we are up to.'

'Who might opposition be?' I asked.

'Well.' Martha looked embarrassed. This was so astonishing I felt worried for the first time. 'Carl heard a rumour. It was when he was asking around about Vilcabamba, trying to check the provenance of the mask. There's some guy in Paraguay or maybe Argentina, we aren't sure. He'd have bought the mask.'

'Who is he? What is he?' I looked at the rest of them, horrid suspicions growing in me.

'International bad guy,' said Rory. 'Someone big. Someone secret. Someone rich. He would loot Vilcabamba and keep the best for his own personal pleasure. The rest would go to fund the sort of politics his sort miss.'

'Great,' I said bitterly. 'How many rifles do we have left?'

'Jacko has one. Pablo has one. We have one up here. The fourth was dropped in the river and ruined.' This was Matheson speaking.

'You think this helicopter might be his crowd?' I asked.

'I don't know,' said Martha. 'I don't see how he could know we are here. We think he heard about the mask. He could have heard of its association with Cloud-maker. But I don't see how he could know an expedition is in progress right now. We drew no attention to ourselves at all. We were just eco-tourists and they come in droves right now. But I want no risks taken. We mustn't draw attention to ourselves up here, now we know the jungle has eyes. They mustn't know if we find the cave.'

The third day was fruitless. That evening Carla put on the mask.

We had dispossessed about a quadrillion bats and scraped out as much muck as we could. We brought water from one of the many streams and falls and washed out the floor after a fashion. We wasted more time collecting firewood. After the floor dried and we adjusted to the smell, it wasn't so bad.

It was not a deep cave. Martha was tired and a little feverish that day. She was worried about time passing and the thought of the helicopter haunted her, I think. She was also missing her daily sex-fix from Rory.

She took aspirin and retired before dark. The rest of us sat outside for a while watching the stars like ice-spots freezing the black sky.

The wind sighed round the mountain and far below the canopy rustled and stirred, a vast, distant sea of sound.

Carla put on the mask. There was a moon and her face shone at the polished cheek-bones. Her eyes were black holes.

She began to speak. The three of us, Matheson, Rory and myself were transfixed.

'When I was ten I was chosen,' she said in a high soft

voice. *'They took me from my mother and my little brothers and sisters and I went with others that were chosen to Ollantaytambo. Ollantaytambo. Incahuasi. No matter. We chosen ones were gathered there to weave, to weave for the Lord-Inca and his coya. We lived to worship the Sun and obey its rituals, to keep its anger at bay so that the people of the Lord-Inca might be blessed with rains and good harvests. We wove cloth of great beauty. The mamacuna taught us. We were handmaidens of the Sun and we lived in the high places where men could not get us. Some of us were taken and married to the high people, close servants to the Inca, men he trusted and relied on. We belonged to the Inca. We were his treasure. So he rewarded those who served him well. Some of us stayed to weave and worship. Till the white men came. They found us women in our temples high at Ollantaytambo, high at Incahuasi, high in the mountains weaving for our Lord, and they took us with force, violating our persons and because they did that, they violated the Lord-Inca and they violated the Sun itself. The Sun then set on the people of the Inca and our day passed.'*

Rory moved round towards her when she stopped. He knelt astride her seated body. He took her masked face between his hands, hunched over her.

I stood up clumsily. Matheson put out his hand and held my arm, preventing me. The wind sang in my ears and I heard voices, the screams of the raped women, running feet softly sandalled, the harsh laugh of the conquerors, the clash of metal, of sword on stone, on flesh.

Rory hunched over Carla and spoke to her. Then he removed the mask.

I stood with Matheson holding my arm, frozen.

Rory kissed Carla's mouth. She stared up at him open-eyed. She was mesmerised. Rory kissed her again and it seemed to me he sucked out of her what it was he wanted.

144

'Tell me,' he said. 'Tell me.'

Her lips moved.

He pressed his groin down and rubbed his sex on her belly. 'Tell me,' he whispered, 'and you can have what you want.'

Carla groaned.

Rory put his hand into her clothes. Matheson said: 'Stop.' He let go of my arm.

'Tell me,' murmured Rory. 'I know you know.' He pressed his groin into Carla, the movements rhythmical, sexual.

Matheson took two long strides towards him and took him by the shoulder.

Rory whirled, breaking his grip. He lifted himself from the girl and struck Matheson hard in the face. Tom staggered back and sat down suddenly. By the time he got to his feet Carla had moved.

She was kneeling at Rory's feet, fumbling with his trousers.

'Stop it,' I cried.

Rory turned to me. His face was blazing. 'It's the way,' he said. 'Can't you see?'

Carla drew out his sex, a silver spear in the moonlight. She began to dance, there on her knees in the moonlight. Her body was taut, swaying. Her head went back. Her eyes were all whites, the irises seemingly disappeared.

I must have started forward. Matheson stopped me, coming behind me and putting his arm across my chest.

The restraint felt protective. What we saw was frightening.

Carla danced on her knees with her arms writhing and her head bent back. Then she climbed with slow grace to her feet and removed her clothing. Her body was pearl in the cold air, her hair emptiness, her eyes mad and white. She twisted and turned in front of Rory, brushing his erect penis with her belly. Then she lifted one leg high, really high, and hopped towards his body.

She stood now hard against him. She had one leg up held between their bodies in the sort of pose a ballet dancer finds hard to achieve. Her exposed sex was a black pit waiting to engulf the silver organ of the man. She came up on the toes of her foot and held Rory's shoulders. He clasped her lightly round the waist, supporting her in a position that would have given me enormous pain, but one that Carla apparently could maintain with ease.

She eased herself onto his cock. It disappeared into her pit. Rory held still, bracing her, and she began to quiver her body against him.

Matheson put his hand under my chin and bent my head back. I looked up at the moon. Across it in black silhouette hung something bird-shaped, something so enormous it did not belong to our time, this time.

Maybe it belonged to the time that held Carla in its grip.

She was speaking again in that high, nasal sing-song tone. '*Ollantaytambo. Incahuasi.*' She said the long polysyllables as a chant, a song. Her body swayed its sexual dance, a butterfly flutter of vagina sucking cock.

'*They taught us to pleasure men. They taught us to bend our bodies to the man's will, that we were vessels of pleasure to a man. We were taught to make our muscles move in strange ways so that the life-giver a man has might be conjured to bring forth the foam of life in abundance.*'

She placed her hands against Rory's shoulders and drew herself away from him, his penis sliding out of her body. He had not come to climax and the heavy

146

thing gleamed with a membranous skin of sexual mucus. Carla put her hands round his neck. '*Ha,*' she said suddenly and jumped.

Her legs were round his waist, crossed at his back by her ankles. Her arms held his neck. She leaned back and he did likewise, bracing himself against her weight.

It seemed to me his face was white with shock. Had her opening missed, she might have broken his penis with the slam of her body.

She shook herself rapidly on him, bouncing her sex against him so that she screwed him while he held still. Suddenly he gave a cry and his own hips jerked hard, several times.

Carla waited till he was still. Then she let go of his neck. She sat held by him, his hands under her buttocks. Then, very slowly, she arched her back.

He staggered as her weight pulled. A moment later she had her hands over her head, her body tightly arched, and she was able to support herself on the ground with her hands. She still had his sex in her body.

He stood stiffly, as if shell-shocked.

Carla undid her legs at the ankles. Gradually she opened her legs wide. Using her own balance, she drew herself away from the man, off his sex, until she stood on her hands, upside down, her legs, one forward, one back, doing the splits in the air.

The moon shone on the black pit between her legs. Gradually it came into vision. The long, snaking vulva was swollen and pouting. The lips stood up, seeming to writhe in the chancy light. The clitoris stood free, at least an inch big, triumphantly erect. Slowly the mouth of her vagina inverted itself till padded puckered flesh puffed out, as if looking for the next penis to suck in.

Rory took a step back. A wisp of steam ascended into the cold air. Matheson let go of me. 'I . . .' he said in a strangled voice. I felt his body sway towards the girl.

I caught him and hit him round the face. His put his hand to his cheek and looked at me, aghast. 'It's witchcraft,' I said hoarsely. 'Don't do it.'

The thing in the sky cawed suddenly, a great raucous call of derision. I resisted the impulse to kiss Carla's cavorting flesh. Rory had adjusted his clothes and backed off slightly.

Matheson said: 'Sydney.'

'No,' I said.

The moon sailed behind a cloud. The wind whirled noisily and sucked up our hair on end. The bird thing left the sky, its absence palpable. Carla came down onto her feet and grabbed her clothes.

Rory helped her dress. No one said anything. They went into the cave.

'What happened?' said Matheson in a strange voice.

'You should know.' My voice was harsh.

'Why should I know?'

'You got the thing. You and Carl. You had the copy made. You can tell the difference between them. You know what happened when I wore it in your room.'

'When we fucked.'

'Because of the mask.'

'Sydney,' he said desperately, 'you've got me wrong.'

'The hell I have. What I do know is that everything is wrong. Every damned thing is wrong. There's something very cock-eyed about this business, as you full-well know. What the hell was Carla on about. Olly, something. Inca hooarzi.'

148

'I don't know.' The fire went out of him. 'I'm tired. I'm going to bed.'

The following day Martha, looking unwell and coughing slightly, allocated our search areas. We left her there by a small fire with a plentiful supply of fuel. The cold and wet were getting to us all.

Outside, Rory called Matheson and myself over. He looked at us, his own face a little strained. 'I suggest we follow Carla,' he said.

'Why?' said Matheson.

Rory said with bitterness: 'You do what you damned well please. Sydney, come with me.'

I looked at Carla. She had wandered off in a direction quite different from the one given her by Martha. She appeared to be singing. The sky was very blue and the sun shone warm. Little wisps of cloud littered the sky like torn tissue. Far below us the forest smoked, sending long pillars of ghostly vapour up from between the clinging dampness of the trees into the wide blue warmth of the sky.

'I'll follow Carla, I guess,' I said slowly. 'I'm worried about her.'

We set off absurdly, all three, antagonisms along as well, following the girl.

She made straight for nowhere and she didn't look back. She could hardly not have known we followed her, yet she seemed oblivious to our presence. Occasionally she stopped and picked a little mountain flower. She zigzagged backwards and forwards, ambling without purpose, until she came to a short cliff face rearing above her.

Water flowed over the edge and made an arc in the clear air. Rainbows decorated the broken edge of the water, jewelling the air. On wet rocks slimy green moss grew with tiny blue flowers starring it. Little rust-coloured birds hopped and chattered noisily in the rocks.

I saw a hummingbird and heard the sweet buzz of its wings.

To the left of the waterfall a deep cleft in the rock led upwards in a series of staggered steps. Carla began to climb this.

I came up it between the two men. I was glad of help from either of them. The crack narrowed to a chimney and the rock crumbled and broke sometimes under our boots. Carla went up as if her feet were winged. The rest of us had to work at it.

I couldn't make the last bit. How Carla did it was a mystery. Rory couldn't do it either till Matheson took him perilously onto his shoulders and that gave Rory the chance to haul himself over the lip of the crest.

For a moment I wondered coldly if he would leave me there with Tom. But he leaned over and held a hand down. I stood with my back to the rock jammed against it. I cupped my hands, my knees slightly bent. Matheson put one booted foot in my hands, let me gather myself, and then threw himself upwards. Rory caught him and hauled and a moment later the agony stopped and his weight was off me.

Both men took off their belts and sliding the end through the buckle, let the loop this formed hang down to me. I slid my hands through the loops and let the belts be pulled tight on my wrists. The men then hauled me up using brute strength.

I released my wrists and returned their belts. Matheson grinned. 'You look good on a leash, Johnson.'

'I expect it's the only way you can keep a woman,' I riposted.

Carla had ignored all this and gone off. Suddenly we lost sight of her.

Rory looked worried. 'I should have left you two. She mustn't get away. Not when we are so close.'

We began to cast about, looking for her. Suddenly there was a vast chittering noise and a cloud of bats issued straight out of solid rock.

We almost fell into them, so desperate were we not to lose sight of the entrance.

The mountain bulged out. In the bulge was an overlap, the rock folded and pleated back on itself in a gummy way. This left a narrow vertical crack. We slid in.

Matheson said: 'Martha should be here.'

'Go back and get her, hero,' I said.

Up ahead of us, in the dark, Carla screamed.

'Hang on,' shouted Tom. 'We're right here.'

Rory took a candle from his pocket and lit it. We looked around us.

We were in a narrow passage. It bent to the right immediately and we moved close together around the bend. More bats came out and I ducked foolishly against Matheson's chest as they rushed, chittering, by me. I jammed my hat more firmly on my head. I didn't want my hair caught up with them.

Rory's candle led the way. The floor began to drop sharply and our booted feet slithered.

'Help,' shouted Carla.

'Faster,' I said in agony.

'No.' Rory's voice was cold. 'We don't want to end up in the trouble she's in.'

We edged forward trying not to slip down the steep slope. The passage widened a little and we held the rocky sides as we went to steady our progress.

Carla was sobbing.

'We're coming,' shouted Rory.

A great wind suddenly blew up in our faces raw and rank with ammonia so that I felt faint and dizzy.

The wind laughed, batting backwards and forwards between the walls of the passage and I found myself clutching Rory's belt suddenly.

He laughed. 'It starts,' he said softly. 'Jesus, it starts.' I realised he was suppressing an enormous excitement.

'What's happening?' I said. My voice sounded scared.

'Go with it, Sydney. Don't fight it.' His voice crackled with excitement. I let go of him.

He stopped dead. The floor stopped at our feet and there was a hole. Carla's sobbing came up from the hole.

Rory set the candle carefully on the floor. He laid himself down and peered over the edge. He took a torch out of his pocket and shone it downwards. 'Are you hurt, Carla,' he said quite softly.

'Rory,' she said, snivelling.

'There you are, darling. Tell me, what's down there?'

'Get me up. I don't like this. Pull me up.'

'It's the cave, sweetheart. No turning back now.'

The wind boomed up the hole, *ho, ho, ho.*

'Which way, Carla? Down past you or across this hole and along the passage again?' Rory flicked the torch up and shone it across the top of the chute. On the far side the passage continued, narrow and winding.

'Pull me up.'

'What did the mask tell you?'

My blood ran cold. I slipped my knife out of its sheath and pressed it to Rory's neck. He was on his front, hanging over the hole. He was so surprised he went rigid.

I took a fistful of his hair and pulled his head back against the tip of the knife. 'Carla,' I called.

'Yes. That's Sydney, isn't it? Is Martha there?'

'No, sweetheart. Hold tight. We'll have a rope down to you in two seconds. Are you hurt, darling?'

'No. Not much. I'm scared, Sydney.'

'We'll have you safe. There are three of us here. Don't be frightened.'

'What am I doing here?' she whimpered. 'How did it happen? When I fell I thought it was a dream.'

I moved back from the edge and let Rory sit up. He stared at me in the candlelight, foxy-faced and bright. 'Get the girl up,' I said.

'Sydney. She knows where to go.'

'Get the girl up.'

He laughed. 'I can take that knife off you.'

'If you go for me, Matheson will push you over the edge. He's looking for an opportunity. We'll apologise to Martha afterwards for losing you.'

Rory reached into his pack and took out a rope. He tied a loop in one end and then ran the rope round a rocky outcrop. He backed away from the hole and braced himself against the wall of the passage, digging his feet in.

'Drop the end over, then,' he said. His voice was calm and friendly. I was just an obstacle to be overcome, no more.

I leaned over the edge. I shone my torch down and lowered the rope to where I could see Carla's frightened white face turned up at me. All around was profound blackness.

'Tell her,' said Rory, 'to drop the loop over her body until she can sit in it. She's to hold the rope above the loop then, and we'll pull her up.'

Matheson took his place on the rope, ready to haul.

I passed the instructions on to Carla. She was calm now. She did as she was told, arranging the loop under her backside. She squatted on her little ledge, holding the rope so tightly that I could see her knuckles shine fleshless, like a skeleton's.

'Ready?' I asked.

'Ready.' She gave me a small scared smile. 'OK,' I said to the men.

They hauled slowly and Carla jerked up. As soon as I could reach her I put out the torch and helped to steady her. Finally I was able to help her up over the edge.

I put my arms round her and hugged her, brushing her hair back from her face. 'OK, now?' I murmured.

'I'm fine. Sorry to be such a baby.'

'You've been a bit dreamy today,' I said carefully. 'We saw you wander off. We followed you and then you found this cave. That's brilliant, Carla. This is probably the cave. The special one. The one the mask was in.'

'Not down that horrid hole.'

'Of course not.'

Suddenly excitement ran hot through me, liquefying my veins. For the first time I knew the desire to find out. This was the first moment I believed: believed in the mask, believed in the cave, believed in the possibility of finding Vilcabamba.

I turned to the men. 'Listen,' I said. 'This is Martha's privilege. Jacko and the others could well be back this afternoon. I vote we go back to the camp and tell Martha. Then we get equipped for this. I know we can't use the torches too much. We'll bring more candles and the kerosene lamps. We need a means of crossing this damned hole. We need to be roped for safety. Come on, don't let's get greedy now. Let's do this right.'

'We haven't seen the drawings yet,' said Matheson. He fingered the camera. I knew he was carrying colour film and a flash for this.

'We know this is the right place,' said Rory. His eyes were glittering. He grabbed Carla and kissed her smackingly on her lips. 'You sweet darling,' he crowed. 'You led us right here.'

Carla went pink. It occurred to me she didn't remember last night, she didn't know what she had done.

'It is across the hole,' she said uncertainly. 'How do I know that?'

Rory said: 'I'm sorry. I'm so hungry to know. I can't bear the suspense.'

'Sorry? What for?'

'Not bringing you up immediately. I wanted to know if we should come down.'

'Well, of course.' She stared at him, delighted. 'It's what we've come all this way for. It's wonderful. Quickly, let's tell Martha. She'll be over the moon. Then we can come back like Sydney says, and do it properly.'

So that was what we did.

Things got better. Martha felt rested and well again. We ate a late lunch, a little careless because we were expecting the others back with more food. Meanwhile, we described in minute detail what we had seen.

We were all virtually ill with excitement. The fever to investigate the cave had me in its grip as tightly as it did the others. Up until now I had taken none of this seriously. I didn't forgive Rory his treatment of Carla in the cave but I understood it.

It was a fever.

We forced ourselves to wait. We decided to move the camp the following morning up to the cave. We would leave a message for the others and mark the route. We had a tin of white paint with us, for just this sort of problem.

As it happened, they came straggling up the mountain an hour before sunset. Almost we were tempted to bundle on up, but they were tired and hungry, and as we calmed down, we realised how much we all wanted to eat.

We fed luxuriously, talking all the time. After a while Rory took a short walk with Martha. I could guess what for, but as it happened I was wrong.

When it was dark and we were full fed, lying with bloated stomachs in the smoky cave listening to Matheson shiver our ears with the sadness of the blues, Rory asked me to step outside.

'I don't think so,' I said pleasantly.

'Don't be silly, Sydney. I need to talk to you in private.'

'Still wet from Martha, babe?' I said softly.

'We talked.'

'Solomon knew. Strange how many euphemisms screwing has.'

'Sydney, give me a minute in private, please.'

I looked at him. 'Keep the belt buckle tight, huh?'

We went outside. We sat side by side looking at the moon and the moonlit void below us. 'I had a talk with Martha,' Rory said. 'It's about Carla.'

'What about Carla?' I made my voice admiring. 'She's very athletic, isn't she?'

I felt his head turn. 'She scares the cock off me, if you want to know.'

I felt his groin. 'You grow them *that* quickly.'

He laughed unwillingly. 'So to speak,' he amended. 'Look, let's admit there is something spooky about the mask. It can show the way.'

'How would I know that?'

156

'Because you wore it. That's how you knew the way out of the lagoon.'

It was funny. I had not so much forgotten that episode as suppressed it. I hated it. I hated the thought of being out of control.

I kept quiet. 'It takes over,' he said quietly. 'I've tried it too.'

In the forest?

'Are you prepared to try it again, Sydney?'

'No. No way. I like to control what happens inside me, lover.'

'Carla is. She doesn't remember, see. I remember. You remember. She doesn't. So she's the safe one to use. It won't hurt her.'

Indignation ballooned in me. 'Hey, hey, hey,' I said sharply. 'This is a little exploitative, isn't it?'

'Carla agrees. Martha agrees.'

'Martha is pandering her step-daughter to the mask?'

'Don't talk rot, Sydney. Don't you understand why I am telling you this? It's because I will guard her when she is under its influence.'

There was a short silence. 'You mean you will fuck her,' I corrected.

'I mean that, yes. That's why I'm telling you. Explaining. I owe you that much.'

'You owe me nothing.'

'You might not think so. I know different. You are a very special person, Sydney. I'm close to wondering if this game is worth the candle.'

I was silent. Did he mean I was the candle? Was I the price?

'Martha is accepting that you'll fuck her girly,' I said at last.

'Yes. Obviously our games will stop. I know there is no blood relationship. Carla isn't adopted, either.

But even so, it's uncomfortably close to incest. I start with Carla, I stop with Martha.'

'You ever have a problem,' I drawled, 'telling the women you have sex with when you might or might not be available?'

'I have enjoyed Martha's company immensely. She is a talented, sexy lady any man might feel proud to share a bed with. She's ten years my senior but it's still been a privilege. It is a relationship I end with regret. I hope she regrets it, too. I tried to please her. Even so, giving it up to increase our chances of finding Vilcabamba is an easy decision. I'm not so sure about you.'

'Me?'

'Giving up you. I might not get you back. Afterwards.'

I shifted on my rear. The ground struck cold up through the bones of my backside. 'Who says you have me?'

He reached round then, and put his warm hand on my face. 'Sydney,' he said in a low chiding voice, full of amusement.

I pulled back irritably. 'So this with Carla is a monogamous deal all of a sudden?'

'I don't want it to be. But I don't think Carla will tolerate me being with you, and at the moment, the object of the exercise is to have her compliance. The bonus for being out of her skull with the mask, frankly, is sole access to my body. As for sneaky ones, I don't think that's good enough with you. I want you properly, Sydney. I want you all the time. I want bed and champagne and restaurants and bed and more bed and being in your company, laughing with you, sliding it into you, making you cry.'

'I'm having trouble believing this conversation.'

'Of course you are. Other women are gullible with

158

me. Carla is. Does it ever occur to you I find your cynicism refreshing? Not many women can resist me.'

'Huff puff.'

'Don't give me that big bad wolf line. Of course I'm the big bad wolf. But the little piggies leave their doors open and the lights on. Except you.'

'I thought you'd eaten at my table. Maybe my memory's playing me up.'

'You've allowed me in, true. But you can say no. You've said no tonight.'

'You give the word cocksure a whole new meaning.'

'I don't pretend with you. I don't lie to you. This is how I am. Arrogant. Boastful. Excitable. Devious. Ambitious. Manipulative. And I like danger. I mean I like it. I snort danger, Sydney. It's my vice.'

'You chose a funny career, glueing old pots together.'

'I knew what I wanted, what I could do. I can be patient when I have to be. My job is my *entrée* into some very dangerous places in the world. I don't do Roman mosaics or Viking burial ships, Sydney. I've been working on and off in South America for ten years now. I've been shot, I've been arrested, I've been whipped, I've been bitten by snakes, by scorpions and once, by a tarantula.'

'Coo,' I said. 'Can I have your autograph?'

He burst out laughing. 'I could fall in love with you,' he said. 'Don't let me. Stay fireproof, babe. I'm bad medicine.'

We moved camp the next day. We honestly had no idea what the cave would tell us or how the mask might help, yet each one of us was keyed up and taut with excitement.

We rigged a rope in the rock chimney that had

given us trouble on the way up before. Poor Carla couldn't believe she had made it alone and we didn't push it with her. We didn't want her disorientated or frightened. As it was she had changed in character. She had developed a kind of sly confidence, as if she had access to some secret knowledge. I guess this was a pretty accurate way of looking at things. She had become a little commanding, too. The rest of us were her inferiors, now. We had to look to her for progress and she tolerated us with condescension.

Frankly, she needed her bottom smacking.

I don't know how Rory stood it. With him she was proprietorial. She flaunted him, especially to Margie and me. This was crazy. Margie didn't go for him best I could tell, and I couldn't see how she knew anything about him and me. We had been discreet. The uncomfortable feeling that Rory might have said something crept over me but I dismissed it. At least Carla had the sense not to antagonise Martha. With her she remained the same, docile, gentle and affectionate.

So Martha didn't see what the rest of us saw, how much the girl had changed.

Big Jacko saw. His light eyes would dwell on Rory for minutes together. I think Jacko was immune to Rory's charm.

Although we had been there the previous day, we found the cave entrance very hard to locate. The fold of rock was very unobtrusive and we were bemused at how tricky it was, till Martha put her hand in it, leaning on the rock face in exasperation.

'Hey folks,' I said as we prepared to enter. 'Um, what happens if we all go in together and there's a rock fall or something? Who goes for help?'

There was a silence.

'What help?' asked Rory. 'You mean the emergency telephone we passed in the cloud forest?'

'It's only two days down to Pablo. That's about the time it takes to get a 999 call answered in London these days. We've got food and water on us. We know the place has air vents, we felt enough wind yesterday.'

The wind that laughed. Not pleasantly, either.

Margie said: 'Martha, I'm claustrophobic. I don't fancy this bit at all. Tom will show me the photographs afterwards. I'll wait outside. I'm tired, anyway. I could do with a rest.'

So it was agreed. She made herself comfortable with her pack and our hammocks, the cooking gear and all our spare clothing. The minimal caving and climbing equipment we carried, cooked food and chlorinated water, we took with us.

We entered the cave. We went single file. Martha led because it was her expedition. She was roped to Rory who followed her. He in turn was roped to Big Jacko. This was in case Martha fell, the two men could save her.

The rest of us, drawing up at the rear, were unroped. We crossed the pit Carla had fallen into and once again I felt the rush of air bouncing round the cavern, air full of consciousness, it seemed to me. It was as though the cave breathed. The truth was, I was spooked.

We used two kerosene lamps, carrying a spare can of fuel. They were more economical than candles or torches. Our supply of batteries was limited. Martha carried one, and Colin, who led us rearguard, carried the second.

The passage remained narrow and wound down into the heart of the mountain. It was dry and quite warm. The walls glittered, little quartz crystals reflecting the lamplight with a thousand points.

There were more holes in the ground and we were able, with care, to skirt their rims. My bladder demanded a little attention and I dropped back, with maidenly modesty, to deal with things.

I was just settling my pack afterwards when a blast of air came down the passage towards me, down the way we had come. It was warm and sour. There was a noise.

A tiny meep of fear escaped me. The others were gone ahead. With my torch off the darkness was infinite.

It couldn't be Margie following. Not alone, after what she had said.

I flicked my torch on.

We looked at each other. 'Oh,' I said feebly. 'Hi, there.'

Some time passed. I said: 'We don't have to do this,' but there was no response. 'Shoo,' I added.

It moved, easing more legs forward.

I took a step backward. This was a mistake. More of it moved towards me, with speed.

'I'd prefer a car accident,' I offered. I'm not immortal, I know that. But there are ways and ways of going.

'Sydney,' said a voice behind me.

'Movement,' I said breathlessly, 'excites it. Not noise, it seems.'

'It's probably deaf. I mean, no ears to hear with.'

'Conversationally, it's been a barren experience,' I agreed. I was unable to stop myself stepping back against Matheson.

The thing heaved some more of its body out of the pit. The clubby head swayed, puzzled by the torchlight. No ears maybe, but the eyes were dinner-plate sized.

'Why don't you get the other side of me,' said Matheson.

'I can see the benefit from my point of view,' I said. 'What's in it for you?'

'Do it, Johnson.'

'I'm setting back the cause of feminism here,' I said, easing myself so that Tom was between me and the monster.

Each segment had a set of legs. Three or four more segments worked their way towards us.

The Nikon was tucked in Tom's shirt. He had the Minolta rigged with a flash. He lifted this now.

'This for Vogue?' I said. 'The fashion in Chitin.'

'When I yell, run for Colin. He has the rifle.'

I touched his shoulder. 'Tom?'

'I know. You're pregnant. If it's a boy, will you name it after me?'

'Hero's a girl's name.'

The thing opened its jaws. A hissing noise escaped and the acrid smell of it assailed my nostrils. Tom set off the flash and yelled. I ran.

As I ran, desperate not to trip on the uneven, rubbly ground, my torchlight bobbing, I shouted. I yelled. I screamed. Quite soon I cannoned into Colin. 'Back there,' I screamed. 'This thing. Tom's there. Shoot it.'

I turned and ran with Colin, using my torch as well as his lantern. Tom came into view.

The thing was reared like a vast centipede over him. His machete was out and he was slashing at its face. One of its eyes was already cut. It was hissing and the stench was terrible.

Colin gasped. I took the lantern from him and he raised the rifle, working the bolt.

163

'Don't hit Tom,' I yelled.

Pretty fatuous, huh. My mind wasn't its sharpest.

'What kept you?' yelled Tom, back-pedalling towards us. The thing darted its head at him and its jaws closed over his shoulder.

He roared, stabbing at it with his machete. The rifle went off, an enormous explosion in that confined place. Behind me the others were running to see what was going on.

The rifle went off twice more. The thing began to sag. Tom was trying to break its grip on his shoulder. I was there, then, with my knife, cutting its jaw so that it released him.

It began to slither backwards, falling down into its pit. We never even got to see how long it was.

Tom sat on the floor. I could smell the rifle, a clean, beautiful smell. Other people made a hell of a noise behind me. I pulled Tom's shirt open and inspected his shoulder.

The skin wasn't broken. 'The skin isn't broken,' I said idiotically.

'Just the bones inside,' he said.

I touched it. 'Not really,' I pleaded.

'Feels like it,' he said grumpily. He fell over in a dead faint.

Big Jacko had unroped himself. He ran expert fingers over Tom's shoulder. It was turning yellow and puffy in front of our eyes. 'I think it's just bruised,' he grunted.

Tom opened his eyes. 'I want a drink,' he said crossly. 'Rye. And bed. And lots of small compliant women looking after me.'

I grinned lopsidedly. My heart was starting to hammer with delayed shock. 'Welcome back, you bastard.'

'Help me up, frog. You frighten me this close. I might ask Colin to shoot you too.'

On his feet, he punched Colin lightly with his undamaged hand. 'Great shooting, John Wayne. I can't thank you enough.'

Colin gave a small, tight smile and suddenly I remembered what Rory had implied about him. About his sexual orientation.

We went on, down into the mountain. Jacko carried Tom's pack as well as his own. Tom held his shoulder stiffly and was evidently in pain.

Somewhere a heart boomed. Deep and regular the pulses sounded, like the mountain was alive.

'What's making that noise?' I asked Colin nervously.

'Dunno. Wind, I expect.'

'This place gets indigestion?'

He didn't respond. I found him very taciturn. 'Is this all sandstone?' I asked.

'Limestone,' he grunted. 'The Amazon basin's very old shield rock. All this was an inland sea once. Most of the deposition has been worn away since. Odd outcrops like this remain.'

'What do you think of the mask?' I said. He was not a man I found easy to read. He kept himself closed and locked in, the reverse of the extrovert Rory.

Colin said nothing for a while. Then he said almost brusquely: 'It doesn't matter what I think. Or what you think. Nothing is what it started out to be. Things evolve. Time and circumstance change them. Meaning changes. The balance between things is in constant flux. That's why I'm an archaeologist.'

'You lost me, Wittgenstein.'

He gave me a brief contemptuous look.

* * *

165

We arrived at a chamber with several passages going off it. The walls were wet and shiny, and stalactites hung from the roof almost meeting the stalagmites growing up from below. Tom walked round tapping them with his knife, making cave music while he whistled through his teeth. He still held his shoulder funny.

We ate some meat and biscuits while we decided what to do.

'Carl would have helped us here,' said Martha, giving me an accusing look. 'The men he bought the mask from described this place to him.'

'They mention giant insects?' I asked as if I didn't really care.

'No,' said Martha balefully. 'I'm certain that was a one-off. A freak.'

'My biology's uncertain,' I said, 'but usually baby has a mum and a dad. Not to say siblings. And aunties and uncles. Only the phoenix does it alone.'

'You had a *mother*?' queried Tom. 'I thought they assembled you from parts.'

'At least a centipede hasn't tried to kiss me.'

'Even centipedes have too much sense,' he retorted.

Big Jacko started to laugh. 'Children, children,' chided Martha. 'We have serious work to do.'

Carla said: 'I will wear the mask.'

Chapter Five

They made me stay with Carla. Martha insisted. She felt responsible for Carla and she didn't want her alone. Alone with Rory, that is. Margie wasn't there. That left me.

She didn't know about Rory and me, of course.

I stationed myself as far from them both as I could. The others all went back some way up the passage we had come along. All the time we went down in this damned mountain, down into its grumbling bowels.

I still heard that booming noise, so soft and low I felt it rather than picked it up with my ears.

Rory took the mask from his pack. Carla faced him, smiling. He swayed into her and kissed her lips. Her face in the lamplight was dreamy. She liked having him do this. She liked the power she had over him.

He put the mask on her face.

Inca!

Copper bodies, round and hard as a barrel. Tunics of wool and cotton. Leather sandals. Ears pierced, the holes enlarged, and golden discs inserted.

Sweat of the sun, tears of the moon.

Carla said: '*You have gone with her.*'

'Gone?' said Rory.

'*You and she have gone together. Make her come forward.*'

There was a silence. 'I think she means you, kiddo,' said Rory.

I came unwillingly forward. Carla was terrifying.

'*I will see you,*' she said. She crossed her arms.

Rory turned to me.

'Oh no,' I said 'There are games I don't play.'

Carla waited.

'She's having us on,' I said huskily. 'This is perverted.'

'Sydney, don't be coy. This isn't the time.'

'I won't do this thing.' My vision swam. *Tears of the moon.*

I began to fall forward, half-fainting. Rory caught my body and held it against him. My head bowed back but my lower body was firm against his.

'Is this what you want?' he said to Carla.

'*This is what I must have,*' she replied.

The golden seat. The Lord-Inca. His sons and councillors. Above us the peak of Intihuatana, the hitching place of the sun.

'I'm not wearing the mask,' I whispered dry mouthed. 'Why must I suffer this?' Rory's groin was hard against me, demanding.

Rory undressed me. I had no control over my body which was plastic, deformed. Visions and strange music beat in my mind. All the time the boom boom boom of the beating heart of the mountain sounded in my blood.

I lay on the ground. Rory was above me, naked. His face was lit and exultant. Two arms, not his own, wove round his body. Carla stood behind him and their bodies blended.

'No,' I cried, pitifully.

The hands held his penis. He stood with his own arms outspread. The hands masturbated him so that his penis grew enormous, swelling and pulsing.

The end flowered open. I was wet.

They turned me on my hands and knees. My head hung down, my loosened hair all round my face. Hands softly pulled my breasts, milking them. My buttocks were opened. Fingers entered my vulva.

Something wet crawled over my anus. I sobbed. My vagina was penetrated. I heard laughter. There were fingers in my body, stirring me, forcing a response from willing flesh.

Only my mind was reluctant. Only one corner of it was still my own. They possessed me. The mask possessed me.

Lips caressed my nipples. Lips pressed against my melting labia. Everywhere was kissed, puckered flesh, pleading flesh. Aroused and swollen flesh, moist with anticipation.

I was entered. Slim the thing that entered my sex. Slim and long and wriggling. I swayed, tears mingling with my hair.

Now something large was pushing at me. I cried out my distress. Large and slippery it pushed. It kept pushing. My puckered flesh yielded and I howled.

They laughed. It was a sibilance, quick and sly, this laughter of theirs. The mask held me and the violation of my rear commenced.

All the time Rory took his pleasure, fingers played in the constricted space of my vagina. Her fingers. I hated her then.

I would have escaped if I could. My limbs were lead, weighted to the ground.

She teased my clitoris. My rear spasmed. Rory was grunting, pressing harder, his hands holding my buttocks apart so he could see in the lamplight the ravishment he made.

I felt him swell and subside. His climax beat in time with the pulsing boom of the mountain. He drew back out of me.

The spell retreated. I sobbed with my face in the muck of the floor.

I rolled over, my face smeared with dirt and tears and mucous. 'You bastards,' I sobbed.

Carla had removed the mask. Her eyes slanted almond and dark in the high-cheeked paleness of her face. Her body arched across mine till she lay over me, her naked back across my stomach.

She dug her heels in and lifted herself. Rory knelt between her legs. His long, firm, wet cock was hard erect again. He slid it into her and she moaned and writhed.

He took her quickly. She was ecstatic, greedy for him, blazing with her triumph in having him before us all, above us all. As soon as I could I got out from under them.

I was trembling when I picked up my clothes. I hated what had happened. I had not owned my own body. It had obeyed other minds than mine. They had violated my personality, ravished my integrity, taken away my freedom of decision – I had been powerless to prevent it.

My mind was still full of the images of a culture long dead. I saw the waterfall and knew I had to wash. I could not stand my body as it was, smeared with their games.

I left the chamber. The waterfall was there, falling from the rocky roof through a fissure to land in a pebbled pool. It drained out through cracks in the floor.

I stood under it, naked, letting its icy flow bring balm to my filthed skin. The impossible coldness was bliss. I froze in cleanliness. It poured through my hair, over my face, into my mouth.

'What the hell are you playing at?'

Tom was there, watching me. 'Go away,' I said. The water ran icy between my breasts. They might have been marble, so cold and pale they were in the low uncertain light. I had lodged a candle on a shelf, leaving the lamp with Rory and Carla. The lovers.

The taste was sour in my mouth. I let more water run in.

Tom ignored my nakedness. 'Get out of that,' he said. 'What happened back there?'

'Filth,' I said and snickered.

'You're playing these games too?'

'Inca,' I said. 'Can't you feel it?'

He pulled me out of the waterfall. 'You're frozen, you stupid bitch.' He worked his shirt off awkwardly and began to rub me with it.

Water ran out of my hair, between my breasts, and was caught and held by my fleece. It dripped from the base of my belly to the floor.

Tom rubbed me harshly all over with his shirt, using the one hand. 'Get dressed,' he said. 'I didn't reckon this from you. I thought you valued yourself. Playing sluts' games with that slime-bag.'

I shivered and began to pull my clothes on. I felt tired and frightened. I wanted to go home.

He watched me dress, his face set and angry the whole time. When I was ready I said: 'The water might help your shoulder. Let me look at it.'

'I don't want you touching me.'

'Don't be childish. Let me look.'

171

His shoulder was patchy purple and black, the edges of the bruise yellow. I wadded the scarf I bound my hair with and soaked it under the flow. I began to wash the shoulder, pressing the cold material against it. Then I manoeuvred him so the water fell over the shoulder, holding him where he knelt so that only his naked chest and arm got wet.

His face was pressed into my stomach. My hands held his head, I felt his hair against me.

'That's enough,' he said, muffled in my clothes. I drew him out of the water and knelt by him, patting the excess water off the shoulder.

His shirt was wet from drying me. There was a moment where we knelt together, my arms round him, his head bowed and against my breast.

I worked his shirt on with him standing up and then slung his cameras aboard his back.

'That feel any better?' I asked.

'Sydney,' he said wearily. 'I shouldn't have interfered with the centipede. It would have spat you back out.'

We walked back to the central chamber. 'Oh, good,' said Carla brightly. 'We go this way, Sydney.'

So we came to the cave of the paintings, where the gold miners told Carl they found the mask.

Colin and Rory were overwhelmed. Tom took photographs and Martha clapped her hands with joy. Carla sat down on the floor smiling and appeared to go to sleep. Big Jacko stood quietly watching. I had the feeling he didn't approve of the way things were going.

Neither did I.

They were llamas and guanacos, mostly. The flat-backed, long-necked, shaggy prick-eared llamas were unmistakable. They all had their short tails up in a little arch, making them life-like and fluent. Under

172

one a little humanoid figure reached, clearly milking the huge beast. A calf nuzzled up beside the milker.

'These are very old,' exulted Rory. He had a scalpel-like thing and was scraping a minute amount of pigment into a little plastic phial.

'You mean the ones who fled from Vilcabamba, they did it?' I said.

'No. That was the 1570s. This is older than that, by hundreds of years.'

'How can you tell?'

'This is Tiahuanaco. You agree, Colin?'

'Of course. We'll get it dated. The scrapings will tell us. And we'll come back.'

We'll come back with authority,' said Martha. 'You will have the right to claim discovery.'

'I thought it was supposed to be Inca.' I was unsettled and grouchy at what had happened. I wasn't so much mad at that silly bitch Carla or even at Rory. I was mad at myself, at my loss of control.

Martha said: 'Put the mask on that shelf.'

'No,' said Carla. 'It goes here.'

A pillar of rock stuck up in the middle of the cave. Carla took the mask and set it on the top. It fitted beautifully. The height of the pillar was maybe four and half, five feet.

If you stood back, it looked like a person.

Carla said: 'I would like you all to leave. I will stay and meditate for a while, alone.'

We did as she said. I got myself by Martha. 'A word,' I said.

She was bright-eyed. 'Yes, Sydney? You're really earning your keep now. I appreciate that. I appreciate all you're doing to help us achieve what we want.'

'I don't want to help. I don't think this is right. Can't you see what's happening to Carla?'

She was silent a moment. 'Carla is not like other

girls,' she said quietly. 'She is very shy and diffident. I'm glad to see her assertive. Rory won't do her any harm.'

'Rory wouldn't give toe-fluff to keep a vagrant warm,' I said. 'He only cares about Vilcabamba. He uses people.'

She turned her head to look at me. 'I'm surprised to hear you say that, you of all people.'

'What do you mean?' I said stupidly. Was the cow insinuating I spoke from spite because the man fucked elsewhere?

'Sydney. You work for a newspaper. Everyone uses everyone. It doesn't have to be bad. I think this will prove a very good experience for Carla. Very life-enhancing.'

'What about the sex?' I said brutally. I was getting annoyed.

'Are you jealous?' Martha looked at me with lizard eyes. 'I don't see why you should be.'

'I don't think this is the way for Carla to experience sex.'

'She is no virgin, if that's what you mean. I find your attitude astonishing. You sound like a Sunday School teacher.'

I was getting nowhere. Perhaps Martha was right. I hate the manipulative power-play scene myself when it's tied up with sex. Sex is for fun. Work is for power. Not everyone agrees with me, though, and Carla didn't work.

The truth was, Carla was having herself a ball. I didn't like it because I was getting pushed around. I doubt I would have been as concerned if I'd been able to stay on the sidelines.

It was very late by now. The decision was that we would split up, some of us staying the night underground, some returning to reassure Margie that all was well and we had achieved our first objective.

Carla elected to stay in the chamber of the mask alone for the night. The rest of us staying would retire along the passage a little. Martha wanted to stay as did both Colin and Rory. Big Jacko always went with Martha, unless she sent him with Carla.

Matheson and I would return up top. I was profoundly grateful. I was tired and sleepy, but my wish to be out of that terrible place was stronger by far than any desire for rest. None of them seemed to take the attack on me and Matheson seriously. I did. I rather thought Tom did.

We ate. We had left our exit roped over the dangerous places, so we could get out in a hurry if need be. Tom and I shouldn't have any trouble.

We took one of the kerosene lamps, freshly filled, and we took a rifle. We would bring extra food back in with us the following day.

It seemed to me the others couldn't wait to be rid of us. They were excited like children over the cave of the mask. I struck a cracked note in this excitement, perhaps Tom did too. They wanted to wallow in their discovery. I now found the thought of the flies and the humid river positively delightful. I hated the mountain.

Tom and I set off quietly. Since we disagreed about almost everything, we didn't talk much. We plodded up the steep slopes in near silence, making our way back to Margie outside.

The silence grew. My heart pounded steadily, or maybe it was the mountain. Tom led, his head down watching his footing. His pack was hooked over his good shoulder. I carried the rifle. This was a strange feeling, like I'd grown a penis or something.

It was warm, the air muffled and heavy. My boots

felt weighted. The black silence pressed on me and my shoulders bent tiredly.

I thought about fragrant baths and satin sheets. I stumbled slightly and put up my arm. Something touched it, feather-light.

I flinched but I could see nothing, no bats, no creepy insects. My bare hand touched something else that stuck to my fingers.

'Tom,' I called. I pulled the stuff off me and wiped my hands on my trousers. My vision was blurred.

'Tom,' I said sharply.

'Yeah?' He looked misty in the gloom, his edges ill-defined.

'What's the matter?' I meant, what the hell is happening here, but that sounded too panicky.

'Apart from being in your company?'

'What's this stuff hanging down?'

He reached out and touched the grey nothingness. 'Cobweb, I think,' he said.

I edged closer. 'You reckon,' I said huskily, 'they grow the spiders like they grow the centipedes here?'

'I like to see you frightened, Sydney. Not other women. I don't like women frightened in general. But on you it looks good. I figure you should take the lead here. Strike a blow for equality, huh?'

I took the lead. We plodded on, our boots rattling and occasionally slipping on the rough, steep ground. The cobwebs got thicker. Finally I took Tom's machete and cut them away.

'Why wasn't all this here on the way in?' I asked.

'Search me.' He lit a cigar.

'I don't have rubber gloves.'

We went on. The cobwebs got thicker and thicker. I stopped again. It was very warm and I was sweating, partly from the exercise and partly from naked fear.

'Tom.'

'Yes, frog.'

His casual air didn't deceive me. The son of a bitch was enjoying my crumbling nerves. 'Have you been keeping an eye on the time?'

'Since you went in front I've been watching your butt. It waggles delightfully. I'll warn my children how looks deceive.'

'Because I think we should be out by now. I think we should be passing those damned holes where the centipedes live. I don't think we should be in this spider's parlour.' I stopped, appalled at what I did think.

'You mean,' said Tom softly, 'you think we're lost.'

'We'd better go back,' I said huskily. The mountain boomed softly.

'I think you're right. The air's a little stuffy. You go first again, pussy-cat. It gives me the best view of you.'

The webs I had cut were repaired. I told myself the webs were sticky and self-mending. I kept the machete in front of me all the time, the lamp in my left hand.

I really didn't like this.

The webs got thicker. When I cut them they swung like soft curtains and brushed my face. I tripped and felt sour web on my tongue. I crouched on the floor, trembling.

A hand touched me. 'Giving up already, frog?'

I turned in my crouch and took the hand, pressing it to my face. It was dry and warm. 'Damn you, Matheson,' I said. My voice was shaky.

He lifted me using his good arm, keeping it lightly round me. 'Calm down, princess. We've got food, water and weaponry. Who could ask for more?'

'Me,' I said in a stifled voice. 'I could ask for fresh air and the outside.'

177

'You're going to hate me later for letting me see you like this.'

'I hate you already. Rory told me about your weasel plan to sell Martha short. You stink, Matheson.'

There was a silence. I continued to stand with his arm around me, my body greedy for the reassurance of his solid physical presence.

'All the details, frog?'

'Enough.'

'Such as?'

'Planning to hide Vilcabamba when you found it and going back later.'

'That plan.'

I wanted to lean aginst him. I wanted to let the greasy skin of my face rest against his. I wanted to be soothed and to feel safe. I had expected him to deny Rory's accusation.

He didn't. Rory was velvet-pawed, panther-bright, tricksy and darkly golden, a man with the sexual grace of a fallen angel. He should be the villain of the piece. It stood to reason.

Rough-cast, witty, dry and nagging Matheson ought to be fine underneath. Mentally I had him as Humph Bogart in *Casablanca*.

This wasn't the movies. Rory was a man with an education, an international trade and the ability to make good in the eyes of the world, to earn respect.

Matheson was a free lance photog, a Joe Nobody. I, of all people, had been deluding myself. I was with the bad man now. He wasn't a very bad man. He wasn't very anything. Mr Second-Rate, we had here, and the contrast with Rory's grace and fire could not have been stronger.

I stood back and laughed. 'Sorry,' I said lightly. 'I'm fine now. I'll recognise the web-maker when I see it but make sure you stay behind me so I don't get muddled.'

Later still we sat silent, side by side, resting. We had put out the kerosene lamp to conserve it. Matheson was smoking again, the red tip to his cigar a pleasant sight in the nothingness of the underground cave. The webs were gone and we had met no spider.

We had met nothing. I hardly knew whether we went up or down, I was so tired. We were hideously, hopelessly lost.

Matheson reached into his pack and after some rustling about, handed me something.

'What's this?' I said, but I knew. It was the counterfeit mask.

'Put it on,' he said gently.

'Why? The others have the real one.'

'That is absolutely and unutterably true. The others have the real one. Put it on, Sydney. Don't argue, just this once.'

'Put it on yourself.'

'It won't go on me. I've tried.'

If he spoke the truth, it really had been Rory that day in the forest.

'This is pointless,' I said feebly.

'Sydney. You don't like me very much, do you?'

'I didn't mean to let it show.' My voice was coyly amazed.

'You screwed hell out of me in Manaus.'

'We all make mistakes.'

'Cut the wise-cracks. You wore the mask and it made you lusty, even for me. It made me want you. And you saw the lagoon, the lagoon in our future.'

I shifted uncomfortably. 'OK, OK.'

'It was this mask you wore.'

I ran my ears over this a couple of times. 'Come again.'

179

'It was this mask you wore. Martha had the original by that stage.'

I was suddenly angry. 'Don't con me, you snake. I saw you paying for it the night before. Remember?'

'I remember, babe. I was buying a copy. The woodcarver had already returned the original. He didn't want to turn in the copy and he took some persuading.'

'Why?'

'How the hell should I know? What I do know is the difference between them. We have the copy here. You had the copy that day in my room. Now put the mother-fucking thing on and get us out of here.'

I wouldn't do it. It scared shit out of me. I didn't want dreams and visions. I didn't want carnal abandon when I was almost gibbering with fear deep in a damned mountain that breathed and had a pulse. A mountain that ate people. I wouldn't do it.

'I won't do it,' I said.

There was a silence. The man sucked on his cigar. I could feel he was trembling with tension but when he spoke again, his voce was calm enough. It was absolutely expressionless. 'Sydney,' he said and stopped.

'Yeah.' My voice was sulky.

'I'm not into forcing women to screw me. Whether you believe me or not, it does not turn me on.'

I stayed silent.

'You don't want to wear the mask because a side-effect is that we're likely to screw. That is, the side-effect to the mask saving our lives by getting us out of here before we meet the spider or another of those centipedes, is that we might fuck. Again. And you so hate the thought of this that you would rather die.'

I could have said many things. The man's voice was deadly cold. I was inflicting damage on his ego, of course, and if men had penises the size of their egos, we women wouldn't bother to come out of the bedroom.

'Look,' I said, equally calm. 'Stop thinking with your gonads. Really, a screw with you is neither here nor there. It is not a big deal. The earth doesn't move, sunshine, *comprenez*? What matters more to me is the grey matter. I don't like it scrambled. I'm not me with someone else inside my skull, so the death of my body is neither here nor there either, if I have to hand over control of the hardware to some four hundred year old ghost.'

'You get control back.'

'No,' I said softly. 'It comes with a virus, baby, and you know it and I know it. Carla is not the same girl, is she, even when she doesn't wear the mask?'

'You don't think the change in her is down to Duncan? That is an evil guy, Johnson.'

I stood up. 'I guess the rest period is over,' I said.

The wind sobbed along the passage as Matheson struggled to relight the kerosene lamp. It whirled round me, stuffy and warm, full of news and chatter, all of it malignant.

'That wind must come from outside,' said Tom.

'You fool,' I said, trying not to cry. The wind came from the bowels of the mountain, it was foul and filthy with whisper and menace.

I put out my hand in the gloom. My fingers closed round a perfectly smooth boss. It was so unnatural I stopped and looked at it properly.

The sides of the passage opened with a grating roar. I yelped and leaped backwards cannoning into Tom. Choking dust rose in clouds and it was a moment before we saw there was an inner chamber, hewn and shaped.

I felt eagerness leap in Tom. 'No,' I said sharply.

'This is amazing,' he said, pushing past me.

I stood alone on the threshhold. 'Get out,' I said, my voice cracking with urgency.

'For heaven's sake, Sydney. Come and look.'

'Tom, it's a bad place.'

He chuckled. The light swept round. There was a carved frieze running round at just above head height. 'I need some pics, Sydney. Don't stir up the dust again. This is fantastic. Pinky and Perky will go berserk when they know this is here.'

I looked behind me. There was nothing, only blackness stretching either way, ahead and behind. The wind teased along and stroked my face.

I rubbed the feeling away and stepped in after Tom, keeping by the doors.

He was using flashes and working his way round the chamber. The walls were smooth up to the frieze and smooth again above it though the ceiling was rough, about eight feet above us. A vast stone seat sat silent in the dark, empty, opposite the walls.

It was so creepy my hair wanted to stand on end. I looked at the chair and wondered why I was so chicken-hearted. I should have been thrilled. Then this funny noise started.

'Tom,' I said sharply. His flash went off again and I was momentarily blinded.

'Tom,' I said again on a rising note.

'Yeah?' He was working and his voice was absent.

'That noise?'

Then I knew what it was. 'The doors,' I screamed.

He looked then. We both looked. The doors were closing.

Tom bent to pick up the lamp which he had taken from me when he entered the room. Instead he kicked it over. 'Shit,' he said, fumbling for it, holding his swinging cameras.

I stood at the doors watching him. I pushed but I might as well have tried to push a building. For a split second I thought of going through alone with only my failing torch for company.

The doors shut. Tom stood holding the lamp. 'Ah,' he said and I had nothing to say back.

There was no exit to the chamber that we could find. The wind made little trickles in the dust about our feet but we couldn't find the crack it came through. The slight shuffling, gritty noise got on my nerves. I felt played with, laughed at. Cruelly so, at that.

Tom felt various projections. We figured reasonably enough that if there was a handle for coming in, there was a handle for going out. We couldn't find it. My hands felt raw from being scraped over rough stone surfaces.

After a while we sat back to back in the middle of the floor. Neither of us fancied the great stone chair, me being an upholstery fiend, it seemed.

We were warm, dry, hungry and exhausted. We weren't thirsty, yet.

Tom leaned his head back onto my shoulder. I felt the roughness of his unshaven cheek. 'Sorry about this, Sydney,' he said in a light voice.

I'd been believing for a long time we wouldn't find our way out. It was not reassuring to know that at long last he had come to the same conclusion.

I leaned my own head exhaustedly back on his shoulder. We were cheek to cheek in the darkness. 'I'm not a woman to hold a grudge,' I said. I turned my face to his in the darkness so that I could feel his breathing and burrow slightly into his skin. I needed human comfort, even his.

I almost went to sleep. Little furtive scraping noises interrupted my sad and dismal dreams. 'What's that?' I asked blearily, half-believing I was imagining it.

183

We had put out the lamp without really considering who we were conserving the oil for. Now Tom produced his torch and flicked its yellowing beam on.

He put it straight off. I felt his body suddenly hard, rigid with emotion.

'What is it?' I said again, trying to control the leaping fear in me.

'Sydney,' he said with an effort.

'Tell me.' The suspense was unbearable.

'Are you good on snake recognition?'

I moaned softly, closing my eyes.

'See,' said Matheson as if his lips had suddenly cracked because his mouth was too dry, 'they're big and they're patterned brown. Now the fer-de-lance is only a mere eight feet or so in length but has this venom that causes rapid and severe internal bleeding. If, however, we have bushmasters here, they can grow up to eleven and half feet. Their venom isn't so poisonous, which you might think would make them the better option. However, they make whole quantities of it and they have these really enormous fangs. I mean huge. So generally the consensus of opinion is that they are the more dangerous. In fact,' croaked Matheson, 'they are considered to be right up there with the world's most dangerous snakes.'

During this, without being aware of it, I had turned round and put my arms tightly round Matheson's shaking body.

'Perhaps,' I whispered, 'they can't see in the dark.'

Matheson shuffled so that I lay more or less in his lap, his arms round me as I looked upwards into his face, though I saw nothing because of the dark.

'I'll tell you a secret,' he whispered back.

'I don't want to hear it.'

'They're both pit vipers.'

'They live in pits. The dark doesn't bother them.' I

was trying to sound intelligent. My heart ballooned rhythmically under my shirt.

'The pits referred to are between their eyes and nostrils. They are infra-red detectors. They hunt by heat, sweetheart. The heat the prey gives off.'

I was sweating like a pig. Now, too late, I knew the point of that deodorant that keeps you dry. I made a little whimpering noise and pushed my face into Matheson's chest.

'I have a final request.' Matheson's voice was so croaky I almost couldn't hear it.

'Won't smoking raise our temperature?' I husked back.

'Wear the mask.'

Very carefully I sat up, my back muscles tensed against the bite of the unseen snakes. Matheson reached out and poked me in the eye. Having located my face, he stroked my cheek briefly. 'It was always wrong time of the month for us, huh?' he said awkwardly. He put the mask on my face.

The wind whirled and I heard the snakes hiss in fury. The world rushed upwards and I felt myself soaring in the dark. Things laughed playfully, spitefully, and old voices voiced old wrongs, old grievances. All the ills of a conquered people lay on my shoulders but still I was pushed up on gusts of foul, hot air belched out of the pit of past history.

My hands struggled up against the intolerable weight. My fingers scrabbled vainly. I wanted to tear the thing from my face. My will and my mind denied everything but still I was tossed upwards grazing my tender human flesh on harsh stone and old lies.

For a moment I saw him. He sat in the royal chair, commanding me. His tunic was woven vicuña and his cloak was fastened over his right shoulder. Jewels and gold glittered in his clothing. On his head was the royal fringe, his crown of red wool encrusted with gold. He held in his left hand the mace of gold, symbol of his office. Golden sun-discs filled his ears.

I saw him and was afraid. For he saw me. He saw me and knew me and all were subject under his absolute authority.

My nakedness was absolute. I was nothing. I had nothing. Nothingness embraced me.

In the void we embraced, chest to chest, belly to belly, my long legs locking behind his back, my buttocks resting upon his crossed legs. As suited an ancient god, his phallus stood proud and awesome, not a mortal's shaft. It had the look of alabaster and the feel of sun-warmed silk. Beneath it hung balls of golf-ball proportions, plump, taut in their soft draperies.

We stared into each others eyes, held in a trance, his hands lifting my buttocks, my arms snake-like about his neck, keeping us steady.

He opened me, splayed the globular flesh of my backside, exposing my damp pinkness, lowering me in offering, to his desire.

He rose within me, going deeper than all previous man-flesh, so full it seemed he would rend me, yet he did not. We became one, moulding closer still, his shaft unmoving, possessing, yet being possessed. I felt at one with the ancients and the universe, felt as though I died, ascended to some higher state of being. Was he Tom, or was he the Inca? It was impossible to say, for they merged, became one, confusing still further my already suspect visions.

Chapter Six

'You're not dead. You're not dead. You're not dead.'

This has to be the ultimate reassurance. I woke up and found it was true.

'What happened?' I said. I hutched myself further into his body. Matheson held me against him and it was very good.

'We're safe. We're outside the cave. The mask got us out.'

My hand crept up. My face was free.

'I took it off,' said Tom.

'I'm cold,' I said.

'You don't have any clothes on.'

Astoundingly, this was true. My mind worked slowly. 'You raped me,' I said in a voice thick with rage. 'You raped me while I was out cold with that thing.' I struggled free of his body and began feebly to hit him.

He caught my fists. 'No. No, no, no. Of course I damn-well didn't. It just happened as we got out of that place.'

I stared at him. It was dark but not totally so. The air was keen and cool. 'How did we get out?'

'I don't know. I don't understand.' His eyes fell away from mine. He wasn't lying. He was looking at my naked, exposed breasts. He released my wrists and I hugged myself, shivering.

He picked my arms apart and looked at my breasts again. 'You don't think much of men,' he said. 'Understand this, though. We don't all like our rides to be broken-spirited. Horses we saddle, where I come from. Not women.'

My teeth drew back in a snarl. I came up on my feet feeling the power glow through me. I reached out and grabbed the man's belt, lifting him. His back arched and he fell. I tore his clothes open and laid him bent-backed over a mound. I held his hands away from me effortlessly. I crouched astride his body, standing bent-kneed. Then I laughed. My body gulped his organ into its hot fastness. I sucked and squeezed and milked him till he came. Then I sat on his straining stomach and rubbed myself.

I released him and walked away. The dim stars faded in the steel-blue vault of the sky. The far distance was lit by a deep glow. Across this paler patch was a long, jagged-tipped silhouette.

The planet rolled. The ball of the sun hung low behind the mountains. Night was giving way to the coming day.

I stood with my arms open, watching. The sky brightened. The mountain tops were steel white. Below was the great black sea of the eternal forest.

'You bitch,' shouted Matheson. He came round between me and the rising sun. I took his hair and forced him to his knees. Then I stood astride his face, keeping him there. The smooth and rough textures of his skin, the projections and dips of his features, were very agreeable to my swollen vulva.

The snow-capped peaks led infinitely to my left and to my right. The sky swelled with light. Behind me, above me, Cloud-maker's summit turned from dull grey to rose-pink.

The sun's disc tipped up over the jagged peaks. White snow glinted and became red fire. My body was suffused with red. The sun grew and light streamed over the world. The vast heaving sea of trees took on faint colour and definition. White vapour began to smoke upwards in spirals, clouds forming in the trees and dissipating upwards into the platinum brilliance of the new sky.

I was cold. I wanted my clothes. I looked down and cried out. A moment later I was crouched face to face with him.

He looked terrible. His unshaven face was streaked with dirt and sweat. He was grey with exhaustion and fear, fear of me. His golden eyes were muddy and opaque.

'Tom,' I whispered.

'You bitch,' he said again, his voice hoarse and shocked.

'It was the mask. You made me wear it. I didn't want to.'

'It got us out of there.'

He went out of focus. 'I saw the Inca,' I said, my voice high and strange.

'Jesus,' he whimpered and put his face on my shoulder.

My clothes lay scattered on the mountain side. We collected them wearily and I dressed.

'We're looking east, Johnson,' said Tom casually

189

over his shoulder. We were having trouble meeting each other's eyes.

'It's where the sun usually rises.'

'I get saddle sores talking to you . . . Oh,' I said, catching on. 'We're on the other side of the mountain.'

'First base, kiddo.'

I walked over to where my other self had sun-worshipped after raping the man. The mountain dropped steeply to the soft writhing basin of greenery below. Things shrieked and gobbled and howled and chittered, their wordless cries rising thinly on the hollow air. Far beyond it, at the horizon, the white-capped rampart of the Andes marched endlessly north and south.

Matheson joined me, not too close. I was sufficiently divorced from that other, demented self to feel a sly amusement at this.

'Fifteen million years,' he said.

'I usually feel about that old before my first coffee of the morning,' I agreed.

'Are you incapable of feeling awe, Johnson?'

Pompous pig. 'I believe in nothing,' I hissed. 'Nothing. And I will not change my mind.'

He turned away and I watched the mountains sulkily. He came back with a telephoto lens from his pack, he watched the forest and the mountains for a bit, then he handed it to me.

Our fingers touched and we almost dropped the precious lens in our anxiety to break the physical contact. I took a deep breath, staring at the ground. 'I won't do it again. It was the mask.'

He made a big effort and got a grip of my shoulders. He really didn't like touching me. 'Tell you what,' he said. 'Let's pretend it never happened. Let's wipe it. As you say, it was the mask. You didn't want to do it, you weren't responsible, you didn't like it and I hated it.'

I looked crossly at him, eyeball to eyeball. 'It wasn't me. For a start, I'm not that strong.'

A queer look came over his face. He pulled me close to his body and looked into my face. 'So escape,' he said.

I felt the pressure of his unkind grip. 'I'd hit you with your lens,' I explained. Men are dumb.

'Yeah. Sure. Right.' He released me hurriedly. I looked through the lens.

The forest canopy was alive with colour. The flowers that grew rooted up in it, the epiphytes, glowed from this height like tiny gems. Birds of every colour flitted here and there feeding on the canopy fruits. I saw a troupe of monkeys.

I saw Vilcabamba.

I pulled the lens away from my eye. With considerable effort, I put it back. I searched where I knew it to be. I saw nothing.

I took the lens away again. I looked with my naked eyes and stopped analysing what I saw.

There it was, cloaked in vines, choked in equatorial flowers, stifled by the insidious growth of trees taking the stone wonders back deep into their green embrace.

It was a vision, but I knew where the real thing was.

'What's the matter?' asked Matheson. With a tremendous effort I tore my gaze away. I looked at him feeling huge with knowledge.

For the first time in a long time, too long by far, my training reasserted itself. Information is currency. You can buy anything with it. Sometimes, in extreme times, you need it to buy your life.

'Nothing,' I said. 'Vertigo. I felt as if I was falling.'

'Liar.'

'Hoo, boy,' I said and smiled. Frontal attacks were easy. 'Time we joined the others.'

Matheson looked at the Andes again. The sun was high now, the forest unshadowed and brilliant. 'Not so many people have seen sunrise over the Andes,' he said.

I was sickened of novel sights but I didn't say so. I didn't want to sound cowardly.

We stopped and washed on the way over the mountain, stripping unselfconsciously. I desperately wanted to get clean. I washed my pants and sat naked in the sun while they dried on a rock. By this stage in our relationship I reckoned we both would have preferred nestling up sexily to a pit viper than to each other.

We met Big Jacko first, moodily collecting firewood. When he saw us a grin of pure pleasure lit up his ugly mug and my own spirits suddenly lifted. With simple naturalness of feeling, the guy was glad we weren't dead or lost, living in the tomb below.

We explained shiftily we missed the right way back and wandered all night, coming out on the far side at dawn. We stumbled into camp. I was too tired to answer questions, groping for my hammock while someone blessedly gave me coffee to drink. Matheson did the talking with Margie hanging affectionately on his arm.

I had changed into clean clothes before passing out with tiredness. While I slept, Margie washed my clothes at the waterfall nearby and laid them out to dry. That girl had a heart of gold and deserved better than Matheson. I wasn't going to tell her that, though. It had belatedly occurred to me that his affectionate cuddle in the sealed room when we thought we were about to die was not what it seemed at the time.

We had had a machete and a rifle. I never saw the snakes nor how many there were, but with me between him and the beasts, Matheson could have picked them off almost at leisure.

If I'd refused the mask a second time, is that what he would have done?

I woke in the evening, ate and went right back to sleep. My exhaustion was of the spirit as much as of the body. I didn't want to think about the mask, either.

The following morning we left the mountain. Over breakfast I detected a certain amount of excitement in my fellow adventurers. Martha was nice to me, acting very concerned, but I could tell her mind was chiefly elsewhere.

There was no way I was going to tell anyone what had happened inside the vile mountain we were about to leave. I was busy with denying it even to myself. But at the same time I felt a responsibility to Carla, not so much for the girl herself but to Martha, her mother-substitute, whom I respected.

I approached the subject carefully. I'm not a tactful person, it's a liability in my field of work, but I did the best I could.

'Uh, about the mask,' I said.

'I recognise your contribution, Sydney.'

'What?'

'That business in the painted cave, where you stayed to make sure Carla wasn't abused. Don't think I don't trust Rory, honey, but we girls always need to look after each other, huh?'

'I am concerned about Carla. I don't understand this mask business, but it seems very potent. Should she really be wearing it, Martha? Aren't we tinkering

with things we don't know about? Our rational Western minds might be blocking us from seeing there is
real trouble here. You wouldn't let the girl take mind-
altering drugs to find this lost city, would you? But
that's what the mask does. We're interfering with
Carla's mind.'

Martha looked at me oddly, as well she might. She
didn't know I'd worn the horrible thing.

In the suspended seconds before her reply, a
thought dropped crystal clear into my mind.

I'd worn the potent mask last night. So what was
Carla wearing when she screwed Rory in the painted
cave, when she ordered Rory to screw me?

Was Carla playing games with us all. Was she no
diffident little rich girl, but on the contrary a sly
pussy-cat out to get her man and her perverted sexual
thrills any which way she could?

I'd felt strange in the painted cave but then I was
frightened of the real power of the mask which I had
authentically experienced. Also, I undoubtedly had
the hots for Rory Duncan. But Carla could have been
play-acting and snickering to herself the whole way
through, as we danced puppet-like to her orders.

I'd begun to feel very cold, but Martha was speaking to me. 'I appreciate you worrying,' she said,
looking at me a shade oddly as if such worry was out
of character for someone like me. This was true
enough. 'But there are things you don't know.' Suddenly all her repressed excitement came bursting out.
'I don't see why you shouldn't be told. You deserve
to know. She's seen it, Sydney. She's seen Vilcabamba. She knows the way.'

I gaped. I was struck dumb.

'The mask is a map,' said Martha. 'It tells the
wearer, I don't know how, the way to go. Carla will
lead us now. It's west of here. It's between us and

194

the Andes. We'll go some of the way by boat but then we'll have to walk. We've done it, Sydney. We can find it. Do you understand?'

'I understand,' I said faintly. I struggled a moment. 'Good,' I forced out. 'That's great news. Perhaps she won't have to wear it again.'

Martha was sober. 'I've tried it myself, you know. It won't stay on me, something about my face shape, I suppose. Don't you and Margie try it, dear. You're right, we don't understand mystical things. I've spoken to Carla and I'll speak again to her. She mustn't become addicted. She is an adult, though, and I know she's desperate to help. She wants to do this, Sydney.'

'She wants Rory Duncan,' I said flatly. 'The mask means she can have him.'

Martha was shrewd as they come. Her face shuttered and she took her time answering. Finally she said: 'Not many women would turn down a man like that. Maybe he isn't one to marry but you're adult enough, Sydney, to know that a man like him makes a woman feel good, as long as she keeps control of herself and doesn't become addicted. He's sweet flesh and we both know it. I'm not begrudging Carla feeding on him for a while. I trust him not to be a bastard any more than he naturally is, being an attractive man. I'm sorry if you feel you're getting the short straw here.'

A kind of black rage seized me. 'I was not,' I hissed, 'speaking through jealousy.'

'Good,' said Martha calmly and left me.

We broke camp and moved down the mountain. I gathered the others had returned uneventfully after sleeping underground, meeting no strange beasts.

When I spoke casually to Colin about the wind and the booming I had experienced, he looked blank.

We re-entered the cool damp embrace of the cloud forest. It was like a landscape out of a Spielberg film: cloaking, primitive, infused with a hooded silence. The moss gave wetly under my hands. The gnarled trees assumed the shapes of ancient beings. Moisture-starred webs broke softly at my passage. Underfoot the ground was crevassed and broken, as if longing to swallow the warm meat of my body into its clammy fastness.

Johnson, I told myself sourly, you've got the creeps.

We dropped lower into the warm bath of the equatorial rain forest. The heat and humidity made me feel battered and weary. Insects began to feast on any unprotected skin again. My temper got filthier as we struggled on. I wanted to be home among the back-biting fun of work, hustling for stories, doing my job.

Rory picked me off that night as we camped. 'I want to talk to you,' he said.

'I'm tired. Let's leave it, huh?'

'If I have to, I'll say it in front of the others. Maybe Carla won't play then. You know she knows the way, she says.'

'Martha told me. OK, what is it? You finding it a problem screwing one woman at a time, big boy?'

He took my arm and led me a little away from the camp. The familiar nocturnal forest shrieks and rattles bounced among the trees. We sat down after checking the immediate area for snakes and scorpions. I really hated this forest.

Rory suddenly went on his knees in front of me. To my astonishment he opened my shirt and pressed his face on my breasts. I felt his warm hair on my sensitive flesh. Instinctively, my arms went round his shoulders. He bent to me, his voice muffled, his arms about my waist.

'Sydney,' he said.

'Hey, hey, what's this? Is the man confessing to something awful? Been fiddling your luncheon vouchers, darling?' I kept my voice light. I was sick of heavy emotion.

He lifted his face and grinned up at me. 'I'm confessing to something awful,' he said. 'Something terrible. I find this very hard to say.'

'Then don't say it. You'll regret it. That's good advice from one toughie to another.'

'I'm not as tough as I thought, Sydney.'

His voice had a little shake of emotion in it. I felt panic rising. 'I don't want this,' I said sharply.

He held me firmly. 'You're going to have it, though. Sydney. Sweet Sydney. Gorgeous foul-mouthed abrasive Sydney. Darling, this is real for me. I mean this. I don't want it, it's a damned nuisance, but it's a fact.'

'I don't know what you are talking about.' My own voice was starting to shake. *Damn him!*

'Yes, you do. You are far too clever not to understand. I'm telling you, you damned bitch, I'm telling you I love you. I love you. I want to marry you. When this is over I'm going to do my damnedest to make you want to marry me. There now. I've never proposed before. I want you and I will have you.'

The silence went on and on. Finally, I said: 'This is a very unfunny joke.'

'This is no joke. I'm on my knees to you.'

He drew my head down with an effort because I held my neck stiff. His lips grazed mine. He touched my closed lips several times, sweetly, gently. Then he pressed harder. He began to open my mouth. His hand went up and he loosened my hair so that he held me in it, his hand over the back of my head. He held my face against his and he kissed me with passion and sincerity.

It felt sincere. How was I to know?'

I began to respond though my whole nature rebelled. This was wrong. I didn't want this. Men were a vice, like booze. The trick was to have the vice, not let it have you.

He broke the kisses and dropped his face into my breasts, nuzzling my cleavage. His warm breath flooded me. I sat doing nothing, my arms lightly on him, my senses unable to react.

He did up my shirt again and then stood. He lifted me and held me against his body. His lips were close to my ear and when he spoke, my hair was ruffled.

'We will find Vilcabamba now Carla knows the way,' he said. 'I'll do what she wants me to do, though I don't think it has anything to do with the mask. I think the poor girl just lusts for me and knows she can't get me any other way.'

My feelings entirely, buster, I thought.

'Then, when this is over, I'm going to get back into civilisation with you and court you, for want of a better word. Pester you, maybe, if you continue to resist me. I have the strangest old-fashioned feelings about wanting to prove I can support you, that I can give you something. But Vilcabamba will make me. You must understand that. As an archaeologist, this will be the peak of my career and it will keep me from now on. You will do as you please, of course. But I tell you, Sydney Johnson, I want with you what I have never wanted before. Stability. A shared life. Babies.'

I broke from him. 'I can't handle this,' I said.

He laughed delightedly and released me. 'Of

course not, darling, or you aren't the sort of girl I took you for. But let the idea grow on you. Think about it. I'm at your feet. I'm putty in your hands. You can tread on me and I'll lie on my back with my paws in the air and beg for more.'

'That's disgusting.'

'For two pins I'd club you over the head and haul you off to my cave and take you by force. I'm going to have you, whatever it takes. You can come protesting or you can come gracefully. It makes no difference in the long run.'

'I don't see,' I said feebly, 'why you are coming out with all this now.'

'Because I'll burst if I don't say it. Because I'm staking a claim. I know I've hit pay-dirt and no one else is going to get it. Because Matheson is running a campaign with you against me and I know you listen to him.'

'I don't like the man.'

'Sex isn't to do with liking. The man is clever and he wants your body and he doesn't like me.'

'He doesn't like me.'

'There you go,' said Rory softly. 'That's what I'm afraid of. You're gullible with him. He might say that because he senses you recognise he's a shit. But the man is crazed for you. I can't blame him. I'm in the same state myself. Most curiously, I'm being honourable for once. Not my style at all, Sydney. All I can say is that he is offering a bit of ham-fisted screwing. I want to make love to you for as many years as you'll permit me. Maybe the difference doesn't seem so much to you. But I'm begging you here. Don't take the cheap poke he offers. He's a bloodsucker. A base coin.'

Rory sank to his feet and bit the front of my trousers so that I felt a sexual jolt go through me. 'I don't want him here,' he said. 'I won't be responsible for my behaviour if you let him. He's croc meat, Sydney. Carrion. Don't let his flesh enter yours. Please.'

We got back to the others somehow. I wanted to be alone in my hammock, furled in my mosquito net. I was on overload, emotionally-speaking. And physically. And I was afraid. Afraid of Vilcabamba.

I went to sleep that way but I slept heavily, in considerable comfort now I was strung up again. I could see why these hammocks were absolutely the way to be in this part of the world. You could lie in them and watch the leaf-cutter ants tramping past with their little flakes of leaf in all kinds of weird geometrical shapes. You could watch the vicious biting ants out foraging, the army ants, the veinte-cuatro whose bite lasted an agonising twenty-four hours, and all the other kinds. I was fast becoming an ant expert here, a useless qualification back home in Wapping. You could watch the termites, the scorpions, the lizards, the tree frogs (apparently they live in the trees because the Amazon and tributaries are so infested with carnivorous fish that the frogs have got the hell out of it) and even, I suppose, the snakes, in comparative safety. A hammock is just the business when every solid surface around you is coated thickly with animals who consider you as prey.

This deep and relaxing sleep changed things for me some. I stopped being frightened about the mountain, Cloud-maker, now permanently a piece of my past. I put the truly weird man-situation on hold. Sydney knows when to sit back and let events slog it out around her. And I began to lust after Vilcabamba myself.

I knew where it was. So did Carla, it seemed. Only, no one knew I knew and that was just the way I

200

intended to keep things. I had no edge on the situation I found myself in, a naked and uncomfortable situation, except this one piece of knowledge. I was going to keep it very private.

Vilcabamba. The last Inca stronghold. Where they were reputed to have buried or hidden their treasure, such that they had saved from the rapacity of the Spanish. There had been various expeditions throughout the last three hundred years to identify the ruins positively but no one was sure. It might have been Machu Picchu, or Vitcos, or Espíritu Pampa – all these places had their expert adherents but no one had found the treasure. If it existed.

We were gong to find it. Common sense told me we would be just one more crazy bunch asserting we 'knew', and no one was going to take any notice of the mask, but for the moment I was blinded by the thought of fabulous golden artefacts set with precious stones. That would be the proof, of course. None of the treasure would come to me personally and I had no desire to be rich as long as I could work and have fun. But finding the treasure would tell the world we had it right and everyone else was wrong.

I wanted that. Not just for Martha's sake. Not for Rory's sake, though he was attempting to tie his future to mine. No, it was for my own sake. When else would I go treasure hunting? This was a unique event in my life. I wanted it to end good.

We came back to the boats and Pablo, waiting patiently for us, on the following day. We all exchanged excited greetings. Early the following morning we would be off. We wanted speed now.

We knew where we were going.

We had three days in the boats, chugging against the increasingly turbulent stream. We were closer to the

201

mountains that bred this great river and all its little sisters. We were close to the borders of Peru now, a long way south and west of Manaus.

Before us lay the Andes. In geological terms they were babies, a mere fifteen million years old. Originally the Amazon basin had drained into the Pacific. The Andes, made from crustal plate sinking under the continent of South America down the Pacific seaboard, making as a knock-on effect the volcanoes that were the mountains, had turned the rivers round and pushed them out into the Atlantic after a period of being a vast inland sea trapping primitive marine dolphins and manatees and all those horrible fish, and giving them time to evolve into fresh-water versions. That was the history of the place in a nutshell.

Now we were done with the boats for the second time and I was damned sorry. It was the way to travel despite the flies, wasps, crocs and piranhas. The birds were great, I had to admit it, from the marvellous hummingbirds right up to the absurd toucans. I had even seen some monkeys now, the long skinny-limbed spider monkeys, the red howler monkeys, the squirrel monkeys – there were other kinds and I had to struggle against becoming an expert.

I saw mud-banks impregnated with salt, covered with scarlet macaws and thousands of green butter-flies attracted to the mineral. I saw the beaches in the river thick with vast blue butterflies or littered with the huge evil bodies of the caymans. I saw too much, it was too hungry, too desperate to live, too alien to me, too keen to eat me, but the place was getting under my skin. It ravished me, even as I hated it and feared it. I was on sensory glut suspended above the coffee-brown waters, swaying in my hammock while Pablo guided us nearer and nearer to our goal.

All the time Margie made a quiet and dignified play for Matheson. I think he responded. I didn't care. I wrote up some notes, read them and tore them up. I would write this afterwards. At the time it was too much.

Carla set herself up like some kind of figurehead in the lead boat. When the moment came to abandon the river, I was ready.

After all, I knew. I knew every bit as much as Carla. I knew where Vilcabamba was. The knowledge, gained with pain, lay warm in me and fertile, ready to grow as the time for its use arrived.

This was to be no two-day walk into the jungle. We would be away from the river for maybe a couple of weeks or more. We had to back-pack everything with no Pablo to help because his duty was primarily to the boats.

Come the time to set off I was equal parts fear and anticipation. The jungle frightened me. My companions frightened me too, all bound up with the lust for glory and underpinned with hot sexual currents that weren't healthy in a company such as ours. Most of all I was frightened of myself. This wasn't the me I knew, I understood. I was behaving out of character, which might be due solely to my extraordinary environment or it might, on the other hand, be because of that damned mask.

Then there was Rory, ever attentive to Carla. Sometimes he met my eyes and then he would smile at me, intimate, aware, possessive. I should have hated it. Instead, I was passive, receiving through my antennae but not sending any signals if I could help it. It wasn't so bad having such a panther of a man bound to me by golden chains, but I wasn't sure I could control the beast if he got a little out of hand.

Did I want to? Any relationship worth a damn has

tension in it. Rory Duncan was no peaceful homecoming to love in the sunset. He was offering fire and passion and difficulty. It was up to me what I did about it, and I think the man laughed inside himself, watching me struggle with his proposition. His proposal.

His arrogance, his confidence in himself licked my soul like a man licks the vulva of a woman he craves for. It made me hot and lusty, swirling with dark thoughts.

I kept these dark thoughts to myself, naturally enough. The truth was, I wanted marriage like I wanted backache. The proposal left me amazed but emotionally cold. What was getting to me was the desire under the proposal, the lust for me that had moved such an obvious non-marrier to change his spots.

I wanted to tap that lust and I wanted the tap fully turned on. These little dips in the jungle away from prying eyes were almost worse than useless. I wanted a fortnight in satin sheets while we screwed ourselves into exhaustion using every sexual permutation the pair of us would tolerate. I didn't just want him in me, I wanted to be in him tearing a glut of sensual pleasure from his strong-limbed beautiful body. I wanted to be croaking and sweaty, star-fished on a bed with him hung over me, feeding off me and rousing me to new excesses. I wanted to wake feeling his cock thick in my backside and for me to fall asleep again with him still jerking beyond thought, beyond sense, beyond reason.

Then I would be purged and my own self again, free of him and my lust for him and ready to get on with my life. There was no room in my life for a partner and I would not and could not share how I ran things. I had plenty of men friends, I had no hang-ups about working with male colleagues and I only took male lovers, but a lover need be neither a friend nor a colleague.

I wanted Rory as a lover, an inspired and inspiring lover, but as nothing else. It would be nice, very nice, to manage this before leaving South America. Though I found it hard to take his proposal seriously, if he meant it I had a tiger by the tail and it might be better to resolve things this side of the globe than in my own familiar quadrant.

Meanwhile, I had to admit that penetration was on my mind. We left the boats to penetrate the trackless, dark, thickly-humid jungle, maybe stepping where no human had set foot before.

We were going to penetrate the secret of Vilcabamba. I believed that totally and I believed the secret was complex and at least in part, dangerous.

And of course, I thought about male penetration of female orifices. I thought about Rory, my self-confessed lover, penetrating Carla and submitting to her strange commands. I thought about Matheson poking Margie when maybe it was me he wanted, if Rory had the rights of it. I thought about Martha pandering her daughter-substitute to the man she wanted herself, to get what she wanted. Vilcabamba.

We were a hell of a sick bunch when you thought about it. Maybe we were treasure crazed. None of us was poor, but the gold glittered through the green gloom, enticing us forward, demanding we respond.

So we did.

I worried about Indians. Tribes had lived here since the great migration of peoples across the Bering Strait and down through Alaska, Canada, North America and South America. Maybe no particular piece of ground I set foot on had been trodden before by a human, but the land was not entirely uninhabited and they had never taken kindly to foreign intervention here. the Incas had tried and failed. The Spanish had tried and failed. The modern governments had tried and failed. The Indians stayed hidden or they died. There were people ancient and modern failing to live alongside each other here in the rain forest. Modern man predated on the forests, logging, slashing and burning, mining and filling the rivers with toxic mercury. For the most part the Indians suffered and died, few being assimilated. You could harldly blame them for using their blow-pipes with curare-tipped darts, but I didn't want to carry the can for man's beastliness to man.

Colin laughed at me like I was a dumb bimbo scared of spiders. No one seemed to have told him the spiders in these parts dined on fair-sized birds. That's what I didn't like about the place. All the familiar things I knew and didn't fear, ants, fish, spiders, lizards, had massive proportions here, voracious appetites and venom sacs frequently as designer accessories.

We saw no Indians though, and if they saw us they weren't letting on. We continued to walk through the endless trees in the oppressive damp heat, two men in front always slashing our way through, Carla stalking regally behind them to direct our path.

She had the direction right. I didn't need a compass. Vilcabamba was calling me and I faced it like it was Mecca.

I didn't like the call. It was wrong, very wrong. I didn't believe in the supernatural, I didn't believe in non-rational explanations.

But that damned city in the jungle called me and I answered, inching closer and closer over the ball of the planet, day by day.

I told no one.

One night Martha said: 'How close are we, honey?' to Carla.

Carla turned to her with a face so suffused with smug superiority I could have smacked her. 'We're closer, Martha, closer. Can't you feel it. It rings in me like a bell, like a sweet, silver bell.'

I snarled *sotto voce*. Pretentious cow.

'How long before we get there?' said Martha.

Carla closed her eyes and swayed esoterically. I yawned. Carla lifted her hands and sort of drew her fingers apart across her face. 'I can't tell,' she said in a high voice. 'The veil is too thick.'

I couldn't tell either but veils didn't come into it.

Rory watched her through slitted eyes. It occurred to me he looked more like an exploiter than a lover. Matheson watched too but I could tell he only half-believed she knew the way. Big Jacko watched with concern, he was genuinely fond of the girl, I think, and unhappy about how she was being used both by the mask and by Rory. Colin kept himself to himself as usual, his thought processes private.

Margie watched Matheson. She had become sallow and tired-looking. It was in this state of mutual discomfort that on the following day Rory slashed with his machete through one of the long, conical, hanging wasp nests.

We had met these on the river. The wasps, if disturbed, flew out and attacked savagely. It was true that a wasp sting wasn't near as bad as a hornet's, but there were always more wasps than hornets, though with care they could be avoided.

Rory had failed to see this nest in the greenery. His machete chopped into it and immediately the air was filled with a furious buzzing, stinging riot.

We were too well trained to scream. No one was

fool enough to open his or her mouth. But we scattered at incredible speed hoping someone else would bear the brunt of the attack. I crashed solo through undergrowth and found myself at the top of a steep slope. At full speed I hurtled down it. It became a mud bank before I could stop myself and I went over.

A moment later I hit flat ground. It was not painful. It was positively comfortable in its way. I hit it full force and struggled upright.

Upright. Upright and with half my body underground. A hysterical bubble rose in my throat. It was a quagmire. A swamp. I had fallen into a bog, I was on my own and I was sinking.

Sense returned. I struggled out of my heavy pack and tossed it awkwardly the few yards to where the undergrowth began again. Then I fixed my hat more firmly to my head and tried to walk through the gloop till I could grab a branch.

No dice. The effort of trying to push a foot forward or lift it up sucked me further down. Moreover, a fat bubble of nauseous gas plopped evilly up beside me and burst.

Within the space of several minutes I sank from my thighs to my waist.

'Hey, lady,' I said out loud to myslf. 'You don't go this way. A mugger, maybe. A car accident. Even a plane crash. But alone in an Amazonian swamp, no chance. This isn't in your stars. You are urban born and you will die urban. This is not the death for you.'

I sank to rib level. I began to scream for help. I had five, ten minutes at the most. It was a disgusting death. I would rather be eaten by crocs or bitten by a snake. At least that was animal against animal. Was I to be snuffed out by wet leaf-mould? It couldn't happen.

I screamed as high and as piercingly as I could. They couldn't be far, the bastards. I hadn't gone far. They had to be within earshot.

I screamed and the soft red mud bank absorbed my screams. The thick, choking greenery embraced the noise I made and rendered it douce and ineffectual. The canopy was low here with many trees uprooted and broken by storms admitting far more light than was usual. A morpho butterfly, huge and spectacular in glorious iridescent blue fluttered over the quag and I reached for it, as if its fragile beauty could haul me upwards and transport me into a safe situation.

I was in up to my armpits and I sobbed. My throat hurt.

'There you are,' said a cross voice.

'Please,' I begged, the word dragged out by my sobbing.

'I'm coming as fast as I can.'

I opened my eyes feeling my cheeks wet with tears and my upper lip all snottered with fear. Matheson was sitting grumpily tying himself with vines. Then he threw one to me.

I caught it easily. He hauled and I went face forward into the muck.

I floundered upright. I was no nearer safety. I began to moan hopelessly.

'It's damn sticky,' said Matheson.

'May you rot in hell,' I hissed. The incompetent was going to let me die.

Matheson played boy scout with his knots some more while my elbows sunk in. Then he leaned himself out over the innocent leaf-litter surface and reached for my hands.

We connected. Our hands grasped. He was lying belly down in the swamp holding my hands at full stretch, tied to terra firma by jungle creepers.

He lifted his face and stared into mine. 'I can't pull you in this position. Can you pull yourself up me?' He was grunting with the effort of speaking.

I clawed up his shirt-sleeve. The strong jungle-quality material didn't give. I came very slightly closer to him till our faces, smeared with swamp mud, were side by side. His got pushed in a couple of times but he heaved it up again.

For a moment we rested. We were like strange lovers. I held one shirt-sleeve by the elbow, my face on his shoulder, upright in the swamp, my other arm round him. His two arms were round me under my armpits, his face against mine, flat on the surface.

'You'll have to crawl along me,' he said.

'I'll push your face in.'

'I can keep it up for a bit.'

I drew breath and lunged for his trouser belt. His whole upper body sank but mine came up some till I was angled steeply, heading for safety.

Beside me he wallowed desperately, rolling onto his back and breaking my grip and then doubling his body till he sat in the swamp with his head up.

He gripped the ropes, bunching himself. 'You bitch,' he said hoarsely. 'You'll kill us both.'

I gripped his knees. Then I reached one hand back and he took it, pulling himself towards me. I pulled on his knees and one of the creepers tying us to the bank broke.

We were both, quite literally, in up to our necks. The remaining creepers were tied round his waist under the surface. He began to fish for them with his hands, letting go of me.

My chin touched swamp and my head shot back. I scrabbled for him and hit him in the face. He beat my hands away. 'Let me get the rope,' he yelled.

The mud filled my ears. 'I know where Vilcabamba is,' I said. 'The mask told me.'

My hat sat a yard away, neat and absurd. There was mud on my cheek-bones. I looked up and saw glimpses of the sky, soft and blue, in the low, broken canopy.

Matheson's arm came round under my shoulders and forced my entire body strongly upwards. I was clear to my neck once more.

I kept quite passive. He was upright himself, hauling with one hand on the creepers and holding me with the other. I saw the muscles knot and stand under the straining material of his shirt. Then he had purchase with his feet. His arm was round a root. He was pulling me up, my chest was free and then we were both on firm land, lying with me half on top of him.

Quite a long time went by, I think. Matheson said: 'That wasn't nice.'

I was mostly shut down in the mental sphere and didn't respond for a moment. His words percolated through me. A terrible trembling started and my fingers scrabbled at his chest. Shirt buttons had given way and I clawed feebly at his bare skin.

He laid a muddy hand on my muddy hair. 'I never thought to see you really scared,' he said. 'Not even in that ghastly pit. So this is the bugbear, is it? This has really got to you. Jeez, it has to be bad. I thought you *were* the swamp monster. It seems I got you wrong.'

I beat his chest and cried weak tears.

'There's water not far. Why don't we go and wash?'

'I can't stand up,' I sobbed.

'Sure you can, vulture lady. Just remember how much you hate me. That'll fire you up.'

I remembered and I crawled agonisingly to my

211

hands and knees. I felt like I'd played mattress to a herd of buffalo. Matheson got to his feet and hauled me upright, the muscles of my shoulders cracking with pain.

He cut through the creepers that had saved us and we plodded the short distance to a rocky outcrop in the mud bank I had fallen over. Water coursed clean and sweet, gathering in a small pool at the bottom. Matheson began to peel off his foul clothes. I stood leaning against a tree. I didn't have the energy to feel afraid I was butting in on a snake.

He stripped quite naked and put his swamp-plastered body under the water. He washed everything, his hair, his ears, round his cock, in the crack of his arse, down his legs and between his toes. When he was done he washed his clothes with the same meticulous care.

I stood and watched, leaning in exhaustion, both nervous and physical, against my tree.

The sun slanted in gold bars. Vast green leaves trembled. The water fell pure and sweet sounding. Matheson turned to me.

'You can't manage?' he asked.

I was miles away. I could see but I couldn't talk, I couldn't act. The naked man before me belonged in the deep stillness of a million trees. He reached out and took my flaccid hand. He drew me forward and removed the mud-stiffened layers from my filthy body with some difficulty. Then he put me into the cool water and washed me.

His hands were large and warm. I felt them in my hair and over my face, gently in my eye sockets, probingly in my ears. He washed my neck clean and my shoulders, his blunt thumbs in the delicate cups of flesh where bone and tendon shaped the architecture of my throat. He turned me, himself wet again, and washed down my back where it narrowed and hollowed into my waist. He washed each arm at a time, opening and separating my fingers, and then he came back to my body and took my heavy breasts in his hands where the water ran forward through courses of black mud and collected on my nipples, to drip from them. He washed the streaking mud away till my pale, smooth skin shone mother of pearl in the green and gold light of the late afternoon.

He said nothing. He washed my ribs and then he knelt in the water and I stood while warm hands stroked my buttocks open and fumbled gently with my anus. Clean hands came between my thighs and I felt fingers gentle and questing in my vulva, at my clitoris, in my vagina, taking the mud away. When he bent to wash my legs and my feet, I saw his wet, brown hair streaked gold and red and amber against my own wet, clean, curling fleece.

Salt tears ran slowly down my face washing minute particles of mud out from the corners of my eyes.

He moved me out of the water and washed my clothes as he had washed his own. Then he looked at me.

'We need to find the others,' he said. 'It'll be night soon.'

'*Forever*,' I whispered. It was my first word in an hour.

He moved against me, his dry, warm, naked body against my damp one. I wasn't cold. I had no feeling. I was numb.

He held my slack arms. We stood stiffly, chest to chest. 'Snap out of it,' he said roughly. 'You were scared. Now it's OK. Cut this out.'

'You were going to leave me there.' My voice was quiet, dead.

His grip tightened. He shook me. 'No,' he said. 'Never.'

I smiled.

He smacked my face suddenly. My head jerked but I didn't feel it. 'You've been poisoned,' he said. 'I can't get through to you.'

I snickered. 'Wanna fuck, big boy?'

He stepped away from me as if I burned him. I saw then he was erect, his penis standing out from his fluffy cloud of toffee-coloured hair. I turned round and leaned forward against the tree, straddling my legs and offering my sex to him like a monkey on heat.

'No,' he said but I could hear how he wanted it.

'Go on,' I encouraged. 'I have to say thank you somehow. Pop it in. Move it about. That's what you like, isn't it?'

He was up behind me, his body pressing against mine. I could feel the fat stalk of his sex bouncy against me. His hands came round to where my breasts hung and for a moment he let them fill his grasp, the nipples soft between his fingers.

He laid his cheek on my back. 'I want to kill you for this,' he said.

'You want to make it in me.'

'That too.'

'No one's stopping you. Either or both.'

Painfully, he turned me round. Now I leaned against the tree. His clubby penis was between my thighs, pressing upwards. 'Can't you, can't you be different?' he said, like it hurt to talk.

I rubbed my breasts against him. My nipples had darkened and come arect. 'When you buy sex,' I said softly, 'you can't expect it to come packaged with love. That's only for the movies. Hadn't you realised that?'

His face was lowered into my shoulder. 'I'm not going to do this,' he mumbled.

I felt his cock move. I squeezed my thighs slightly. 'Whatever you like.' I said, indifferently.

He put his face onto mine with his mouth open. I kept still. Tentatively he tried to kiss me. I did nothing. He drew his head back and for a moment his brown eyes looked into mine.

'You're dead,' he whispered.

'You've got it,' I agreed. 'Back there, when you let me go, I died.'

'No, Sydney. It wasn't like that.'

'Have women loved you?'

'Yes.'

'Does Margie?'

'I don't know.'

'You're like a shadow, a simulacrum. You look like a lovely man once lived in you. Did he go away, Tom, or was there never any substance to you?'

He left me then and dressed himself silently. I dressed myself too and we retrieved our packs before finding a way up the bank and back towards where we thought the others were.

It was strange they hadn't come to find us. Night was falling with deadly swiftness. We had no lamp with us, only our fading torches and some candles and matches. We had no gun either, only our knives and Tom's machete.

He made no suggestion we stopped and camped. It didn't matter if we failed to find the others, we had food in our packs and I knew the direction to go in. I think he was afraid to spend the night alone with me.

I wasn't afraid of him. How could a person, a human, make me afraid? It was the jungle that threatened, not tamed, not brought under control, not taught it was subject to almighty humanity and his beetling concerns.

The jungle could swallow us and not notice the difference. I was afraid of the jungle but I wasn't afraid of Tom Matheson.

Then we found them. We smelled the fire first, then we saw the glow making the forest leap and flare so that the trees became strange moving figures, animated alien shapes. Saying nothing to each other, what was there to say? We stumbled out of nightmare and back into our company of eight.

Martha thumped me happily and wrung Tom's hand. Margie hung onto him, her eyes red and swollen in the firelight. Big Jacko looked honestly happy. Colin nodded amiably and saw about some hot food for us.

Carla said: 'You were away a long time. Why were you away?'

'I fell in a swamp, a quagmire. I was sinking. I started screaming. Tom appeared and got me out. I was shell-shocked afterwards and we found some water and cleaned up. Then it took us a while to find you. No one come looking?'

'We decided to stay together,' said Martha. 'After the wasps it took us some time to gather. Then you were gone, Sydney, and Tom and Rory. Rory isn't with you?'

'No,' I said strangely. 'He's still gone, you say?'

Carla said: 'He serves the mask. I will not go forward without him.'

Tom looked at her like she was some new kind of insect.

'Balls,' I said crudely. I was suddenly full of anger, all the emotion I hadn't been able to feel over the past two to three hours curdling into a tight, hard knot inside me. 'The guy's lost. Bang off a few rounds.

Build up the fire. Burn the bloody mask. You say you know where Vilcabamba is. We don't need it any more.'

Tom looked at me.

Carla said: 'I do not want her along.' Her voice was high and mad.

'I told you it was bad for her,' I shouted to Martha. 'The kid's losing her marbles.'

'She's upset about Rory,' said Martha. 'She doesn't mean what she says.'

Margie put her arms tight round Tom. I could feel as if they were my arms how stiff he was, rejecting her. We were diseased. There was a disaster brewing here.

'Martha,' I said intensely. 'Give this up. We find Rory and go back to the boats, back to Manaus. Carla's going mad. Margie is desperate for Tom and he's playing her around. Rory is fucking anything on two legs and probably telling all of us how much he wants us. You can't see past the glory of finding Vilcabamba. You're obsessed with it beyond reason. Only Colin and Jacko have retained any sense here. Let's get out before one of us kills another. Before the jungle gets us all.'

The silence was stunned. We were a tableau in the firelight, the shadows it made dancing grim and mad between the twisted trees and strangling vines. Margie had released Tom, who stared at me. Carla was blazing. Jacko looked at his feet. Martha was open-mouthed.

Into our silence came the buzzing roar, increasing, unbearable, of a helicopter. The helicopter. I don't think one of us, for an instant, thought of it as anything but malignant.

That was strange, if you like. It shows how far gone we were.

'The fire,' said Martha jerkily.

'I want Rory,' squealed Carla.

Big Jacko picked up one of the rifles and shot the bolt.

I was to remember that as the most shocking thing of all.

The helicopter hovered over the trees. We saw its lights flashing though its shape was obscured by the forest heads.

At that moment Rory crashed into our circle. He grabbed a rifle and pointed it upwards. Then he fired.

Margie screamed and Martha clutched Rory's arm and jerked it before he loosed off a second shot. The helicopter rose slightly. Rory dropped to one knee and sighted upwards. He fired again, the noise a sharp crack over the roaring cacophony of the hovering craft.

The helicopter lifted and began to peel away into the night. Rory dropped the gun and wiped his face. He was filthy and sweating, his face grazed across one cheek.

It seemed to take us a long time to sort ourselves out. I ate, listening. I knew there was real trouble and I was in the care and protection of madmen. I needed to keep my strength up. I might yet have to survive alone.

Rory told us he had been wandering about, lost, thinking of camping for the night when he first heard the helicopter. After that he had trailed it as it quested over the trees. It had been using a searchlight and once he had been caught in the beam. They had shot at him then, grazing his cheek.

He ate hungrily. Then he lay on his back and let Carla hang over him, tending his cheek. She acted like I didn't exist but Martha knew there was unfinished business.

Margie came up to me and spoke low. 'I didn't take you for this, Sydney,' she said.

'I can't help it.' I was weary. 'Look around you. We aren't healthy. We need to get back to civilisation. We don't belong here and it's corrupting us.'

'We're walking through a jungle. Don't mythologise this. Something very basic is going on. I don't think you are nice at all.'

'I don't want the man,' I snarled. 'Have him. He evidently likes you but he's a shit. You care for a shit. That's your look-out, Margie, you run your life your way. But this jungle isn't healthy and both Tom and Rory are playing games with us ladies. Can't you see it?'

'I see what Rory Duncan is. I don't care. He leaves me alone. Carla can look out for herself. She's got Martha and Jacko looking over her and she's a rich little girl so there are phalanxes of lawyers back home in New York as well. It's you, Sydney. It's you stirring the men up. It's you competing. It's you threatening everything. You don't want them for yourself, you won't give them satisfaction, but you won't send them away either. A man needs to know where he is. You give your body and some kindness or you make sure they know there's nothing doing. Has no one ever taught you that? You can't behave, Sydney. You're an alley-cat.'

I closed my eyes. 'Tom has just saved my life, late and reluctant though he was. I can't argue with that. I'd have let the Angel of Mons pick me out of that swamp. I do not want his body.'

She was really close now, almost spitting in my ear. 'You've had him and you aren't bothered any more, is that it? One more conquest. Who are you after now? Colin? Jacko? Pablo?'

'Have you slept with him?' I asked conversationally.

'Yes. It was wonderful. He's a wonderful lover with a woman who cares, who responds, who has something to give. You're a vampire, a succubus.'

'So what are you worried about? He's wonderful. You respond. Sunset and roses, isn't it? He thinks I'm a dung beetle, you know.'

'He admires your strength.'

'My resistance, you mean.' I saw she was crying. It was time for some dishonesty. 'Wise up, Margie,' I said. 'He's trying to make you jealous. There's nothing between us. We don't screw. Do it how the man likes it if that's your bag, but don't take out his failures on me. I screw men like I eat hamburgers, to fill an empty place. Tom knows that and feels insulted. He's punishing you because his ego has been dented. He's not worth a decent girl like you, but if you stop dancing to his tune he might act a bit nicer.'

'We aren't all cold inside,' said Margie, tossing her curls like a heroine in a penny novelette. It was an exit line and blessedly she left me.

Rory lay with his head in Carla's lap. 'It's them, Martha. They're trailing us to Vilcabamba.'

Tom's voice was prosaic. 'How do they know we know the way?'

'They knew about the mask,' said Rory. 'Carl let that much out before he realised the significance of the thing.'

'Who are they?' I asked. Just because I was newly elected leper of the party I didn't see why I shouldn't know who might be shooting at me.

Rory drew breath and then hesitated. Carla stroked his brow. It was nauseating. Rory looked at Martha and she nodded, looking strained and tired herself now.

'It's a businessman in Paraguay. Nominally he's a businessman. He trades in arms, at any rate, that I do know. He has this vast estate with a private army on it in the hills back of Asunción. Well, Asunción's in a swamp, really. This man has a higher bit.'

'What's his name?' I asked, the journalist in me struggling briefly to make a reappearance.

'Mendes. They just call him Mendes. No one ever seems to see him though they say he likes to interfere in his businesses and run them hands on. There's some mystery about him, manufactured to create fear, I should think. No one knows where he's come from, who his family is, how old he is, how rich he is.'

'What's he care about Vilcabamba? It sounds small beer compared with international business and gun running.'

My voice was unemphatic. The rat I smelt was huge.

Colin and Rory looked at each other. Then they looked at Martha. 'Honey,' she said. 'You haven't got this at all, have you?'

'I deputised for Carl, under threat of dismissal, hours before he was due to fly to Miami,' I said. 'I did no reading, no research in this area. My editor told me none of that was necessary. I could write about the rain forest as a non-specialist, without all the background information, just like, quotes, an ordinary member of the public, unquotes.' My voice was very dry. 'I didn't want to come. I threatened to resign. I don't want to be here. I don't like travel even as far as Wapping where I work, let alone across the globe. In the circumstances I think I've behaved very well. I don't complain about being bitten, stung, attacked and nearly drowned. I do not belong here and I don't pretend any different. To add to my troubles, I mean the troubles of not belonging here, not wanting to be here and having an editor who needs a new brain, I find there's a conspiracy going on. We aren't here to snap the bird life and have an eco-experience. I'm in the middle of a bunch of screwballs chasing lost cities and treasure like we were a second-rate Hollywood movie. In addition we have a helicopter gunship with a crazed Paraguayan madman aboard shooting at us. I think the mask is sick, I think Carla's losing her marbles, I don't like the sexual undertones of this trip but I'm stuck with you all. For two pins I'd walk back to Pablo and wait till you all get back, or not as the case may be, but I kind of took a shine to Martha and if she wants me along as an independent witness, I'll come. I think we'll find some ruins, yeah. So what? There isn't going to be any treasure. Can't any of you see that? It's a dream. Wake up, kids. Get your heads straight. Before we all get killed.'

I had not raised my voice but my audience held completely still, listening to me. When I was done, Rory began to speak.

'There is the solid gold statue of Viracocha, some fifteen inches tall, taken from Pachacamac before the Spanish got there and hidden by the priests thereafter. There is the sun image, Punchao, meaning daylight or dawn. This is described in contemporary accounts as being of great size, beautifully made in gold and impregnated with precious stones. The Spanish lost track of it, it was never melted down. There is Coricancha, the garden of the Temple of the Sun in Cuzco, with full size golden ears of maize on silver stems. There is real doubt it was lost to the Spanish now. There is a full-sized effigy in gold of the first Inca, Manco Capac, with a gold and silver banquet; crayfish, snakes, all the animals they ate. There are sentries in gold; vicuña, llama, alpaca. All this exists, Sydney. It's somewhere. The most reasonable place for it to be is Vilcabamba, probably hidden in the silver mines they dug near there. Even if one piece is found, its worth is unimaginable both in real terms, in the weight of gold contained in it, and in archaeological terms, as lost artefacts of the most superb goldsmiths the world has ever known. Against Vilcabamba, Sutton Hoo is a wart on the face of Everest. We are trembling on the biggest find ever, a slice of documented history missing for four hundred years. We might look a tacky bunch to you, Sydney, but if this expedition, Martha's expedition with all the clout of the Turner Trust ready to line up behind it, is successful, we will all be in the history books for ever. This isn't Tutankhamen, Sydney. That was small. This is big. This is billion-dollar stuff. If it's in Brazil, they could pay off their international debt with it. It shouldn't be bought and sold, of course. It mustn't fall into private hands. I'm sorry you don't believe us, I'm sorry you can't see the glittering prize that is almost in our grasp. Of course Carla is dazed with it all. She knows where it is. As to what else you said, that's your poroblem, not ours. We're OK. We're holding things together. The problem we have now is to throw Mendes off the track and find Vilcabamba. That's what we should be discussing here. Really, what you say is an irrelevance.'

I had nothing to say. There was nothing I could say. It could all be true. Meanwhile, I had offended most of them and was close to being *persona non grata*.

I felt very lonely in my hammock but that wasn't so bad. I don't rely on other people very much, not for what I think and how I go on. Causing offence is

223

second nature to me and I'm uneasy if all my company like me. I wouldn't want to lose the edge.

I was lonely because the environment was wrong; this jungle, Mendes, guns, treasure. It wasn't me. It didn't fire me up. I didn't belong.

I lay listening to them discussing ways of travel that would not reveal our presence from above. I had already thought the helicopter could have dropped off a small platoon of gun-hungry goons to follow us on the ground, but it took them an hour to get around to discussing the possibility.

Carla kept Rory's head possessively in her lap, stroking his hair and his forehead in a nauseous manner. Margie hung affectionately on Tom who ignored her and spent the evening in silence fiddling with his cameras.

We didn't hear the helicopter again that night but I felt its sinister presence like a great bug hanging over me. Oppressive was the word, and it was an understatement.

So the others thought nothing of the internal currents operating in our group. I disagreed. There was trouble ahead and we were a divided house.

One other little problem stuck in my craw. We were out in the wilderness in a fertile desert of millions of trees.

So how the hell did the helicopter know where to find us? I didn't hear the others discussing it and I didn't say anything myself. But in my cynical eyes we had a traitor along.

Now who could that be?

Chapter Seven

*P*rogress was slow, the vegetation thick, impenetrable sometimes, so that the men had to work in a gang, attacking the stranglehold of gnarled roots, vines and strange plants that even Colin sometimes had trouble identifying.

For three days we made hardly any progress at all, covering less than five hundred yards. Tempers frayed, suspicion as to the identity of the traitor took up most of our thinking time. Mostly though we were too damned tired to think overmuch at all.

I leaned back into a tree trunk, almost asleep on my feet, the humidity of the rain-forest floor draining me. I thought it would be just my luck to go down with malaria as well; the bugs seemed to flock to me whilst totally ignoring the likes of Martha and Big Jacko.

I watched Tom, my tormentor, as Martha sagged beside me into the cushion of greenery, oblivious to the ants, took out her canteen and drank sparingly, mopping her brow with a dampened handkerchief. Her face was pink with the heat, like my own, damp, hot, her features drawn with fatigue. She watched him, too, though not covetously. Rory was her man of the moment. Not exclusively, of course, but that didn't seem to bother her.

'Neat ass, huh?'

I nodded faintly, begrudgingly, watching Tom. 'I suppose so.'

'Strong too.'

'Um.' I watched him, sweat stained, hair slicked back, his chin covered in spiky stubble that was several days old. Physically, he out-laboured them all.

We all stank just a little now, hadn't found a fresh water source for several days. We carried our drinking water with us, a very precious commodity.

Matheson hacked and pulled, dragging the vines sideways off the path we cleared, always after hourly checks with Carla to make sure we were on course. We were, I knew, but there was no way that I was letting on to all and sundry that she wasn't the only one with weird powers. I didn't want demands made upon me, was determined that the mask shouldn't take me over the way it had Carla. She was not a better person for the experience. In fact she was a major pain in the arse, a slightly crazed prima donna with a stupendous ego. I kept out of her way just in case I gave in to my instincts and slapped her around a little bit; that wouldn't have gone down very well with my fellow travellers who seemed to want to humour her no matter what. I'd already blotted my copy-book by calling into question the very reason for this, as I saw it, foolhardy expedition.

I kept to myself and so did everyone else. And that wasn't altogether healthy either. I'd seen Humphrey Bogart and Walter Houston in *The Treasure of the Sierra Madre* more than once, knew what the prospect of unimaginable wealth did to people's minds. They became paranoid, suspecting everyone around them of coveting their portion, plotting to cheat them out of it, kill them for it. Maybe I was being alarmist, but somehow I don't think so. For myself, I didn't believe there was going to be any crock of gold at the end of our particular rainbow. It was a gut feeling.

When night fell the nocturnal beasties came forth, flying and biting, slithering and squeezing. The noise they made was all around us and above. I needed ear-plugs.

We tried to sleep, recharge our batteries, but it was difficult to get comfortable and the jungle noises were too loud, even with the improvisation of cotton wool in our ears.

I sighed heavily, exasperated, turning this way and that, tried to ignore those around me. Oh how I missed Brixton and Wapping, celebrity stake-outs and dustbin searches for info, doorstep sieges on dis-graced MPs or High Court judges. There I came into my own. Here I was lost, overwhelmed, my news-hound instincts buried beneath anti-bug cream and the need for self-preservation. What am I doing here? I want to go home. I felt like indulging in a bout of snivelling, but wouldn't let myself, for Matheson was too close, was, I'm sure, watching me surreptitiously. I couldn't give him the satisfaction of seeing me in less than total command of myself – smarmy, ugly bastard. I turned again, presenting him with the back of my head.

Someone screamed. I think it was Martha. I didn't go in for that kind of thing. We all jumped about in alarm. All, that is, except Big Jacko who was clutching at a feathered dart protruding from his neck. He gave a strangled cry then went down heavily, like a tran-quillised elephant.

Carla shrieked, 'Indians.' And we all scattered.

My heart thudded, blood pounded up past my ears, my lungs felt as if they would explode, as I struggled, stumbling and falling more than actually running, scrambling behind Colin. I was certain he had no idea where he was going, any more than I did. This was blind panic. I hadn't even seen an Indian, only had Carla's word for it. Feeling, suddenly, like a complete idiot, I slowed, tried to be rational.

I called ahead, voice no more than a whisper. 'Colin, where are you?' There was no reply. 'Colin?' I creeped forward, thinking it made more sense if we stayed together, even if our witless flight meant we no longer knew where we were.

I pulled aside the fronds of a giant fern and spied furtively between, seeing Colin ahead of me in a rocky clearing where the jungle hadn't been able as yet to take a complete hold. My whole body relaxed with relief and I started forward. Then stopped dead.

What at first appeared dense vegetation began to move before my very eyes, showing, when seen against the stony background, the shapes of men, bodies daubed, green and grey . . . the Indians. I held my breath. Hiding behind the giant fern I crouched fearfully, biting my nails.

There were still several Indian tribes in the upper reaches of the Amazon, so Rory had said only yesterday, as if it were gospel, who had never seen white men, were completely untouched by civilisation. And there were the odd expeditions who lost contact with the outside world and were never heard of again. Just our luck.

Poor Colin. They were going to kill him. It was obvious. I didn't want to watch, scared of what I might see, scared that they'd see me, that I'd be caught, wouldn't be able to save my own skin. Even then I didn't give much for my chances. This was their forest. I certainly didn't belong. They were invisible, while I, I didn't doubt, stood out like the proverbial sore thumb.

I crouched low, hardly daring to breathe, watched the drama unfold in the clearing. It was dark now and the greens were deepening to greys and blacks, but a moon was beaming down through the gap in the trees, a strong shaft of light silvering all.

Colin had tried to flee, had been quickly caught and manhandled. The natives clustered around him, poking and prodding, tearing his clothes away. Colin looked pale and slim, moonlight whitening his flesh still further – a somewhat frail, almost delicate, man. He must have known he was done for, didn't even bother to fight against the many arms and hands of his captors. They were seven in all. They led him away.

Scared witless though I was, I knew I had to follow at a distance, see what became of him, and if indeed it was possible, somehow, to save him. If I found my way back to the others perhaps I could get help.

More unseen beasties gobbled, chittered, shrieked and howled. The um um um ooh ah bird called raucously.

Their makeshift camp was small, little more than a cleared area around a cooking fire. They prodded the naked Colin into the clearing, chattered amongst themselves with much gesticulation and eloquent looks.

Colin knelt where they'd shoved him, in the trampled undergrowth. I'd always thought him harmless and sort of boring, a man for whom zoology and botany were the main delights. Now, as I watched, feeling like snivelling again but not daring to, I reappraised the man, decided that he was acting far

229

more bravely than I could ever have imagined. My heart went out to him.

The group of Indians were all male, young and agile, a hunting party. On the outer perimeter of their cooking fire where the ashes were barbeque hot, they placed several fresh fish wrapped in vine leaves.

While these cooked they produced leather water-bags and proceeded to drink, even, to my utter surprise, offering Colin their refreshments. He sipped, found it pleasant, obviously, and took a deeper gulp, saying 'thank you' politely and making a point of smiling friendly-like. So like Colin. He was no anthropologist but it was clear that he found them fascinating.

One of the Indians, with dead straight raven hair, and golden ear circlets, smoothed the white flesh on Colin's shoulder, wonderingly. He might well have been their very first white man. Whatever, they were treating him with some deference, hadn't filled him full of poisoned darts as I'd fully expected.

I was on the opposite side of the camp to him, knew that I couldn't circumvent swiftly and silently. I could either move fast and noisy or dead slow and, hopefully, silent. I chose the latter, being no hero, keeping my eye on the picnic party all the time.

They ate, offering fish to Colin. He graciously accepted, throwing the burning-hot food from palm to palm until it cooled. They laughed, showing rows of dazzling white teeth. My stomach growled. Replete, they lazed about a while, belching and casting curious eyes over their unexpected catch, then some slept, curling close to neighbours for warmth, and others coaxed companions to get on their hands and knees so they might mount them in a no-fuss manner and find quick relief for their sexual urges.

I paused to watch, as goggle-eyed as Colin. They

were nicely hung, generously endowed, sliding easily into bottoms that were evidently thus accommodating on an easy, regular basis. The fact that Colin was impressed and excited became pretty obvious when he took up the hands and knees position himself with his cock sticking out rigidly. The Indians nudged each other, pleased by such actions, laughing low. One of them positioned himself before Colin, his rear in the air, his legs wide, his bottom muscles contracting and relaxing playfully. Colin fell upon him greedily, touching the buttocks, inserting a fingertip into the native's anus. The rear wriggled about, enticing, his wishes clear. The scholarly, serious young white-man took the native by the hip and eased into him, looking down and seeing himself buried to the hilt. The Indian pushed back against him, obviously delighted, and Colin began to pump, hurriedly, greedily, like a man too long denied.

I knew how he felt. He'd been watching and desiring Rory for days, seeing him with Carla, wanting him himself, craving his tight little hole. But Rory was calculating and manipulative, wouldn't screw or be screwed by anyone for no good reason. Everything he did had a purpose.

Colin came with a joyous cry, his pent up longings satisfied, his soft penis slipping out of the fleshy passage. He stayed on his hands and knees, panting heavily, a smile on his face.

The Indian who had offered himself to the white-man now moved around behind, sporting, I noticed and becoming wet myself, the most impressive erection. It was fat and at least nine inches. He caught Colin by the hips and filled him without preamble, thrusting swiftly towards relief. Colin looked to be in Blissville, his rear held high, his face radiant. He issued a never-ending stream of appreciative 'ah's'.

When all thirsts, appetites and sexual desires were sated, the group fell asleep, Colin too. I couldn't believe it; I was scared witless myself while he, apparently, had nerves of steel, and slumbered like a babe.

I worked my way around to him, the procedure taking another half an hour at least, every footfall taken with the greatest care. I called softly, voice trembling with fear.

'Colin?'

Nothing. He didn't even stir.

'Colin?'

One of the Indians stirred instead, tickled the tip of his brown nose and was still again.

'Colin!'' My whisper was more insistent this time.

He opened one eye, then his mouth, looked as if he was about to speak. I put a finger to my lips fearfully, warning him to be quiet.

I beckoned him with a hand signal, mouthing the words silently. 'Come on, we can escape.'

But he shook his head. 'No. I want to stay.'

I shook my head in consternation. The man was mad. 'You can't. They'll kill you.'

'Maybe. Maybe not.'

My head was still shaking, though now with disbelief. 'Why?'

'I can't explain. You go. Find the others. Forget me.'

'You fool.'

He smiled mildly. 'Yes, probably.'

Another Indian stirred, threw an arm across Colin affectionately, and I drew away, was lost in the jungle night.

No one could blame me, I reassured myself, stumbling back through the infuriating maze of greenery. I'd done my best, had risked my life to try and persuade Colin to escape. No, it wasn't my fault. Even so, it didn't rest well with my conscience.

It was late morning of the next day before I found the expedition campsite. There knelt Martha, her face tear stained, laying orchids on the giant leaf-shrouded chest of Big Jacko. She looked up as I collapsed nearby and drank some water, managing a wan smile of welcome.

'Thank God you're safe, Sydney. Colin?'

'The Indians got him.'

'Oh dear.'

Hugging her knees to her chest, Margie looked much the same as I did, I guessed. Shit scared. Her eyes were staring, her face pale. She couldn't even speak. Somehow I'd expected to see Matheson with her, safe.

I looked to Martha. 'No Rory or Tom?'

'No sign of them yet. But they're safe, I'm sure,' she said, willing it to be so.

Carla stood at the edge of the clearing, looking off into the impenetrable greenery, off to where Vilcabamba beckoned her. I knew, because it drew me too.

I'd almost succeeded in digging a grave deep enough for Big Jacko with one of the shovels brought along for archaeological purposes, when Rory staggered back into camp. He was scratched and bloody, and limped a little.

'Rory!' cried Carla, with overwhelming relief. 'Thank God you're safe.' She flung her arms around him, hugged him tight, spattering little kisses all over his face.

Over her shoulder he shot me a reassuring smile. I smiled right back. But where was Tom? Not that I cared a jot about the ugly bastard, you understand, I just wished him no harm.

Martha asked the question and Rory, putting an arm around Carla, sat back on his heels between us and sadly recounted what had befallen them since the incident with the Indians.

'We ran, Tom in front, me close behind. Didn't stop till we felt pretty sure that we weren't being followed. We started back here, but we went off course, got lost. Then at first light this morning Tom lost his footing, fell down this ravine we were skirting. As it grew lighter I could see him, but he was dead, wasn't moving or showing any signs of life. I couldn't get down to him. It was awful.'

He smiled miserably but there were no tears. Maybe he didn't think that they were manly. Anyhow, Margie cried enough for everyone.

I was staring at him with my mouth open. Tom dead? My insides seemed to turn in upon themselves and crash down upon my pelvis.

Martha was shaking her head, stunned. 'Colin, Big Jacko and Tom. What a night.'

I sat myself down silently and never said a word, chucking the shovel into the hole.

We huddled close that night, no plans made for tomorrow, a state of depression descending. Martha and I exchanged worried glances over the heads of Rory and Carla, who seemed as single-minded as ever in their quest to find the lost city, the black, unlucky day quickly put behind them.

Three men were dead (well Colin wasn't but I doubted he'd last long with the natives) and yet they treated it as a mere hiccup.

Rory cuddled into Carla until satisfied that she slept, then crawled over to me and snuggled down the length of my back. His hands were everywhere, unbuttoning my top, working inside my trousers. I let him do as he pleased, glad of his nearness, confirming that I was still alive, but sex was the last thing on my mind. He tried harder to rouse me, working on my breasts and clitoris like some eager schoolboy, clumsy because of the clothes that were in the way, but endearingly persistent.

'God, I adore you, must have you, Sydney. You don't mind, do you, darling? I sense you're sad about the deaths. And that is partly why I want you . . . need you. Loving you as I do and joining our bodies in the act of love is proving we still live, that we cannot be beaten.'

He was echoing my own thoughts. I moved onto my back, obediently accommodating, unzipped him, hot and heavy with lustful longing, wriggled down my trousers and let my knees fall apart. He ran his fingers through my hot dampness and then lay heavily atop of me, sliding that fat member of his into me, moving gently and with no noise so that we shouldn't wake the three women huddled nearby.

Rory was all male, Mr Charisma himself and I lusted after him like no other, but this night I couldn't respond, my mind on other things, like: why did the Indians only kill Big Jacko with the poisoned dart? There were enough men in the band that had captured Colin. Each one of them could have targeted one of our number and we'd have been wiped out. Why only Big Jacko? And then there was the business of Tom. I'm not a believer in the supernatural, in messages being sent from one being to another via the telepathic telephone. Nope. When I read in *Jane Eyre* where Mr Rochester called to her across miles of moorland and she'd heard the voice on the wind and, silly bitch, answered, I was ever the one to scoff and label it romantic tosh. But this night as Rory rolled off me, kissing me on the mouth and forehead and saying: 'Thank you, darling, thank you,' something in me knew Matheson was still alive, or yes, damn it, some signal reached me.

Rory snored beside me, wearing a contented smile, not a care in the world. He was a man of great self-assurance, a manipulator and, supposedly, he loved me, wanted to marry me, fill a house with our babies. Alarm bells rang at the thought and I inched away from him, rearranged my clothing and took off, my back-pack slung over my shoulder. I headed off in the direction from which Rory had returned, determined that I'd see for myself what had befallen my tormentor.

The moon was out again, an ally, thank God, and I carried my knife tightly grasped in my right hand, as nervous as hell, starting at the slightest movement or noise around me, sighing heavily with relief when I found that a bird or monkey or suchlike were the culprits, disturbed by my clumsy progress through their habitat.

Dawn was about to break when I found the ravine. At least Rory hadn't lied about that. Maybe I did him a disservice by suspecting him. It might have happened just as he said: Tom fell and didn't move, looked dead. Dead he might be.

I walked to the edge of the rocky drop with care, the scree quick to slide and take more with it on the way down to the rocky, sparce scrub at the bottom.

The sun came up, hazy, sending the humidity soaring once more so that I felt damp and uncomfortable within my jungle gear. I looked where I walked for safety's sake and divided my gaze equally between feet and ravine, painstakingly thorough. Nothing. I never thought to look up to the tree-line above the ridge. So the voice startled me and I slipped and had to scramble to safety, away from the edge.

'What took you so long?' Tom wanted to know, a cynical eyebrow arched.

'Tom!'

'Do I take it you missed me, couldn't go on without me?'

'Don't be stupid. I only came looking so's I could bury you and dance on your grave.'

He laughed, warmly, I noticed, while striving to conceal my joy at finding him alive and relatively unscathed, by the look of him. He was sitting on a large boulder, holding his head, his legs and arms showing grazed and bloody through tattered clothing. His face was cut and grazed too.

'You hurt?' I asked, closing the distance between us, prodding a finger at the swelling on his head.

'God! Hell, no,' he snarled. 'What do you think?'

'I think I was a silly bitch to come back looking for you. I should have left you for the wildlife. You'd make a good jaguar's dinner,' I muttered, slinging my back-pack down and searching for my first-aid tin. I pulled out antiseptic and a wad of cotton wool. Soaked it. I hoped it was the sort that stung like hell. It was. I felt better.

He sucked in fast past his teeth, grimacing, but didn't once comment on my sadistic approach to nursing. So close to him as I dabbed at his sore bits and applied sticky plasters to the more severe cuts, my breasts jigged about, straining at the fabric of my shirt. He reached out and squeezed. I slapped the hand away. His fingers sent a thrill through me, but there was no time for that, not now. I needed answers to questions. Some I could already guess at.

'Did you fall or were you pushed?'

'Pushed, I think, though not before I'd been clunked over the head with a handy rock. Hence the bump.'

'Rory'

'Who else?' He looked at me as if I was an idiot even to ask. 'Being unconscious probably saved my life, 'cos I fell like a drunk, all relaxed.'

'I don't understand what's happening. It's weird.'

'Your Rory's up to something.'

'He's not mine. I don't want him. Don't want any man full-time. Just shut up and listen, Tom,' I insisted, impatient and worried. 'Big Jacko's dead, Poisoned dart. You know that, of course. But *why* just Big Jacko, why not all of us? I can't figure it. Colin and I ran off in the same direction and he was taken by the Indians, but, Tom, they didn't really look like bloodthirsty killers, didn't, now I come to think of it, carry blowpipes at all. They had spears and bows and arrow.'

'If Duncan's up to something then it's likely that he ran in my wake after we scattered from camp, deliberately followed me to try kill me. But that implicates him in Big Jacko's death. I don't like the man, true, but would he be in league with . . . well, with whoever . . . God, thinking about all that is making my headache worse. What happened to Colin?'

'He . . . well he kind of decided he'd like to stay with them. I couldn't persuade him otherwise. I did try, honest, risked my neck to talk to him. But he seemed to take a fancy to them and was delighted to find that they practised sodomy on a daily basis.'

Tom was chuckling. 'I hope he's happy.'

'Can you walk?'

'I think so. I managed to climb out of the ravine. Mind you, it took me most of the night. I just go dizzy from time to time.'

'What shall we do? What do you think Rory'll do when he finds out I've gone?'

'He'll forget all about you. He's only got one thing on his mind – Vilcabamba.'

I nodded. My thoughts exactly.

'That's where they'll head. Nothing will stop them. And that's where we'll be going too. Mister Rory Duncan probably thinks we'll perish without Carla to guide us through the jungle. We'll prove him wrong, won't we, viper-pants?'

I gave him a cagey look. 'What do you mean?'

'That you know the way. You can get us to Vilcabamba as assuredly as the irritating Miss Carla.'

'Maybe. Maybe not.'

'Don't you start playing games as well. I'm in no mood for more double-crossing, so beware.'

'All right, all right,' I capitulated. 'I know the way. I'll get us there. But don't expect me to trust you. I'm not gonna trust anyone; its safer.'

I started to do up the top of the antiseptic tube. He caught my hand.

'You haven't finished. Look, I've got a cut lip, a scratched cheek . . .'

'You'll survive.'

'Perhaps you could kiss 'em better?'

'I think that clunk on the head has made you delirious. I'd sooner kiss a pot-bellied pig.'

He made a snorting noise and pulled me to him, between his legs, holding me tight, pulling out the tails of my shirt from my trousers and nuzzling beneath with his mouth and nose, making disgusting piggy noises all the while. I started laughing, squealing as he scraped his stubbly chin over my midriff.

'Argh! Don't! You're like sandpaper.'

He quit momentarily, standing up too quick and going dizzy.

'You all right?'

He laughed wolfishly, picked me up, laid me down

on the hard ground, pinned me there and half undressed me, leaving me with my shirt on but unbuttoned. My trousers and panties he threw aside.

Why was I letting him do this? I didn't even like him, did I? He was sexy, yes. I'd already admitted that much to myself, but his irritation factor more than outweighted that. Maybe sex was the sealing of a pact between us, the combining of allied forces. Ah what the hell, I just wanted him, plain and simple. That was the truth, I was showing how happy I was to find him still alive. I might feel differently tomorrow, but that was then and this was now. And, of course, that should really go without saying.

He'd just got his trousers down to reveal a splendid erection that made me instantly desirous, when he had another dizzy spell and fell over sideways. I rolled over, straddled him, taking the thick shaft between my hands and running its sensitive head back and forth through my sex.

He grinned and groaned.

I narrowed my eyes, looked cunning, taking him into me and lowering slowly, watching the look of anticipation and pleasure on Tom's face, sliding down over him, swallowing him up.

His head hurt something awful, it was obvious and he made noises in pleasure-pain. 'Ooh my head. Ah, that feels *so* good. Ah, God . . .'

I rode him, my ugly, beautiful man, his face and torso all sweaty and dusty from the fall, reached out and stroked the bloodied, craggy contours of his face as he reached up and cupped my heavy breasts, caressing their plump warmth to firm, hard-nippled arousal.

I moved upon him, muscles tightening about his shaft, making him cry out in delight. Rode him at a quickening pace as my mound began to pulse, became the central object of my consciousness.

Tom grabbed me about the hips, held on tight as I took us both on a fleeting, crashing wave of bliss.

Progress was slow, very slow. So what was new about that? We had no machete, only my knife, and I reluctantly, very reluctantly, let Tom borrow it to try and aid our passage through the rain forest.

We had only the meagre supplies in my back-pack, which consisted of three dehydrated meals, a couple of changes of clothing, endless pairs of knickers and a totally useless map of the London Underground. I had no idea what that was doing in there.

Matheson muttered and grumbled, carrying on as if it were my fault that he'd left his belongings in camp when fleeing, so he'd believed, for his life.

'The mask was in my rucksack. They'll have found it, no doubt, and will have a double helping of whatever power comes from those things. And besides the mask there were my flares and cameras.'

'Flares . . .' I gave him an intense, questioning stare. What would a photographer be doing with flares?'

'For emergency use only.'

'Not the sort of thing one usually thinks to pack though, surely?'

'Hey, look, it's no big deal, believe me. And these are not usual circumstances. Truth is, a friend of mine, a deep-sea angler, heard I was coming on this trip and offered them, said that being God only knew where up the Amazon wasn't so very different from being out on the ocean, that he'd never dream of going out without the means to pinpoint his location in an emergency. Satisfied?'

No. My expression became guarded, my thoughts

241

wary. Were my instincts wrong? Was my trust in him misplaced, was I going to be betrayed? Might he have been the one who sabotaged the radio? 'Who'd be likely to see flares all the way out here, hundreds of miles from anywhere, anyone?'

'Hopefully someone. Friends.'

I squinted at him, scrutinising. 'Was it you who signalled to this Mendes guy when he flew over in the helicopter? Yes, it was, wasn't it! It's the only logical explanation.'

I backed away from him, suddenly aware of possible menace. This man might be in league with drug traffickers, gun runners, South American robbing barons, and I was showing him the way to Vilcabamba, a potentially fabulous find, so others kept telling me. Damn, damn, damn, how could I have been so stupid! And I'd given him my knife!

He frowned at me, shook his head. 'I'm disappointed in you, Sydney. I thought you knew me better than that. Do I look the sort to be involved with Paraguayan henchmen?'

'Frankly, yes.'

'Hasn't the possibility accurred to you that our Mister Walking Talking Penis, Rory Duncan fired his rifle off that day he was away on his own, as a signal to our pursuers, so that they knew near enough where we were, huh?'

I shrugged my shoulders, only a teensy bit convinced, said, hoping to catch him out, 'Then how did Rory get wounded . . . he had a scar on his cheek, remember.'

'Anything could have done it. A branch probably sprang back and whipped his cheek. Hell, I'm not gonna stand here thinking up possible explanations. You either believe me or you don't. I'm not bothered one way or t'other personally. You're stuck with me,

242

dear Sydney, dear Sydney . . .' And he went on to sing every tedious verse of 'There's A Hole In My Bucket', not always getting them in the right order.

He was right. I was stuck with him. And I knew it.

The rest of the day passed in near silence, I was so suspicious. I found myself watching everything he did, reading things sinister into the slightest quirk of his behaviour.

It rained, gloom descending beneath the canopy of foliage long before dark, and we made camp feeling decidedly miserable. We tried to do something with the dehydrated meals – it was a total disaster. He scowled at me, unimpressed and irritated by my total lack of culinary expertise.

I scowled right back. 'Trust me to get lumbered with a man who can't cook. Tut, *honestly*!'

He looked savage, spat out something that bore a passing resemblance to an oxo cube and decided to try to sleep instead, curling up beneath a layer of giant, rubbery leaves to try and keep the dripping trees from soaking him.

My stomach was growling so much that I persevered with the lumps of muck that someone with a sense of humour called food. They bore no resemblance to anything I'd ever seen come from an animal or vegetable.

Thoroughly miserable, time passed slowly. I copied Matheson and settled down to try and sleep. But the raindrops were so heavy and landed with such forceful thuds upon our covers, that I just couldn't relax. I kept waiting for the next thud . . . then the next.

Matheson growled, 'If you don't stop huffing like that I'm gonna throttle you, d'you hear?'

'Um.'

'Count sheep.'

'I can't. I'm too damned busy counting raindrops.'

Ten minutes later, I gauged, he turned to me in the dark. I couldn't see his face but could feel his hot breath. 'Damned if you haven't got me counting them as well, now!'

I grinned in the dark, safe in the knowledge that he couldn't see me.

'And you can take that smile off your face.'

I chuckled. Obviously he was a carrot lover too. Gosh, we actually had something in common – high beta carotene levels. Either that or he was beginning to know me, my habits. My laugh was cut off by his mouth. In the dark I couldn't see how ugly he was, his face all craggy and sprouting with whiskers. In the dark I had to admit that he could kiss better than any other man on earth, even Rory, the man who'd sworn he loved me above all others, wanted to marry me, and who had then, just as casually, forgotten all about me, it seemed, in his singular desire to get to Vilcabamba.

I warmed to the kiss, began to feel for Matheson beneath the layers of vegetation, to insinuate my body against his. His erection was impressive, my fingers eagerly tried to make it bigger still, working delicately on him so that my tormentor was vanquished, putty in my hands, or so I liked to think. He caught his breath, he quivered, I tongued him lightly in the darkness.

He threw me off impatiently, unzipped and dragged off my trousers, rolled me onto my stomach and ran the palms of his hands up my back, dragging the shirt with them. His fingers were feather-light, his palms calloused and strong as they sort of massaged my lean back. His hand then travelled over the dipping small of my back, to my buttocks and my sex.

I reached out a hand as I lay face down in the fern

leaves, circled it around his now huge member, stroked and squeezed it possessively.

His breath caught. 'Bitch . . . witch,' he whispered against my nape as fingers invaded me, stroked me, made me wetter still. I raised my bottom enticingly, pushed against the fingers.

'Slob . . .' I ran a finger over the head of his penis.

'Serpent . . .' He kissed my nape, licked my backbone, all the while fingering my bottom and sex, trailing around to my clitoris and stroking gently, making me jerk in exquisite response.

'Bastard . . .'

'Siren . . .' The tongue travelled on down, between my buttocks, on until it found my womanly place and buried itself, wet and luscious. I gasped, my nipples so hard . . . my senses all atingle. There was just that one plunge, making me want to scream with pleasure, then he covered my body with his own, slipped a hand around to the front of me so he could play upon my clitoris, and pushed his mighty erection steadily into me.

I was wetted by the rain, warmed by the humidity, his naked body lying down the length of mine as he took deep possession, the loveliest and, oddly, the most comforting feeling I had ever known with a man. So why did I have to feel it with Matheson of all people? I must be going nuts.

He thrust at me with fulsome, measured strokes, a hand cupping my breast, caressing the hardened nipple, taking me like a dog with a bitch, yet not crudely. He was gentle, he was loving. I shied away from the thought yet I couldn't altogether deny it.

'Dog . . .'

'Bitch . . .'

'You've already used that one,' I reminded him,

trying to get myself and, hopefully, Tom, back onto a less affectionte course.

'Demon, then,' he whispered, close to my ear. 'Shut up, Sydney. I'm in no mood for swapping insults.'

'But *you* started it!' I snarled, full of mock indignance.

'I'm not gonna argue,' he replied, and, to my utter amazement, clamped his hand over my mouth. 'That's better.'

I made a cutting remark, but with his hand so tight it came out as a garbled muffle. I gave in, magnanimous in defeat, gave myself over entirely to pleasure. I'd get even with Mr Matheson another time. I had other things on my mind right then, like: Do it harder, deeper, yes, oh yes. And: I can't stand it any more, I'm coming, yes, now, right now.

My body relaxed, my lungs taking air in gasps.

Tom came on cue, well trained, groaning against my neck, his loins jerking, his shaft twitching deep inside me. He was gasping, too, and once the waves of sweet sensation died away he collapsed where he was, the pair of us a hot and sticky, wet fusion of flesh beneath the emerald canopy. We had no trouble falling off to sleep then, our minds and bodies sated and drained, no longer aware of the steady dripping of rain from above.

Umm, that tasted so good. Next to sex chocolate was my favourite thing. I devoured another square with guilty relish, letting it melt in my mouth and coat my tongue.

Up ahead Tom hacked and sawed pathetically at the tough vines and branches with my knife, his hands sore and bloody.

I'd used the need to take a pee behind a tree as my

excuse for disappearing. I must have taken longer than I realised, because he came looking for me.

Quick as lightning I hid the remainder of the bar behind my back, tried to affect an innocent expression.

He frowned, sweaty, his bristly face red with exertion. 'What you doing?'

'Nothing. Just sitting a moment.'

'Really?' He cocked an eyebrow. 'What's that around your mouth?'

Instantly my hand shot up to wipe away the telltale evidence, the Cadbury wrapper rustling metallically behind my back. He caught the hand, glanced a sore finger over the corner of my mouth, examined it closely, licked it.

'Chocolate! Where the hell did that come from?'

'It was in my back-pack. I found it just now. Had forgotten all about it. Honest.'

'Honest my ass! You knew it was there and you weren't going to share it, were you? You rotten little sneak. You were gonna guzzle it all on your ownsome.'

I stood up, all petulant, my aggression growing the more guilty I felt. 'So what? It's mine. I brought it from England. All the way here. And I'm damned if I'm gonna share it with you!'

'That right?' he said, challengingly, eyes flinty.

'Yeah.' We glared eyeball to eyeball. 'It's hardly my fault, is it, that you lost your rucksack?'

'I didn't lose it, you know that.'

'Well, you haven't got it now, have you?'

'No . . .' He wavered, then rallied, determined that I shouldn't get the upper hand. Men, they were all the same, couldn't stand a woman having the final word. 'Now look here,' he said, patronisingly, 'your argument doesn't make sense, and you know it. If

247

I'm hacking a way for both of us to get through this jungle, the least you can do is share your rations *fairly.*'

'My rations, yes. My chocolate, no.'

He grabbed for it, forced it out of my hand, unpeeled the indigo foil and crammed the whole damned lot into his mouth. I wrestled with him and then, when I saw that all was lost, that he was chomping and slurping over his booty, I could only stare at him in shocked horror, my mouth open.

'Ooh, lovely,' he drooled, voice velvety from the chocolate around his tongue, his eyes rolling upwards in mock ecstasy, showing only the whites.

'You bastard.' I was close to tears.

He laughed the harder at my distress. 'Hell, I'll buy you a box of chocs every week, guzzle-chops, when we get back to civilisation.'

I stamped my foot and screamed. 'You know where you can stick your chocolates! I hate you.'

'Now there's a novel idea,' he mused, smirking.

'Hate you,' I repeated, so that he should be in no doubt.

He swallowed down the last residue of chocolate in his mouth and gave a faint, unconscious nod of appreciation. 'That was delicious.'

Incensed, I grabbed for his testicles, thinking to take his smile away in a most thorough fashion. But he read me pretty well and hopped agilely out of reach, tut-tutting. 'Ooh, you are a vicious little bitch, Sydney.'

I opened my mouth –

'Please, don't say you hate me again. It's getting tedious. And the feeling's mutual.'

'It can't be. You couldn't possibly hate me as much as I hate you!' I declared.

'Wanna bet?' he chuckled.

'Yeah.' I smirked.

I tried to control it but this enormous burst of laughter erupted from me and I couldn't stop. I had to cling to the detestable man, just as he clung to me. I hoped he'd laugh his head clean off.

He clapped his arms around me, holding me in a bear-hug. Mine snaked about his neck. We kissed as if superglued, mouths sucking like sink plungers (yes, I know that's not very romantic), bodies pressing, lust building. We fumbled with buttons and zips, our trousers dropping. And then he lifted me, let me glide down over his excited body, rubbing against his hard cock, stimulating my clitoris to a state of hungry abandon. I tightened my stranglehold on his neck and he hoisted me once more, his strong hands cupping my buttocks, then lowering so that his manhood found me, inched in blissfully and then slid up in one fluid stroke. He staggered, in me to the core, every available inch, his neck cording with exertion, his dark eyes ablaze with passion. He moved to the nearest tree, backed me up against it and took me with animal intensity, grunting with each powerful thrust and making me cry out. We came almost immediately, no break then in the crying out and grunting, the crescendo scaring the birds from the trees.

Three days later we lay belly down, side by side on the ridge of an outcrop of rock. Neither of us spoke. We were intent on watching the fatigued foursome progressing very slowly beneath us.

Rory carried the rifles, one slung over his shoulder by means of a strap, the other held firmly in his hand, pointing ahead. He looked wary as well as weary, but not half as belaboured as the three women who carried the baggage and supplies.

The jungle was thinning now, the terrain rocky and sterile in parts save for a few tenacious plants that had rooted in crevices and ledges. Far off in the distance, blue and hazy, were the Andes, a most spectacular backdrop. And before them, still hidden by a vast expanse of trees, was Vilcabamba. We were close now. Perhaps only a day and a half away. I kept that information to myself. It paid, I'd found, to keep your cards close to your chest, especially when you had a couple of aces. Besides, I still didn't trust Matheson.

'Margie's carrying my rucksack. Good girl. At least I know my cameras and stuff will be looked after,' whispered Tom.

I should have liked to make some acid comment about his devoted admirer, but my thoughts were occupied. Carla lead the way, carrying the lightest of the loads, and looked now to be so full of her own importance as to make one nauseous. But she was going the right way. I had to give her credit for that.

I had the feeling that any woman who donned the mask would land up in a similar mental state to Carla and myself. It seemed to endow its ancient secrets indiscriminately on the wearer, yet affected each person differently. Certainly I didn't think myself as self-important or irritating as Carla. Matheson would have probably disagreed, mind you.

'They look pretty tired,' he observed. 'Rations must be getting low.'

I gave a vague nod, shifted position. Something rumbled beneath me. I gave Tom an odd, concerned look, then yelled with fright as the rock beneath me fractured and began to slide, cleanly separated.

Tom snatched for me but was too late. The four people below looked up, exclaimed to see me reappearing before them in so unorthodox a fashion. And Rory trained the gun on Matheson.

'Come on down, Matheson.'

Faced with the barrel of a gun, Tom had no option. Meanwhile, I was trying to decide which way was up after rolling down the slope like a rather-too-solid snowball. I couldn't see anything for the dust cloud that engulfed me. I coughed and choked, emerging to spit and sneeze, amazed to find that I'd broken nothing but a fingernail.

'Sydney,' cried Martha, warmly, putting her arms around me as I blinked to clear the dust from my eyes. 'Thank God you're safe. Since Big Jacko . . .' She couldn't bring herself to say 'died'. 'We've been *so* worried.'

'I'm fine, Martha, really. Something just told me that Matheson wasn't dead and I knew I wouldn't be at peace until I found out. And, as you can see . . .'

Martha nodded, looked genuinely impressed.

Rory kept the rifle trained on Tom, who was working his way gingerly down the slope amid an ever-shifting avalanche of scree.

'You should have left well alone, darling,' said Rory, speaking to me as a father would to a foolish daughter, and a very young daughter at that. 'The man's trouble, has been letting off flares to signal to Mendes and his men. *He's* the traitor.'

It sounded logical when put like that. I desperately wanted to believe Rory, still had the hots for him something awful.

'I didn't want to kill him, you must believe me, just wanted to immobilise him so that he'd no longer be a danger. You do understand, don't you? You're an intelligent woman, you can see why I did it.'

I nodded, thinking it politic to do so. Matheson looked at me with utter contempt, while Rory handed the rifle to Carla and quickly tied the photographer's hands behind his back.

'Keep an eye on him, Carla dear,' instructed Rory. 'I need to have a private word with Sydney.' He lead me away, out of sight and earshot.

'Darling,' he exclaimed, wrapping his arms about me, startling me. 'Darling, thank God nothing happened to you with him, that you're still in one piece. Whatever made you do it?'

'It's like I told Martha – I just had a feeling,' I reiterated, feeling uncomfortable crushed in his arms, and pulled away as much as I could, which wasn't much, maybe an inch. All of a sudden I felt as if I were suffocating. Rory shook his head with obvious concern. 'If anything had happened to you . . .'

'But it didn't. Here I am safe and sound.'

'Did he . . .?' He squirmed, couldn't ask, but wanted to know.

'Have sex with me, do you mean?'

He nodded. 'I don't like asking but – '

'Yes, we did, Rory. These things happen when you haven't got a TV or personal stereo to keep you occupied during the dark hours,' I said, flippantly.

'You poor baby. You talk tough but I know you're a tender little thing really. What did he do? When?'

There was something extremely repellant about his voice, his questions. 'I don't want to talk about it.'

'I could kill him,' he declared with theatrical jealousy.

Alarm bells sounded. 'That would be a bit drastic, I think. He didn't rape me. I wanted it.'

'Did he make you cry out like I did? Use your beautiful lips, worship your pussy with his mouth?'

Jee, this was getting creepy. I was finding it hard not to let my disdain show, sensed that to humour him would be best at present, though. His hands stroked me, his mouth kissed my forehead, my ears, nuzzled at my nape. When he tried to kiss my lips I pretended I needed to cough.

'He screwed me regular. Nothing weird.'

'I hate to think of it, his hands on you, his fingers in you. His cock invading you, mastering you. You're mine. I love you, Sydney. I want you as my wife.'

His hand groped between us, cupping my mound through the impenetrable stuff of my trousers, his chest squashed against my breasts. He kissed me hard, bruisingly, his teeth gnashing possessively against my lips. I allowed him that. Felt nothing. Certainly I didn't want to have sex, though it was obvious that he did. He strained against my belly, his penis hard, demanding against my belly, his tongue slithering against my lips.

I pushed him away, wiped my mouth. 'I'm sorry, but I can't, not now. I'm too – too tired, confused. Please, not now.'

He pulled away, looking a little hurt, but with a great more understanding than I had hoped for, hugged me affectionately, then released me, nodding. 'It's OK. I understand. Let's just forget it for now. I was being thoughtless. It's just that I love you so much. You do see, don't you?'

'Of course. And I'm very flattered, Rory. Just give me time, please.'

'As much as you need,' he reassured, clapping an arm around me as if we were best buddies.

We walked calmly back to camp. I caught Tom looking at me again the moment I reappeared, could almost hear his mind ticking over. We'd been gone no time at all, certainly not long enough for sex. His look was stony. But I somehow detected relief as well.

Rory crooked a finger at Carla, whispered in her

ear, then they moved off a short distance, hidden by thick foliage from the rest of us. I had no doubt as to what they were doing. Rory needed a woman. He couldn't have me, so he'd signalled to Carla. I could hear them, very faintly, the little noises a woman makes when a man strokes into her, could see them in my mind's eye. Carla on her knees, Rory taking her from behind as seemed to be his overriding preference. The more I thought about it, the hotter I became and the more I thought perhaps I'd been foolish to turn the gorgeous Rory down flat.

Chapter Eight

I gave the tied-up Tom a wide berth the next day as
we struggled on through the vegetation in search
of the Eldorado I was still heartily convinced existed
only in the minds of fools. Gold-hungry fools.

Martha looked at him often, shaking her head, full
of reproach. Her comments always along the con-
demning lines of: 'I never thought you'd be mixed up
with the likes of this Mendes, Mister Matheson. I'm
so disappointed. How could you betray us? Why?'

'Missus Andersen Turner, you got the wrong man,'
he'd protest calmly, as if endowed with exceptional
patience, as if Martha were a child who could not or
would not understand what really should have been
obvious.

Then she'd get angry. 'You had the flares. It had to
be you who signalled to the lookouts on that helicopter gunship.'

I kept my thoughts to myself, though, for whatever
reason – and I didn't want to bother with self-analysis
– I couldn't believe one hundred per cent that Matheson was our man. I was beginning to have my doubts

about Mr Rory Duncan. He was a charmer. Too much so? He worked real hard at keeping the ladies sweet, yet did very little in the way of flora and fauna study. There wasn't a day went by when we didn't encounter some extraordinary specimen of orchid or some particularly yucky looking stalk-eyed frog. But he hadn't bothered to enter a note in his book for days, or shown the expected interest in such varieties. Then again, it could be argued, I had to acknowledge, that Matheson didn't take many photos even when he wasn't tied up or being pushed down ravines.

Anyhow, I kept away from him, from everyone else too. I felt uncomfortable and longed to be home.

At around sunset Carla took the unilateral decision to stop, declaring that she was having difficulty in receiving directions from her ancient and ghostly guides. I had to bite my tongue not to say something sarcastic, but frankly I thought she was full of shit, was playing the oracle bit way over the top.

We were all hungry, yet no one had much of an appetite for the dehydrated cubes which, when thrown into a pan of boiling water, as demonstrated by Martha, turned, Hey Presto, into beef stew. It was the worst beef stew I was ever going to taste, I knew that with certainty. We ate in silence, Margie taking it upon herself to spoon-feed Matheson who was still bound up.

He was in a right old state, having fallen face-first into a silted up river-bed that afternoon. He was caked in mud. A few days ago such a disaster befalling him would have cheered me up no end, but not now.

After the excuse for a meal we sat around, or rather Rory and Carla had their heads together again in a manner I'd come to find irksome, and the rest of us watched them, waited.

'If you're not sure of the direction, you *must* put on the mask,' Rory was imploring in his winning way.

Carla put the back of her hand to her forehead *à la mode* Sarah Bernhardt, and looked anguished. 'Must I? Oh, no no no, please don't ask it of me so soon after the last time.'

Oh how I could have slapped her! Eat yer heart out, Gloria Swanson.

'You have to, Carla, for us. Darling, don't you see. We're all relying on you.'

'Yes, but the sacrifice – '

'Will be worth it,' said Rory, emphatically, taking the masks from Martha.

Yes, they had both masks now, of course. I wondered curiously as to which they'd choose to use. And I wondered a lot as to why Carla felt the need to wear it again. Her communing with the ancient past wasn't, presumably, as strong as my own. For I knew exactly which way and how far Vilcabamba lay; we would be there tomorrow. Or perhaps she did know and this mask-wearing nonsense was for another reason. Certainly it did seem that Rory was insistent that she don it, and that she wanted to please him more than anything, would meddle with powers whose strength was an unknown quantity in order to please him.

She put on the mask. I averted my eyes, determined not to watch, not to be drawn in by its power. Yet even so, I could feel it seeping into my brain, flashes, images, inhabiting a different time and space.

They – Martha and Margie – tied Tom to the overhanging bow of a tree, his body taut, feet just touching the ground. They opened his shirt, unfastened his trousers. I also undressed, had no control over my actions, moving towards the group in nothing but my shirt. The mask acted like a drug on us all.

I saw the Lord Inca, the wealth at his feet, the fountain of gold that erupted from his mighty phallus, heard the roar of the wind, felt it over my naked body, bowed before him, all covered in gold myself. Bracelets around my wrists and ankles, my throat and waist, in my hair.

Rory held me down – bowed as I was in respect to my lord – his body swaying over mine, half dressed, penis hard and eager. He cupped my breasts, finding the nipples already hard with excitement and the prickle of fear. I could feel the length of him between my buttocks, knew what he would do, didn't want him. Wanted Tom.

Tom, who grew less ugly to my eye as time passed, whose roughness I had come to trust. I tried to crawl to him. I couldn't make myself move, was being held by Rory, could see Margie licking Tom's manhood, taking him all into her mouth. I could see him struggle as if he didn't like it, then he saw that I watched, snarled contemptuously, and let the devoted secretary have her way, to spite me.

Carla stood in the mask, trembling trance-like, talking mumbo-jumbo, and as I watched the mask changed, the thing's expression becoming a leer, a look of cunning, controlling us, determining the mood.

I was hot, sexy as hell, needed to be taken and used badly. I squirmed around so that Rory couldn't push that big thing of his into my anus, which I knew he wanted, lay on my back and opened my legs especially wide in invitation. He was wild-eyed, as crazed as I, controlled completely by something over which we had never had control.

Rory held my knees wide apart and put the head of his penis into me, moving it so slightly in that sensitive opening that quickly I was at fever pitch. Then he stroked into me, long and deep, taking my breath, ramming, grinding, animal. I wrapped my legs around him, locked my ankles across his back. He tried to kiss me. I turned my head away.

I felt the pleasure build, let out a series of little throaty noises as I came, clenched the man the tighter through the throes, then relaxed.

Rory wasn't done. He turned me, pulled me up and back on my knees, fingering my anus, lubricating it so that he could stuff me with his member. He liked my backside, I knew. It was obvious. I was tight, resistant, squirmed when he moved his finger out then in, and all the while masturbated his shaft to keep its handsome rigidity. Finally, he made his move, did what he'd been itching to, one hand guiding the bulbous head of his engorged penis past my wetted bottom-mouth muscles, the other drawing against my belly, pulling me close. He pushed all into me, holding me tight against it, was looking down, I didn't doubt, and watching himself wedged, huge and stretching between my buttocks. I felt him tremble with delight, squeezed him deliberately hard so's I could hear him groan. He did.

He drew out of me, only the head still buried, and shoved in again, out of control. I stayed still and accommodating, my rear high in the air, letting him use it, lifting my head and looking up to see what the others were up to.

Carla was close to Matheson, her hands held high, in the middle of some ancient incantation. Martha and Margie caressed him everywhere, his penis rearing its head again despite the worshipping blow job that Margie had given him. The two women's actions seemed totally controlled by the mask wearer.

Martha swayed against him, rubbing a nice pair of

breasts against his shirted back, Margie standing in front of him and shimmying up and down, her rump playing against his manhood. It must have been a very pleasant sandwich.

He did seem to be enjoying it, as much under a spell as the rest of us, yet his eyes kept looking across the separating distance to me and there was torture in those eyes and rage at Rory for using me.

I reached out a hand, using the other to keep my balance, reached out to him, wanted to shake Rory off my tail but could not. I wanted Tom. And from the look in his eye I knew he wanted me.

With strength that came from I knew not where, I pushed hard against Rory then pulled forward, his member slipping from me, and I half scrambled, half ran to Tom.

I kissed him deeply, ran my hands over the dark, lean chest, shoved Margie aside when she acted possessive.

'*Down*,' ordered the imperious voice from Carla's mask. It didn't sound like Carla's voice at all, was far too masculine for that slip of a girl.

Margie instantly obeyed, lying prostrate at the feet of Matheson. The human step was heaven sent and I hopped up, my arms snaking Tom's neck, my body sliding down his, taking his shaft sweetly into me.

From behind us came Martha, intercepting Rory who staggered over, his penis all hot and huge with nowhere to go. He had tunnel vision, me thinks, had eyes only for my secret hole.

As if the thing controlling Carla now charged Martha with super strength, she caught the sizeable Rory by the shoulders and all but threw him to the ground, straddling him and gobbling up his sex with hers. She was laughing like a lunatic, pinned him down by the shoulders. Poor Rory looked frightened half to death. I had no sympathy for him whatsoever. It was about time he learned what it was like to be on the receiving end of someone else's obsessive demands: to be powerless.

Meanwhile, I gave Tom an endless kiss and moved my body leisurely up and down against his, the friction exquisite. We were a long time in coming, but the wait was worth it. Then afterwards I just kept my arms around him, hugged him, our eyes closed, our brains tranquil, upon the same subconscious plane.

It was with some surprise that I felt the ground move from under me and looked down to find that I had been standing on Margie. What was I doing? I hopped off apologetically. She came to her feet in confusion, as nonplussed as I, dusting herself off. Rory and Martha had broken apart and Carla had removed the mask. The spell was broken.

I pulled away from Tom, reality rushing in. I had the comradely presence of mind though to pull up his trousers for him and zip him up before finding my own clothing and covering my nudity.

No one spoke. No one caught anyone else's eye. Such a surfeit of abandonment, no matter that it had occurred whilst we were held under a spell, made us all a might awkward to say the least. In fact I'd say we were all as embarrassed as hell.

Rather than just hanging around trying to think of something – anything – to talk about *except* what had just happened, we all had an early night, dear Margie remembering to release Tom from the tree.

We seemed to be climbing. Very gradually, hardly noticeable really. The vegetation thinned still further and the humidity lessened, so that by sunset of the next afternoon we were in rocky terrain, the air arid.

I put on a camouflaged, brimmed hat to stop the back of my neck burning. I sensed we were near.

We entered a canyon, high gorge on both sides, rising sheer to approximately one hundred and fifty feet, I guessed, the twisting, white baked course of an ancient river seeming to beckon us, always promising something around the next bend.

Eventually it delivered, as I'd known it would, and Vilcabamba, or rather, its impressive gateway, lay before us.

There were several moments of excitement and expectation as we quickened our step, raced, all wanting to be the first there, just like kids. Then came the great disappointment.

Carved into the foot of the gorge was an unmistakably ancient entrance of impressive dimensions – Lord Inca's head, bedecked in ceremonial head-dress, still discernible despite the weathering of several centuries, looking down at us, huge, forbidding.

Torches at the ready, we moved inside, through a narrow passage, into a large chamber, then a larger one still. There were eight chambers in all, hewn from the bowels of the rocky gorge. Each was more splendidly carved than the last, the majority seeming to act as antechambers to the final, ceremonial setting.

In the last room an altar was hewn from its far wall, the sides of which were delicately carved to show a frieze of native animals – snakes, jaguars, monkeys, that kind of thing. Around the walls, where the yellow beams of our torches penetrated patchily, were carved faces. Ugly as sin. The Inca's version of gargoyles, I was thinking.

Beside me Margie shivered, turned up her nose. 'Nasty looking lot, aren't they?'

On the other side of me Tom agreed. 'Bogey men.'

Martha was crouching, her flashlight trained upon

a detailed panel depicting a human sacrifice. Time had left the carvings as crisp and new as the day they were carved. The heart being held up by the priest and the writhing victim were vivid. Too vivid. Martha swallowed and switched off her light.

We stood there. Not knowing what to do next: anti-climax is a crushing thing indeed. There was no treasure, no anything, just empty, sometimes ornately carved rooms. Even the carvings were not unique; South American museums were full of similar examples.

'We must have the wrong place,' said Rory, turning accusingly on Carla. 'You've made a mistake.'

She shook her head, as disappointed as the rest of us and feeling, I could tell, as if somehow it was all her fault. 'No, this is it. I know it. Feel it.'

I felt it too, but said nothing.

Angry, Rory stormed out. The others followed dejectedly behind, leaving me with Matheson to bring up the rear.

He looked at me archly. '*You* see anything?'

I shook my head.

'Shame.'

'I feel something though, like Carla, It's here, Tom. This *is* Vilcabamba.'

'Pity it didn't live up to the legend.'

I nodded faintly, my mind a fuzz of confusing thoughts. I lit the way back for the tied-up American. 'We'd better catch up the others.'

He walked ahead, asking over his shoulder, 'I don't suppose you'd care to untie me?'

'Nope.'

'Don't tell me that ass-loving Duncan has convinced you I'm the traitor? Tut, I thought even you couldn't fall for that.'

'I don't know what I think, so I'm not taking any

263

chances. Frankly, I wouldn't trust you an inch,' I told him, coolly.

'You trusted me with quite a few yesterday, as I recall,' he quipped, smirking.

The taunt was so contemptuous that I really shouldn't have risen to it. But what the hell . . . I stuck out my foot and tripped him, watched him fall, unable to save himself, with a fleeting satisfction.

He landed with a grunt, painfully hard. I stood over him, mouth tight-lipped, eyes dangerously sparkling. 'Confucius say: "He who in tight spot should mind his manners".'

Matheson rolled, struggled and staggered, finally making it onto his knees and hence to his feet. He glowered.

I smiled sweetly, pushed him against the wall and kissed him hard, enjoying the surprised look that widened his soulful brown eyes. He certainly hadn't expected that.

Back outside and in the first chamber, we made camp in a subdued manner. This wasn't how we'd expected things to be at all. Even I, who'd been the chief cynic all along, had to admit that I should have liked to find *something*, even if it was only a cruel message left by whoever had found the place ahead of us and cleared it out, saying, 'Sorry, Suckers, we beat you to it'.

'Oh well,' said a despondent Martha, 'this was something we knew might happen. It's very often the case when dealing with antiquities. There are always site robbers. Look at the pyramids – empty.'

'Not always,' corrected Rory, bitterly. 'You're forgetting about King Tut.'

'That was good luck,' she said, philosophical now. 'We had bad. It's just one of those things.'

'Oh, shut up!' he shouted, throwing away the

flashlight he was holding with violent fury. He strode off, needing to be alone, it seemed.

'Huff-puff,' I mumbled, watching his irate back grow smaller, watching the devoted miss, Carla Mignari, hurry after him to try to console him.

I'd fleetingly thought about doing so myself but something held me back. I didn't feel the same way about him any longer. Tasty he might be, but he was a flawed Adonis, weird in some ways, his character dubious. I think the rot set in when he'd started spouting all that lovey-dovey crap. It was a put-off. He liked to talk sweet nothings in my ear but then had to overpower me when it came to sex. He needed to dominate. I needed an overbearing man in my life like I needed headaches and food-poisoning. Matheson came and stood beside me. 'Not going after him too, kiss-in-the-dark? Aren't you worried Carla might gobble up your main course?'

I sniffed disdainfully. 'Another little trip can always be arranged, y'know. And I don't mean the sightseeing variety.'

I helped Martha carry most of our gear into the first chamber where, it had been decided, we would bed down for the night. It wasn't too bad, the hard rock floor softened by centuries of dust that had blown in through the open, ancient portal; the air easy on the nostrils. The same couldn't be said for all the chambers. Some were unpleasantly rank as if animals used them as storm shelters and latrines.

It was dark by the time Rory and Carla returned. She looked sheepish still, while he didn't so much look angry now as worried. Why?

After our meagre supper I fell further into a state of despondency, finally wriggling into my sleeping bag and giving into a weariness that seemed doubly intense because of the recent disappointment.

265

If we'd found Eldorado, our treasure, we wouldn't have slept at all, that was for certain. We'd have partied all night, Martha opening the alcohol rations that she carried for just such an occasion. But it wasn't to be. There was no drunken revelry. It was, however, despite the cancellation of the party, going to prove an eventful night.

I slept fitfully, my mind full of ancient images, flashes of a culture long gone, and woke feeling too hot and claustrophobic in the confined darkness. I unzipped my sleeping bag and allowed my body to cool.

The voices I heard were very low, the whisperings reminding me of cartoon mice – fast and squeaky, I groped for my torch, lit up, running the beam around the room. Tom was snoring, looking uncomfortable, trussed up as he was, like an oven-ready chicken. Martha was frowning, disappointed, it seemed, even in her dreams. Margie slept soundly, a lock of hair travelling back and forth on her cheek as she breathed. Rory and Carla were missing.

Lately they seemed to be forever disappearing for private conferences. I decided to go do a bit of spying.

The whisperings came from the inner chambers. I kept my torch focused on the floor ahead and felt my way falteringly along the cool stone walls. By the time I'd crept as far as the sixth chamber I could make out what they were saying.

'It's not working,' Carla was saying, voice miserable, apologetic.

'It will, darling, it will. Don't fret. Just relax, empty your mind. Come here, let me massage your shoulders. You're *so* tense.'

'It's because I know how important this is to you, Rory . . . darling.'

'Just relax. There, now doesn't that feel good.'

'Umm.'

I got the distinct impression that he was now toying with something other than her shoulder. I was in chamber seven, switching off the light and feeling my way cautiously forward, heading towards the faintest of light sources.

'Ooh, that's good,' gurgled Carla.

'I peeped around the corner, then moved quickly back out of sight until I could decide whether it was safe to do so again. Yes, it was. Carla was sitting perched upon the edge of the stone altar, her trousers off, her legs wide. Rory was crouched between them, paying her court with his tongue, ever the one to know how best to get what he wanted from a gal. I moved slowly, watching them with one eye peeping around the corner.

Their flashlight was lying on the altar behind Carla, her body blotting out most of the light. I felt quite safe, was in deepest shadow.

She leaned back, taking her weight on her hands, arching delightedly as Rory held her folds open with his fingers and stroked her with his tongue, then plunged it as deep as he could within her. She gurgled deep in her throat.

He pulled away. 'Try the mask again.'

'Oh, don't stop, darling,' she pleaded, all glistening where he'd abandoned his slobbery caresses.

'Try the mask again,' he bargained.

She held it to her face, fitted it on.

My heart beat faster with apprehension for I knew how easy it was to fall under the spell of that damned thing. But this time I seemed to be immune, felt nothing. The mask had lost its power. Carla, it appeared, was reluctant to tell Rory so, perhaps afraid that he wouldn't gratify her sexually if she did so.

'Anything?' he wanted to know, insistent, stroking

her from thighs to knees as his tongue flickered over her bud.

'I'm not sure . . .'

She was, the crafty bitch. She just didn't want him to stop.

'Do it for me, darling,' said Rory, unzipping his trousers and holding her legs wide as he filled her. 'Do it for me because I love you. I want to marry you. I've never proposed before, not to anyone. I want you and I will have you.'

I drew in my breath, gasped, amused rather than indignant. The slimy bastard. He'd used exactly those same words upon me! Even the meaningful kiss he bestowed afterwards was a carbon copy of the smacker he'd given me.

I snuck away in disgust. By the time I'd reached the second chamber I was muttering in cynical irritation. I didn't think I'd be able to go back to sleep, I needed a drink.

I put on the torch as I enterd our temporary dorm and searched visually for the booze bag. It was a heavy duty, army issue back-pack which Big Jacko had taken charge of until his untimely death. Not really caring whether I was caught or not, I rummaged and found the metal flask of brandy, taking one – blimey it was strong – two – not so bad – three – that's much better – good gulps.

In moments I could feel it coursing my veins, and felt a bit better. Just a bit. I might as well go take a pee while I was up, I decided, wandering outside.

At irregular intervals along the walls of the canyon there were small outcrops of rock like cathedral buttresses. It was quite ludicrous because no one was going to see me but I walked along until I reached one, hid behind it and pulled down my trousers, squatting and doing what came naturally, looking at the rocks all around and feeling very small and quite insignificant. I longed for crowds, London in the rush hour, hell on the tube.

Relieved, I stood up and zipped up, took a step out from behind my natural screen and stopped dead with fright.

Up above, the purple, star-studded sky burst with white-orange light, lighting up everything with a stark and ghostly whitness.

Someone had let off a flare.

Automatically I looked towards the entrance of the Inca shrine, and saw Rory Duncan as plain as day, clearly illuminated. After the initial 'whoosh' of the rocket-like projectile there was no noise at all, only the blinding light that seemed to last for minute upon minute. It would be seen for hundreds of miles. He was signalling to someone, using Tom's distress flares. How convenient, and so much more effective than a gun shot!

I didn't like it. Not one little bit. I was certain then that Matheson had been right about Rory. The rifle shot *had* been a signal to Mendes's helicopter.

I needed to get back to the shrine to warn the others, however Duncan stood in my path, the light from the flare dying but his fluttering torch beam betraying his position.

He moved off down the gulley, standing at a widened section of the dried river-bed where, I surmised, he'd calculated that it was wide enough for the helicopter to descend and land.

I creeped along like a spider on a wall, quick and flat, diving into the first chamber and shaking Matheson urgently whilst cutting the rope around his wrists with my knife.

'Ssh,' I warned him, 'Rory's up to something . . . let off one of your flares. I think he's signalling to that

269

chopper . . . to Mendes. They might be here any minute.'

It wasn't even that long. We heard the familiar noise of the rotar blades, getting louder all the time.

Carla, who'd only just fallen back off to sleep after an unsuccessful attempt to commune with the ancient ones, blinked awake and grumbled.

Martha was instantly awake. 'Helicopter,' she warned, woken by its noise rather than us.

'We know,' said Tom, brandishing the torch and trying to locate the rifles. I had a nasty feeling they were outside with Rory.

'What's happening?' wondered Margie.

'Rory's betrayed us. Mendes is coming,' Martha explained calmly, showing little of the fear she was truly experiencing. Once again I found myself admiring her.

Carla was shaking her head in disbelief and crying. 'I don't believe it. Not Rory. He told me he loved me. We're to be married.'

'Carla,' I told her bluntly, no frills, 'our Rory is a liar too. He's said exactly the same thing to me. He wanted to keep us sweet, knew that we were useful. You helped him find this place.'

'It *can't* be true,' she sniffed.

'Apparently it is,' said Martha.

Margie nodded. 'Yes. He even used those tactics with me. *And* I believed him until, that is, I spied him canoodling with Sydney.'

'Looks like we've all been had.'

'Somehow I don't think that's the worst he's capable of, either,' said Tom warningly, filling us all with foreboding. 'He has the rifles. We can't even defend ourselves.'

As if on cue, Rory appeared in the doorway. It was

almost dawn and there was just enough light to make out his silhouette in the greyness.

'Sorry for the early awakening. Can't be helped, I'm afraid. Please, step outside, all of you.'

The helicopter came down slow and smooth, landing within the torch-lit area Rory had hastily prepared. It was a huge grey-green camouflaged thing, blinding us with dust and deafening us with its rotars. The moment it touched down the door slid open and guerillas in jungle combat gear spewed out, lining up in a precise row of twenty, sub-machine-guns pointing at us, the epitome of South American Bandidos. Speaking for the others, I think I can say that we all quaked in our boots. Though oddly enough, it was Rory, herding us around at rifle point, who seemed in danger of messing in his trousers.

The pilot cut the engine, the rotars slowing, and at last we could open our eyes properly again and spit out the gritty content of our mouths.

I was looking for Mendes, the drug baron, master criminal, general Mister Nasty, who I expected to look like Anthony Quinn with Groucho Marx touches, puffing on a big Havana cigar. Then this tall, leggy (yes, even longer than mine) beautiful Latin bird climbed out and slapped her thigh with a riding crop. I almost giggled; this could not be for real, it was high camp. She was amazing, all in white, her designer cat-suit paling any of Martha's tailor-made jungle outfits to mere ordinariness.

She strode at us, full of herself, oozing confidence. No wonder Rory trembled.

'Good grief!' exclaimed Martha, 'I do believe Mendes is a *woman*.

Rory ran to greet her, welcoming her in an obsequious gush. It was stomach-churning stuff. And to think I'd had the hots for him! Perhaps it was a side-effect of all those anti-malaria tablets I'd been taking. It was a lame excuse but I was sticking to it.

I looked at Tom. His eyebrows were quirked. He looked wrily amused. How he must be enjoying this in his own hideous way. Oh, how I'd be reminded later – if there was to be a later – that my main course was merely a soufflé full of hot air. I wanted to groan.

Evidently Mendes – for this female could be none other – didn't like what she was hearing from the jabbering, attentive Rory. At one point she stopped dead, fastened him with a stare that could have frozen a lava-gushing Mount Etna at fifty paces, and then snapped out a half dozen choice words of contempt.

Rory was sweating now, looking miserable. He nodded, he wrung his hands, he begged her pardon. It was obvious what they were talking about. Treasure. Or, rather, the total lack of it. She seemed to be holding him personally responsible for the failure.

Mostly they spoke in a Latin lingo and I was none the wiser, but now and then there were irate sentences in English and it was possible to get the gist of things.

'Nothing?'

'No. Nothing. I'm sorry. We were misinformed.'

'Not even a little something?'

'Not a scrap.'

More cursing and speed talking in the foreign lingo, then, 'But this cannot be,' ranted Mendes, ordering her men to make a search of the shrine in the rocks. Ten minutes later they were back, their leader shaking his head negatively and reporting that Duncan spoke the truth.

She struck him – Rory I mean – once across each cheek, stamping her foot in a fury. Rory wrapped his arms around his head for protection. I noted her gorgeous boots of beige kid leather; undoubtedly Italian.

'Imbecile!' was one of the nicer things she called him.

'Do you get the feeling she's not well pleased!' wondered Tom under his breath, as caustic as ever when it came to Duncan.

'I wonder if he used the "I love you, I want to marry you" line on her too?'

'Somehow I don't think he'd have dared.'

If we hadn't been in such a tricky predicament we might well have found the pantomime enacted before us amusing. As it was though, all those loaded and pointing sub-machine-guns tended to dampen the humour somewhat.

The fact that Rory was the traitor was no surprise. That Mendes was a woman certainly was.

We were herded back into the first chamber and made to sit in a tight bunch in a corner, watched over by a swarm of mean-looking mercenaries.

Mendes came to stand over us, legs planted wide, that crop she carried flicking lightly off her thigh in high theatrical style; she'd have made a great Principal Boy. She was a performer, wanted us to enjoy the show or, at the very least, be impressed as hell.

She smiled, teeth white and perfect in the dusky face. It wasn't a trustworthy or friendly smile. If a rattlesnake could smile, that's how he'd look.

'My associate, Mister Duncan, tells me there is no treasure . . . no gold. I am so disappointed. I say this cannot be. We must try harder. Miguel,' she looked to one of her soldiers, held out her hand, 'the mask.'

I half expected him to click his heels, Nazi fashion and was disappointed when he didn't.

From a straw bed in a wooden crate he lifted a

mask. Another mask. Us captives in the corner exchanged bemused looks. Just how many masks were there? Was this latest one real or fake?

'Now,' said Mendes, 'which one of you has the gift?'

'It's her,' said Rory, pointing at Carla.

She gave him a disgusted look. 'You jerk.'

Such name calling was evidently the least of his worries. He was trembling something awful and sweat had broken out on the forehead I had thought so ideally handsome only a week ago. Now words like, 'scumbag' and, 'slimeball' sprang to mind.

'Stand,' ordered Mendes.

Mouth set determinedly, Carla stood up. She was plucky, I had to give her credit for that. She showed no fear.

'Put on the mask.'

Carla complied. Nothing happened.

'You are not trying,' said Mendes, voice low and threatening.

Carla removed it, and informed the woman frostily, 'I don't have to try. If the spirits want to send their message and pictures, they just do. I have no control over it. There's nothing, hasn't been since we reached this place.'

Mendes eyeballed her intensely. 'You are a very lippy girl. I no like your attitude. Sit down again. Where is the other mask?'

Rory produced the other two like lightning, desperate to please in any way possible. 'Matheson brought one as well.'

'Three?' She was thoughtful. 'Where did this Matheson get his?'

Tom chirped up, 'I met a man in Manaus who said he could sell me the key to Vilcabamba. I gave him the equivalent of a months wages for it and, frankly, I think I was robbed.'

'Huh,' Mendes was heard to faintly dismiss. 'Let the women wear them together. Perhaps the magic will be stronger.'

I was ordered to my feet, so was Martha. We put on the masks. The three of us stood together, full of trepidation, willing something, *anything* to happen. It would buy us time. I don't know if the other two experienced the same as me, yet I'm pretty sure they must have. Certainly we all acted the same.

For several moments, while Mendes stood before us, waiting impatiently, slapping the crop into her palm, nothing ocurred, then, very gradually, I felt myself being transported back, back, fragmented moments in history flitting before my eyes, colourful, confusing. When wasn't it?

I was with the Lord Inca. No, no, I was the Lord Inca. I looked down from my lofty throne of stone, down to my people. They were prostrate before me, trembling in fear. The traitor was dragged before me, handsome, black haired. He held his hands out to me beseechingly, his eyes imploring. I was deaf to his entreaties, ordered him to be sacrificed. He was dragged away, his screams sounding through the vaulted chambers of stone.

After the sacrifice came the nights of fertility. Bodies swayed, joined, my ears filled with the excited cadence of their breathing. They writhed at my feet, legs coiled, bodies entwined, a sea of pistons firing, of cries and sighing, adoration of human flesh.

Gradually the mists cleared. I was drawn forward, away from that far off place and became aware bit by bit of my confined surroundings, of the people who inhabited it.

Tom, Rory, the mercenaries, Mendes, Margie, were doing the most extraordinary things to each other, held beneath the spell that those of us in the masks had conjured for them.

Rory lay writhing and jabbering, apparently tormented by some unknown nastiness, clawing at the dusty rock floor of the first chamber.

Tom was at my feet, kneeling, his face pressed against my trousered sex, his hands wrapped around me, holding me tight, like steel bands. I couldn't move at all. Was trapped, yet felt very safe.

The mercenaries were on their hands and knees, trousers down, cocks out and pushed home, deep in the bottoms of their immediate neighbours. There was much jerking and grunting from these slim blades, long blades and fat blades all working away in tight, eagerly offered rears.

Tom was pulling me down, onto my knees, was fumbling blindly with my trousers, deep in a trance. The sight of so much humping and pumping had really got to me by then. I helped him.

On my knees, I moved my legs wide apart, took his hot and swollen member and guided the glistening head to my opening, rubbing its seeping pearliness against myself. He groaned, impatient, mad even to be in me. I didn't try to hold him back, was ready, willing. He pushed into me, fulsome, adoring. We moved together, breaths ragged, hands holding the other possessively tight.

Over his shoulder I could see Carla now kicking Rory. Martha was very still, just like a statue, the faintest of trembles running constantly through her. Her trance was deep indeed. But most startling of all was Margie with Mendes.

They lay closely curled upon the hard floor, each lovingly tongueing the other's sex, searching out its most intimate folds and sensitive spots, lapping, probing with tongues made rigid and pointed. They were oblivious to all, lost in rapture, under the ancients' spell.

Tom thrust hard, making me cry out, and cling to him all the tighter. His hands cupped my buttocks, holding me wide to his assault of demanding strokes. Our crisis was quick in coming. We scratched, kneaded, swayed and clenched, my muscles milking him, drawing – it seemed then at the height of ecstasy – the very life and soul from him, the pair of us becoming one.

One by one the other occupants of the room came back to their senses, wondering at their own actions with confusion and embarrassment. I couldn't help noting with amusement that some of the mercenaries were obviously appalled at their own behaviour. They zipped themselves up, red-faced with shame, unwilling to make eye contact with anyone around them.

Carla ceased kicking Rory, and Martha's body relaxed from its rigid tremble with a drawn out groan. She staggered, then clutched at the wall for support.

The only two who showed no discomfort were Mendes and Margie. Long after their bodies' cravings had been satisfied and they'd broken free of the trance, they still clung to each other, tenderness in their eyes, their smiles, their gentle caresses.

From Tom there was a look that said, 'Well, well, what d'you think of that?'

'At last she's showing some taste,' I snorted, infuriated with myself for having sex with him again. It was getting to be too much of a habit. I detested him yet I couldn't seem to say no.

He cocked an eyebrow. 'And that from the woman who just tried to screw my brains out.'

I was opening my mouth to deliver a particularly razor sharp retort when Mendes demanded, 'Enough you two. What did you see? Where is the gold?'

'Sorry, nothing,' I said, shaking my head.

'The same,' said Carla.

'And me,' the ashen-faced Martha concluded. It was her first time wearing the mask and the experience had evidently shaken her.

'You lie!'

The three of us shook our heads, emphatically.

'Look,' I said, patronisingly patient, addressing her as if she was a cretin without the capacity to take in even the simplest scrap of info, 'there was nothing. Just an orgy. That's why we all acted the way we did . . . all the rutting and sex . . . Rory getting himself a kicking. In the vision he was actually a sacrifice – his heart cut out of his living body. But there was no gold.'

Rory swallowed hard, plainly uncomfortable.

Her eyebrows knotted, her lips thinned. 'You are lippy also. I no like you, no want to hear from you again.'

'But you asked – '

The crop snapped around the side of my head, making my ear ring.

'Hey,' shouted Tom, 'enough . . .'

Soldiers surrounded him, machine-guns pointing, so that he put his hands up in supplication and gave Mendes an insincere smile. 'OK, OK.'

Mendes raised an eyebrow. 'She your woman?'

'Hell no,' laughed Tom. 'Of course not!' I exclaimed, as if that was the most ridiculous suggestion I'd ever heard.

Mendes looked really out of sorts, muttered at Rory, at her men, left two guards and went outside. It was fully light now.

'Suppose you tell us what's going on, Rory? It can't hurt you now,' said Tom.

278

'The others will soon be arriving. She's going out to meet them.'

'Others?'

'The ground troops. They're a day behind us because an injured soldier had to be air-lifted out.'

'Sounds like she's got an army,' I muttered.

'Thirty guerilla for this operation.'

'You'd have thought we would at least have heard them in the jungle, felt we were being followed, or something,' said Martha.

'In a way you did,' said Rory, dispassionately. 'They killed Big Jacko.'

Martha looked at him aghast. It was patently clear that the man's death didn't bother him at all.

Tom snarled, 'Scum!'

'He was a threat . . . had to be eliminated,' said Rory. 'I never had anything against him personally. But the man was an ex-commando, knew how to use a gun.'

'Mendes' men killed Big Jacko?'

Rory nodded. 'A man with a blowpipe, so's you'd think it was natives.'

'But there really were Indians,' I said, confused but not wanting to admit to it.

'Colin's stumbling upon them was pure coincidence. Convenient for me because it backed up the Indian theory.'

'And what's this Mendes to you, Duncan?' Tom wanted to know, his voice full of snarled threat – not that he could have done anything with the guards present.

'We are lovers, go way back. I met her in Belize many years ago when serving with the British Army. She was a revolutionary then, gun-running, supplying mercenaries to back up Marxist rebellions against fascist dictators. There were, and still are, plenty of those in Central and South America. This particular little escapade has been a long time in the planning. We knew there was something tangible to the legends of Vilcabamba, collected scraps of info. We tried to piece things together but had no real success. So when we heard about Martha's venture we decided that the explorers could do the hard work – find this place, at which point we'd arrive in force and relieve you of all the cumbersome treasure.'

'Except there isn't any,' said Martha, bitterly reminding him, 'and Big Jacko died for nothing.'

'No, there isn't,' he agreed, stonily.

'And this Mendes woman doesn't srike me as the type to accept such a disappointment philosophically,' added Tom.

'No. She's greedy. It's one of her biggest failings. Greedy and unforgiving.'

'Tough,' I said, finding it impossible to find even the teeny-weeniest speck of sympathy for him. He'd betrayed us all, as a group and individually; there was blood on his hands, as they say.

'What's her real name?' Tom wondered, curious.

'It is Mendes, though Chiquita, not Chico. She has always fuelled the lie that Mendes is a man. It is safer, amuses her.'

'Interesting.'

'Interesting, yes, but of no help to you, Matheson. Such information will go to the grave with you, you see, because you'll never leave here alive. We couldn't allow that. Foolish talk costs lives. And when those lives are mine and Chiquita's, I have no qualms about silencing you poor unfortunates. You knew the risks. Your luck has run out. Too bad.'

'What about your luck, scumbag?' I reminded him. 'Snow White and the Wicked Stepmother have amalgamated it seems to me. She's not happy with you, Rory, old boy, not happy at all.'

He took on a confident air. 'I have a way with women, as you well know, Sydney. I'll talk her around. What's one treasure more or less. She's already fabulously wealthy.'

'I wish you all the luck you deserve.'

He'd almost said 'thanks' until he thought more carefully about the wording. His stony look returned and he strode out.

Thereafter, events passed with alarming speed. We heard the helicopter burst noisily into life, heard Mendes shouting orders. Then she appeared in the doorway, jerked her head to signal the guards to leave and smiled at Margie.

'I can promise you a life of luxury and sweet loving. Will you come with me?'

Margie was torn, wanted to go but didn't want to desert her friends in their darkest hour.

Martha encouraged her. 'Go, if you want. We'll none of us think the worse of you. Choose life, Margie.'

'Life and love,' said Margie, nodding madly, face radiant, running into Mendes' arms. The white-suited woman gave her a hard, passionate kiss, then pushed her out through the doorway. She looked at her watch.

'What's happening?' Tom asked, getting a prickle of apprehension and foreboding down his backbone.

'Do not move for precisely two minues or it could be dangerous, even fatal.'

'What have you done?'

She ignored him. 'Goodbye.'

'I'm not just gonna sit here,' riled Tom, scrambling to his feet.

Frantically, I rugby tackled him around the legs,

brought him down. 'Don't be a fool. If you go outside they'll probably kill you, they might be waiting with guns.'

'I doubt it,' he argued. 'Can't you hear the chopper? It's taken off.'

He was right. Still I was reluctant to loosen my grip. 'Please wait. She was so precise; it was a definite warning.'

There was an explosion that made the whole gorge rumble and shake around us.

Carla screamed, clung to Martha and tried to make herself as small as possible.

'Christ!' shouted Tom, galvanised.

'What the hell – '

'An explosion.'

The dust hit us in a blast-wave, dense and choking. Suddenly there was no light. Martha clung to Carla, who was half shrieking, half sobbing with fright, in fear of her life.

'Is it two minutes yet?' Tom shouted over the crashing and rumbling.

'Yes, it must be,' I shouted back, nodding in case he couldn't hear me.

Cautiously he went forward with me following, out into the entrance of the Inca's shrine. It was obvious what had been done. Explosives had been placed at the main portal, had been detonated, bringing down tonnes of boulder-sized rocks and rubble.

'We're buried alive,' I cried, aghast, telling myself not to get hysterical.

'I can see light. Just a crack. See?' he said hopefully, climbing up the pile of rubble.

He was right, there was a small chink, just enough so he could see out, but the rock around it was huge, unmoveable. I scrambled up beside him, put my head beside his and looked out, taking in great mouthfuls of dust-free air. I was in danger of snivelling, could feel a sob at the back of my throat.

We could hear the helicopter hovering above now, probably having completed its ascent clear of the gorge. We were both thinking that they were going, leaving us to die, the swines, when this spooky cry pierced the air, grew louder, unending. There was a thud, then silence.

'My eyes widened. 'Good God!'

'It's Rory,' said Tom, in case I was in any doubt or had my eyes closed, for it was not a pretty sight. 'Main course is off.'

'Ho-ho, very witty. Now that was one unforgiving, no nonsense kind of woman,' I said, swallowing down the bile in my throat. He'd been thrown out of the helicopter and plummeted two hundred feet and more to his death.

'We'd better go tell the others,' said Tom, averting his eyes from the pulverised body with a grimace.

'Which they gonna get first, the good news or the bad?'

Chapter Nine

We'd started off with four women and five men. Now there were just four of us. And we were not a happy bunch of adventurers, not even the indomitable Martha who'd always managed to somehow lift us with her enthusiasm. We were miserable and we did nothing to hide it. We all thought we were going to die.

We were thirsty, hungry, cold and full of a sense of failure. We had found Vilcabamba and it was a gigantic disappointment. As far as archaeological finds went, this was a bummer. Only Tom made any attempt at trying to save us, and even he had to admit defeat when the larger boulders, which made up most of the barrier between us and the outside world, wouldn't budge an inch. He sat at the bottom of the pile and held his head in his hands. Not even a half-hearted verbal assault from me was enough to rouse him to a lively reply. We needed Superman.

We passed that day and the next in miserable inactivity, each of us with our own morbid thoughts, nobody speaking. On the third day I wandered off on my own, cheesed off with the glum faces of my companions. Carla kept on about how hungry and thirsty she was and how she detested our meagre rations. Martha's patience was gone and she'd ranted at the girl:

'Shut up your endless complaining or I'll wring your miserable scrawny neck!' Not like Martha at all. Carla started crying in earnest then and I decided I'd had enough.

The batteries in my torch were growing weak now, the beam an uncertain yellow that illuminated only in half-light, nothing clear. I had to get away from them, at least for a while. They were driving me nuts. So I was irritated, to say the least, to hear footsteps behind me. I turned to find Tom in my directed beam of light.

'I vant to be alone,' I said in my most unwelcoming Greta Garbo voice.

'So do I. Let's be alone together.'

'Don't be stupid.'

'Why not? I don't see that it matters at this sorry stage of our lives. I can be stupid if I like.'

'Suit yourself.' I moved off, ignoring him, feeling him close behind me, following in the wake of my light. That began to irritate me too. 'Look, if you're gonna be with me, walk with me, not behind me. You make me uneasy.'

He laughed. It was a little bit hollow, fatigued. 'Why? Do you expect me to do something despicable to you in the dark?'

'I wouldn't put anything past you, not even at this sorry stage.'

I should have been expecting it, he'd warned me, after all, yet when he did grab me I yelled in surprise, lashed out at him in the darkness, my torch having been knocked to the ground and gone out.

He pinned me against the wall. I struggled, wasn't in the mood. He kissed me, hard, long and deep, as only he seemed to know how, until my knees wobbled and I had to hold on to him for support. He undid his clothing and then my own and pressed against me kissing me again in the pitch black, deeper, draining me of indifference, filling me with fire. I moaned, mouth working bruisingly against his, my hands roving over him, his back, his buttocks, his strong thighs. He was hard against me, hard and big . . .

'Quick,' I pleaded, grinding my hips against him.

'No. Slow. Nice and slow,' he insisted, nudging my legs apart and finding me with his hand, stroking so delicately, so slowly that I wanted to whimper in exquisite distress, mad with longing for what he wouldn't give.

He lowered his head, licked my breasts leisurely, each flicker of the tongue measured and precise, torturously slow. He raised himself again and, as he did so, impaled me upon his shaft, taking me with a hard, deep stroke that took my feet clear off the ground. He cupped my buttocks, let a finger stray into my bottom and took me against the wall, with lethal precision, each stroke making me cry out, gasp with intense pleasure that was almost pain. I called out his name but it was lost in a gasp. I clung to him, tugging at his hair as all too soon I felt the heat build, knew the joy of a throbbing, prolonged climax, momentarily losing my hold on reality. For a while we were happy, at peace. But the real world was quick to flood back and with it, despair.

I sagged a little in his arms. 'Y'know, if I'd died just then of pleasure it would have been a wonderfully neat end to my life. I shouldn't have minded at all.

But no, fate is never that kind, is it? It's orchestrated things so that we're gonna be a long time dying.'

His breath on my cheek was warm, faintly comforting. 'Do we have to talk about that now?' muttered Tom, 'I was feeling pretty damned happy till you opened your mouth.'

I was hardly listening, my tongue running on of its own accord, spilling out all the black thoughts in my head. 'How will we die, d' you think? Starvation? Will we resort to cannibalism to survive a little longer, and if so who would we eat? Or will some of us go mad? Yes, probably I would, I'm a head-case at the best of times.'

'Now *that* I wholeheartedly agree with.'

Half-heartedly I tried to knee him where it hurts most, but he was ready for it, fended off the aggresive limb and laughingly tut-tutted in the dark.

We searched for our trousers, could only find one pair. Tom's. I had to make do with my lacy Marks & Sparks knickers. I shrugged off the loss. It really didn't matter now. Or it wouldn't in a week or so's time when I'd snuffed it. We had very little water and you couldn't survive long without it. We'd be dead in a sealed tomb and no one would ever find us. My newspaper would carry an exclusive, probably make a mint. Bad news was good news in the newspaper business. Having no real idea what had happened to me and the rest of our party, they'd make it up as they went along, following their one and only maxim: never let the truth get in the way of a good story. Pablo would tell how he'd waved us off from the boats on the final leg of our journey, watched us disappear for ever into the jungle. From there on they could give vent to their lurid imaginations without restraint. The story I was supposed to write, the headlines I'd envisaged making, now some other hack would do the job, get the glory, promotion . . .

On returning to the first chamber we found Martha in tears, shaking her head in lamentation. 'I chose him . . . chose him for his neat butt, not his suitability . . . this mess is all my fault. We're gonna die because I chose the wrong man. I was a fool.'

'Don't blame yourself,' soothed Tom. 'He had a way about him, knew how to exploit his looks and manners. And your being foolish is in no way exclusive, is it? Sydney, Carla *and* Margie, all fell for his charm.'

I looked daggers at him. It was true but I didn't want to be reminded.

'But I should have known better. I'm no giddy teenager. And I believed him when he said that you were the traitor, even swallowed that guff about him trying to eliminate you by "helping" you down that ravine because you were a danger to the rest of us. I *am* a fool. Forgive me, Tom.'

'Forget it. I have.'

Carla sniffed, eyes red-rimmed with crying. 'I don't wanna die.'

'We're not gonna die. Not yet, anyhow,' Tom promised her.

I raised an eyebrow. 'Oh yeh, how come? You into miracles or something?'

He scowled. 'There's always a chance. Always hope.'

'What, you mean if I go shout endlessly through the gap in the rocks someone might hear us?' I laughed crazily. 'Who? There is no one, not for several hundreds of miles, or has that obvious fact escaped your memory?'

'Well aren't you a cheery soul,' snarled Tom. 'I can see we'll have to put you in charge of morale.'

288

'Ah, drop dead!'

'You likewise.'

'Stop it, you two,' hissed Martha. 'Squabbling doesn't help.'

Tom and I stared at each other, me determined not to look away first. 'I hope you die first, so's I have something to cheer me up in my final hours.'

'Sydney!' gasped Martha, shocked. 'That was a terrible thing to say.'

'My, aren't we ultra-sensitive all of a sudden,' I hissed.

Tom's look was full of disdain. 'Viper.'

'Amoeba.'

Carla jumped up and screamed, 'If you keep on like this I won't wait for your to die. I'll murder you both in your sleep!'

I moved out in a huff, deciding that I wanted no company but my own. Of course I didn't go very far. That wasn't possible in the present circumstances. I took off to chamber six, or was it seven? Hell, whose counting! I couldn't be bothered with things like that. I was going to die; that was the only thing in my head.

Feeling a right bitchy Miss Anti-social, I thought, *Stuff 'em and sod 'em*, putting down my bed-roll and sleeping bag and going through the contents of my back-pack by torchlight. Rory's torch; he wouldn't be needing it any more.

I had a little water, a little dehydrated foodstuff, several writing pads and ballpoint pens, a dozen pair of knickers and my anti-bug sprays and creams. Toiletry articles were minimal: a brush, flannel, soap, lipstick and a teeny vanity mirror.

I looked at myself and recoiled with shock. Great Scott, that couldn't be me! Never! I was a disaster, one helluva mess, a dog. I felt the snivels starting, knew that once I started I probably wouldn't be able to stop. I wasn't razor-sharp, sassy Sydney, ace reporter any more. I was a gaunt wreck of humanity. It would be better if I died; I didn't want anyone to see me like this. Not even that rat, Matheson.

I shook my head in disbelief, hurled the mirror away. How could he bring himself to have sex with me? He must keep his eyes closed! Poor Tom. I almost had to admire him. Either that or pity him – maybe he had some weird mental defect and only liked doing *it* with uglies.

I cried in the empty darkness, switching off the torch to conserve the batteries, eventually fell into a drained, deep sleep.

The place was bathed in sunlight, patches of dappled shade looking cool and inviting. The trees and shrubs all luscious green, the pool aqua and ultramarine, the white sandy bottom glimpsed as clear as crystal.

There were people there. Dusky skinned and blue-black haired, they were natives, at one with their surrounding. Their clothes were ornate and highly coloured, reds and golds dominating.

Upon his stone throne sat the Lord Inca, splendidly robed and wearing the crown and mantle of office. Gold dripped from him – his arms, neck and ears.

Everyone was in awe. The scene was one of ordered homage, the subjects laying offerings at his feet, kissing the hem of his mantle.

His throne seemed to rise from a sea of gold, emeralds, furs and fruits. From a hollow gourd he drank nectar and wine, his eyes raking his subjects, all seeing, terrible.

His people quaked, held in thrall, not daring even to murmur. He was a descendant of the very sun in the sky and the setting was heaven on earth.

In the cool waters of the magical pool a harem of beautiful women bathed in the nude, their bodies every size and shape. Their nipples rouged, their eyelids kohled. They were the most beautiful girls from the Andes and the Amazon and they were the Inca's, his women of pleasure.

When it came to breeding, he could only mate with a direct descendant of the sun, like himself, which meant he had to wed his own sister, but for sexual contentment he had his pick of a vast country.

He watched them as he drank, studious, spoilt for choice. Who should it be today? Did he feel energetic or did he just want to lie back and be pandered to? Did he want to fill her mouth, her woman's place or the resistant and tight passage between golden globes of buttock? He smiled thinking of yesterday and the girl-woman he'd had. He'd filled her mouth with soft, luscious fruits, until she struggled to eat, juice running from the corners of her mouth, laughing and choking all at the same time. Her mouth full, he'd started to push them up her bottom, watching how they pressed past her muscles, stretched her for a moment and then disappeared, were swallowed. He'd been captivated, forced more and more into her, her mouth and anus, kissing her and thrusting his shaft in where he'd filled with fruit, to see what it would feel like. It was luscious, wondrous, juices oozing from her everywhere.

Now he pondered, his elbow on the carved stone arm of his throne, his chin in his hand, watching them, trying to decide.

They knew they were being watched, pleasured themselves with false phalluses of beautifully grained mahogany, forever ready to couple, but must never pleasure themselves to the point of bliss. Only the Inca could do that. Should they get carried away they would be punished.

A servant approached, interrupted his pleasant predicament. The Inca frowned.

The servant kept his eyes downcast and trembled. 'Lord, the men in grey metal demand to be bid entry.'

Black eyes fastened upon him. 'Demand? Demand.' He was heartily sick of them. The men in grey metal were always coming. They pretended to be friends of the Inca, but he was not fooled.

'Send them away.'

'I will try, lord, but I know not if they will go.'

'What do they want this time, do you think?'

'Our yellow metal, lord; they always ask for the same. These men in grey metal, conquistadores they would be called, call it gold. For them it is of great value.'

'For us also.'

'If we give them some, mightn't they go away, lord?'

'Aye, but for how long? They always return, demand more. Will not be satisfied, I fear, until they have all.'

'We could stop them having all, lord. We could hide it.'

The Inca nodded. 'It may well have to come to that. Now, though, I will fix on a smile so warm that they shall never guess at the anger in my heart. Send them in. But first tell my women to go hide themselves.'

I awoke with a start, blinking at the strong light in my eyes, my shoulder feeling pinched and bruised where someone shook me. 'Wha . . . what is it?'

'Sydney, I had a dream,' said Martha, full of enthusiasm, Tom and Carla peering over her shoulder.

'Big deal,' I muttered, more than a little put out by the rude awakening.

'It was about Inca gold. And it was as vivid and clear as if I was there.'

'Did it happen to have a pool of naked nymphets in it?' I asked, joking.

'Yes!'

I sobered instantly, frowned at her. 'What else?'

'A . . . well, a sort of throne-room setting, only it was out of doors. And there was this absolute dish of a guy who couldn't make up his mind about which woman he fancied.'

'And the conquistadores arrived and demanded to be allowed in to see him, yeh?'

Martha nodded wildly, amazement stupefying her. 'We both had the *same* dream!'

I shook my head. This was all a bit too weird for my liking.

'It's not possible. You know that.' A shiver ran down my spine.

'Not possible, yet it happened,' laughed Martha, slightly hysterical I thought, like an over-excited child. 'And I knew, somehow, had to come find out while it was still clear in your head as well as mine.'

'Right, so it was weird. But it didn't mean anything, did it? It's not gonna help us get out of here, is it?' said I, all common sense and joy-killing.

'Well, no, it doesn't tell us anything specific, or mean anything that I can think of, but . . . aw, dammit, Sydney, you take the fun out of everything,' said Martha, deflated.

They stared at me, all of them, grim, glum, irritated. I stared right back, more irritated than the lot of them put together. 'What's for breakfast?'

Tom frowned thunderously, his craggy face lining around the mouth and eyes. For once he didn't say anything and so I had no reason to fling a stinging, clever reply in his face. I felt odd, cheated.

Martha had given up on me in disgust, putting her arm around Carla's shoulder and leading her away. I put my own flashlight on as Tom moved away with his, following behind the others to light their way. Apparently I was to be ostracised.

I turned my back on him. Let 'em go. I didn't care. I'd never wanted to come on this silly expedition in the first place. Why couldn't Martha spend her wealth on charities like other tycoon's widows, instead of getting a notion in her head to go swanning off up the Amazon in search of some mythical treasure. No, I needn't feel bad and I wasn't going to let them make me.

I stared at the wall behind the altar as I searched my back-pack for something – anything – to eat, looking over the frightful faces there with utter dislike. Inca. I hated the word, anything to do with it. If I ever got out of here . . . But of course I wouldn't.

That choking lump in my throat again. I swallowed it down, took a loose chunk of rock from the altar top and hurled it at the middle face. The stone disappeared, went straight through the eye socket. I stepped back and blinked in surprise.

I shouted, 'Tom, Martha, come back! Quick!'

They responded immediately to the urgency in my voice, came at a run, Carla in their wake because she didn't want to be left in the dark on her ownsome.

'What?' they trumpeted in unison.

'There's thin air behind that wall. I just threw a stone and it . . . it disappeared through the eye-hole,' I stumbled in excitement.

He handed his torch to Martha and she and I illuminated the wall while Tom climbed onto the altar, felt around the faces, tentatively put his hand, then his whole arm through the hole.

'If you start yelling,' I jibed, 'don't expect me to jump up there and try to save you and your arm; I've seen Gregory Peck and Audrey Hepburn in *Roman Holiday*.'

'Tee-hee', he laughed sarcastically, mimicking me. 'Give me your torch.'

With it he cast a beam through one eyehole and looked through the other. 'Can't see a thing. The light can't seem to penetrate it. It's a black void, no walls, no nothing.'

'If only we could find a way through,' said Martha, hope in her voice. 'It might be another way out.'

'Then again, it might not,' I added.

Tom had jumped back down from the altar, was standing contemplating it, hands on hips, like the rest of us. 'We've got nothing we can use to smash our way through. It's darned thick . . . six inches and more of solid rock.'

I was looking at the faces, hateful things, and then I gasped. 'Oh my God, why didn't we see them before? They're staring right at us!'

The other there looked at me as if I'd really flipped this time.

Martha snatched at my shoulder, spun me around, staring with wild hope into my eyes. 'What is it? Do you see something? Another vision?'

'They've been staring me in the face. The faces. See?' I moved my torch beam as I pointed out, 'One . . . two . . . three. They're a key. It's obvious!'

'Feel her forehead,' said Tom, acidly. 'Sounds like she's cracking up.'

'No, Tom. Look. Its a fail-safe device. Just like with a nuclear missile in its silo. No one man has the key and the right combination. Two men have to punch in the code simultaneously or it won't activate. Got it?'

'Uh . . .' He was thinking, digesting, nodded, but wasn't totally clear though, I could tell.

'I've got it,' whooped Martha, delighted. 'Three faces, three masks. The masks were scattered, no one person given them by . . . the Inca, do you think Sydney?'

I nodded emphatically. 'It has to be. That's why we had the dream. It was the clue. He had the treasures of Vilcabamba hidden away from the conquistadores. Only he and, perhaps, one other – his most trusted servant – knew where it was and how to retrieve it. The masks went their separate ways and the treasure was never seen again, the secret dying with the only persons who had been privy to the deed.'

'Get the masks, Carla dear,' Martha bade her step-daughter 'and hurry.'

'I've got it,' said Tom, gripped with excitement.

'Oh good,' said I, 'I knew you would . . . *in the end*.'

Carla returned with the three masks and once again Tom mounted the altar block and placed each in the corresponding carved recess. They fitted perfectly.

'It was an ace bit of luck that Mendes also had a mask, and left it behind for us,' said Carla.

'Yes,' agreed Martha. 'When it wouldn't tell her where the gold was she discarded it as useless.'

I watched Tom, waiting, hoping, as the last mask was fitted in place. He moved back and watched, but nothing seemed to happen.

'Give the wall a shove,' I said desperately. 'Perhaps it needs a bit of help, has seized up after all these years.'

He put his back into it, pushed with all his might and then, yes, we could heard the deep rumbling of something huge and mechanical coming ponderously to life. But it wasn't the wall that moved; it was the carved top of the altar. It slid away, surprisingly quickly once its momentum had built and Tom, watching the wall instead of his feet, fell down into the altar with a yell.

Carla shrieked. We all ran forward, pointing our torch beams below.

Some ten feet beneath us was Tom, struggling to

his feet and slapping the dust from his clothes. He didn't look any the worse for his unexpected descent.

'Chuck me a torch,' he called up, his voice echoing in the emptiness.

I dropped mine, careful to do so directly over him so that he'd have no trouble catching it. We couldn't afford another broken torch.

He checked around, visibly relaxed. 'It's OK. Nothing nasty, creepy or otherwise. There's a staircase carved out of the rock to my right. If I've got my bearings correct, it's heading directly away from the gorge, up through the heart of the rock. It's an incredible feat of engineering. And it just might be a way out of here.'

'We're coming down,' Martha said, speaking for all of us.

She dangled Carla first, so that Tom could grab her from beneath and set her down safely, then me. Finally, she climbed over herself, hung and dropped, Tom catching her sure and steady.

We counted the stairs as we went. My torch failed on the two hundred and sixty-fourth and we were left with only Martha's weak, yellow beam to show us the way. We all stared ahead intently, as if by doing so we could penetrate the evasive gloom.

'Two seven two, two seven three . . .' rattled off Carla.

She was beginning to get on my nerves. Though that was nothing new. 'Can't you count in your head like the rest of us?'

'Two seven five . . . I'll do it which ever way I please . . . Two seven seven . . .'

'No, it's two seven six, dear,' Martha corrected.

I groaned in exasperation, raced ahead several

steps to hopefully get out of earshot, but pretty soon I could hear her again.

'Two eight four . . . two eight five . . .'

'How much further do you think?' I asked Tom.

He shook his head vaguely. 'Not sure. The air's still pretty stale. When – if – we feel fresh air, then it shouldn't be too far to the summit.'

'And what if we reach there only to find that we still can't get out? The exit may be grown over, sealed even . . .'

'The one thing I most admire about you is your optimism,' said Tom.

'I just like to consider all eventualities, know the facts. For a start we now have only the meagre supplies in my back-pack because the rest of you forgot to collect yours before leaving the altar chamber. We've no more batteries for the torch and about one cupful of water left in my canteen. I reckon that's about two sips each. I'd kill for a half of lager or a shandy. Damn, why did I think of that? Now I won't be able to think of anything else, it'll be torture.'

He laughed, not unkindly.

Martha's torch went out. 'That's it,' she said, somewhere in the dark, as if we needed telling. 'From here on up we're in the dark. We'd better stay close. Hang on to the tail of my jacket if you like, Carla, honey.'

'I don't like being last,' mumbled Carla, afraid.

'It's better than being first,' I reminded her, groping my way forward, then around a bend.

The stair changed course every so often, spiralling right then left, sometimes going straight on and narrowing so that I could feel the walls on both sides without holding my arms out from my side.

Carla had long since given up counting either in

her head or aloud. She was gasping, pulling Martha back. 'Can we stop, just for a bit? I'm exhausted.'

'Yeah, OK, said Tom, lighting up a cigarette. He leaned back against the wall and took a long, deep drag, looking at me by the light from his match.

'I think . . . yes, there it is again. Fresh air, Tom. Do you feel it?'

The match he was holding went out. Down the stairs howled a sudden, ferocious wind, taking our breaths, whipping at our clothes. Carla clung to Martha who flattened herself against the wall.

Tom yelled, I cried out, stupefied, and I could hear Martha screaming faintly, all but drowned out by the roaring noise that was all around us, centred on us and didn't seem to pass by.

It snaked my breath away, coiled around me, howling like a beast, ripping at my jacket, my knickers.

Martha screamed. 'It's ripping off my clothes!'

Carla just screamed, high and endless.

'Christ!' exclaimed Tom. 'What the hell's happening? It's going up my trouser leg, ripping, tearing . . .'

I could hear him slapping at it, trying to fend it off. Then he started to gurgle, just as if the thing had invaded his mouth.

'Tom!' I shrieked, 'Tom!'

'What is it? What is it? wondered Martha, voice trembling with horror. 'I can feel it at the top of my legs, hot, slippery. It's trying to get between . . .' She broke off, was obviously struggling with it. Her voice was full of disbelief. 'It's in me . . . my bottom, my sex . . .'

'And me,' cried Carla. 'My clothes are all gone. Is it a snake?'

'No, it can't be.'

It seemed to have as many tentacles as an octopus, yet when I tried to stop it invading me, squirting cream up my bottom and sex, I could find nothing to attack or get hold of. It was like a phantom.

I dripped with cream, could feel it running down my legs, could feel the ghostly, slithering shafts, as long and supple as rubber, snaking into me, wriggling, tasting and teasing at the very core of me. It snaked over slimy arms, up around my body, circling breasts, slithering over my ears, nose, into my mouth. Its possession was total. It took away my breath; I had to struggle to stay conscious.

We were all of us consumed, our every orifice filled, stretched, tested and caressed by the wind thing.

My feet weren't on the ground. I was borne up by the phenomenon that was wedged deep in my backside and vagina, engulfed by it, cocooned. It rubbed those slimy arms within me, bringing me to one shattering climax after another, filling me, squirting its supernatural essence into me, still filling me, still hard, demanding.

'Oh dear, oh . . .' cried Martha, but it was with delight now instead of terror.

It bore into me, filling me as no man ever had, rubbing on my clitoris until I cried out for the umpteenth time, felt as if on fire, the thing was causing so much lovely friction. And then, as suddenly and alarmingly as it had come, it vanished, moving off with a mighty whoosh down the stairs.

We collapsed in a messy heap, trembling, choking with relief and shock over words that just wouldn't come.

Eventually Tom managed to speak. 'You ladies all right?'

Exhausted sighs were our collective reply.

I felt myself where it had been in me. I was as dry as a bone but tingled with excess. 'Whatever was that?' I wondered.

No one else spoke. I guessed they were shaking their heads in puzzled amazement.

'Hell,' breathed Tom, awe-struck, exhausted, 'No one's ever done a job on me like that before! It nearly worked me to death! So much wet and slime. It felt like it was shooting up my ass a hundred miles an hour, and yet now . . . I'm totally dry. It's incredible.'

'Carla, you all right, honey?' asked her step-mother, gaining enough control to speak rationally.

'I guess so. It didn't seem to harm me none.'

'Was it real?' I asked, though I'd already made up my mind, I wanted confirmation.

'No,' they all said.

'How could it be?' said Martha. 'I could feel it and yet I couldn't find anything to get hold of.'

'A sex-maniac poltergeist then?'

'Whatever it was,' said Tom, 'it sure knew how to strip-search. If it ever fancied doing something other than scaring people shitless in the dark, it could get a job at customs.'

We three ladies groaned. 'Tee-hee.'

Further on the steps grew uncertain, the stuff from which they were hewn crumbly, no longer solid rock. We continued cautiously. Tom thought it was sand-stone turned to dust with age and water erosion. Then we could smell earth, good old-fashioned soil, and knew that the surface lay not too far above.

Our climbing accelerated accordingly, all of us eager for daylight, for escape from an unsettling, incomprehensible darkness.

Tom, taking the lead, pulled up. 'Whoa, something's in the way.'

301

'What?' wondered Carla in alarm. She didn't want any more surprises.

'By the feel of them I'd say tree roots. Got your knife handy, Sydney?'

I extracted it from the remains of my jacket pocket. It's a wonder I still had it on me at all. I handed it over, bumping uncertainly into Tom in the total, unvaried darkness. He felt for my hand, carefully extracted the knife, then let his other hand travel down over my belly, the sly dog. I felt for his nuts, then had a better idea, slyly withdrawing and nudging Carla into my place.

'Sydney?' There was a definite query in his voice.

Over Carla's shoulder I murmured softly, 'Um?'

'Doesn't matter.'

He pulled her close, was doubtless clutching at her buttocks and pressing his hard cock against her navel. Carla was breathing fast and having trouble not murmuring and giving the game away.

'What's taking so long?' Martha wanted to know.

'A tough root. Gonna take some time. Sit down and have a rest.'

Carla was entering heartily into the spirit of the game, holding her hands out in the dark so I could substitute my own, fondle Tom, feel where he rubbed against her, take his thick tool to slip it down through her mound, into her wetness. She trembled, he bucked, plunged into her, working with urgent hungry thrusts, his meatiness full in her, the very root of him trying to force an entry.

I touched where they were joined, her stretched sex, his greedy manhood, let my fingers play there until I'd driven the pair of them wild.

He started to pound, buried in her, hardly withdrawing, just stabbing, stabbing, filling her, friction building, building, bursting . . .

He groaned, couldn't keep quiet, no matter what.

'What're you up to above?' wondered Martha, though the amusement in her voice led me to believe that she already had a pretty good idea.

'Nothing,' I said, coyly, so close to Tom's ear that he still believed, I was certain, that he'd just had a quicky with yours truly in the dark.

Carla staggered away, probably wearing a look of crafty satisfaction, slipped a step and clung to me so she wouldn't fall. 'Thanks,' she whispered.

For what? Saving her or sharing Tom?

We continued our escape. The slender water root of some no doubt huge mahogany or similar hardwood bypassed, we soon reached daylight. We looked at each other, all of us tattered and virtually nude, blinking against the glare. Another tree's root system criss-crossed the ancient opening, the mighty slab of stone that would have once hidden the staircase, fractured by the growth of the tenacious roots. The gap through which we must pass was very narrow.

Carla went first, Tom behind her to give a helpful shove.

'Be a gentleman and close your eyes,' she insisted. 'I don't want you staring up my backside.'

'Just as if I would.' He adopted an offended expression.

It was a tight squeeze but the slim Carla was soon up and out on the surface, turning to take a good look around. 'Wow! What a view.'

'What can you see?'

'The whole world!'

'I want to go next,' insisted Martha, eager to see what had got Carla enthusing. She turned to Tom. 'Same rule applies to me – keep your eyes shut.'

'You have my word on it as a gentleman,' he vowed, hand over heart.

It took a little bit more effort and hefting on Tom's part to squeeze and then expel Martha through the opening. Once above she instantly forgot about us two below and wandered off after Carla. Tom and I could hear them eulogising over the view.

'Fantastic.'

'Breath-taking.'

'They've forgotten all about us,' I said huffily.

I was beneath the opening now, ready to be borne up by a strong and capable Tom, boosted back into the world again.

'Nice 'n convenient,' said Tom, that horny edge to his voice, his hand gliding up my leg. His face, squashing against my buttocks, teeth playfully nipping.

'Cut that out,' I said, sternly, playing Miss Indignantly Reluctant, knowing he'd do no such thing.

The hand slipped between my legs, cupped my mound, drew me back towards him, bent me a little so his penis could play between my cheeks, tease my little hole. He was hot, rigid, I was on fire from the play-time earlier, all juicy.

He sheathed himself in me, pushed me hard against the wall, kissing my nape hungrily, stroking between my sex-lips while he very quickly satisfied his urge. His fingers brought me to a crisis, his penis pumping hard and relentless, my buttocks splayed to allow him full measure.

'Ooh, yes,' I gasped at each thrust, tightening my muscles about him, pushing down to meet the onslaught happily, greedily.

His breath was hot on my ear, making me tingle. 'You're insatiable,' he observed huskily, pinning me

304

against the wall, holding me captive, holding me as if he never wanted to let me go.

I felt all-powerful, all woman, his equal any day. 'You got a problem with that? Scared you won't be able to keep up with me?' I teased, certainly not about to tell him it had been Carla instead of me on the stairs. Hell no, where was the fun in that? Let him think, worry even, that he couldn't completely satisfy me. Yes. I didn't want him too cock sure. Just because we were comrades at the moment, I didn't want him to get the wrong idea about me, think I was a pushover.

'I love a challenge,' he breathed, lips on my ear, shaft deep within me, our bodies rubbing, hot and damp.

I came, gasping, softly groaning, my body all aquiver. He followed close behind, with yelps and moans, his hands squeezing me reflexively. Sated, we found it difficult to find the energy to climb out afterwards, him shoving me and then me attempting to haul him dragging my back-pack behind. Eventually we made it, collapsing on the grass, blinded by the sun.

We forgot our virtual nakedness, the view diverting, magnificent, to say the very least. Carla was right, it was like being on top of the world. Only the distant pale blue peaks of the Andes were higher. We were on a tabletop, like an island in the middle of the jungle, sun-baked and sparcely grassed, looking down onto the tops of centuries old trees, while above us a condor wheeled on a thermal.

I turned one hundred and eighty degrees, taking it all in.

'Amazing.'

Tom nodded.

Martha's eyes were wide with wonder. 'Breathtaking or what?'

'Too much. How could I do it justice in a newspaper column?'

Martha looked at Tom, whose remaining scrap of clothing was the collar of his shirt, and laughed uproariously. 'No. They'd likely be more interested in the fact that we were all naked as we took in the view.'

'What a cynic you are, Martha,' I said in mock defence of my profession, then remembered something. 'That reminds me.' I knelt down and undid the fasteners on my back-pack. 'They're not much but they're something.' I produced several pairs of pretty, not practical, panties, and held them out so they could take their pick. Martha and Carla were ever so grateful. Tom, however, told us plainly that there was no way he'd wear women's knickers. Carla took pity on him and gave him the shreds of her T-shirt. From this he fashioned a loincloth and had us all rolling around in hysterics when he modelled it *à la mode* Cindy Crawford.

Our spirits were high. We began to think that maybe, just maybe, we had a chance of coming out of this thing alive.

Climbing the stairs had taken most of the day. Within half an hour of our coming to the surface the sun set, the whole sky ablaze with salmon, magenta and cerise.

We four huddled into a depression in the plateau to watch, an ancient felled tree our windbreak but a chill night wind making us painfully aware even so of our lack of clothing. The spectacle done, the sky dark and star lit, we lay like sardines for warmth, too exhausted to even savour the sensuality of such closeness.

I awoke shivering, my empty stomach making hideous gurgling noises. My movement woke Martha who, in turn, woke Carla. Tom was nowhere to be seen.

We sat up, looking bleary-eyed, mussed and grouchy. Tom's cheeriness when he rejoined us was irritating in the extreme. He was whistling, carrying a gigantic bunch of bananas, almost as vast as himself, and beamed us a smile like the husband in the Persil ad: whiter than white and nauseatingly sweet.

'Breakfast, ladies.'

Martha, ever the thoughtful one, tried to act pleased and gracious. 'Thank you, Tom. How nice of you. I, for one, am starving.'

He picked the fruits with the yellowest skins and handed them around. 'We can keep the green ones for later. They'll keep us going for days.'

I made myself eat slowly so's I wouldn't get indigestion later on. I froze, my eyes on stalks.

Tom noticed. 'What's up Doc?'

I pointed. Creeping out of the bananas was the biggest, hairiest spider I had ever seen. We're talking colossal, tea-plate size. My whole face distorted with horror. I could feel it prickling. I hated spiders, was the original arachnophobic.

Tom laughed. Beast!

I shivered, goose bumps coming up all over me, a chill running down my spine. I was frozen, gripped by a fear I knew I'd never conquer, not till my dying day. Carla saw it now, began to squeal. I had an ally; that made me feel a little better, not such an idiot.

'Do something, Tom,' I pleaded, watching the multi-legged thing ambling over the bananas.

He raised his foot, I assumed to step on it. 'No!' I cried, 'Don't kill it. Just get rid of it.'

He rolled his eyes, doubtless thought me the silliest bitch alive, took up the stalk of fruit and carried it a suitable distance away, flicking off the spider with the banana skin he carried, having devoured the contents. 'All right now?'

I nodded my head, grateful. 'Thanks,' I said, grudgingly.

'What d'you do at home when you've got one in the bath?'

'Run for the neighbour.'

'Why not just drown it?'

'Just because I've got an irrational fear, doesn't mean I want the things dead.'

His eyebrows were quirking. He was obviously amused.

'Yeah, OK,' I muttered, before he had a chance to open his mouth. 'So I'm a closet Friend of the Earth. Don't spread it around.'

He laughed and unzipped another banana.

Breakfast done, Tom said that we should follow him, see what he'd discovered whilst finding food.

One side of the plateau had a sheer drop, we knew, but the other sloped gently away into the encroaching jungle. Me carrying my back-pack, Tom the bananas, we set off.

On the slope were the ruins of some centuries-old building site. The stone canopy had collapsed and its pillar supports were broken, scattered about, but I knew the place. I looked at Martha, she at me. 'The Lord Inca's throne,' we said together. 'Snap!'

'How do you know?' said Carla, who felt nothing, for some reason, no longer able to tap into the mystic source. Consequently, she was inclined to be a bit huffy.

'We've seen it in our dreams,' said Martha, pointing out the different structures before us. 'That was his throne. In fact it looks to be still pretty well intact. It had a stone canopy over it to protect him from the sun. Below was a pool where his women bathed. And over there, where the vines have got a stranglehold, was a crescent-shaped, terraced structure cut into the rock where his subjects would sit on ceremonial occasions, not unlike the Roman seating in an amphitheatre.'

Tom was listening intently, taking it all in, picturing it in his mind.

We climbed on down, carefully, through the rubble and overgrowth, to inspect the throne close up. It had suffered from the ravages of time, its exquisite carving all but obliterated by the rain and wind of centuries. Corners were chipped badly where the canopy had collapsed upon it.

I smoothed its arms, where the Inca had touched five hundred or so years before me, during the final chapter of his people's supremacy in their own land, the century of the conquistadores.

I had to sit upon the throne, just had to, was drawn, transfixed. Martha nodded, felt it too. She sat at my feet, held my hands. The charge I felt ran through into her via her arms.

Tom and Carla had wandered on down the slope, were beginning to climb up the tiers of stone seats facing us. I looked at them, yet I saw the native people, ghosts, decked in their finery in honour of their deity, the King of the sun, every seat filled.

It was as if Martha's and my hands joining doubled the power. In my mind the picture was crystal clear. I needed no mask as my passport. *I* was the Inca. I gave the orders. The gold was hidden where the Spaniards should never find it, buried deep, its very existence henceforth uncertain, the stuff that legends were made of.

I leaped out of the stone seat, raised my hands to the sky, the sun, incantation pouring from my lips. Martha knelt in homage at my feet. Tom and Carla stood watching me from the crescent, nudging each other, highly amused by my theatrical outburst. Their voices carried, bouncing around the walls of the amphitheatre.

'Do you think that she's flipped?' wondered Carla, acidly.

'Nah, she's always been nuts,' said Tom.

The spell was broken. My arms dropped, head cleared.

Martha and I hugged, our faces full of joy. At last we knew the answer, the secret, we had been chosen to receive it. Yes, even a flippant, arrogant bitch like me. I was humbled.

We ran, tumbling and sliding, to the bottom of the slope, stood on the paved area where once there had been a bathing pool for the Inca's beauties. We stood there and we knew that right there, beneath our feet, was one of the great, perhaps even the greatest of treasure troves in the whole world.

The Lord Inca had emptied the pool, placed in it the greater part of his gold and jewels, then had the pool filled and grassed. Later it was paved, I didn't know why, yet. Conquistadores had come and gone, walking over that very pavement but never guessing. Each time the Inca saw them do so he would chuckle to himself, pity the poor fools.

Still holding hands, Martha and I danced and skipped in a circle like kids, shrieking and laughing. It's difficult to describe the euphoria I felt. I'm sure I shall never ever feel that good again.

'It's here, It's here,' we sang. 'Right beneath our feet, it's here.'

'She definitely flipped,' muttered Carla, sour-faced. 'Look at her, the silly bitch. And look at my step-ma, in a pair of borrowed knickers with her tits jigging all over the place.'

'Nice tits, though,' said Tom, kindly, descending to the pavement to try get some sense out of Martha and me.

'All right, come on, enough's enough,' he insisted, getting between the pair of us, breaking up our crazy dance. 'What's gotten into you both?'

Stopping suddenly, with nothing to hold on to, I staggered, awfully dizzy, and tottered. With a squeal, Martha did likewise. Flat on our backs, we roared with laughter.

'It's here . . . the treasure. He emptied the water out of the pool and filled it with his worldly wealth,' I said.

Tom turned all alert and interested, pointed at the slab beneath his feet. 'Here?'

'Yes.'

'You sure?'

'Positive.'

'Certain,' said Martha. 'But it's deep. God only knows how we'll dig it out. The sensible thing to do is get back to civilisation, equip ourselves properly, get the right backing and come back for it. Trouble is, I'm finding it very difficult to be logical and sensible. Heck, I must have gold-fever.'

She wasn't in the least serious, and even giggled. Tom's look towards her was appraising. I looked beyond him to Carla, who stood several rows back in the cheap seats, frowning our way, looking, if anything, embarrassed by our antics. Her disapproval didn't bother me at all.

My eye was caught by a sudden movement in the upper regions of my vision and I watched, alarmed and agog, as a line of native faces showed above the summit of the seating crescent. After the heads came torsos, then legs. All deep brown, golden touched, save one. He was pale, delicately handsome and fair. He waved.

'Colin!' I cried, genuinely happy to see him. 'Why aren't you dead?'

Chapter Ten

Colin was in love. I was envious. I was sceptical. Even hard-as-nails me longed to feel that elusive emotion. Yet I didn't believe it existed at all.

He kept staring into the eyes of one particularly handsome Indian and holding his hand. It was touching, and I mean that. The dusky one returned looks of adoration.

We sat on the slabbed pavement, the natives' food shared generously amongst us, drinking a disgusting brown concoction that was, seemingly, a mix of cold coffee grounds and river silt. Still, I was thirsty, hungry, hadn't eaten anything much for several days. And on my tall and lanky frame the loss of a few pounds made me look positively scrawny.

We told Colin what had happened with Rory and Mendes and he, in turn, told us of his and his new friends' encounter with the ground troops that the helicopter had set down. It was one of the guerillas, Colin told us, though of course we already knew, who had killed Big Jacko with a poisoned dart. And it was his little band of natives who had dogged the progress of the mercenaries through the jungle, laying all manner of booby traps in their path.

'They have many ways of making unwelcome visitors feel less than at home,' he said. 'They covered pits with twigs and greenery so an unsuspecting chap would fall in, finding himself face to face with a commune of poisonous frogs. They set up snares, so a foot in the wrong place meant some luckless guerilla was left dangling upside down amongst the trees. They fired darts from blowpipes no bigger than flutes, so well camouflaged that no one could see them, just felt these horrid pin pricks all over their bodies.'

'But the mercenaries had an Indian with them,' I queried. 'How come he never spotted your friends?'

'He was only half Indian, they say. Probably Yanomamo. Not as clever as my boys,' said Colin, proudly.

'How do you communicate?'

'My friend here,' he told us, hugging his lover's shoulder, 'spent several months at a mission post in the Amazon Basin when he was a boy. His Spanish is adequate. So's mine, just. We get by. Anyhow . . . back to the mercenaries. When one of them fell into a pit and broke his leg, they radioed for help and the chopper came and picked 'em up. We, or rather, *they*,' said Colin, casting an encompassing glance over his new friends, 'followed your tracks to the gorge. But we were quite evidently too late to stop Mendes, as we found a huge pile of rock blocking the entrance to the Inca shrine, and we found Rory's body. We decided to search the vicinity in hope of finding further trace of you and stumbled on this place. Not even the Indians knew this existed.'

'This place, Colin, is Vilcabamba.' The Indians started jabbering in awe at mention of the name. 'And right here, beneath us, is the Inca's gold,' I told him.

'Amazing,' he enthused, drawing out the word.

'Wow. They said they felt something here . . . you know, vibes, spooks. Seems they were right.'

'Do you think they'd help us retrieve it? Might they object? I feel odd about disturbing it . . . feel it belongs to them more than us. This is their land after all.'

'We can't *not* dig it up,' said Carla, looking at me as if I was nuts. 'It's why we came. The whole reason for this expedition. If we don't, all the awful days we've just endured will have been for nothing. And, anyhow, how come you're acting the idealist all of a sudden?'

I shrugged, her scathing comment like water off a duck's back. Verbally I could beat her any day. It was too easy, no challenge. I just gave her a look of contempt.

'I know how Sydney feels,' said Martha. 'I understand what she's saying. We've had the visions, the pair of us. They were special, an honour . . . Yet it's conceivable that perhaps we were given those insights so's we could find this place, so that we'd pinpoint the gold. I think we are meant to do this, to dig it up.'

I didn't feel strongly one way or the other, so I capitulated, 'Yeah, maybe you're right.'

Martha was man-hungry. I could see it in her eyes, in her provocative gestures. There hadn't been anyone since Rory, or *anything* since that weird episode on the underground stairs, which defied all possible explanation. She was looking over the natives, trying to decide which one she'd make herself available to.

Colin, ever the gentleman, had handed around his jacket, T-shirt and vest so that we females could cover our top halves. All the men had bare chests thereafter

315

and the two whites amongst them began to pinken and tan in the sun as they laboured at the dig.

They worked in shifts, six or so at a time, those who had done their stint wandering off to the shade to recuperate.

Martha wandered off too, though never so far away that I couldn't see clearly what she was up to.

A native lazed beneath a tree, his back propped against the trunk, his legs drawn slightly up.

She sauntered by, giving him the once-over, seeing how well endowed he was. Evidently he passed the test, because she smiled ever so friendly and bent over to retrieve some imaginary object in front of her, affording him a tantalising view of her rounded rear and lacy Marks & Sparks panties.

He sat up straighter, alert, running his tongue over his lips, the dark shaft between his legs growing before my very eyes, fatter, longer, cumbersome almost.

He threw away the sugar cane he'd been stripping with his teeth and chewing, and crept silently up on Martha. She knew he was there, of course, but wasn't letting on. It was all part of the game.

With a triumphant cry he grappled with her, wrestling as if she were some wild animal he'd been stalking through the undergrowth, one arm capturing her around the midriff, the other grasping at an ample breast. She was juicy with expectancy and hope, it was just as well, for he was poking at her rear without preamble. He pulled her panties down around her thighs, filling her woman's place, then, after a while, switched to her other entrance.

Martha hadn't been used there before, was a little alarmed, tried to wriggle away from the bulbous head that had pushed past the tight opening. But he wasn't about to be deterred, pushed all in, his hips working in delicious rythmn, taking deep, fluid strokes, shea-thing himself.

The worried look left Martha's face. She found that she liked it, held her bottom high for him. He gave a low rumble of pleasure and came, jerk jerk jerk, then withdrew, his interest in Martha over.

She was mortified, looked about frantically. Her eyes fastened upon another man lying on his back in the long grass, sucking on a green stem. He'd been watching her and his friend, was sporting a chunky erection. She smiled, wandered his way.

I was feeling hot, sexy, found my gaze wandering from Martha's antics to Tom, who was digging doggedly with a wooden scoop, several of which the Indians had quickly fashioned to make the excavation slightly easier. Tom's wiry body gleamed with sweat, rippled with modest muscle. I could glimpse his wedding tackle beneath his skimpy loincloth. He was nicely hung, I had to admit, ripe and silken, just waiting to be aroused, or so it seemed to my fertile imagination. I fancied him. Correction. I fancied anyone!

I decided to follow Martha's example.

She had tried to straddle the aroused native and take his skyward pointing tool up into her, to ride him. But he was having none of that. In his culture it was obvious that the man dominated and woman was there simply as a receptacle. He caught Martha by the shoulders, all but threw her onto her back, and slid into her, burying himself deep, all in the blinking of an eye. OK, so I'm exaggerating a bit, but only a bit. He was pretty damned quick. This was sex of the most basic kind. They did it because it came naturally to them, an animal instinct, an urge. They did it to women and if there weren't any available –

317

as I'd already witnessed the day they captured Colin – they did it to other men.

I decided I wouldn't mind some of that. I was wearing Colin's vest. It was big on me, its shoulder staps repeatedly falling down. Now I didn't bother to pull them up in irritation but let them droop, one side dangling lower than the other, showing off a pert, full breast, hard-nippled with longing. I wandered Martha's way, where most of the men seemed to be resting, prior to or after a strenuous time at the dig.

I noted, as I wandered amongst them, that they were all erect, all watching Martha and the native coupling.

I moved past Martha, hips swaying, winking at her as I did so. She winked back, lying beneath the grunting Indian. He took his weight on his arms, only his penis and thighs in contact with the woman beneath him. Soon his grunting became loud and quick and he cried out, thrusting at her wildly, then rolling off. Her desire still wasn't quenched. She groaned. Poor Martha. I hoped I was luckier.

I lazed against a tree, one hip thrust out, belly sucked in and breasts large and hard-nippled with excitement. I didn't have long to wait and neither did Martha.

Another Indian was already between her legs, with a thumb on her clitoris and a finger in each of her secret places. I was pleased to see that they could, on occasion, be a *little* bit adventurous. She groaned happily almost immediately, no doubt contracting in waves of pleasure around his artful digits. She lay back, relaxed and content. He wasn't about to leave her alone though, had his own needs to think of, drew her knees up and slipped his shaft into her accommodating wetness.

Meanwhile, I was being perused by a passing native with the most delightfully big hard-on. I smiled, issued an unmistakable invitation. He stopped, came up to me, a hand grabbing my exposed breast, pulling roughly on the nipple, then drawing it into his mouth to suck. It was wonderful. My belly ached, my sex got all twitchy, I pushed my pelvis at him, felt his hard shaft, so substantial, so long, I groaned.

He didn't even bother to pull down my knickers, just caught at the gusset and ripped them open, a finger finding my spot straight away through the opening in the fabric, his lust-heavy penis followed straight behind.

He filled me, his hard, hot member stretching me to the limit, then withdrawing with every quick and violent thrust of his hips. I held him around the neck, his tall body raising me from the ground by some three or four inches, his shaft impaling me. With each thrust I cried out, the sensations exquisite, intense, even brutal.

He came, so did I, my vulva still throbbing as he withdrew. He smiled his thanks and strode off. I sagged to the floor, legs wide, trembling like jelly. I felt good, fancied a nap.

Probably only a minute or so later, my mind empty and tranquil, I opened my eyes to find another native between my legs, raising them, pinning them back against my torso and sinking his sizeable member into me. Feeling all languid and easy going, I let him do what he wanted, which I didn't doubt was to quickly screw me. I was right. Another smile of thanks another drowsy interlude.

Then I must have rolled, or been rolled, onto my belly. A dark body lay down the back of me, inserting himself into my bottom-mouth. I mumbled an objection at being woken up, tightened so he couldn't enter. He sank himself into my vagina instead, wriggled a finger into my bottom and let it play therein while he screwed me.

319

Oh my, it felt so good. I raised myself for him just a little, feeling more kindly disposed as he took me with leisurely skilfulness, snaking a hand down beneath my body and stroking my bud. So thoroughly stimulated, I came quickly, tightening about him, clenching my muscles to heighten his pleasure, bring him to a climax quickly behind me.

The digging went on all through the day, layers of rubble and soil shovelled aside by the hundred-weight. Beneath was sand and dust and, at long last, the first clunking sound was heard as something metallic was struck by their primitive spades.

Everybody started babbling excitedly, Tom cautioning the natives to take care, go gently. We didn't want anything damaged. Digging stopped. They took to scraping and scooping.

At sunset that night the first artefact was laid partially bare. Colin and a native strenuously pulled it clear, everyone else gathered around, watching, breath bated. I think we all gasped. My heart was beating with excitement. Martha was wringing her hands anxiously. 'Careful with it. *Careful!*'

They held forth a golden wine jug, tilting it so that it poured forth its dry load of sand. There were oohs and ahs in appreciation of its beauty. It was a cere-monial piece, deliberately large, its spout decorated with a hetero-sexual copulation.

I reached out a trembling hand, ran my palm over the curve of the body. It was cool, unblemished.

'It's pure gold,' said Colin, 'and very heavy. In Europe we tended to have silver gilt. That is, silver that's had mercury gilding in gold over the top. Not gold at all, just silver that's given a protective coating of non-tarnishing metal. Fools a lot of people.'

'Damn and blast,' snorted Tom, regretfully, 'I *wish* I had my camera.'

Colin nodded in commiseration. 'It would have been nice to do a photographic record. See the decorated spout, the entwined lovers? This is a favourite form of enhancement, and usually it was the Inca women who had the skill to craft the pots and vessels.'

They continued their careful plundering long into the night, the natives fashioned torches on stakes, the flames adequate enough to work by.

Martha and I tried to be useful, to concoct a sort of soup out of the diminishing rations in my back-pack and some wild plants that the Indians insisted were good when cooked. The best that could be said about it was that it was hot and wet. The men who drank it when they came off shift were too exhausted on the one hand and too euphoric on the other to give a damn anyhow.

Thereafter, the finds came thick and fast, hardly any interval between them. All beautiful, as fabulous as the first. I shook my head in wonder, poring over more jugs, flasks, lidded pots, plates, knives, plaques, porringers, caskets made of gold and full (once the sand had carefully been removed) of cabochon rubies, uncut emeralds as big as grapes and baroque pearls like pigeons' eggs.

Carla and I filled our hands with the precious stones, set them in our navels, held them to our ears and looked over our reflections in mirrors of highly polished silver. We had more gems in our reach than were in the whole of the British Royal Regalia.

'I've died and gone to heaven,' laughed Carla with delight, 'and heaven is like Fabergé, Cartier, Tiffany's, Worth and Aspreys all in one.'

Then I slept because there came a time when I just couldn't keep my eyes open any longer.

The sun was just up, a red fireball over the far horizon. The commotion woke me.

Martha, Carla and I raised ourselves on our elbows, blinking at the highly excited natives. It was hard to say whether they were angry, happy or downright nuts. Mostly, as I said, they just seemed excited, their words coming in a rush, loudly broadcast, their arms flying around all over the place.

Lying amid our sea of gold, the three of us looked quizzical, finding it hard to come fully awake.

'Colin? Tom?'

They were standing over the hole where the bathing pool had once been. They'd gone much deeper since I'd fallen asleep, and had unearthed chests of ceremonial robes studded with gems and sewn over with gold discs. Golden head-dresses, golden daggers, golden buckled shoes; clothes fit for a king, the King of the Sun.

The mosaic-like flooring of the pool was now revealed, yellow, white and orange-red, like sunbursts. And exactly in the middle stood a hewn stone coffin. It could be nothing else. There were flashes in my brain and I realised why I had been confused earlier, had seen the pool grassed over, though we had found it paved. It had been opened again, a place excavated for a coffin. Only a man of the greatest importance would be buried in such a place.

I rose, eyes riveted, went forward as if drawn by a magnet, unaware that Martha and Carla moved in my wake.

Tom and Colin flanked the sarcophagus, the natives now falling *en masse* to their knees, a sudden breeze whipping through the hidden glade. A cloud passed over the sun. Above, four condors wheeled where yesterday there had been only one. We all shivered.

This was getting heavy, I felt. I wasn't comfortable with it. I seemed to have lost control of my life, of my body. I wanted that control back, but knew it wasn't to be, not till I'd put a great distance between me and this place.

The stone lid was carved like a sunburst. A shock ran through my body. I felt terror and yet I ordered them to remove the lid. I knew who was in there, was so afraid I honestly felt on the verge of blacking out, even hoped for it so I could escape.

Carla and Martha flanked me. Compared to myself they seemed calm. I envied them, admired them. The lion hearted Sydney had fled. There was just me in her place. And I felt totally inadequate.

Colin and Tom hefted, sweat breaking out on their foreheads. It must have taken two dozen men to place the lid on top five centuries before. The natives would have made the task of removing it easier but they weren't budging. There was no power on earth stronger than the one in their immediate vicinity and they bowed to it, were prostrate.

The stone grated, slowly shifted, tottered and fell with a thunderous boom that shook the earth all around. And there he was, the Inca, the Sun personified, uncorrupt, as if asleep, bedecked in the robes of majesty. There were golden discs in his ears, rings on his fingers, bracelets on his arms, emeralds in the golden belt around his waist.

There was silence all around. We all seemed to be in shock. My mouth had dropped open. He was so well preserved, so perfectly intact, that I half expected him to sit up. My heart pounded right up to my ears. I couldn't swallow.

Carla swayed beside me. I put out an arm, fastened

it supportively around her. Martha had gone down on her knees, entranced by the spectacle.

I've always been of the opinion that people who hear voices in their heads should be quickly and quietly taken away by burly minders in white coats. Yet I was hearing voices now, as plain as if the orator was beside me, so clear, in fact, would you believe, that I *did* actually turn around to see if there was anyone there. No one. So it was him. But of course. I'd known *that* all along. I was just trying to kid myself. Because I needed this kind of communication like I needed a hole in the head, couldn't see why I was being singled out. Why couldn't it be Martha? she'd be thrilled.

So, anyhow, this voice in my head, deep and strong, his voice, was saying, 'Take my head-dress. It is yours. Bestow it on the one most worthy. Take it, take it . . .' It was repeating itself, very insistent.

I took two reluctant, unsteady paces, and stood at his side. His flesh had dried to parchment, the bone clearly defined. I saw the man of my dreams when I looked down upon that husk, a handsome man, a man whose eyes had burned with a dark passion. Then I looked at Tom, dusty, sweaty, his dark hair raked back by his fingers, his eyes dark and intense. The three faces merged, superimposed, became one. That got me terribly confused. I was in one helluva state.

I reached down and, ever so carefully, gently, slipped the crown from his head. It was brittle with age, shaped like a fan, the red and yellow wool fabric stiffened with some antique animal glue. Bits of it disintegrated where my finger touched it.

'Tom,' I said, making him jump. He'd been watching me so intently, he'd gone into a world of his own. 'Tom, I've been asked to choose. I choose you.'

'Chosen for what?' He raised an eyebrow, very serious, wary even.

'To wear the crown of ceremony.'

He shook his head in alarm. 'Hell, no, I wouldn't feel happy about that. I'm an outsider, a foreigner in this land. Ask one of the locals,' he suggested, pointing to the floored Indians.

'I'm not asking you to take on the duties of king-ship. Just to don the head-dress. *He* wants it. Don't be difficult.'

I expected him to shoot me one of those 'poor bitch, she's as nutty as a fruit-cake' looks of his, but to my surprise he didn't.

He looked a little uncertain, but he nodded. 'OK.'

I exhaled in relief. I sensed that our communing with the Inca was drawing to a close. This might be the last thing we were ever asked to do. I'd have hated to let him down right at the final hurdle. 'Thanks.'

Tom circumvented the coffin, and stood before me. 'I want it to be known that whatever happens to me in the next ten minutes, I hold her totally respon-sible,' he joked, lamely, pointing at me.

I ignored that, reached up, placed the flamboyant line in headgear squarely on his crown and stood there waiting, wondering.

A minute passed, the waiting beginning to feel silly. Perhaps *nothing* was supposed to happen. I could see Tom's feet begin to shuffle restlessly; his patience was running out and doubtless he felt a fool. Perhaps the voice in my head was dreamt up by me. After all, I hadn't had proper food in days. It could very likely be that it was affecting my brain, that I was, quite simply, imagining things.

A fierce and prolonged gust of wind came howling through the glade, whipping Colin's hat off his head, plastering our clothes to our bodies. The sun had been hot, now we were in the shade beneath a cloud which seemed to have appeared from nowhere, black, thunderous, emitting forked lightning. It chilled us, right down to our souls.

Air rushed and swirled past me, making my vest flap, tearing at Tom's head-dress.

I looked at the Inca. He was disappearing before my eyes, disintegrating, blowing away as dust on the wind, his clothing and flesh, until there were only his bones and the gold and jewels from his clothing.

Tom's head was bare, save for a sprinkling of dust. He shook it out.

And the wind that had rifled amongst us so furiously, died away as suddenly as it had come.

Emotion welled up in me, burst like water through a break in a dam, sobs tearing at me, tears running in rivers down my cheeks. I retreated, knelt with Martha and Carla, all of us crying under the dreadful weight of a terrible grief. We could see, knew why he was here, amidst his treasure.

The Inca had refused to tell the conquistadores where the treasure had been hidden. And they, gold-hungry, religious fanatics that they were, had put him to death with a barbarity that eclipsed anything the Inca could have devised. In death, his secret safe and the Spaniards pulling out, having grown weary of the jungle-locked citadel, his most trusted servants had buried him with his gold, then melted away into the jungle, leaving Vilcabamba deserted, inhabited only by ghosts.

I was so wound up in my own emotions, at first, I didn't see Tom standing like a statue, tall, straight, eyes sparking. He was still Tom, but he was different.

For many moments he stood, arms outstretched, staring up at the darkness, the forks of lightning. I began to be afraid. It was almost as if he defied the elements to smite him.

My tears dried and I went to him, shaking him by the shoulders. 'Tom? Tom! Speak to me. Are you OK? Stop messing about, you bloody idiot.'

He focused his gaze on me then and I pulled back, gasped. His eyes were black, smouldering. The Inca's eyes. He caught me around my back and under my knees, scooped me up in his arms.

'Tom, what're you doing? Are you mad? Put me down. Now! Tom, I mean it. Tom . . .'

He carried me to his throne. The Inca's throne, I mean. Sat down and nestled me in his lap, arms like bands of steel, kissed me as only Tom could, deeply, persuasively, until I no longer protested indignantly, but was wet with lust for the hard bulge of him I could feel against my buttock. He pulled me around to face him, astride now, and shifted the insubstantial rags of his loincloth. His penis reared, erect, hard, the skin pulling back from the head. He ran a thumb gently back and forth between my sex-lips, and I lowered my head, teased him with my tongue.

He moaned as if in agony and I looked up, could see that I had Tom back now, that the Inca had gone, for ever. I was sure, he had found a kind of peace at last.

Tom said my name softly, yes, called me by name rather than something scathing like viper-pants.

'Syd . . . Syd . . .'

'Yes, Tom. It's OK. All over.'

I took his thick shaft and eased it into me, slowly, softly, tenderly.

Our movements were in harmony, slow, measured. We had all the time in the world. There was no race, no frantic clamour to get to the finishing tape. He kissed me again, his arms enveloping me, making

327

me feel warm, safe. Considering our present situation, the latter feeling was one to cherish.

It felt as if we were lost in each other for hours. Very likely it was a matter of minutes. I lost all sense of time when having fun. But no, fun wasn't the word. Fun was what I usually had when I had sex. Tom and I were not having fun. We were . . . Hell, it's so confusing! It wasn't a fun-filled atmosphere, that's for sure, not with some five hundred year old bones dominating the proceedings.

My feelings were all ajumble. I was happy about the treasure. Sad about the Inca. Worried about Tom – briefly. Tired. Hungry. That's why, when he took me in his arms and carried me off, deaf to any protest, I had felt secure and happy inwardly. It was this place. It was bewitched. I'd be my old self again once I got back to polluted old London. Yeah, that was it – I was starved of carbon-monoxide!

I pressed real close to him, only that over-sized vest between us. My breasts squishing against his hard muscles, I snuggled my face around the nape of his neck, kissing his ear, breathing warmly over him until I could see the hairs on his skin standing upright and excited. Then I let my lips travel back to his, sucked his upper lip, then his lower one, finally kissing him the way he kissed me. He kissed like nobody else. Even his shaft, moving so deeply within me, bringing me closer to bliss with each moment of possession, couldn't compare with the sensations of that kiss. It brought us together like nothing else ever could. Some really weird things had happened to me during the last few weeks, but the thrill we felt when we reached the pinnacle of delight that day at Vilcabamba was sure to be one that lingered for ever in the memory. It changed us. Or rather it may have been the occurrence – our joining – which made us realise we had changed.

Afterwards we lazed by the throne, watching the last of the artefacts being exhumed. Martha had gone off and collected flowers, laid them all around the remains of the Inca lord. There were no more voices in our heads. All that was done with.

The natives mumbled awed prayers and blessings for the dead, hefted the massive lid up between them and closed the coffin.

'Do you think Colin's Indian buddies might be descended from the old ones of Vilcabamba?' I said.

'It's possible,' said Tom, nodding positively.

'We've found the treasure. What happens now?'

His head shook, he gave it careful thought. 'I really don't know. It was tentatively agreed that in principle we thought it best that we should hand over the trove to the authorities in whichever country Vilcabamba lies, that the stuff should go on display in a museum.'

'You don't sound so sure now,' there was query in my voice.

'I'm not,' he admitted. 'Something happened to me along the way or, more likely, here. I don't like the idea of things being taken away.'

I was nodding enthusiastically. 'I know what you mean. I feel exactly the same. I've told myself I'm stupid, that the rest of the world has a right to see all this stuff, that a museum is the right place for it, that it'll help the economy of Peru or Brazil, whichever country we finally find we're in, by increasing tourism. But even so, I don't like it.'

We smiled at each other. Allies. It was so nice not to be arguing for a change. Sniping and bitching did get a bit tiresome sometimes. Not that I'd given it up completely, you understand. I was just taking a breather.

Martha and Carla approached looking purposeful. They were smiling as well. My, but weren't we all of a pleasant disposition today!

'Carla and I have been talking,' said Martha, in her most authoritative tones.

'Yeah . . .'

'Discussing the find . . .'

'Yeah . . .'

'And we feel wrong about taking it away.' She put up a hand as if she expected me to immediately start arguing. 'I know it's what we always said we'd do, but . . . well . . . feelings change . . . we've changed.'

Carla nodded emphatically. 'This place is magical, full of vibes . . . good vibes now . . . I don't want us to do anything that would make it change. I feel we were allowed to see the past, find the treasure so that we could be part of it . . . here. The magic will go if we remove it all.'

'What about Colin?' asked Tom.

'He will stay. He's adamant. Wishes to be the custodian of this place.'

'Then it's settled,' I said, with glee. 'Vilcabamba keeps its secrets. Colin is the guardian and we make our way back to Pablo and the boats. We can perfect a suitable story on the way. If we tell about reaching the shrine, but it being a dead end, of Rory's betraying us to Mendes, of his death, it'll make a good enough story for my newspaper, should satisfy our readers taste for sensationalism.'

'Good thinking, Sydney. Yes, the adventure ended with the disappointment at the shrine and Rory's death.'

'Yeah,' said Carla, warming to the theme. 'We can say the party was jinxed, that Big Jacko, Colin and Rory died because of malevolent spirits.'

'Um,' Martha was cautious. 'Yes, but remember,

dear, we don't want to make things so interesting that some other collective of adventurers decided to come in search of Vilcabamba. The discovery of King Tut's tomb and the bad luck allegedly associated with it kept interest going indefinitely. We want Vilcabamba forgotten, a legend without substance.'

And that's how it was. Colin and the natives guided us back to within a few miles of where Pablo would be waiting for us with the boats. We made camp there, shared a last meal, talked about all that happened, still fresh with amazement. It would fade with time, just like the memories, but for now it was heady, exhilarating. We each carried a memento, the only plunder we would allow ourselves. We were sure the Inca wouldn't have begrudged us such modest keepsakes. Rubies, emeralds and pearls, just one each of whichever we fancied. I had a ruby, kept it held tightly in my hand.

And even though my head was still chock full of wonder, there was a small portion that felt a poignant sadness. We'd made friends, lovers, enemies. None of us would ever be the same again.

We couldn't sleep, reclined around the fire, me with Tom, Colin with his lover whose name was unpronounceable. I don't remember consciously selecting Tom for a last night of passion. It just sort of happened. I just sort of drifted his way and he mine.

I lay on my side, a hip thrust up in tattered panties, my weight taken on an elbow. He was behind me, his fingers in my hair, his breath on my neck, his chest against mine. I sighed. His hand came to rest on my hip, smoothing it, coaxing it to move back a little, apply pressure to his loins. He was big and hard. Just knowing it made me hungry. I entwined my legs with his, raised the upper one so that he had access to my sex, half turned my head so he could kiss me.

His fingers found me, gentle, then insistent, stroking me, probing me, working me to a heightened state of readiness. Then I felt his rigid flesh snaking between my buttocks, probing my hidden place, pushing in. I sighed again, noisier now. He was hard, determined, his strokes deep and measured, so that I made little noises of appreciation at each thrust, ground against his loins. Soon I was panting, and Tom's sheathing of flesh grew violent, wild, making me come, trembling with reaction, throbbing then making me come again with his fingers playing at my bud.

The others had supposedly been talking, snoozing or eating, but they couldn't resist watching Tom and I surreptitiously. Colin's lover decided that he had an urgent need as well, took Colin by the hand and lead him to a felled tree. Colin draped himself elegantly over it, trousers dropped and the Indian came up behind him, rubbing his loins and hips against Colin, teasing him for minutes on end till Colin was begging for it, caressing his back and his rounded, though attractively neat, buttocks. When he knew he'd driven poor Colin to distraction, he lifted his tiny excuse for a loincloth, showing off a splendid erection, and eased it into the white-man's bottom-mouth, pushing it home with a grin of pleasure. He held Colin down by the shoulders, plundered him quickly and efficiently, then when he'd come with much yelling and humping, changed places and offered Colin his own rear.

Colin was in heaven. The white-man's world was full of homophobes, he'd found. He'd despaired of ever finding true love. Now he was sure he had it, without shame or censure.

Martha watched unobtrusively, not wishing to seem impolite or voyeuristic. It was really turning her on, I could tell by her body language. She was all slinky, all seductively draped, leaning back non-chalantly against a none too comfortable rock. She smiled ever so friendly at any native who caught her eye. Two of them really got a come-on, her come-to-bed look between narrowed lids unmistakable, no matter what the culture. They sidled up, sat down and proceeded to play footsy with her, vying for attention. Pretty soon it was all getting heated and she was rolling around with them on the floor, the two males exploring her all over. They saw little of the women of their tribe – though there were some somewhere, Colin had said – so Martha and Carla and I were a real novelty, especially as we were an odd colour. Women took second place in the pleasure top-ten to hunting. And hunting was really a euphemism for just bumming around and doing precious little.

One of them pulled Martha back into his arms, stuck a finger up her bottom and followed that swiftly with his turgid shaft. She gasped, delighted by his initiative, squealed when the other opened her legs and knelt before her, burying himself in her woman's place. She whooped like a Texan, and gave herself over to a truly licentious bout of pleasure. She felt this was her swan-song as far as unrestrained adventures went. Was determined that, in every way, it would be one that she never forgot.

Carla was tired, had fallen asleep soon after finishing supper, which the natives had generously furnished us with. It had no name, Colin said, after it was consumed, and added, 'I think it's best you don't know what was in it. It was palatable; that's the main thing, surely?'

'I suppose so,' I said, feeling benevolent. 'And stop calling me Shirley.'

Everyone who knew how old that joke was groaned loudly.

Later, as I was dropping off to sleep, Tom had given me a quizzical look. Our time was running out, we both knew, for somehow, tomorrow, when we met up with Pablo once more, we'd be back in the other world, the modern world. And I'd be in London while he was in the USA – exactly where I couldn't say.

'What'll you do without your main course?' he wondered lightly, referring, presumably, to my ill-conceived infatuation for Rory Duncan.

I yawned. 'Main courses can be too much sometimes for the digestion to cope with. I'm quite partial to leftovers, my big heap of Bubble and Squeak,' I told him, hugging his arm more tightly around me.

He was a little pleased, a lot confused. 'Your answer doesn't make a whole lot of sense to me. Bubble and what . . .?'

I palmed the back of his head, pulled him to me, kissed him, deeply, deeper . . .

The next morning we waved goodbye to Colin, having kissed and hugged and been hugged and kissed by everyone. We took one last look behind us, back to the distant hills, and then headed for the river.

Pablo was there, lazing on the deck of his boat with his legs hanging over the side.

Martha yelled loudly.

He clambered to his feet. A smile split his face, he laughed. 'Mees Martha . . . Seed-nee . . .' Then he faltered as he counted our number, looked behind us for the missing three, his eyebrows knitting.

That was where our adventure ended and the lying began.

'Merry Chrishmash,' I slurred, piling into the crowded lift, leaving the chaos of the office party behind me, and pushing one particular man who tried to follow me back into the newsroom.

'Merry Chrishmash,' Brian Sheehan shouted back, burping as the doors closed, separating us.

He wanted to come back to my flat, I knew, but I had other plans, had no time for canoodling over the Xerox machine or drunken fumblings in my private domain.

I was going home. Home to my box of chocolates. Tom had been true to his word, expensive Belgian temptation landing on my doorstep, not once a week as he'd once promised ('cos, well, that really would have been excessive and he didn't want me getting fat) but once a month. They were always beautifully wrapped inside their condom-like, protective bubble-bag, and tied up with ribbon. Beneath the wrapping was a note, a note that always said the same non-mushy, cryptic thing. 'How About It?'

I wasn't stupid. I knew what it was. I'd just not felt ready over the last months. I'd had to adjust. It hadn't been easy. Not for Tom either, I didn't doubt. And, besides, there was no way that I wanted him to think that I was a pushover. It would do him good to wait. A thing was more highly valued the harder it was to obtain.

My present had arrived that morning, bearing, as American's always insist on doing, the sender's address. I'd written it down in my address book months ago when the first chocs arrived, and double-checked that I'd done it correctly. That address was of vital importance.

At home I drank coffee and sobered up. Then I stuffed a couple of suitcases and left a note pinned to Tyrone's door so he'd cancel my papers. I didn't want to see him, didn't want to have to say 'no' to a good friend. I'd called a taxi and it was waiting down below on the cold, gloomy street.

The ride to Heathrow was a nightmare (when isn't it) and the driver kept pushing down the cab window and shouting, foul-mouthed, at any and everyone.

Tom was in Vermont. I'd remembered to pack my snow boots. And in my cosmetics bag was a huge ruby that looked too big to be real. I fancied that sometime during my indefinite stay I'd have a chance to model it in my navel and rekindle some delicious memories.

BLACK
lace

NO LADY
Saskia Hope

30-year-old Kate dumps her boyfriend, walks out of her job and sets off in search of sexual adventure. Set against the rugged terrain of the Pyrenees, the love-making is as rough as the landscape.

ISBN 0 352 32857 6

WEB OF DESIRE
Sophie Danson

High-flying executive Marcie is gradually drawn away from the normality of her married life. Strange messages begin to appear on her computer, summoning her to sinister and fetishistic sexual liaisons.

ISBN 0 352 32856 8

BLUE HOTEL
Cherri Pickford

Hotelier Ramon can't understand why best-selling author Floy Pennington has come to stay at his quiet hotel. Her exhibitionist tendencies are driving him crazy, as are her increasingly wanton encounters with the hotel's other guests.

ISBN 0 352 32858 4

CASSANDRA'S CONFLICT
Fredrica Alleyn

Behind the respectable facade of a house in present-day Hampstead lies a world of decadent indulgence and darkly bizarre eroticism. A sternly attractive Baron and his beautiful but cruel wife are playing games with the young Cassandra.

ISBN 0 352 32859 2

THE CAPTIVE FLESH
Cleo Cordell

Marietta and Claudine, French aristocrats saved from pirates, learn their invitation to stay at the opulent Algerian mansion of their rescuer, Kasim, requires something in return; their complete surrender to the ecstasy of pleasure in pain.

ISBN 0 352 32872 X

PLEASURE HUNT
Sophie Danson

Sexual adventurer Olympia Deschamps is determined to become a member of the Légion D'Amour – the most exclusive society of French libertines.

ISBN 0 352 32880 0

BLACK ORCHID
Roxanne Carr

The Black Orchid is a women's health club which provides a specialised service for its high-powered clients; women who don't have the time to spend building complex relationships, but who enjoy the pleasures of the flesh.

ISBN 0 352 32888 6

ODALISQUE
Fleur Reynolds

A tale of family intrigue and depravity set against the glittering backdrop of the designer set. This facade of respectability conceals a reality of bitter rivalry and unnatural love.

ISBN 0 352 32887 8

OUTLAW LOVER
Saskia Hope

Fee Cambridge lives in an upper level deluxe pleasuredome of technologically advanced comfort. Bored with her predictable husband and pampered lifestyle, Fee ventures into the wild side of town, finding an an outlaw who becomes her lover.

ISBN 0 352 32909 2

THE SENSES BEJEWELLED
Cleo Cordell

Willing captives Marietta and Claudine are settling into life at Kasim's harem. But 18th century Algeria can be a hostile place. When the women are kidnapped by Kasim's sworn enemy, they face indignities that will test the boundaries of erotic experience. This is the sequel to *The Captive Flesh*.

ISBN 0 352 32904 1

GEMINI HEAT
Portia Da Costa

As the metropolis sizzles in freak early summer temperatures, twin sisters Deana and Delia find themselves cooking up a heatwave of their own. Jackson de Guile, master of power dynamics and wealthy connoisseur of fine things, draws them both into a web of luxuriously decadent debauchery.

ISBN 0 352 32912 2

VIRTUOSO
Katrina Vincenzi

Mika and Serena, darlings of classical music's jet-set, inhabit a world of secluded passion. The reason? Since Mika's tragic accident which put a stop to his meteoric rise to fame as a solo violinist, he cannot face the world, and together they lead a decadent, reclusive existence.

ISBN 0 352 32907 6

MOON OF DESIRE
Sophie Danson

When Soraya Chilton is posted to the ancient and mysterious city of Ragzburg on a mission for the Foreign Office, strange things begin to happen to her. Wild, sexual urges overwhelm her at the coming of each full moon.

ISBN 0 352 32911 4

FIONA'S FATE
Fredrica Alleyn

When Fiona Sheldon is kidnapped by the infamous Trimarchi brothers, along with her friend Bethany, she finds herself acting in ways her husband Duncan would be shocked by. Alessandro Trimarchi makes full use of this opportunity to discover the true extent of Fiona's suppressed, but powerful, sexuality.

ISBN 0 352 32913 0

HANDMAIDEN OF PALMYRA
Fleur Reynolds

3rd century Palmyra: a lush oasis in the Syrian desert. The beautiful and fiercely independent Samoya takes her place in the temple of Antioch as an apprentice priestess. Decadent bachelor Prince Alif has other plans for her and sends his scheming sister to bring her to his Bacchanalian wedding feast.

ISBN 0 352 32919 X

OUTLAW FANTASY
Saskia Hope

On the outer reaches of the 21st century metropolis the Amazenes are on the prowl; fierce warrior women who have some unfinished business with Fee Cambridge's pirate lover. This is the sequel to *Outlaw Lover*.

ISBN 0 352 32920 3

THE SILKEN CAGE
Sophie Danson

When University lecturer Maria Treharne inherits her aunt's mansion in Cornwall, she finds herself the subject of strange and unexpected attention. Using the craft of goddess worship and sexual magnetism, Maria finds allies and foes in this savage and beautiful landscape.

ISBN 0 352 32928 9

RIVER OF SECRETS
Saskia Hope & Georgia Angelis

Intrepid female reporter Sydney Johnson takes over someone else's assignment up the Amazon river. Sydney soon realises this mission to find a lost Inca city has a hidden agenda. Everyone is behaving so strangely, so sexually, and the tropical humidity is reaching fever pitch.

ISBN 0 352 32925 4

VELVET CLAWS
Cleo Cordell

It's the 19th century; a time of exploration and discovery and young, spirited Gwendoline Farnshawe is determined not to be left behind in the parlour when the handsome and celebrated anthropologist, Jonathan Kimberton, is planning his latest expedition to Africa.

ISBN 0 352 32926 2

THE GIFT OF SHAME
Sarah Hope-Walker

Helen is a woman with extreme fantasies. When she meets Jeffrey – a cultured wealthy stranger – at a party, they soon become partners in obsession. Now nothing is impossible for her, no fantasy beyond his imagination or their mutual exploration.

ISBN 0 352 32935 1

SUMMER OF ENLIGHTENMENT
Cheryl Mildenhall

Karin's new-found freedom is getting her into all sorts of trouble. The enigmatic Nicolai has been showing interest in her since their chance meeting in a cafe. But he's the husband of a valued friend and is trying to embroil her in the sexual tension he thrives on.

ISBN 0 352 32937 8

A BOUQUET OF BLACK ORCHIDS
Roxanne Carr

The exclusive Black Orchid health spa has provided Maggie with a new social life and a new career, where giving and receiving pleasure of the most sophisticated nature takes top priority. But her loyalty to the club is being tested by the presence of Tourell; a powerful man who makes her an offer she finds difficult to refuse.

ISBN 0 352 32939 4

JULIET RISING
Cleo Cordell

At Madame Nicol's exclusive but strict 18th-century academy for young ladies, the bright and wilful Juliet is learning the art of courting the affections of young noblemen.

ISBN 0 352 32938 6

DEBORAH'S DISCOVERY
Fredrica Alleyn

Deborah Woods is trying to change her life. Having just ended her long-term relationship and handed in her notice at work, she is ready for a little adventure. Meeting American oil magnate John Pavin III throws her world into even more confusion as he invites her to stay at his luxurious renovated castle in Scotland. But what looked like being a romantic holiday soon turns into a test of sexual bravery.

ISBN 0 352 32945 9

THE TUTOR
Portia Da Costa

Like minded libertines reap the rewards of their desire in this story of the sexual initiation of a beautiful young man. Rosalind Howard takes a post as personal librarian to a husband and wife, both unashamed sensualists keen to engage her into their decadent scenarios.

ISBN 0 352 32946 7

THE HOUSE IN NEW ORLEANS
Fleur Reynolds

When she inherits her family home in the fashionable Garden district of New Orleans, Ottilie Duvier discovers it has been leased to the notorious Helmut von Straffen; a debauched German Count famous for his decadent Mardi Gras parties. Determined to oust him from the property, she soon realises that not all dangerous animals live in the swamp!

ISBN 0 352 32951 3

ELENA'S CONQUEST
Lisette Allen

It's summer – 1070AD – and the gentle Elena is gathering herbs in the garden of the convent where she leads a peaceful, but uneventful, life. When Norman soldiers besiege the convent, they take Elena captive and present her to the dark and masterful Lord Aimery to satisfy his savage desire for Saxon women.

ISBN 0 352 32950 5

CASSANDRA'S CHATEAU
Fredrica Alleyn

Cassandra has been living with the dominant and perverse Baron von Ritter for eighteen months when their already bizarre relationship takes an unexpected turn. The arrival of a naive female visitor at the chateau provides the Baron with a new opportunity to indulge his fancy for playing darkly erotic games with strangers.

ISBN 0 352 32955 6

WICKED WORK
Pamela Kyle

At twenty-eight, Suzie Carlton is at the height of her journalistic career. She has status, money and power. What she doesn't have is a masterful partner who will allow her to realise the true extent of her fantasies. How will she reconcile the demands of her job with her sexual needs?

ISBN 0 352 32958 0

WE NEED YOUR HELP . . .
to plan the future of women's erotic fiction –

– and no stamp required!

Yours are the only opinions that matter.

Black Lace is the first series of books devoted to erotic fiction by women for women.

We intend to keep providing the best-written, sexiest books you can buy. And we'd appreciate your help and valued opinion of the books so far. Tell us what you want to read.

THE BLACK LACE QUESTIONNAIRE

SECTION ONE: ABOUT YOU

1.1 Sex (*we presume you are female, but so as not to discriminate*)
Are you?

Male ☐
Female ☐

1.2 Age

under 21 ☐ 21–30 ☐
31–40 ☐ 41–50 ☐
51–60 ☐ over 60 ☐

1.3 At what age did you leave full-time education?

still in education ☐ 16 or younger ☐
17–19 ☐ 20 or older ☐

1.4 Occupation _____

1.5 Annual household income
       under £10,000 ☐   £10–£20,000 ☐
       £20–£30,000 ☐   £30–£40,000 ☐
       over £40,000 ☐

1.6 We are perfectly happy for you to remain anonymous; but if you would like to receive information on other publications available, please insert your name and address

_____

_____

_____

_____

SECTION TWO: ABOUT BUYING BLACK LACE BOOKS

2.1 How did you acquire this copy of *River of Secrets*?
       I bought it myself ☐   My partner bought it ☐
       I borrowed/found it ☐

2.2 How did you find out about Black Lace books?
       I saw them in a shop ☐
       I saw them advertised in a magazine ☐
       I saw the London Underground posters ☐
       I read about them in _____
       Other _____

2.3 Please tick the following statements you agree with:
       I would be less embarrassed about buying Black
       Lace books if the cover pictures were less explicit ☐
       I think that in general the pictures on Black
       Lace books are about right ☐
       I think Black Lace cover pictures should be as
       explicit as possible ☐

2.4 Would you read a Black Lace book in a public place – on a train for instance?
       Yes ☐   No ☐

SECTION THREE: ABOUT THIS BLACK LACE BOOK

3.1 Do you think the sex content in this book is:
    Too much   ☐   About right   ☐
    Not enough   ☐

3.2 Do you think the writing style in this book is:
    Too unreal/escapist   ☐   About right   ☐
    Too down to earth   ☐

3.3 Do you think the story in this book is:
    Too complicated   ☐   About right   ☐
    Too boring/simple   ☐

3.4 Do you think the cover of this book is:
    Too explicit   ☐   About right   ☐
    Not explicit enough   ☐

Here's a space for any other comments:

SECTION FOUR: ABOUT OTHER BLACK LACE BOOKS

4.1 How many Black Lace books have you read?   ☐

4.2 If more than one, which one did you prefer?

4.3 Why?

SECTION FIVE: ABOUT YOUR IDEAL EROTIC NOVEL

We want to publish the books you want to read – so this is your chance to tell us exactly what your ideal erotic novel would be like.

5.1 Using a scale of 1 to 5 (1 = no interest at all, 5 = your ideal), please rate the following possible settings for an erotic novel:

Medieval/barbarian/sword 'n' sorcery ☐
Renaissance/Elizabethan/Restoration ☐
Victorian/Edwardian ☐
1920s & 1930s – the Jazz Age ☐
Present day ☐
Future/Science Fiction ☐

5.2 Using the same scale of 1 to 5, please rate the following themes you may find in an erotic novel:

Submissive male/dominant female ☐
Submissive female/dominant male ☐
Lesbianism ☐
Bondage/fetishism ☐
Romantic love ☐
Experimental sex e.g. anal/watersports/sex toys ☐
Gay male sex ☐
Group sex ☐

Using the same scale of 1 to 5, please rate the following styles in which an erotic novel could be written:

Realistic, down to earth, set in real life ☐
Escapist fantasy, but just about believable ☐
Completely unreal, impressionistic, dreamlike ☐

5.3 Would you prefer your ideal erotic novel to be written from the viewpoint of the main male characters or the main female characters?

Male ☐ Female ☐
Both ☐

5.4 What would your ideal Black Lace heroine be like? Tick as many as you like:

Dominant	☐	Glamorous	☐
Extroverted	☐	Contemporary	☐
Independent	☐	Bisexual	☐
Adventurous	☐	Naive	☐
Intellectual	☐	Introverted	☐
Professional	☐	Kinky	☐
Submissive	☐	Anything else?	☐
Ordinary	☐	_____	

5.5 What would your ideal male lead character be like? Again, tick as many as you like:

Rugged	☐		
Athletic	☐	Caring	☐
Sophisticated	☐	Cruel	☐
Retiring	☐	Debonair	☐
Outdoor-type	☐	Naive	☐
Executive-type	☐	Intellectual	☐
Ordinary	☐	Professional	☐
Kinky	☐	Romantic	☐
Hunky	☐		
Sexually dominant	☐	Anything else?	☐
Sexually submissive	☐	_____	

5.6 Is there one particular setting or subject matter that your ideal erotic novel would contain?

_____

SECTION SIX: LAST WORDS

6.1 What do you like best about Black Lace books?

_____

6.2 What do you most dislike about Black Lace books?

_____

6.3 In what way, if any, would you like to change Black Lace covers?

_____

6.4 Here's a space for any other comments:

_____

_____

_____

_____

_____

Thank you for completing this questionnaire. Now tear it out of the book – carefully! – put it in an envelope and send it to:

> **Black Lace**
> **FREEPOST**
> **London**
> **W10 5BR**

No stamp is required if you are resident in the U.K.